P9-EGK-738

Heartless

Heartless

Marissa Meyer

THORNDIKE PRESS
A part of Gale, Cengage Learning

Farmington Hills, Mich • San Francisco • New York • Waterville, Maine
Meriden, Conn • Mason, Ohio • Chicago

Recommended for Young Adult Readers.

Thorndike Press, a part of Gale, Cengage Learning.

Thorndike Press® Large Print The Literacy Bridge.
The text of this Large Print edition is unabridged.
Other aspects of the book may vary from the original edition.
Set in 16 pt. Plantin.

LIBRARY OF CONGRESS CATALOGING-IN-PUBLICATION DATA

Names: Meyer, Marissa, author.
Title: Heartless / by Marissa Meyer.
Description: Waterville, Maine : Thorndike Press, 2016. | Series: Thorndike Press Large Print. The Literacy Bridge | Summary: In this prequel to Alice in Wonderland, Cath would rather open a bakery and marry for love than accept a proposal from the King of Hearts, especially after meeting the handsome and mysterious court jester.
Identifiers: LCCN 2016035012 | ISBN 9781410494375 (hardback) | ISBN 1410494373 (hardcover)
Subjects: LCSH: Large type books. | CYAC: Characters in literature—Fiction. | Love—Fiction. | Fantasy. | BISAC: JUVENILE FICTION / Fantasy & Magic.
Classification: LCC PZ7.M571737 He 2016b | DDC [Fic]—dc23
LC record available at https://lccn.loc.gov/2016035012

Published in 2016 by arrangement with Feiwel & Friends, an imprint of Macmillan

Printed in Mexico
10 11 12 13 14 15 23 22 21 20 19

For Mom

I pictured to myself the Queen of Hearts
as a sort of embodiment of ungovernable
passion — a blind and aimless Fury.

— LEWIS CARROLL

Chapter 1

Three luscious lemon tarts glistened up at Catherine. She reached her towel-wrapped hands into the oven, ignoring the heat that enveloped her arms and pressed against her cheeks, and lifted the tray from the hearth. The tarts' sunshine filling quivered, as if glad to be freed from the stone chamber.

Cath held the tray with the same reverence one might reserve for the King's crown. She refused to take her eyes from the tarts as she padded across the kitchen floor until the tray's edge landed on the baker's table with a satisfying thump. The tarts trembled for a moment more before falling still, flawless and gleaming.

Setting the towels aside, she picked through the curled, sugared lemon peels laid out on parchment and arranged them like rose blossoms on the tarts, settling each strip into the still-warm center. The aromas of sweet citrus and buttery, flaky crust curled beneath her nose.

She stepped back to admire her work.

The tarts had taken her all morning. Five hours of weighing the butter and sugar and flour, of mixing and kneading and rolling the dough, of whisking and simmering and straining the egg yolks and lemon juice until they were thick and creamy and the color of buttercups. She had glazed the crust and crimped the edges like a lace doily. She had boiled and candied the delicate strips of lemon peel and ground sugar crystals into a fine powder for garnish. Her fingers itched to dust the tart edges now, but she refrained. They had to cool first, or else the sugar would melt into unattractive puddles on the surface.

These tarts encompassed everything she had learned from the tattered recipe books on the kitchen shelf. There was not a hurried moment nor a careless touch nor a lesser ingredient in those fluted pans. She had been meticulous at every step. She had baked her very heart into them.

Her inspection lingered, her eyes scanning every inch, every roll of the crust, every shining surface.

Finally, she allowed herself a smile.

Before her sat three perfect lemon tarts, and everyone in Hearts — from the dodo birds to the King himself — would have to recognize that she was the best baker in the kingdom. Even her own mother would be forced to admit that it was so.

Her anxiety released, she bounced on her toes and squealed into her clasped hands.

"You are my crowning joy," she proclaimed, spreading her arms wide over the tarts, as if bestowing a knighthood upon them. "Now I bid you to go into the world with your lemony scrumptiousness and bring forth smiles from every mouth you grace with your presence."

"Speaking to the food again, Lady Catherine?"

"Ah-ah, not just any food, Cheshire." She lifted a finger without glancing back. "Might I introduce to you the most wondrous lemon tarts ever to be baked within the great Kingdom of Hearts!"

A striped tail curled around her right shoulder. A furry, whiskered head appeared on her left. Cheshire purred thoughtfully, the sound vibrating down her spine. "Astounding," he said, in that tone he had that always left Cath unsure whether he was mocking her. "But where's the fish?"

Cath kissed the sugar crystals from her fingers and shook her head. "No fish."

"No fish? Whatever is the point?"

"The point is *perfection.*" Her stomach tingled every time she thought of it.

Cheshire vanished from her shoulders and reappeared on the baking table, one clawed paw hovering over the tarts. Cath jumped forward to shoo him back. "Don't you dare! They're for the King's party, you goose."

Cheshire's whiskers twitched. "The King? Again?"

Stool legs screeched against the floor as Cath dragged a seat closer to the table and perched on top of it. "I thought I'd save one for him and the others can be served at the feasting table. It makes His Majesty so happy, you know, when I bake him things. And a happy king —"

"Makes for a happy kingdom." Cheshire yawned without bothering to cover his mouth and, grimacing, Cath held her hands in between him and the tarts to protect from any distasteful tuna breath.

"A happy king also makes for a most excellent testimonial. Imagine if he were to declare me the official tart baker of the kingdom! People will line up for miles to taste them."

"They smell tart."

"They *are* tarts." Cath turned one of the fluted pans so the blossom of the lemon-peel rose was aligned with the others. She was always mindful of how her treats were displayed. Mary Ann said her pastries were even more beautiful than those made by the royal pastry chefs.

And after tonight, her desserts would not only be known as more beautiful, they would be known as superior in every way. Such praise was exactly what she and Mary Ann needed to launch their bakery. After so many years of planning, she could feel the dream morphing into a reality.

"Are lemons in season this time of year?" asked Cheshire, watching Cath as she swept up the leftover lemon peels and tied them in cheesecloth. The gardeners could use them to keep pests away.

"Not exactly," she said, smiling to herself. Her thoughts stole back to that morning. Pale light filtering through her lace curtains. Waking up to the smell of citrus in the air.

Part of her wanted to keep the memory tucked like a secret against her chest, but Cheshire would find out soon enough. A tree sprouting up in one's bedroom overnight was a difficult secret to keep. Cath was surprised the rumors hadn't yet spread, given Cheshire's knack for gossip-gathering. Perhaps he'd been too busy snoozing all morning. Or, more likely, having his belly rubbed by the maids.

"They're from a dream," she confessed, carrying the tarts to the pie safe where they could finish cooling.

Cheshire sat back on his haunches. "A dream?" His mouth split open into a wide, toothy grin. "Do tell."

"And have half the kingdom knowing about it by nightfall? Absolutely not. I had a dream and then I woke up and there was a lemon tree growing in my bedroom. That is all you need to know."

She slammed the pie safe shut with finality, as much to silence herself as to prevent further questions. The truth was, the dream had been clinging to her skin from the moment she'd woken up, haunting and tantalizing her. She wanted to talk about it, almost as much as she wanted to keep it locked up and all to herself.

It had been a hazy, beautiful dream, and in it there had been a hazy, beautiful boy. He was dressed all in black and standing in an orchard of lemon trees, and she had the distinct sensation that he had something that belonged to her. She didn't know what it was, only that she wanted it back, but every time she took a step toward him he receded farther and farther away.

A shiver slipped down the back of her dress. She could still feel the curiosity that tugged at her chest, the need to chase after him.

But mostly it was his eyes that haunted her. Yellow and shining, sweet and tart. His eyes had been bright like lemons ready to fall from a tree.

She shook away the wispy memories and turned back to Cheshire. "By the time I woke up, a branch from the tree had already pulled one of the bedposts full off. Of course, Mama made the gardeners take it down before it did any more damage, but I was able to sneak away some lemons first."

"I wondered what the hullabaloo was about this morning." Cheshire's tail flicked against the butcher block. "Are you sure the lemons are safe for consumption? If they sprouted from a dream, they could be, you know, *that* kind of food."

Cath's attention drifted back to the closed pie safe, the tarts hidden behind its wire mesh. "You're worried that the King might become shorter if he eats one?"

Cheshire snorted. "On the contrary, I'm worried that I will turn into a house should *I* eat one. I've been minding my figure, you know."

Giggling, Cath leaned over the table and scratched him beneath his chin. "You're perfect no matter your size, Cheshire. But the lemons are safe — I bit one before I started baking." Her cheeks puckered at the sour memory.

Cheshire had started to purr, already ignoring her. Cath cupped her chin with her free hand while Cheshire flopped deliriously onto one side and her strokes moved down to his belly. "Besides, if you ever did eat some bad food, I could still find a use for you. I've always wanted a cat-drawn carriage."

Cheshire opened one eye, his pupil slitted and unamused.

"I would dangle balls of yarn and fish bones out in front to keep you moving."

He stopped purring long enough to say, "You are not as cute as you think you are, Lady Pinkerton."

Cath tapped Cheshire once on the nose and pulled away. "You could do your disappearing trick and then everyone would think, *My, my, look at the glorious bulbous head pulling that carriage down the street!*"

Cheshire was fully glaring at her now. "I am a proud feline, not a beast of labor."

He disappeared with a huff.

"Don't be cross. I'm only teasing." Catherine untied her apron and draped it on a hook on the wall, revealing a perfect apron-shaped silhouette on her dress, outlined in flour and bits of dried dough.

"By-the-bye." His voice drifted back to her. "Your mother is looking for you."

"What for? I've been down here all morning."

"Yes, and now you're going to be late. Unless you're going as a lemon tart yourself, you'd better get on with it."

"Late?" Catherine glanced at the cuckoo clock on the wall. It was still early afternoon, plenty of time to —

Her pulse skipped as she heard a faint wheezing coming from inside the clock. "Oh! Cuckoo, did you doze off again?" She smacked her palm against the clock's side and the door sprang open, revealing a tiny red bird, fast asleep. "Cuckoo!"

The bird startled awake with a mad flap of his wings. "Oh my, oh heavens," he squawked, rubbing his eyes with the tips of his wings. "What time is it?"

"Whatever are you asking me for, you doltish bird?" With a harried groan, Catherine ran from the kitchen, crashing into Mary Ann on the stairwell.

"Cath — Lady Catherine! I was coming to . . . the Marchioness is —"

"I know, I know, the ball. I lost track of time."

Mary Ann gave her a fast head-to-toe

glance and grabbed her wrist. “Best get you cleaned up before she sees you and calls for both of our heads.”

Chapter 2

Mary Ann checked that the Marchioness wasn't around the corner before ushering Cath into the bedroom and shutting the door.

The other maid, Abigail, was there already, dressed identical to Mary Ann in a demure black dress and white apron, attempting to swat a rocking-horsefly out the open window with a broom. Every time she missed, it would nicker and whip its mane to either side, before flying back up toward the ceiling. "These pests will be the death of me!" Abigail growled to Mary Ann, swiping the sweat from her brow. Then, realizing that Catherine was there too, she dropped into a lopsided curtsy.

Catherine stiffened. "Abigail — !"

Her warning was too late. A pair of tiny rockers clomped over the back of Abigail's bonnet before the horse darted back up toward the ceiling.

"Why, you obnoxious little pony!" Abigail screeched, swinging her broom.

Cringing, Mary Ann dragged Catherine into the powder room and shut the door. Water had already been drawn in a pitcher on the washing stand. "There isn't time for a bath, but let's not tell your mother that," she said, fiddling with the back of Catherine's muslin dress while Cath dipped a washcloth into the pitcher. She furiously scrubbed the flour from her face. How had she managed to get it behind her ears?

"I thought you were going into town today," she said, letting Mary Ann peel off her dress and chemise.

"I did, but it was fabulously dull. All anyone wanted to talk about was the ball, as if the King doesn't have a party every other day." Taking the washcloth, Mary Ann scrubbed Catherine's arms until her flesh was pink, then spritzed her with rose water to cover up the lingering aroma of pastry dough and oven fires. "There was a lot of talk about a new court joker who will be making his debut tonight. Jack was bragging about how he's going to steal his hat and smash the bells as a sort of initiation."

"That seems very childish."

"I agree. Jack is such a knave." Mary Ann helped Catherine into a new chemise, before pushing her down onto a stool and running a brush through her dark hair. "I did hear one bit of interesting news though. The cobbler is retiring and will be leaving his storefront empty by the end of this month." With a twist, a dish full of pins, and a touch of beeswax, a lovely chignon rested at the nape of Catherine's neck and her face was haloed by a cluster of jovial curls.

"The cobbler? On Main Street?"

"The very one." Mary Ann spun Cath around, her voice dropping to a whisper. "When I heard it, I immediately thought what a fine location it would be. For us."

Cath's eyes widened. "Sweet hearts, you're right. Right next to that toy shop —"

"And just down the hill from that quaint white chapel. Think of all the wedding cakes you'd be making."

"Oh! We could do a series of different-flavored cobblers for our grand opening, in honor of the shoemaker. We'll start with the classics — blueberry cobbler, peach cobbler — but then, imagine the possibilities. A lavender-nectarine cobbler one day, and the next, a banana-butterscotch cobbler, topped with graham cracker crumble and —"

"Stop it!" Mary Ann laughed. "I haven't had supper yet."

"We should go look at it, don't you think? Before word gets out?"

"I thought so too. Maybe tomorrow. But your mother . . ."

"I'll tell her we're going shopping for new ribbons. She won't mind." Cath swayed on the balls of her feet. "By the time she finds out about the bakery, we'll be able to show her what a tremendous business opportunity it is and even she won't be able to deny it."

Mary Ann's smile turned tight. "I don't think it's the business opportunity she's bound to disapprove of."

Cath flitted away her concern, although she knew Mary Ann was right. Her mother would never approve of her only daughter, the heir to Rock Turtle Cove, going into the men's world of business, especially with a humble servant like Mary Ann as her partner. Besides, baking was a job fit for servants, her mother would say. And she would loathe the idea that Cath planned on using her own marriage dowry in order to open the business herself.

But she and Mary Ann had been dreaming of it for so long, she sometimes forgot that it wasn't yet reality. Her pastries and desserts were already becoming renowned throughout the kingdom, and the King himself was her grandest fan, which might have been the only reason her mother tolerated her hobby at all.

"Her approval won't matter," Cath said, trying to convince herself as much as Mary Ann. The idea of her mother being angry over this decision, or worse, disowning her, made her stomach curdle. But it wouldn't come to that. She hoped.

She lifted her chin. "We're going forward with or without my parents' approval. We are going to have the best bakery in all of Hearts. Why, even the White Queen will travel here when she hears word of our decadent chocolate tortes and blissfully flaky currant scones."

Mary Ann bunched her lips to one side, doubtful.

"That reminds me," Cath continued. "I have three tarts cooling in the pie safe right now. Could you bring them tonight? Oh, but they still need a dusting of powdered sugar. I left some on the table. Just a teeny, tiny bit." She pinched her fingers in example.

"Of course I can bring them. What kind of tarts?"

"Lemon."

A teasing smile crept up Mary Ann's face. "From your tree?"

"You heard about it?"

"I saw Mr. Gardiner planting it under your window this morning and had to ask where it came from. All that hacking they had to do to get it unwound from your bedposts, and yet it seemed no worse for wear."

Catherine wrung her hands, not sure why talking about her dream tree made her self-conscious. "Well, yes, that's where I got my lemons, and I'm certain these tarts are my best yet. By tomorrow morning, all of Hearts will be talking about them and longing to know when they can buy our desserts for themselves."

"Don't be silly, Cath." Mary Ann pulled a corset over Cath's head. "They've been asking that since you made those maple–brown sugar cookies last year."

Cath wrinkled her nose. "Don't remind me. I overcooked them, remember? Too crisp on the edges."

"You're too harsh a critic."

"I want to be the best."

Mary Ann settled her hands on Cath's shoulders. "You are the best. And I've calculated the numbers again — with the expected costs attached to Mr. Caterpillar's shop, monthly expenses, and the cost of ingredients, all measured against our planned daily output and pricing. Adjusted to allow some room for error, I still think we would be profitable in under a year."

Cath clapped her hands over her ears. "You take all the fun out of it with your numbers and mathematics. You know how they make my head spin."

Mary Ann sniffed and turned away, opening the wardrobe. "You have no trouble converting tablespoons into cups. It's not all that different."

"It *is* different, which is why I need you on this venture. My brilliant, oh-so-logical business partner."

She could almost feel Mary Ann's eyes roll. "I'd like to get that in writing, Lady Catherine. Now, I seem to recall we had chosen the white gown for tonight?"

"Whichever you think." Stifling the fantasy of their future bakery, Cath set to clipping a set of pearls to her earlobes.

"So?" Mary Ann asked as she pulled a pair of drawers and a petticoat from the wardrobe, then urged Cath to turn around so she could adjust the corset laces. "Was it a good dream?"

Cath was surprised to find that she still had pastry dough beneath her fingernails. Picking at it gave her a good excuse to keep her head lowered, hiding the blush that crept up her throat. "Nothing too special," she said, thinking of lemon-yellow eyes.

She gasped as the corset tightened unexpectedly, squeezing her rib cage. "I can tell when you're lying," said Mary Ann.

"Oh, fine. Yes, it was a good dream. But they're all magical, aren't they?"

"I wouldn't know. I've never had one. Though Abigail told me that once she dreamed about a big glowing crescent shape hovering in the sky . . . and the next morning Cheshire showed up, all grinning teeth hovering in the air and begging for a saucer of milk. Years later and we still can't seem to get rid of him."

Cath grunted. "I'm fond of Cheshire, yet I can't help but hope that my dream might portend something a bit more magical than that."

"Even if it doesn't, at least you got some good lemons out of it."

"True. I shall be satisfied." Though she wasn't. Not nearly.

"Catherine!" The door swung open and the Marchioness floated in, her eyes saucer-wide and her face purple-red despite having been recently powdered. Catherine's mother lived her life in a state of constant bewilderment. "There you are, my dear darling! What are you — not even dressed yet?"

"Oh, Mama, Mary Ann was just helping me —"

"Abigail, stop playing with that broom and get in here! We need your help! Mary Ann, what is she wearing?"

"My lady, we thought the white gown that she —"

"Absolutely not! Red! You will wear the red dress." Her mother swung open the wardrobe doors and pulled out a full gown overflowing with heavy red velvet, an enormous bustle, and a neckline that was sure to leave little unexposed. "Yes, perfect."

"Oh, Mama. Not that dress. It's too small!"

Her mother picked a waxy green leaf off the bed and draped the dress across the covers. "No, no, no, not too small for my precious little sweetling. This is going to be a very special night, Catherine, and it's imperative that you look your best."

Cath traded a glance with Mary Ann, who shrugged.

"But it's just another ball. Why don't I —"

"Tut-tut, child." Her mother scurried across the room and framed Cath's face in both hands. Though her mother was bony as a bird, there was no sense of delicacy as she pinched and squeezed Cath's face. "You are in for such a delight this evening, my pretty girl." Her eyes glimmered in a way that made Catherine suspicious, before she barked, *"Now turn around!"*

Catherine jumped and spun to face the window.

Her mother, who had become the Marchioness when she married, had that effect on everyone. She was often a warm, loving woman, and Cath's father, the Marquess, doted on her incessantly, but Cath was all too familiar with her mood swings. All cooing and delighted one moment and screaming at the top of her lungs the next. Despite her tiny stature, she had a booming voice and a particular glare that could make even a lion's heart shrivel beneath it.

Cath thought by now she would have been used to her mother's temperament, but the frequent changes still took her by surprise.

"Mary Ann, tighten her corset."

"But, my lady, I just —"

"Tighter, Mary Ann. This dress won't fit without a twenty-two-inch waist, although just once I'd like to see you down to twenty. You have your father's unfortunate bones, you know, and we must be vigilant if we're to keep from having his figure too. Abigail, be a dear and bring me the ruby set from my jewelry cabinet."

"The ruby set?" Catherine whined as Mary Ann undid the corset laces. "But those earrings are so heavy."

"Don't be such a jellyfish. It's only for one night. Tighter!"

Catherine pinched her face together as Mary Ann tugged on the corset strings. She exhaled as much air as she could and gripped the side of the vanity, willing away the sparkles dancing before her eyes.

"Mother, I can't breathe."

"Well then, next time, I hope you'll think twice before taking a second helping of dessert like you did last night. You can't eat like a piglet and dress like a lady. It will be a miracle if this dress fits."

"We could — wear — the white one?"

Her mother crossed her arms. "My daughter will be wearing red tonight like a true . . . never you mind that. You'll just have to go without dinner."

Cath groaned as Mary Ann cinched the corset one more time. Having to suffer through the bindings was bad enough, but going without dinner too? The food was what she looked forward to most during the King's parties, and all she'd eaten that day was a single boiled egg — she'd been too caught up with her baking to think about eating more.

Her stomach growled in its confinement.

"Are you all right?" Mary Ann whispered.

She bobbed her head, not wanting to waste any precious air to speak.

"Dress!"

Before Catherine could catch her breath she found herself being squashed and wrangled into the red velvet monstrosity. When the maids had finished and Catherine dared to peek into the mirror, she was relieved that, while she may have felt like an encased sausage, she didn't look like one. The bold color brought out the red in her lips and made her fair skin appear fairer and her dark hair darker. When Abigail settled the enormous necklace onto her collarbone and replaced her pearls with dangling rubies, Catherine felt, momentarily, like a true lady of the court, all glamour and mystery.

"Marvelous!" The Marchioness clasped Catherine's hand in both of hers, that peculiar, misty-eyed look returning. "I'm so proud of you."

Catherine frowned. "You are?"

"Oh, don't start fishing now." Her mother clucked her tongue, patting the back of Cath's hand once before dropping it.

Catherine eyed her reflection again. The mystique was quickly fading, leaving her feeling exposed. She would have preferred a nice, roomy day dress, covered in flour or not. "Mama, I'll be overdressed. No one else will be so done up."

Her mother sniffed. "Precisely. You look exceptional!" She wiped away a tear. "I could scatter to pieces."

Despite all her discomfort, all her reservations, Cath couldn't deny a hot spark behind her sternum. Her mother's voice was a constant nag in her head, telling her to put down the fork, to stand up straight, to smile, *but not that much*! She knew her mother wanted the best for her, but it was oh so lovely to hear compliments for once.

With one last dreamy sigh, the Marchioness mentioned checking on Cath's father before she fluttered out of the room, dragging Abigail along with her. As the door to her chambers closed, Cath yearned to fall onto her bed with the exhaustion that came from being in her mother's presence, but she was sure she would rip an important seam if she did.

"Do I look as ridiculous as I feel?"

Mary Ann shook her head. "You look ravishing."

"Is it absurd to look ravishing at this silly ball? Everyone will think I'm being presumptuous."

Mary Ann pressed her lips in apology. "It is a bit of butter upon bacon."

"Oh, please, I'm hungry enough as it is." Cath twisted inside the corset, trying to pry up some of the boning that dug into her ribs, but it wouldn't budge. "I need a chocolate."

"I'm sorry, Cath, but I don't think that dress could fit a single bite. Come along. I'll help you into your shoes."

CHAPTER 3

The White Rabbit, master of ceremonies, stood at the top of the stairs with a puffed-up chest, smiling twittishly as Catherine's father handed him their announcement card. "Good eve, good eve, Your Lordship! What a stunning cravat you're wearing tonight, so perfectly matches your hair. Like snowfall on a balding hill, is how I'd describe that."

"Do you think so, Mr. Rabbit?" asked Cath's father, pleased with the compliment. He spent a moment patting his head, as if to confirm the flattery.

The Rabbit's gaze darted to the Marchioness. "My dear Lady Pinkerton, I'm sure my eyes have never seen such rare beauty, such outstanding elegance —"

The Marchioness brushed him off. "Get on with it, herald."

"Er, of course, I am your humble servant, my lady." Flustered, the Rabbit stuck his ears straight up and raised a trumpet to his mouth. As the ditty echoed throughout the ballroom, he proclaimed: "Presenting Whealagig T. Pinkerton, the most honorable Marquess of Rock Turtle Cove, accompanied by his wife, Lady Idonia Pinkerton, Marchioness of Rock Turtle Cove, and daughter, Lady Catherine Pinkerton!"

As the Marquess and Marchioness descended the steps into the ballroom, the White Rabbit's pinkish eyes skipped to Catherine, widening as they took in her voluminous red gown. His nose twitched with repugnance, but he was quick to mask it under another sycophantic grin. "Why, Lady Pinkerton, you look so . . . er. So very noticeable."

Cath attempted a faint smile and moved to follow her parents down the steps, but as soon as she looked down into the ballroom she gasped and reeled back.

A sea of black and white stretched before her.

Ivory-tailed dress coats and ebony elbow gloves.

Pale starfish fascinators and crow-feather bow ties.

Chessboard leggings. Zebra face masks. Black velvet skirts trimmed in rhinestones and icicles. Even some of the Diamond courtiers had pasted black spades onto their stomachs to disguise their identifying red marks.

Noticeable, indeed.

There was still the rare spot of red in the crowd — a rose tucked into a buttonhole or a ribbon lacing the back of a gown — but Cath alone wore red from head to toe. As if her dress weren't enough, she felt sudden redness rushing up her neck and across her cheeks. She felt eyes snagging on her, heard the intake of breaths, sensed the glower of distaste. How could her mother not have known this was one of the King's black-and-white balls?

Realization hit in quick succession.

Her mother had known. Staring at her mother's billowing white dress and her father's matching white tuxedo, Cath realized that her mother had known all along.

Another trumpet ditty muffled in her ears. Beside her, the White Rabbit cleared his throat. "So devastatingly sorry to rush you, Lady Pinkerton, but there are more guests waiting to be presented . . ."

She glanced at the line that had formed behind her, more members of the gentry peeking around one another and gawking at her.

Dread settling at the base of her stomach,

Catherine picked up her skirt and started toward the masses of penguins and raccoons.

The ballroom of Heart Castle had long ago been carved from a gargantuan chunk of pink quartz, from the floor to the balusters to the enormous pillars that supported the domed roof. The ceiling was painted in murals depicting various landscapes from the kingdom: the Somewhere Hills and the Nowhere Forest, the Crossroads and the castle and rolling farmlands stretching to all horizons. Even Rock Turtle Cove was depicted above the doors that led out to the rose gardens.

Large windows marched along the southern edge of the room, heart-shaped and cut from faceted red glass. The feasting table, overflowing with fruits, cheeses, and sweets, stretched the length of the north wall, beside the partition that separated the dancers from the orchestra. Crystal chandeliers encircled the ceiling, warming the walls with the light of thousands of white tapered candles. Even from the steps Cath could hear a few of the hotheaded candles ranting about the ballroom's draftiness and would someone *please* shut the door down there.

Catherine set her sights on the feasting table — a place of comfort in the crowded ballroom, even if her dress was too tight for her to eat anything. Each step was a struggle with her body pin-straight, her corset constricted against her ribs, and the bustle dragging along the stairs. She was grateful to finally feel the hard click of the ballroom floor beneath her heels.

"My dearest Lady Catherine, I did hope you would be in attendance tonight."

Her gratitude vanished. It figured that Margaret would latch on to her first, before she'd hardly taken two steps toward the food.

Catherine schooled her expression into delight. "Why, Lady Margaret! How do you do?"

Margaret Mearle, daughter of the Count of Crossroads, had been Catherine's closest bosom friend since they were toddlers. Unfortunately, they had never much liked each other.

Margaret had the great hardship of being unbearably unattractive. Not the homely-caterpillar-waiting-to-turn-into-a-beautiful-butterfly sort of unattractive, but the sort of unattractive that gave those around her a sense of hopelessness. She had a sharp chin, tiny eyes spaced too close together and overshadowed by an overhanging brow, and broad, inelegant shoulders that were made more prominent by her ill-fitting clothes. If it weren't for the gowns she wore, Margaret would have been frequently mistaken for a boy.

An unattractive one.

Though Margaret's physical shortcomings were a favorite conversation topic of Catherine's mother ("She would not be such a very dreadful case if only she would snug up her corsets a bit more"), Catherine herself found Margaret's personality to be far more offensive, as Margaret had been convinced since childhood that she was very, *very* clever and very, *very* righteous. More clever and more righteous than anyone else. She excelled at pointing out how much more clever and righteous she was.

Given that they were such dear friends, Margaret had long seen it as her role to point out all of Catherine's inadequacies. In hopes of bettering her. Like any true friend would.

"I'm quite well," said Margaret as they shared a mutual curtsy, "but I feel wretched to inform you that your dress is unduly red."

"Thank you so much for that insight," Cath said through her crushing smile. "I have recently made the same observation."

Margaret's face puckered, squinching up her small eyes. "I must warn you, my dearest Catherine, that such an endeavor to capture attention could lead to lifelong arrogance and vanity. It is much wiser to let your inner beauty shine through a drab gown than to attempt to conceal it with physical accoutrements."

"Thank you for that advice. I will keep it under consideration." Cath refrained from casting an unimpressed glance at Margaret's gown, which was drab and black and topped with a sobering fur cap.

"I hope you will. And the moral of that is 'Once a goldfish, forever a goldfish.' "

The corner of Cath's mouth twitched. That was one more of Margaret's delightful quirks — she was a living encyclopedia of morals that Cath could never make any sense of, and she could never tell if the morals were nonsense, or if she was just too dim to understand them. No doubt Margaret would assure her it was the latter.

Not that she was going to ask.

"Hm. So true," Cath agreed, scanning the nearby guests in hopes for an excuse to abandon Margaret before she built up any momentum. She could be impossible to escape from when she got to carrying on.

Not far away, Sir Magpie and his wife were drinking cordials beside a heart-shaped ice sculpture, but Catherine dared not escape to them — it could have been her imagination, but her jewelry had an uncanny way of disappearing around the Magpies.

Cath's father was entertaining the Four, Seven, and Eight of Diamonds. Even as Cath spotted them, her father reached the climax of some joke and the Four fell onto his flat back, laughing hysterically and kicking his legs in the air. After a moment it became clear that he couldn't get back up on his own and the Eight reached down to help, still chuckling.

Catherine sighed — she had never been skilled at slipping easily into a joke half told.

And then there was the Most Noble Pygmalion Warthog, Duke of Tuskany. Cath had often found him to be awkward and distant and a terrible conversationalist. As their eyes met, she was surprised to find that he was watching her and Margaret.

She wasn't sure which of them turned away first.

"Are you looking for someone, Lady Catherine?" Margaret inched closer — uncomfortably close, settling her chin on Cath's shoulder — and followed her gaze.

"No, no, I was only . . . observing."

"Observing whom?"

"Well. That's a fine waistcoat the Duke is

wearing tonight, don't you think?" she asked, aiming for civility as she inched out from beneath Margaret's chin.

Margaret curled her nose in disgust. "How could anyone notice his waistcoat? When I look at the Duke, all I see is the way he insists on turning up his nose at everyone else, as if being the Duke of Tuskany were any great achievement."

Cath cocked her head. "I think his nose does that naturally." She pressed a finger to her own nose and pushed upward, testing it out. It didn't make her *feel* elitist . . .

Margaret blanched. "For shame, Catherine. You can't go around mocking everyone else like that! At least, not in public."

"Oh! I didn't mean to cause offense. It's just sort of snout-like is all. He probably has an excellent sense of smell. I wonder whether he couldn't track down truffles with a nose like that."

Cath was spared from her defense by a rough tap against her shoulder.

She turned and found herself staring at a black tunic covering a puffed-up chest. Her gaze traveled upward to a scowling face half hidden by a single eye-patch and messy hair peeking out of a white beret.

Jack, the Knave of Hearts, who had been knighted out of pity after losing his right eye in a game of charades.

Her mood sank even further. This ball was off to the most horrible of starts. "Hello, Jack."

"Lady Pinkerton," he drawled, his breath smelling of mulled wine. His eye darted toward Margaret. "Lady Mearle."

Margaret folded her arms over her chest. "It is of intolerable impoliteness to interrupt a conversation, Jack."

"I came to tell Lady Pinkerton that this is a black-and-white ball."

Cath lowered her eyes and tried to look sheepish, though with every reminder she was becoming less embarrassed and more annoyed. "There seems to have been some miscommunication."

"You look stupid," said Jack.

Catherine bristled. "There's no cause for rudeness."

Jack huffed, scanning her dress again. And again. "You're not half as lovely as you think you are, Lady Pinkerton. Not a quarter as lovely even, and I've only got one eye to see it."

"I assure you I don't —"

"Everyone thinks as much, just won't say it to your face like I will. But I'm not afraid of you, not one little bit."

"I never said —"

"I don't even like you all that very much."

Catherine pressed her lips tight and inhaled a patient breath. "Yes, I do believe you told me that the last time I saw you, Jack. And the time before that. And the time before that. You've been reminding me how much you dislike me since we were six years old and dressing up the maypole, if I recall correctly."

"Yes. Right. Because it's true." Jack's cheeks had reddened. "Also, you smell like a daisy. Except, one of those awful, stinky ones."

"Naturally, one of those," said Catherine. "Heaven forbid I mistake that for a compliment."

Jack grunted, then reached up and pulled on one of her curls.

"Ow!"

The Knave had swiveled on his feet and marched away before Catherine could think of a response, though she would later wish she had taken the opportunity to give him a good kick in the shins.

"What an oaf," Margaret said after he had gone.

"He most certainly is," agreed Catherine, rubbing her scalp and wondering how long she'd been there and how much longer she would have to stay.

"Of course," Margaret continued, "it is most deplorable of you to encourage such oafish behavior."

Catherine spun toward her, aghast. "I do not encourage it."

"If that's what you believe, I suppose we must agree to be disagreeable," said Margaret. "And the moral of that is —"

But before she could extrapolate some nonsensical proof of ill behavior, a blare of a trumpet echoed through the ballroom. At the top of the steps, the White Rabbit proclaimed in his nasally voice —

"PRESENTING HIS ROYAL MAJESTY THE KING OF HEARTS."

The White Rabbit blew the horn again, then tucked the instrument against his side and bowed. Cath turned with the rest of the guests as the King emerged at the top of his own private staircase. The entire chessboard of aristocrats rippled with bows and curtsies.

The King wore full regalia — a white fur cloak, black-and-white-striped pantaloons, glossy white shoes with diamond-studded buckles, and a heart-tipped scepter in one hand. This was all topped with the crown, trimmed with more rubies and diamonds and velvet and a central heart-shaped finial.

It would have been a striking ensemble, except the fur had some syrupy substance near the collar, the pantaloons were bunching around one knee, and the crown — which Catherine had always thought looked too heavy for the King's tiny head — had slipped to one side. Also, His Majesty was grinning like a loon when Catherine rose from her curtsy.

And he was grinning at her.

Catherine stiffened as the King jostled down the steps. The crowd fanned out to allow him through, creating a direct pathway, and before Catherine could think to move aside herself, the King was standing before her.

"Fair evening, Lady Pinkerton!" He arched up onto his toes, which drew even more attention to his minuscule stature. He stood at least two hands shorter than Catherine, despite the rumor that he had special-crafted shoes with two-inch soles.

"Fair evening, Your Majesty. How do you do?" She curtsied again.

The White Rabbit, who had followed in the King's wake, cleared his throat. "His Royal Majesty would like to request the hand of Lady Catherine Pinkerton for the first quadrille."

Her eyes widened. "Why, thank you, Your Majesty. I would be honored." Catherine dipped into a third curtsy — her practiced reaction to anything that was said in the King's presence. It was not at all that he was an intimidating man. Much the opposite. The King, perhaps fifteen years her senior, was round-bodied and rosy-cheeked and had a tendency to giggle at the most inopportune times. It was his very lack of intimidation that kept Catherine on her best behavior, otherwise it would be too easy to forget that he was her sovereign.

Handing his scepter to the White Rabbit, the King of Hearts took Catherine's hand and led her onto the dance floor. Cath told herself it was a mercy to be swept away from Margaret, but the King's company wasn't much of an improvement.

No, that wasn't fair. The King was a sweet man. A simple man. A *happy* man, which was important, as a happy king made for a happy kingdom.

He simply wasn't a clever man.

As they took the position of top couple on the dance floor, Cath was struck with a surge of dread. She was dancing with the King. All eyes would be upon them, and everyone would think she had chosen this dress for no other reason than to catch his eye.

"You look lovely, Lady Pinkerton," said the King. He was speaking more to her bosom than her face — a result of his unfortunate height, not any sort of ungentlemanliness, and yet Catherine could not keep her cheeks from flushing.

Why, oh why, couldn't she have fought against her mother's wishes, just this once?

"Thank you, Your Majesty," she said, her voice strained.

"I am indeed fond of the color red!"

"Why . . . who isn't, Your Majesty?"

He giggled his agreement and Cath was glad when the music began and they entered into the first figure. They turned away from each other to walk down the outside lines of couples, too far apart to speak. Catherine felt her corset pinching beneath her breasts and she pressed her palms against her skirt to keep from fidgeting with it.

"This is a delightful ball," she said, joining the King at the end of the line. They took hands. His were soft and damp.

"Do you think so?" He beamed. "I always love the black-and-white balls. They're so . . . so . . ."

"Neutral?" Catherine supplied.

"Yes!" He sighed dreamily, his eyes on Catherine's face. "You always know just what I'm thinking, Lady Pinkerton."

She looked away.

They ducked beneath the outstretched

arms of the next couple and released hands to twirl around Mr. and Mrs. Badger.

"I must ask," the King started as they clasped hands again, "I don't suppose you may have . . . by chance . . . brought any treats with you this evening?" He watched her with shining eyes, his curled mustache twitching hopefully.

Cath beamed as they raised their hands so the next couple could duck beneath. She knew the King was stretching up on his tiptoes but she respectfully did not look down. "In fact, I baked three lemon tarts this morning, and my maid was going to ensure they made it to your feasting table during the festivities. They might be there now."

His face lit up and he twisted his head to eye the long, long table, but they were much too far away to pick out three little tarts.

"Fantastic," he swooned, missing a couple dance steps and forcing Catherine to stand awkwardly for a moment before he picked it up again.

"I hope you'll enjoy them."

He returned his attention to her, shaking his head as if dazed. "Lady Pinkerton, you are a treasure."

She stifled a grimace, embarrassed by the dreamy tone in his voice.

"Though I must confess, I have a particular weakness for key lime tarts as much as lemon." His cheeks wobbled. "You know what they say — key lime is the key to a king's heart!"

Cath had never heard that before, but she let her head bounce in agreement. "So they do!"

The King's grin was effervescent.

By the end of the dance Catherine felt ready to collapse from the strain of appearing joyful and attentive, and she felt only relief as the King air-kissed the top of her hand and thanked her for the pleasure of the dance.

"I must find these delectable tarts of yours, Lady Pinkerton, but I hope you'll keep the final dance for me as well?"

"With pleasure. You honor me so."

He giggled, mad as hops as he adjusted his crown, then took off waltzing toward the feasting table.

Cath withered, grateful that the first quadrille was over. Perhaps she could persuade her parents to let her leave before that final dance of the evening. Her plotting made her feel guilty — how many girls would love to receive such attention from the King?

He wasn't an offensive dancing partner,

only a tiresome one.

Thinking a bit of air might help her cheeks recover from the stretched-out smile, she headed toward the balconies. But she hadn't gone a dozen steps through the crowd of black crinolines and white top hats before the candlelit chandeliers flickered as one and went out.

Chapter 4

The music screeched and died. A cry arose from the guests as the ballroom was plunged into darkness.

There was the sound of breathing, the crinkle of petticoats, an uncertain stillness. Then there was a spark and a flicker. A ring of candlelight spiraled around one of the center-most chandeliers and a haunting glow stretched across the domed ceiling, leaving the guests drenched in shadows below.

Hanging from the lit chandelier was a vertical hoop that Catherine was sure hadn't been there before.

Lounging inside the hoop, apparently as comfortable as if it had been a chaise lounge, was a Joker.

He wore close-fitting black pants tucked into worn leather boots, a black tunic belted at his hips, and gloves, also black — not the white dress gloves the gentry wore. His skin glowed like amber in the firelight and his eyes were rimmed in kohl so thick it became a mask. On first glance, Catherine thought he had long black hair too, until she realized that he was wearing a black hat that hung in three points, each tipped with a small silver bell — though he held so still, they didn't ring, and Catherine could not recall the tinkle of bells when the candles had gone out.

When — *how* — had he gotten up there?

The stranger hung suspended for a long moment, dwelling in the stares of the guests below, as the hoop slowly spun. His gaze was piercing and Catherine held her breath as it found her and, at once, seemed to stall. His eyes narrowed, almost imperceptibly, as he took in her flamboyant red gown.

Cath shivered and had the strangest urge to give him a nervous wave. An acknowledgment that, yes, she was aware that her dress was *unduly red.* But by the time her hand had lifted, the Joker's attention had skipped on.

She dropped her hand and exhaled.

Once the hoop had made a full circle, a ghost smile lifted the corners of the stranger's lips. He tilted his head. The bells jingled.

There was an intake of breath from the watchful crowd.

"Ladies. Gentlemen." He spoke with precision. "Your Most Illustrious Majesty."

The King bounced on his toes like a child waiting for the Christmas feast.

The Joker swung himself up in one fluid motion so he was standing inside the hoop. It spun another lazy half turn. They all listened, mesmerized by the hesitant creak of the rope that attached it to the chandelier.

"Why is a raven like a writing-desk?"

The hoop stopped spinning.

The Joker's words blanketed the ballroom. The silence became resolute. With the stranger facing toward her again, Catherine caught a flicker of firelight in his eyes.

Then, upon realizing that a riddle had been posed, the crowd began to rustle with murmurs. Hushed voices repeated the riddle. *Why is a raven like a writing desk?*

No one proposed an answer.

When it became clear that no one would, the Joker stretched one hand out over the audience, closed tight in a fist. Those beneath him took a step back.

"You see, they can each produce a few notes."

He opened his fist and, not a *few* notes, but an entire blizzard of black and white papers burst from his palm like confetti. The crowd gasped, reeling back as the pieces swarmed and fluttered through the air, so thick it seemed the entire ceiling had disintegrated into paper notes. The more that came, the more the crowd cooed. Some of the men upended their hats to catch as many of the notes as they could.

Laughing, Catherine lifted her face to the ceiling. It felt like being caught in a warm blizzard. She held her hands out to the sides and gave a twirl, delighting in how her red skirt ballooned out, kicking up a papery snowdrift.

When she had gone three full circles, she paused and tugged a slip out of her hair — thin white parchment, no longer than her thumb, printed with a single red heart.

The last confetti pieces looped down to the floor. Some spots in the ballroom were ankle-deep.

The Joker was still peering down from his hoop. In the tumult, he had removed his three-pointed hat, revealing that his hair was black after all, messy and curling around the tops of his ears.

"Though admittedly," he said when the crowd had quieted, "the notes tend to be very flat."

The bells on his hat tinkled and up from the base of those three tiny points an enormous black bird arose, cawing as it soared toward the ceiling. The audience cried out in surprise. The raven circled the room, wings so large their flapping stirred up the mounds of paper below. It took a second turn around the ballroom before settling itself in the chandelier above the Joker.

The audience began to applaud. Catherine, dazzled, found her hands coming together almost without her knowing.

The Joker tugged his hat back onto his head, then slipped down from the hoop so he was hanging from a single gloved hand. Catherine's heart lurched. It was much too high to risk the fall. But as he let go, a red velvet scarf had become tied to the hoop. The Joker spun languidly toward the floor, revealing white and black scarves in turn, all knotted together and appearing seamlessly from his fingers, until they had lowered him all the way to the ground, kicking up a swirl of paper notes.

The moment his boots touched the floor, the circle of light from the chandelier spread out through the ballroom, each taper catching flame in fast succession until the room was once again ablaze.

The crowd clapped. The Joker dipped into a bow.

When he straightened, he was holding a second hat in his hands — an ivory beret with a decorative silver band. The Joker sent it twirling on the tip of a finger. "I beg your pardon, but does anyone seem to be missing a hat?" he asked, his voice cutting through the applause.

A moment of uncertainty ensued, followed by an offended roar.

Jack, halfway across the room, was patting his tangled hair with both hands. Everyone laughed, and Catherine remembered Mary Ann saying that Jack had intended to steal the Joker's hat as a means of initiation.

"My sincerest apologies," said the Joker, smiling in a very unapologetic way. "I haven't the faintest idea how this hat came to be in my hands. Here, you may have it back."

Jack stormed through the crowd, his face reddening fast as people chortled around him.

But as he reached for the still-spinning hat, the Joker pulled away and turned the hat upside down. "But wait — I think there might be something inside. A surprise? A present?" He shut one eye and peered into the hat. "Ah — a stowaway!"

The Joker reached into the hat. His arm disappeared nearly to his shoulder — far deeper than the hat itself — and when he pulled back he had two tall, fuzzy white ears clasped in his fist.

The crowd leaned in closer.

"Oh my ears and whiskers," the Joker muttered. "How cliché. If I'd have known it was a rabbit, I would have just left him in there. But as it can't be helped now . . ."

The ears, when he pulled them out, were attached to none other than the master of ceremonies, the White Rabbit himself. He emerged sputtering and peering round-eyed at the crowd, as if he couldn't fathom how he had gotten into a beret in the middle of the ball.

Catherine pressed her hands over her mouth, stifling an unladylike snort.

"Why — I never!" the Rabbit stammered, flopping his big feet as the Joker settled him onto the floor. He swiped his ears out of the Joker's grip, straightened his tunic, and sniffed. "The nerve! I will be speaking to His Majesty about this blatant show of disrespect!"

The Joker bowed. "So very sorry, Mr. Rabbit. No disrespect was meant at all. Allow me to make amends with a heartfelt gift. Surely there must be something else in here . . ."

As Jack made another swipe for his hat, the Joker nonchalantly pulled it out of his reach and jingled the hat beside his ear.

"Oh yes. That will do." Reaching in again, he emerged this time with a very fine pocket watch, chain and all. With a flourish, he presented the watch to Mr. Rabbit. "Here you are. And see there, it's already set to the proper time."

Mr. Rabbit sniffed, but when the glitter of a diamond set into the watch's face caught his eye, he snatched it out of the Joker's hand. "Er — well. I'll consider . . . we shall see . . . but this *is* a fine watch . . ." He gnawed on the watch's hook with his large front teeth, and evidently determining that it was real gold, slipped it into his pocket. He cast another unhappy glare at the Joker before scrambling off into the crowd.

"And for you, Sir Jack-Be-Nimble, Jack-Be-Quick." The Joker offered the hat to Jack, who grabbed it away and slammed it onto his head.

The Joker started and raised a finger. "You may wish to —"

Jack's eyes bugged and he whipped the hat off again. A lit tapered candle was sitting in a silver candlestick on top of his head. The flame had already burned a smoldering hole into the top of the beret.

"Hey, I'm trying to get some sleep!" cried the candle.

"I beg your pardon." The Joker reached

forward and pinched the flame with the fingertips of his leather gloves. A curl of smoke wrapped around Jack's head as the corner of his good eye began to twitch. "That's peculiar. I thought for sure you'd be jumping over the candlestick, but this is all upside downward indeed."

The guests were in fits, many laughing so hard they didn't hear the echoing caw of the raven as it dropped off the chandelier and swooped toward them. Catherine took a startled step back as the raven brushed past her ear and settled onto the Joker's shoulder. The Joker did not flinch, even as the raven's talons dug into his tunic.

"With one last bit of wisdom, we must bid you a good night." Reaching up, the Joker tipped his own hat to the crowd. "Always check your hats before donning them. You never know what might be lurking inside." The bells jingled as he pivoted on his heels, making sure to face everyone in the audience.

Catherine straightened as he turned her way, and — *winked* at her?

She couldn't be sure if she'd imagined it.

His mouth lifted quick to one side and then, before her very eyes, his entire body melted into inky blackness. In the space of a heartbeat, the Joker had transformed into a winged shadow — a second raven.

The two birds fluttered toward a window and were gone.

Chapter 5

The new court joker was all anyone would talk about. Even the dancing went forgotten as the guests realized that the paper notes covering the floor contained more than just hearts — some had black diamonds, red spades, white clubs. Some, the shadow-profile of a raven. Others: a crown, a scepter, a three-pointed joker's cap. Some guests made a game of collecting as many of the different designs as they could, hunting for shapes they might have missed.

The giggle-mug King was jollier than Cath had ever seen him. Even halfway across the ballroom she could hear his pitched voice demanding that his guests confirm that, yes indeed, it was the most astounding entertainment they'd ever known.

Catherine's stomach growled, vibrating through the boning of her corset. She'd been so enchanted with the Joker's performance she'd forgotten all about her gown's constrictions and her deepening hunger. She tried to be inconspicuous as she squirmed inside the dress, adjusting herself in the tight bodice, and sneaked toward the feasting table. She spotted Mary Ann laying out a plate of truffles, standing out from the other maids with her beanstalk height and the straw-colored hair that had slipped from the edges of her bonnet.

Perking when she spotted Catherine, Mary Ann lowered her head and tugged at one corner of the tablecloth as if to straighten it. "What did you think of the performance?" she whispered.

Cath's fingers fluttered yearningly over the platters of food. "I thought court jokers only told bawdy jokes and made wisecracks about the King."

"It makes me wonder what else he might have up that slee— er, hat of his." Mary Ann swept a tray off the table and curtsied. "Truffle, milady?"

"You know I can't."

"Just pretend to be considering it so I can stand here a while longer. The royal servants keep trying to coerce us attendants to bring out more food, and if I have to go back down to that kitchen I'm sure to melt. Besides, there's plenty food out already when taking into account the number of guests here tonight and the rate at which it's being consumed, and they don't need any more no matter what they say. Right awful waste it'd be."

Catherine steepled her fingers. "Are those caramels?"

"I think so."

"How do you think chocolate caramels would be with a touch of sea salt on top?"

Mary Ann stuck out her tongue in disgust. "Why not throw in a dash of pepper while you're at it?"

"Just a thought." Catherine gnawed on her lower lip, eyeing the chocolates. Yes, sea salt, whatever Mary Ann might think. The pantry at Rock Turtle Cove was always well stocked with it, being so close to the shore, and once, being in an experimental mood, Cath had sprinkled a bit into her hot cocoa and found it surprisingly pleasant. It was just the thing for these truffles. A bit of saltiness to brighten the sweetness, a bit of crunch to reflect on the smooth caramel . . . why, she could make a salted caramel chocolate torte. It could be one of the bakery's signature treats!

Her stomach rumbled.

"Cath?"

"Hm?"

"You look as though you're about to start drooling, and I would hate for you to stain that dress."

She groaned. "I can't help it. I'm so hungry." She wrapped her arms around her stomach as another growl rumbled through the velvet.

Mary Ann's brows creased briefly with sympathy, but then her face brightened. "That dress must have been a smart choice all the same. You danced top couple with the King!"

Cath bit back another, deeper groan. No doubt her complaints of having to dance with the King were nothing compared to carrying heavy food-laden trays through a sweltering kitchen.

Her eye caught on a hulking shape at the other end of the feasting table and she jolted. "Who is that?"

Mary Ann glanced over her shoulder, but just as quickly withdrew. She tipped her head closer. "His name is Peter Peter, and the tiny thing beside him is his wife. I haven't caught her name yet."

"Tiny thi— oh."

The wife Mary Ann had mentioned was indeed a slip of a girl, almost invisible beside the massive bulk of her husband. She had a back that seemed permanently hunched —

from work, not age, Cath could guess — parchment-white skin and stringy blonde hair. She looked ill, one hand pressed against her stomach and having no apparent interest in the food before her. Her face shimmered with a thin layer of perspiration.

On the other hand, her husband was as intimidating as a troll. He stood well above the other guests and would have dwarfed even Cath's barrel-chested father. He wore a black riding coat and breeches that barely fit, the material stretched taut across his oxen shoulders. Catherine suspected that if he moved too fast he would split any number of seams. He had frizzing red hair that was in need of both a washing and a comb, and a brow currently stuck in a scowl.

Neither Peter Peter nor his wife looked at all pleased to be at the King's ball.

"But who *are* they?" she whispered.

"Sir Peter owns the pumpkin patch outside of Nowhere Forest. One of the kitchen maids told me they were granted a knighthood after his wife won a pumpkin-eating contest a fortnight ago. I understand Jack came in second place and has been demanding a rematch ever since." Mary Ann harrumphed. "I wish someone would think to give me a knighthood for all that *I* eat."

Catherine chuckled. One wouldn't know

it to look at Mary Ann, but she had an appetite to rival Cath's own. They'd bonded over their love of food years ago, not long after Mary Ann had been hired on as a household maid.

Her laughter was eclipsed by a shadow falling over them. Thick fingers descended on Mary Ann's tray. "What're those?"

Mary Ann squeaked and Catherine flushed, but Sir Peter didn't seem to notice either of them as he popped a truffle whole into his mouth. If he'd heard them talking about him and his wife, he showed no sign of it.

"Er — caramel truffles, sir," said Mary Ann.

"Unsalted," Cath added. "Unfortunately."

Up close, she could make out the start of whiskers on Sir Peter's chin and dirt beneath his fingernails, as if he'd been too preoccupied with his pumpkin patch to bother cleaning up for his first royal ball.

"Sir Peter, isn't it?" she stammered. "I have not yet had the pleasure of making your acquaintance."

His eyes narrowed as he sucked the chocolate from his dirty thumb. Catherine winced.

Beside her, eyes cast on the ground, Mary Ann ducked away from the table.

"Ohm, mwait!"

Mary Ann paused.

Sir Peter swallowed, leaving bits of chocolate in his teeth. "I'll be taking more of those. These are all — what's it called? Compliments of the King, right?"

Mary Ann half curtsied again. "Of course, sir. You're welcome to enjoy as much as you like. Is there anything else I can bring you?"

"No." He claimed another truffle, and hardly seemed to chew before swallowing.

Hiding in his shadow, Lady Peter watched the truffle travel down her husband's throat and turned green before casting hesitant eyes up at Mary Ann. "Might you" — she stammered, her voice barely a whisper — "have any pumpkin pasties? We sold some pumpkins to the royal pastry chefs yestermorn and heard tell they would be making them for the ball, but I haven't —"

"You don't be needing no more pumpkin!" her husband barked, spittle flying from his mouth and landing on the tray of truffles. Cath and Mary Ann both grimaced. "You've had plenty enough already."

Lady Peter shied away.

Clearing her throat, Cath edged in between Peter Peter and the truffles. "Mary Ann, why don't you go see if the Knave would like to sample the caramels? He's so fond of sweets."

She felt Mary Ann's sigh of relief before she retreated with the tray.

Catherine curtsied. "I am Catherine Pinkerton, daughter of the Marquess of Rock Turtle Cove. I'm told you were recently granted a knighthood?"

His eyes darkened beneath his prickly red eyebrows. "Suppose we were."

"And this must be your wife. It's a pleasure to meet you, Lady Peter."

The woman's shoulders hunched against her ears. Rather than curtsy or smile, she shrank away from the introduction and took to scanning the contents of the feasting table again, though Cath thought she saw her gag at the sight of all the food.

Catherine clung helplessly to her manners. "Are you well, Lady Peter? I'm afraid you're looking a little pale, and it is so warm in here. Would you like to accompany me for a turn around the balcony?"

"She's well enough," Peter snapped. Catherine took half a step back, startled at his vehemence. "Just been eatin' some bad pumpkin of late, like she don't know better."

"I see," Catherine said, though she didn't. "Congratulations on your win at the pumpkin eating contest, Lady Peter. You must have eaten quite a lot. I've been longing to make a pumpkin pie lately, myself."

Peter spent a moment picking at his teeth with his nail and Catherine backed away again, having the peculiar sensation that he was trying to figure out the best way to cook and eat *her.*

"She eats 'em raw." He sounded proud of this fact. "You ever eaten raw pumpkin, Lady . . . *Pinkerton*?"

"I can't say that I have." She had made a few pumpkin pies and one pumpkin mousse in the past — the stringy pulp and slimy seeds that she'd had to scrape out before cooking the flesh had been less than appetizing. Glancing around Sir Peter, she asked his wife, "I can see how one might be feeling poorly after such a meal. It's a shame you aren't feeling well enough to partake in the King's table."

Lady Peter's gaze flickered up and she whimpered before letting her head hang again. She looked moments away from being sick all over the astounding feast.

"Are you sure you don't want to sit down?" Catherine asked.

Lady Peter responded meekly, "Are you sure there aren't any pumpkin pasties lying about? I think I might feel a bit better, if only . . ."

"See? No bother talking to her," said Peter. "Dumb as a Jack-O'-Lantern she is."

His wife tightened her arms around her waist.

Catherine's anger burbled. For a moment she imagined him choking on one of those chocolate caramels, and how she and his wife would stand over him laughing, but her fantasy was interrupted by the Nine and Ten of Diamonds squeezing sideways in between them. "Do pardon me," the Nine said, reaching for a honey-drizzled fig.

Cath gladly took a step back.

"These shindies always like this?" Peter asked, snarling at the courtier's back.

The Ten turned to him with a jovial smile and held up a glass of wine as if in salute. "Not at all," he said. "We used to keep standards."

Cath blanched. The courtier was gone in an instant, leaving Peter with a flaming face and searing eyes. Cath forced a smile. "The courtiers can be a tad . . . uppity, sometimes. With strangers. I'm sure he meant no offense."

"I'm sure he did," said Peter, "and I'm sure he ain't the only one." He stared at her for a long moment, before raising his hand and tipping his tattered hat. "Been a pleasure, *milady.*"

It was the first sign of manners he'd shown, and it was about as believable as the Duke of Tuskany claiming he could fly.

Sir Peter grabbed his wife by the elbow and pulled her away. Cath wasn't sad to see them go.

CHAPTER 6

Catherine allowed herself a huff. Sir Peter's presence, combined with the strangling corset, had nearly suffocated her. "A right pleasure indeed."

"He's a sore thumb, isn't he?"

She turned and spotted a silver tray floating in the air above the table, overflowing with golden-crusted hand pies, neatly crimped on one edge.

"Ah, hello again, Cheshire," said Catherine, filled with relief that she might have one encounter this evening that didn't leave her weary and vexed. Though with Cheshire, it could go either way. "Are you supposed to be here?"

"Not likely."

The cat appeared with the tray resting on his tummy, his striped tail like a lounging chair beneath him. His head came last — ears, whiskers, nose, and finally his enormous toothy grin.

"You look absurd," Cheshire drawled, taking a pastry between two sharp claws and popping it into his gigantic mouth. A cloud of savory steam erupted from between his teeth, smelling of sweet squash.

"The dress was my mother's idea," said Catherine. Placing a hand on her abdomen, she took in the largest breath she was capable of. She was beginning to feel lightheaded. "Are those pumpkin pasties, by chance? Lady Peter was asking after them. They smell delicious."

"They are. I would offer you one, but I don't want to."

"That's not polite at all. And unless you have an invitation, you might want to put them down and disappear again before someone sees you."

Cheshire grunted, unconcerned. "I just thought you might like to know . . ." He yawned exaggeratedly. ". . . that the Knave is stealing your tarts."

"What?" Cath spun around, casting her glance around the feasting table, but Jack was nowhere in sight. She frowned.

When she turned back, Cheshire's humongous cheeks were bulging with the entire tray's worth of pasties.

Cath rolled her eyes and waited for him to chew and swallow, which he made quick work of with his enormous teeth.

Cheshire burped, then dug a nail into the space beside his front molar. "Oh, please," he said, inspecting the nail and finding a bit of pumpkin filling stuck to it. "You don't think those tarts would have lasted this far into the evening, do you?"

She spotted the familiar tray, then, near the edge of the feasting table. All that remained of her lemon tarts were a few crumbs, a drift of powdered sugar outlining three empty circles, and a smear of sunshine yellow.

It was as bittersweet as dark chocolate, that empty tray. Catherine was always pleased when her desserts were enjoyed, but, in this case, after the dream and the lemon tree . . . she would have liked to try at least a tiny bite for herself.

She sighed, disappointed.

"Did you try them, Cheshire?"

The cat tsked at her. "I had an entire tart, my dear. Irresistible as it was."

Cath shook her head. "You would have made a better pig."

"How vulgar." He twisted in the air, rolling over like a log on the ocean, and vanished along with the now-empty dish.

"And what do you have against pigs?" Cath said to the empty space. "Baby piglets are almost as cute as kittens, if you ask me."

"I'm going to pretend I didn't hear that."

She swiveled around again. The cat had reappeared on the other side of the table. Or, his head and one paw had, which he began to lick.

"Though I'm sure Lord Warthog would appreciate the sentiment," he added.

"Do you know if His Majesty had a chance to try the tarts?"

"Oh yes. I saw him sneaking a slice — and then a second, and then a third — while you and Mary Ann were chatting about the pumpkin eater." The rest of his body materialized as he talked. "Shame on you, to gossip so."

She lifted an eyebrow. Cheshire was an expert gossip. It was part of the reason why she enjoyed talking to him, though it also made her nervous. Catherine did not want his gossip-milling to ever turn on her. "Does that make you the pot or the kettle?"

"Still a cat, my dear, and not even an unlucky one."

"Actually . . ." Catherine cocked her head. "You may not be a black cat, and yet your pedigree is something changed. You're looking rather orange of a sudden."

Cheshire curled his tail, newly oranged, in front of his crossed eyes. "So I am. Is orange my color?"

"It looks fine, but doesn't match the night's color scheme. What a pair we must make."

"I imagine it was the pumpkin pasties. A shame they weren't fish."

"You want to turn fish-colored?"

"Rainbow trout, maybe. You should consider adding fish to your baking next time too. I'd love a tuna tart."

"Tuna tartare?"

"Why, you'll make a stuffed bird laugh if you go on like that."

"It wouldn't be the first time."

"By-the-bye, have you heard the rumors?"

"Rumors . . ." She searched her memory. "You mean, about Mr. Caterpillar moving to a smaller storefront?"

Cheshire's head spun upside down. "How slow you are tonight. I was speaking of the rumors surrounding the new court joker."

She perked up. "No. I haven't heard anything about him."

"Neither have I."

She furrowed her brow. "Cheshire, that is the opposite of a rumor."

"Contrariwise. I haven't the faintest idea who he is or where he came from. It's all very odd." Cheshire licked his paw and cleaned behind his ear, which struck Catherine as impolite, being so close to the table. "They say he walked right up to the palace gates three days past, already dressed in fool's motley, and asked for an audience with the King. He performed a magic trick or two — something about shuffling the Diamond courtiers and asking His Majesty to pick one card out of the set . . . I couldn't follow the details. In the end, he was given the job."

Catherine pictured the Joker lounging on that suspended silver hoop, almost as if he expected the King's guests to entertain him, not the other way around. He had been so poised. Though she hadn't questioned it before, Cheshire's curiosity piqued hers. Hearts was a small kingdom. Where had he come from?

"Have you heard the other rumors?" continued Cheshire.

"I'm not sure. What other rumors?"

Cheshire rolled onto his stomach and cupped his face in his furry paws. "His Congenial Kingness has chosen a bride."

Her eyes widened. "No! Who is it?" She glanced around the room. Certainly not Margaret. Perhaps Lady Adela from Lingerfoote or Lady Willow from Lister Hill or —

Or . . .

Her breath hiccupped.

A wash of goose bumps spread down her limbs.

Her mother's enthusiasm.

The first quadrille.

The King's flustered grin.

She whipped her head back toward Cheshire. His enormous grin struck her as extra mocking.

"You can't mean it."

"Can't I?" He peered up at the chandeliers. "I thought for sure I was capable of *that,* at the least."

"Cheshire, this isn't amusing. The King can't — he wouldn't —"

A trumpet blared, echoing off the pink quartz walls.

Catherine's head spun. "Oh no."

"Oh yes."

"Cheshire! Why didn't you tell me sooner?"

"Ladies and gentlemen," cried the White Rabbit, his pitchy voice insignificant after the horn. "His Royal Majesty has prepared a special announcement for this evening."

"Shall I congratulate you now?" Cheshire asked. "Or do you suppose premature well-wishes could bring bad luck? I can never recall the proper etiquette in these situations."

A curtain of heat embraced her, from

brow to toes. She could have sworn someone was pulling on the staylace of her corset as her breaths grew shorter.

"I can't. Oh, Cheshire, I can't."

"You may want to practice a different response before you go up there."

The crowd applauded. The King stepped onto the stage at the far end of the ballroom. Catherine cast her eyes around, searching for her parents, and when she found her mother beaming and brushing a tear from her lashes, the reality settled around her.

The King of Hearts was about to propose to her.

But — but he couldn't. He'd never done anything more than compliment her baking and ask her to dance. They hadn't courted . . . but, did kings have to court? She didn't know. She knew only that her stomach had tied itself into triple knots and the idea of marrying him was preposterous. She had never once considered that the silly man could want anything from her but sweets and pastries. Certainly not a bride, and . . . oh heavens, *children.*

A bead of sweat dripped down the back of her neck.

"Cheshire, what do I do?"

"Say yes, I suppose. Or say no. It matters not to me. Are you sure orange is my color?"

He was inspecting his tail again.

Desperation clawed at Catherine's throat.

The King. The simpleminded, ridiculous, happy, *happy* King.

Her husband? Her one and only? Her partner through life's trials and joys?

She would be queen, and queens . . . queens did not open bakeries with their best friends. Queens did not gossip with half-invisible cats. Queens did not have dreams of yellow-eyed boys and wake up with lemon trees over their beds.

She tried to swallow, but her mouth had dried up like stale cake.

The King cleared his throat. "Fair evening, loyal subjects! I hope you have all enjoyed tonight's delights!"

More applause, at which the King clasped his own hands together and bobbed up and down a few times.

"I wish to make an announcement. A good announcement, nothing to be worried about." He giggled at what might have been a joke. "It has come time for me to choose for myself a wife, and for my subjects . . . a most adored Queen of Hearts! And" — the King kept giggling — "with any luck, bring our kingdom an heir, as well."

Catherine stepped back from the feasting table. She couldn't feel her toes.

"Cheshire . . .?"

"Lady Catherine?"

"It is my honor," continued the King, "to call up the lady I have chosen for my life's companion."

"Please," said Catherine, "cause a distraction. Anything!"

Cheshire's tail twitched, and he vanished. Only his voice lingered, murmuring, "With pleasure, Lady Catherine."

The King spread his arms. "Would the ever lovely, delightful, and stupendous Lady Cathe—"

"Aaaagghh!"

As one, the crowd turned. Margaret Mearle kept screaming, swatting at the orange-striped cat who had appeared on top of her head, curled up beneath her fur headdress.

Catherine alone turned the other way.

She fled out to the balcony, running as fast as her heeled boots and strangling corset would allow. The cool night air sent a chill racing across her enflamed skin, but every breath remained a struggle.

She lifted her skirts and slipped down the steps into the rose gardens. She heard a splinter of glass and startled cries behind her and wondered what chaos Cheshire must be causing now, but she dared not look back, not even as she reached the gardens.

The world tilted. She paused at a wrought-iron gate, gripping one of the decorative finials for support. Catching her breath, she stumbled on. Down the clover-filled path between rose arbors and trickling fountains, passing topiaries and statues and a pond of water lilies. She reached for the back of her dress, desperate to loosen the stays. To breathe. But she couldn't reach. She was suffocating.

She was going to be sick.

She was going to faint.

A shadow reared up in front of her, backlit from the blazing castle lights so that the silhouette stretched over the croquet lawns. Catherine cried out and stumbled to a halt, damp hair matted to her neck.

The shadow of a hooded man engulfed her. As Catherine stared, the silhouette lifted an enormous ax, the curved blade arching across the grass.

Trembling, Catherine spun around. A dark shape dropped toward her out of the sky. She screamed and threw her arms up in defense.

The raven cawed, so close she could feel his wing beats as he flew past.

"Are you all right?"

She gasped and withdrew her arms. Her heart was thundering as she peered up into the boughs of a white rose tree.

It took a moment to find him in the dark. The Joker was lounging on a low-hanging branch, a silver flute in his hands, though if he'd been playing it before, she'd been too distracted to notice.

Her lashes fluttered. Half of her hair had fallen from its chignon and draped over her shoulder. Her skin was burning hot. The world was spinning wildly — swirling with lemon tarts and invisible cats and curved axes and . . .

The Joker tensed, his brow creasing. "My lady?"

The world tilted severely and turned black.

Chapter 7

"Lady hath stumbled on this midnight dreary, with a pallor frightfully pale and weary." A somber, melodic voice floated through the encompassing darkness.

"Duly noted, my feathered friend," came a second voice, lighter and quick. "Are you sure we haven't some sal-volatile in there?"

"I know nothing of your hoped-for salt, though with your plan I find a fault. To keep her from awaking groggy, 'twould be most prudent to make her soggy."

Something hard thumped on the ground by Cath's elbow, followed by a quiet slosh of water.

"No, Raven, we are not throwing a bucket of water on her. Keep looking. Haven't we a ham sandwich? Or some hay? That always worked on the King."

Rustling, fumbling, clanks and clatters.

A sigh. "You know what? Never mind. We'll use this."

The rustle of foliage followed by the snap of a branch. Something soft tickled the tip of Cath's nose.

She squirmed, turning her head away, and caught the faint perfume of roses.

"Aha, it's working."

She wrinkled her nose. Her eyelids squinted open. Darkness and shadows swirled in her vision. Her head felt heavy, her thoughts disoriented.

"Hello," spoke one of the bleary shadows, sharpening into the court joker. He lifted the soft-petaled rose away from her face. "Are you all right?"

"Nevermore," said his Raven, who was perched on the edge of a metal bucket.

The Joker cut him a glare. "Don't be rude."

" 'Tisn't rude to rebuke an arbitrary greeting, a nonsense question upon first meeting. To be *all* right implies an impossible phase. We hope for *mostly* right on the best of our days."

"Exactly," said the Joker. "Rude."

The Raven made an unhappy noise. Spreading his massive wings, he leaped up into the air and settled on a high branch of the rose tree instead.

The Joker returned his attention to Catherine. He had removed the three-pointed hat and his wavy black hair was matted to his head in places and sticking out in others. The light from a nearby garden torch flickered gold in his eyes, still thickly rimmed in kohl. He smiled at her, and it was the friendly sort of smile that reached to every corner of his face, drawing dimples into his cheeks, crinkling the corners of his eyes. Cath's heart tumbled. During his performance, she had been hypnotized by his magic, amused by his tomfoolery — but she had not realized that he was also quite handsome.

"I'm glad the rose worked," he said, twirling it in his fingers. "I suspect this would be a different sort of meeting had we been forced to use the water bucket."

She blinked, unable to smile back as the shadows shifted across his face. It wasn't just the firelight. His eyes really were the color of gold. The color of sunflowers and butterscotch and lemons hanging heavy on their boughs.

Her own eyes widened. *"You."*

"Me," he agreed. He cocked his head to the side, frowning again. "In all seriousness, my lady, are you . . ." A hesitation. ". . . *mostly* right?"

She felt it again, that internal tug she'd had during the dream, telling her that he had something that belonged to her, and she had to catch him if she were ever to get it back.

"My lady?" Setting the rose aside, he touched the back of his hand to her brow. "Can you hear me? You're very warm."

The world spun again, but this time in a delicious, time-stopping way.

"Perhaps I should call for a Sturgeon . . ."

"No, I'm fine. I'm all right." Her words were sticky and her fingers fumbling, but she managed to grasp his hand before he pulled away. He froze, dubious. "Though I can't feel my legs," she confessed.

His lips twisted to one side. "Mostly right, after all. Let's not tell Raven he was correct, or he'll be insufferable the rest of the night." He glanced down. "I can almost guarantee that your legs are still attached, though there is an awful lot of fabric disguising them. I'll go searching for them now if you'd like me to."

His expression was innocent, his tone sincere.

Catherine laughed. "That's quite generous, but I'll go searching for them myself, thank you. Can you help me sit?"

Still holding her hand, the Joker scooped his free arm beneath her shoulders and lifted her upward. She spotted his hat lying upside down not far away, and scattered around it an odd assortment of junk. Glass marbles, a wind-up monkey, handkerchiefs, an empty inkwell, mismatched buttons, a two-wheeled velocipede, the silver flute.

With a quick pat, Cath confirmed that her legs were indeed still present. Her toes began to tingle.

"Your hands are like icicles." The Joker draped her fingers across his palm and started to massage them — working from her knuckles, across the pad of her thumb, along her wrist. "You'll feel better when your blood is flowing again."

Cath inspected the Joker, his messy curls, the point of his nose. He was sitting cross-legged on the grass, hunkered over her hand. His touch was shockingly intimate compared to the touches she was used to — those brief, civilized encounters during a waltz or quadrille.

"Are you a doctor?" she asked.

He looked up at her and smiled that disarming smile again. "I'm a joker, my lady, which is even better."

"How is that better than a doctor?"

"Haven't you ever heard that laughter is the best medicine?"

She shook her head. "If that's so, shouldn't you be telling me a joke?"

"As the lady pleases. How did the joker warm up some hands?"

She shut one eye and considered, but was quick to give up. "I don't know. How?"

"By being a warm, handsome joker, indeed."

Her laugh was unexpected, punctuated by the unladylike snort that Mary Ann often teased her about. She tore her hand away from him to cover her nose, embarrassed.

The Joker's entire face lit up. "Can it be! A real-life lady with a laugh like that! I believed you were naught but mythological creatures. Please, do it again."

"I will not!" she squealed, her face reddening. "Stop it. The joke wasn't even funny, and now I'm all poked up."

He schooled his face, though his eyes still danced. "I meant no offense. A laugh like that is richer than gold to a man of my position. I'll make it my life's work to hear the sound again. Every day, if it pleases you. No — twice a day, and at least once before breakfast. A royal joker must set the highest of expectations."

Her pulse skittered. Twice a day? Once before breakfast?

A new sort of blush blossomed across her cheeks.

Noticing the look, the Joker released her

hand, almost sheepish. "That is . . . you are the one, aren't you?"

She stared at him, and in his eyes she saw the lemon tree that had grown in her bedroom overnight, its branches twisted around her bed's canopy, heavy with sun-ripened fruit. "The one?"

"The future Queen of Hearts?"

The giddy euphoria left her in a single, painful breath. "I beg your pardon?"

"Oh, you needn't beg." Doubt crept across his brow. "Shall I apologize? I didn't mean to be forward. It's just that the King intended to ask for a lady's hand in marriage during tonight's ball, and . . . with your gown, I suppose I'd assumed . . ."

She looked down. Her skirt was a bright red nightmare engulfing her. "Did he say which girl he intended to ask?"

"No, my lady. I only know it was to be a daughter of a lord, though that hardly narrows down the list." He leaned back on his hands. "What were you running from before?"

"Running from?" She forced a withering smile. "I was only wanting some fresh air. The ballroom can get so warm on nights like this."

His eyes pinned her to the grass, growing concerned. "The King hadn't yet made his announcement when you left?"

"I've heard nothing of it."

She shivered, not quite guilty at the lie. What was happening inside the ballroom? Had the King called her up? Were they looking for her?

She glanced back toward the castle, surprised to see how far she'd run. The gardens seemed to stretch for miles and the ballroom windows glowed in the distance. She wondered about the crash she had heard and hoped Cheshire wasn't in trouble.

The Joker rubbed the back of his neck. "Maybe it is you, then. Perhaps I should escort you back . . ."

"No! No. Um." She laughed uncomfortably. "I'm sure he meant to ask someone else. His Majesty has never shown me any particular interest."

"I find that difficult to imagine."

"It's the truth." She cleared her throat. "This might be a peculiar question, Mr. . . . er, Joker . . ."

"Jest. My name is Jest. My lady."

"Ah — I'm Catherine Pinkerton."

"It's been a rightmost pleasure, Lady Pinkerton. What was your question?"

Cath fluffed the voluminous red fabric around her legs to give her fingers something to do while they went on feeling tingly and wanton. "Have you and I met before?"

"Before tonight?" He cupped his chin in his hand. "It seems unlikely."

"I thought so as well."

"Do I seem familiar?" His dimples made an appearance again.

"In a way. Most peculiarly, I do believe I dreamed about you."

His eyebrows lifted. "About me?"

"It is strange, isn't it?"

"Quite." The word was subtle, surprised. He looked briefly unnerved, like when he had first spotted her and her red dress amid the sea of black and white. The self-assured visage slipped, just momentarily. "Perhaps we know each other in the future and you're only remembering backward."

She pondered this.

"So?" he prodded.

She blinked. "So what?"

"Was it a good dream?"

"Oh." Her lips puckered in thought, but then she realized he was teasing her. She scowled. "To be frank, I found it rather dull."

"Ah, but you can't be Frank. You've already told me that your name is Catherine."

"I've changed it."

His laugh was unoffended. "At least the

memory of this dream has brought some color back to your cheeks. You were white as a dove when you fainted. I'm sorry if Raven frightened you."

She remembered the shadow stretching across the castle lawn — the hooded, ax-wielding figure towering over her. She shuddered. "No, it wasn't Raven. It was . . . I thought I saw . . . nothing."

"I see nothing all the time."

"As I said before, it was very warm inside, that's all. And I've barely eaten all day."

"No doubt the corset of tortures didn't help."

Her scowl deepened. "A lady's undergarments are not a suitable topic of conversation."

He raised his hands in surrender. "Only a theory, my lady. I'm sure your lack of sustenance is much more the culprit. Here." He reached for a pouch at his belt and retrieved a chocolate. "I was saving this for later, and so I must have been saving it for you."

"Oh no, I couldn't. I'm still a little faint. It will probably make me sick."

"Some say it is better to have eaten and lost than never to have eaten at all."

She furrowed her brows, confused, but his sincerity never faltered.

"In case you do get sick and the sweet makes its way up again."

"That's *horrible.*"

"I know. I should apologize." Rather than apologizing, he held the sweet toward her. "I must insist that you eat, regardless of the risks. Should you happen to faint again while under my care, I'm afraid I won't be able to stop Raven from using that bucket."

Catherine shook her head and placed a palm against her abdomen. She could feel the bone stays beneath the bodice.

Although, the corset didn't seem as confining as it had before. Now that the evening air was reviving her, there was even room to breathe. Not a lot of room, but perhaps enough to fit in one little chocolate . . .

"Please, take it," he pressed.

"Is it from the feasting table?" she asked, knowing better than to sample untested foods. Once, when she was a child, she'd sampled some wild berries and spent two whole days the size of a thimble. It was an experience she didn't care to have again.

"The King's own."

Catherine took it hesitantly, murmuring her thanks, and bit down. The truffle exploded with silky caramel and brittle chocolate on her tongue.

She stifled a pleased moan.

But if one added just a touch of sea salt — oh, *euphoria.*

She devoured the rest, her tongue searching for any missed chocolate on her teeth.

"Better?" Jest asked.

"Much." She tucked a strand of misplaced hair behind her ear. "Well enough to stand, I think. Could you help me?"

He was on his feet before she had finished asking, his movements graceful as an antelope. "Shall I escort you back into the ball?" he asked, lifting her to her feet.

"No, thank you." She brushed off her gown. "I'm very tired. I think I'll call for a carriage to take me home."

"This way, then."

He grabbed his hat off the ground and settled it on his head. The hat looked wrong on him now and she realized it was his fool's motley that had disguised his handsomeness before. Now that she knew otherwise, it was impossible not to see it.

Turning his head up, Jest whistled into the tree branches. "Raven, would you mind . . . ?"

The Raven cocked his head and peered down through the branches, watching them with a single shining black eye. "I thought perhaps you had forgotten your companion in the dark, downtrodden."

Jest squinted up at him. "Is that a yes?"

The bird sighed. "Fine, I'm going." He swooped off his perch and disappeared in the black sky.

Jest offered Catherine his arm and she slipped her fingers into the crook of his elbow. She was baffled at how much easier it was to breathe now. Maybe she'd been overreacting. Well, not to the King's near proposal, but to the way her dress seemed to be strangling her.

They passed through the garden's arches. The rosebushes fell behind, replaced with towering green hedges that thundered with the fiery bolts of lightning bugs.

"I hope you'll understand if I ask for your discretion," she said, wishing her heart would stop pattering. "This has been a most unusual encounter for me."

"Far be it for me to intrude upon a lady's untarnished reputation. But to be clear, which part of our encounter should remain undisclosed?" Jest watched her from the corner of his eye. "The part when you fainted in the grass and I heroically revived you? The part where we took an unchaperoned stroll through the gardens?" He clucked his tongue in mock disapproval. "Or perhaps the part where you confessed to having had a dream about me, and that I must be quite the rake to hope it wasn't as boring as you've suggested?"

She leaned against his arm. "All of the above?"

He brought his free hand to her fingers, patting. "It will be my greatest pleasure to be secretive together, my lady."

They hopped over the guard gryphon's tail — he was sleeping, as always, against the garden gate. His quiet snores followed them halfway across the lawn.

"So long as we're sharing secrets," she said, "may I ask how you did it? The trick with Mr. Rabbit?"

"What trick?"

"You know. When you pulled him out of Jack's hat."

Jest frowned, his expression mildly concerned. "Sweetest Lady Pinkerton, I fear you've gone mad in this short time we've known each other."

She peered up at him. "Have I?"

"To imagine that I pulled a rabbit out of a hat?" He stooped closer, his forehead conspiratorially close to hers, and whispered, "That would be impossible."

She smothered a grin, trying to morph her expression into something equally devious. "As it so happens, Mr. Jest, I've sometimes come to believe as many as six impossible things before breakfast."

His feet stalled all at once, his face turning to her, bewildered.

Her grin fell. "What is it?"

Jest's eyes narrowed, studying her.

Catherine cowed beneath the inspection. "What?"

"Are you sure you aren't the one the King is in love with?"

It took a moment, but when the laugh came, it was honest and unforced. The idea that the King might wish to marry her was one thing, but the thought of him being in love with her was an entirely different realm of absurdity.

"I assure you, he's not," she said, still smiling, though Jest looked unconvinced. "What does that have to do with believing impossible things?"

"It just seems like a queenly sort of thing to say," he said, offering his arm again. Cath took it, though with more hesitation. "And, well, impossible is my specialty."

She peered up at his profile, his angled features, the mask of kohl. "That," she said, "seems entirely believable."

He looked pleased. "I'm flattered you think so, Lady Pinkerton."

They reached the cobblestone drive at the main entrance to the castle, where dozens of carriages were waiting for their lords and ladies. A cluster of liveried coachmen were smoking pipes beneath the torches on the other side of the courtyard. One of them yelled out when they saw Cath and Jest approaching — "Hoy there, what's been all the commotion about?"

"Commotion?" Jest asked.

"Nothing but gasps and squeals coming from the castle for the last half hour," said the coachman. "Been thinking one of them candles might've lit the place on fire, what with their short fuses and all."

Jest glance at Cath, but she just shrugged. "It must be all the hullabaloo over your performance." A carriage pulled up to them, the enormous black raven perched beside the driver. He must have gone ahead to fetch the ride for her.

One of the footmen, a tree frog dressed in a powdered wig and a royal red coat, double-breasted in gold buttons, came hopping across the courtyard to hold the door for her.

Jest offered his hand to help her into the carriage and she was surprised, as her foot hit the second step into the carriage, to feel the press of lips against her knuckle.

She glanced back.

"Ah — I almost forgot!" Releasing her

hand, Jest removed his hat, bells clinking, and reached inside. He produced a bundle of long white cording. "These belong to you."

Cath uncertainly took the ropes. "What are —" She gasped. Her hand flew to her back, feeling around the fabric of her dress, detecting the boning of the corset, yes, but . . . not its laces. The back of the corset was split open the full width of her hand.

Heat rushed into her cheeks. "How?"

Jest danced back from the carriage as if he feared she would hit him, and she was suddenly considering it. The nerve!

He bowed again, as if he'd completed his final encore.

"Fair evening, Lady Pinkerton. I hope you enjoy satisfyingly deep breaths during your ride home."

Part mortified, part despicably impressed, Catherine marched up the last step and slammed the carriage door shut.

Chapter 8

Catherine awoke to the sound of her parents' carriage returning home, the clomp of the horses' hooves on the drive loud and distinct against the muffled backdrop of ocean waves. She didn't know how many hours had passed, but it was still dark outside, and she dug herself deeper beneath her covers, yanking the quilt up past her nose. Her head was drowsy with fog and sleep. She had the sensation of sleepy tendrils clinging to her from some far-off dream. Arms lowering her onto a bed of rose petals. Fingers tracing the contours of her face. Kisses trailing down her throat.

She sighed, curling her toes against the sheets.

He appeared slowly from the mental haze. Messy black hair. Amber-gold eyes. A dimpled smile stretched across teasing lips . . .

Her eyes snapped open, a blush climbing

up her neck.

She'd been dreaming about the Joker.

Again!

Downstairs, she heard the front door crash open, her mother's voice splitting through the still night. She sounded upset, and Cath cringed. Was she angry that Cath had left the ball without telling them? Or that the King's marriage proposal had been slighted?

Maybe . . . *maybe* . . . he'd asked some other girl.

Energized with hope, she pulled the quilt away and peered up at the shadowed canopy of her bed. She gasped.

Not a lemon tree this time, but roses. They were white as swan feathers, their thorny stems strangling the bedposts. Cath inched one hand from beneath the covers and reached for the nearest blossom. A thorn dug into the pad of her thumb and she flinched, pulling back and popping the wound into her mouth before she got blood on her nightgown.

Giving up on the rose, she whipped the blanket over her head again, letting her heartbeat slow.

What did it mean? What were the dreams trying to tell her?

She counted off the things she knew about Jest.

He was the court joker, but no one knew where he had come from.

He was friends with a Raven.

Impossible was his specialty.

The way he had touched her hand had awoken something inside her she had never felt before. Something giddy, but also nervous. Something curious, but also afraid.

And if her dreams were to be believed, he was a very, very good kisser.

The fluttering in her stomach returned and she squirmed farther into the covers, suddenly light-headed. Perhaps his presence in the castle gardens had been unexpected and disconcerting, but Cath was the master of her own whimsies. She began to wrap herself up in the dream of slow kisses and white roses, to find her way back to that small, harmless fantasy . . .

Her bedroom door crashed open. "CATHERINE!"

Startled, Catherine pushed back the bedcovers and sat up. A ring of lamplight shone on the walls. "What?"

Her mother shrieked, but it was an overjoyed sound. "Oh, thanks to goodness. Whealagig, she's here! She's all right!" With a wail, she threw herself across the room, pausing to set the oil lamp on the bedside table before she collapsed onto Catherine's bed and pulled her into a stifling embrace. Catherine realized with a start that her mother was crying. "We were so worried!"

"What for?" Cath struggled to extricate herself. "I left the ball early and came right home. I didn't think you'd be so upset. I wasn't feeling well and . . ."

"No, no, darling, it's fine, it's just —" She dissolved into sobs as Cath's father appeared over them, pressing a hand to his heart. His face was slack with relief.

"What's going on?" said Cath, spotting Mary Ann, too, in the doorway. "What's happened?"

"We didn't know where you were," her mother cried, "and there was . . . there was . . ."

"An attack," her father answered, his voice somber.

Cath stared at him, trying to read his expression in the unsteady lamplight. "An attack?"

"Not just any attack!" Her mother pulled back and squeezed Cath's shoulders. "A Jabberwock!"

Her eyes widened.

"It attacked the castle," said her father, looking strained and exhausted. "Shattered one of the windows and took two of the courtiers right from the ballroom floor.

Then it just flew off with them . . ."

Cath pressed a hand to her chest. The Jabberwock was a creature of nightmares and myth, of tales told by firelight to frighten little children into good behavior. It was a monster said to live amid the twining and tangled Tulgey Wood, far away in the country of Chess.

As far as Cath knew, no Jabberwock had been sighted in Hearts for countless generations. Stories told of them being hunted by great knights centuries ago, until the last of the Jabberwock was slain by a king who carried the mythical Vorpal Sword.

"It was e-enormous," her mother stammered, "and terrifying, and I didn't know where you were!" Her sobs overtook her again.

"It's all right, Mama." Cath squeezed her tight. "I've been home all night."

"And still dreaming, I see," said her father.

Her mother pulled back and gawked at the thorny rosebush. "Not another one. What is going on in that head of yours?"

Cath gulped. "I'm sorry. I don't know where they're coming from."

Her mother slumped back and rubbed the tears still caught in her eyes. "Good heavens, Catherine. If you're going to dream, try to dream up something useful."

Cath knotted her fingers in the blanket. "Well, we can have fresh rose water, at least, and maybe I'll bake up some rose macarons —"

"No, no, no. I don't mean useful as in things you can bake with or cook with. I mean *useful*. Like a crown!"

"A crown?"

Her mother hid her face behind her thick fingers. "Oh, this night has shredded my poor old nerves. First that awful Cheshire Cat appears right when the King is getting ready to make his announcement, then you're nowhere to be found, then the Jabberwock —" She shuddered. "And now a rose tree growing up in the middle of my house. Honestly, Catherine!"

"I don't mean to argue, Mama, but a crown doesn't really do much of anything. Just sits on one's head, quite useless. Oh, I suppose it sparkles."

"Focus, child. Don't you see? The King intended to ask for your hand in marriage. Tonight!"

Mary Ann gasped, and Cath felt like her own feigned surprise was a bit sluggish. "Why, what an absurd suggestion," she said, chuckling. "The King? Certainly not."

The Marquess awkwardly cleared his throat, startling her mother, who spun to him with flapping arms. "Yes, yes, we're done with you, darling," she said. "Go on to bed. We need to have a mother-to-daughter chat."

Her father looked grateful to be sent away. Dark circles were beneath his eyes as he leaned over Cath and placed a kiss on the top of her head. "I'm glad you're safe."

"Good night, Papa."

Mary Ann curtsied to him as he left, then cast an excited smile in Cath's direction. "I'll just . . . bring up some tea?" she suggested. "To calm everyone's nerves."

"Thank you, Mary Ann," said the Marchioness. She waited until she and Cath were alone before taking Cath's hands into both of hers. "My dear, sweet, stupid child," she started, and Cath's shoulders tensed in defiance. "It is not absurd at all. The King means to make you his bride. Now, I am overjoyed that you made it home safely, but that doesn't excuse your absence, not on such an occasion as this. Where were you?"

Memories of chocolate caramels and unlaced corsets flashed through Catherine's mind.

She blinked, all innocence. "As I said, I was feeling poorly and thought I should leave so as not to cause a scene. I didn't want to interrupt the lovely time you and

Papa seemed to be having, so I took one of the royal carriages. Besides, I think you're mistaken about the King."

Her mother's face turned red as a cabbage. "I am not mistaken, you doltish girl. You should be engaged by now."

"But His Majesty has never shown me any preference. Well, other than for my baking. But even if he had, we've had no courtship. No time to —"

"He is the King! What need does he have of courtship? He asks and you say yes, that is all the courtship required." She heaved an exhausted sigh. "Or, it would have been. Now that you disappeared at the most inopportune moment, who knows what's to become of his affections? He could be jilted — his attachment may be permanently severed!"

Catherine pursed her lips, trying to disguise the influx of hope beneath a veil of concern. "If the King wished to request my hand in marriage, I should hope his attachment wouldn't be so flimsy as that. And I'm still not convinced of his intentions."

"Oh, he very much intended. And he had better still intend, or you will be confined to this room until you learn when it is and is not appropriate to leave a ball!" She hesitated. "Wild, murderous beasts notwithstanding. You must fix this, Catherine!"

"What do you expect me to do?"

"I expect you to apologize for leaving the gala prematurely. I expect you to be around the next time a man makes you an offer that will make you a queen. We must think of some way to ensure we haven't lost his good graces. Something to keep him from changing his mind, not when we were so close!"

"But what if I don't . . ." She trailed off, curling her knees up to her chest.

"What if you don't what? Spit it out, child."

She gulped. Hesitated. Sagged. "What if I don't see His Majesty for a while? We can't very well call on the King, and we have no invitations, do we?"

Her mother smugly tilted her nose up. "In fact, we do have an invitation. We have been asked to afternoon tea in the castle gardens in three days' time." She snapped her fingers. "I know! You shall bring His Majesty a gift! That will be the perfect excuse to approach him. He is fond of your sweets." She stood and took to pacing the room, the light from the lamp casting a restless shadow over the walls. "What do you think he'd like?"

"Anything, I suppose."

"Why are you being difficult?"

Cath shrugged. "I don't mean to be,

Mama. What about those rose macarons I mentioned?"

"Yes, yes, perfect! What are rose macarons?"

Cath prepared an explanation, but her mother was already waving off the question. "Never mind, I'm sure they'll be fine. Now, try to get some sleep. You know you plump up when you're not sleeping well." Fluttering her arms, she bustled out of the bedroom, nearly crashing into Mary Ann's tea tray on the way out.

After the Marchioness had gone, Mary Ann slipped inside and shut the door with her foot. She turned her wide eyes on Catherine and abandoned the tray on the nightstand. "Can it be true, Catherine?"

Catherine collapsed back onto her pillows. "I don't wish to believe it, either. A Jabberwock! In Hearts! The attack must have been awful."

Mary Ann froze, her thoughts tripping over the topic. "Oh yes. It *was* awful. It happened so fast — I barely caught sight of the beast as it was flying away with one courtier in each of its big, gangly claws . . ." She grimaced. "No one knew what to do. The ballroom was in chaos, everyone wanting to flee but too afraid to go outside. Then the Joker showed up out of nowhere — he's rather uncanny, don't you think? — and insisted that the King have everyone gather together in the great hall until it was deemed safe to leave. That's when we realized you were missing, and the Joker tried to calm Mama. He told her that he'd seen a girl in a red gown get into a carriage and he was sure you were safe, but we couldn't send a messenger, and we were stuck inside for hours . . ." Her face pinched with worry. "I'm so glad you're all right."

"Well, mostly right." Cath rose up onto one elbow. "The Joker gathered everyone in the great hall?"

Mary Ann nodded. "He was very calm about it, while the King was . . . well, you know how he is." Her lips stretched into a smile. "Or shall we say, your sweetheart?"

"We certainly shall not." She collapsed backward again. "I'm exhausted thinking about it."

Mary Ann laughed. "Oh yes. It must be tiresome, being a favorite of the King himself."

"Are we speaking of the same man? The short one with the funny curled beard? The one who never stops wiggling?"

Mary Ann settled onto the bed beside Catherine. "Don't be mean. To think, if you had been trapped in the castle with the rest of us, the King would have had to protect you from that beast. Or, at the least, he would have ordered the Clubs to protect you, as is much more practical, given the circumstances. It's very nearly romantic. Why, we would be discussing your engagement right now." She lay down beside Catherine, fluffing a pillow beneath her head.

Catherine pried open one eye. "You can't mean it."

"Mean what?"

Shoving away the blankets, Catherine flopped off the mattress. "Have you met the King?" she asked, adjusting her nightgown. "Practical? Romantic? Rubbish! I can't marry him!"

Mary Ann sat up, eyes wide. "Why not? You would be the Queen."

"I don't want to be the Queen! I want . . . I don't know. If ever I get married, I want there to be romance, and passion. I want to fall in love." Cath poured some tea into a cup, annoyed at how her hands shook. She was flushed — from talk of the King, from news of the Jabberwock . . . but mostly, she knew, from the dream.

Romance. Passion. *Love.*

She had never experienced them before, but she imagined they would leave her feeling like that dream had. Like the Joker did, with his quick smiles and witty remarks. She felt like she could talk to him for hours, for days and months and years, and never tire of it.

But . . .

He was a court joker. He was an impossibility.

She gulped, hard, and tried to tether her emotions back to the ground.

"None of that matters anyway," she said, half to herself. "Marry the King — bah! What I want is to open our bakery. That's what I've always wanted."

Mary Ann scooted to the edge of the bed. "I want that too, of course," she said. "But . . . Cath. The bakery, much as we've talked of it, has always been, well . . . something of a silly dream, don't you think?"

Cath spun to face her, surprised at the jolt of betrayal the words caused. "Silly?"

Mary Ann held up her hands in defense. "Not like that. It's a good dream. A lovely thought, truly. But we've been discussing it for years, and yet we're no closer to having any money, not without selling off your dowry. We don't have any support. No one will think we're capable of it."

"I refuse to accept that. I am the best

baker in all of Hearts and everyone who has tasted my pastries knows it."

"I don't think you understand."

Cath set down the cup without taking a drink. "What don't I understand?"

"You're the daughter of a marquess. Look around. Look at the things you have, the life you're accustomed to. You don't know what it's like to work every day so you can feed yourself and keep a roof over your head. You don't know what it's like to be poor. To be a servant."

"We'll be businesswomen, not servants."

"Or," said Mary Ann, "you could be a queen."

Cath inhaled a sharp breath.

"I can run any amount of calculations, consider every angle of profits and losses, but our little, insignificant bakery will never come close to providing what the King could offer you. The clothes, the food, the security . . ." Mary Ann's eyes glazed over and though her words struck Cath as boringly practical, she could see this was not the first time Mary Ann had considered what life must be like for someone who was more than a maid.

"Yes," said Cath, "but I would be married to the King, and I can hardly stand to be near him for a five-minute waltz. How could

I stand an entire lifetime?"

Mary Ann looked like she meant to defend His Majesty, but she hesitated. "He is ridiculous, isn't he?"

"The worst."

"You don't think there's any hope of you coming to love him?"

Cath thought of the King — squat and impish and flighty as a butterfly. She tried to imagine being wed to him. Stooping down to kiss him, her mouth tickled by his curled mustache. Listening to his giggles as they bounced through the castle corridors. Watching his childish, gleeful expressions every time he won a round of croquet.

She shuddered. "I'm sure that I couldn't."

Slipping off the bed, Mary Ann poured a cup of tea for herself. "Well, you have three days to think on it. Perhaps your heart will soften in that time."

Cath shut her eyes, glad that Mary Ann was ending the conversation. She never wanted to think about it again, but she knew she would have to. In three days her mother expected her to bring a gift of rose macarons to afternoon tea at the castle. In three days she would have to face His Majesty.

"You came home by yourself last night?" Mary Ann asked, heaping each cup with sugar.

"Yes."

"How did you manage to get the corset off?"

Catherine looked away. "The ties had come loose during the ball. All that dancing . . ." She trailed off, accepting the improved cup of tea, and deigned to change the subject. "I think we should go look at the cobbler's shop this morning. I want to see the home of our future bakery."

Mary Ann smiled, but there was restraint behind it. "That sounds like a nice outing, Lady Catherine."

For the first time Cath could see that she, alone, believed wholeheartedly their plan could work. *Would* work. She had never thought she might have to persuade Mary Ann of it too.

But then she pictured the King of Hearts standing before her, holding her hand. She grimaced to think of that small, clammy hand in hers. And then, his request. To be his bride. To be his wife. There would be no passion, no romance, no love. But she could picture precisely how he would smile at her, so hapless. So hopeful.

Her stomach roiled.

Could she ever say yes to that?

As she took a sip of tea, a more important

question struck her.

Could she ever say no?

Chapter 9

Closing sale, read the wooden sign posted in the cobbler's window. WALK IN BEFORE THE SHOES WALK OUT.

Catherine and Mary Ann stood beneath Cath's lace parasol, admiring the storefront across the street and building their courage to go inside.

"It's perfect," Cath whispered, the first to break the silence. She pointed at the large picture window. "Imagine a collection of crystal cake plates there, with wedding cakes and birthday cakes and, oh, the best unbirthday cakes. Plus a centerpiece — a five-tiered showpiece done all in latticework and scalloping, with sugared berries and flowers piled on top."

Mary Ann leaned into her. "I would have to measure the window dimensions to be sure, but I bet we could display upward of a dozen cakes right up front. That would attract plenty of foot traffic, and if we posted flyers throughout town . . . Oh, Cath. I'm sorry I called it silly. This really is our bakery, isn't it?"

"Of course it is. We'll paint a banner on the glass to read SWEETS AND TARTS: THE MOST WONDROUS BAKERY IN ALL OF HEARTS."

They shared a unified sigh. A passing froggy footman gave them an odd look, before licking his eyeball and continuing on.

The shop was on a cozy street lined with flower boxes and thatched roofs, a cobbled road that clattered with passing carriages. The morning was fair and the town seemed more crowded than usual. Passing baskets overflowed with onions and turnips from the nearby market. A crew of carpenter ants were whistling along with the beat of their hammers as they erected a schoolhouse around the corner. Overheard bits of conversation bustled with news of the Jabberwock, though they talked of it more like a long-passed fairy tale than a recent horror, which was the way of the people of Hearts.

Cath had the overwhelming sense that she would be happy to come here every day. To live a simple life here on Main Street, away from the manor at Rock Turtle Cove, away from Heart Castle.

Her attention caught on a street performer on the corner — a trumpet fish, playing for the passersby with an open case gathering coins in front of his musical mouth. Normally the sound of his music would have brought to mind the White Rabbit, but now Cath's first thought was of Jest and his silver flute.

A new dream weaseled its way into her thoughts, unbidden and unexpected.

Her and Mary Ann. Their bakery. And . . . him. Entertaining their customers, or returning home after a day of making merriment at the castle.

It was so absurd she immediately chastised herself for the thought. She barely knew the court joker and had no reason to think he would ever be anything to her beyond a couple of unusual dreams.

And yet, if she was only a simple baker, and not the daughter of a marquess, and not the King's intended . . . then the thought of the court joker becoming something more to her no longer sounded so impossible.

Could this be her future? Could such be her fate?

She was surprised at how encouraged she was by the prospect.

"Cath?"

She jumped. Mary Ann was watching her with a furrowed brow, her face shaded by the parasol.

"Do you know him?" Mary Ann asked.

"Who?"

"The trumpetfish?"

"Oh no, I just . . . thought it was a pretty tune." She dug a coin from her purse. "Let's go inside and take a look around, shall we?"

She didn't wait for Mary Ann to respond, dropping the coin into the trumpetfish's case as she made her way toward the cobbler's shop.

The moment they opened the door, a cloud of sweet-smelling smoke spilled over them and drifted into the street. Cath waved it away with her hand and stepped inside. There was a bell on the door handle, but it was fast asleep and only went on snoring even as they shut the door behind them.

Taking down the parasol, Cath let her gaze drift around the smoky, haze-filled shop. The floor was covered in shoes of all sizes and shapes, from ballet slippers and riding boots to iron horseshoes and flipper covers, piled like snowdrifts and spilling into the pathways. The plain beige walls were sparsely hung with painted advertisements that showed foot-dressings thirty years outdated. The lighting was dim and dusty;

the air smelled of blacking and leather and dirty stockings.

Behind a counter, Mr. Caterpillar, the cobbler, was perched on a stool and smoking from a large hookah. He blinked sleepily at Cath and Mary Ann as they made their way through the mess. A pair of leather-soled boots sat on the counter in front of him, and though he seemed more interested in the pipe than the shoes, Cath busied herself by giving the space a closer inspection, not wanting to interrupt his work.

In her mind, she cleared away the cobbler's shop from this dingy little space. She imagined the walls painted in candy stripes of cream and turquoise, and the window hung with breezy peach-sorbet curtains. Three small cafe tables waited by the entrance, each with a sprig of yellow posies in a milk-glass vase. The stained and musty carpet was replaced with waxed marble tiles, and the cobbler's old wooden counter would be exchanged for a glass case overflowing with cakes and gingerbreads, pies and strudels and chocolate-filled croissants. The back wall would be hung with baskets, each stuffed with fresh-baked bread. She saw herself behind the case, wearing a pink-checkered apron still dusted with that morning's flour. She was filling a jar with biscotti while Mary Ann, in matching yellow checkers, wrapped up a dozen shortbread cookies in a lime-green box.

Cath took in a long breath, then promptly started choking on the hookah smoke that filled her lungs, when she had been expecting spices and the chocolate and the steaming, yeasty buns. She covered her mouth, trying to muffle the coughing fit as well as she could, and turned back to the cobbler.

He was staring at her and Mary Ann. He had not touched the boots on the counter, though coming closer she could see that he was wearing an assortment of shoes himself — all different styles of boots and slippers taking up his many small feet.

"Who," he said lazily, "are you?"

Cath attempted her most charming smile — the persuasive one she'd learned from her mother — and picked her way past the piles of shoes. "My name is Catherine Pinkerton. My maid and I happened to be passing by when we noticed the sign outside. I was wondering what's to become of this shop once you've vacated. It would be a sore shame if it were to stay empty for long."

"It would *not* be a sore shame," Mr. Caterpillar said, rather gruffly, before taking another puff off the hookah.

"Oh, indeed, I only meant for the neighborhood, you know. One always hates to lose an established business, but I'm sure you're looking forward to, er . . . retirement, is it?"

He stared at her for so long she wondered that he would answer at all, or if she had offended him, when finally he said, "I have purchased a small plot of land in the forest, where I shall finally have quiet and solitude."

Cath waited for him to go on, but that seemed to be the end of it. "I see," she finally said. "That sounds lovely." She cleared her throat, still tickling from the smoke. "Are you the owner of this building as well?"

"No," said Mr. Caterpillar. "The Duke has long been my landlord."

"The Duke! You mean Lord Warthog?"

"The same, that bore." He yawned, as if growing bored by their conversation. "I like him well enough, though. He's aloof-like. Not so nosy like the rest of you."

Cath tried to disguise her frown, not only at the unjustified insult, but also because she'd been hoping the building's owner would be someone she had no association with. Someone who wouldn't be apt to discuss her business with the rest of the gentry, or her parents, until things were settled. She still hadn't had the brazenness to ask her father about a loan to start up her bakery — or permission to use her dowry for the funds.

At least Mr. Caterpillar was right about one thing. Lord Warthog didn't seem the nosy sort, so perhaps she could trust him not to gossip about her plans.

Mary Ann stepped closer. "Do you know if there's been much interest in someone leasing out the space once you're gone?"

Mr. Caterpillar slowly shifted his gaze to her. "Who are you?"

Mary Ann folded her hands in front of her skirt. "I'm Mary Ann."

The Caterpillar yawned again. "Whosoever leases this space will be the Duke's concern, not mine."

"I see," said Mary Ann. "But . . . would you happen to think that a bakery would do well here? Say, the most wondrous bakery in all of Hearts?"

The Caterpillar scratched at his cheek with the end of the hookah, pushing the skin around like overstretched marzipan. "Only if this bakery should serve clootie dumplings, which I prefer to all other dumplings."

"Oh, we would," said Cath. "I'd hunt

down the treacle well, even, to ensure it's the best clootie dumpling this side of the Looking Glass."

She beamed, but the Caterpillar only turned his solemn gaze back to her and said, without humor, "The treacle well is naught but a myth."

Cath deflated. "Yes. Naturally. I meant it as a joke."

It was an old myth — that drinking from the treacle well could heal a person's wounds or age them in reverse. Only problem was, no one had the faintest idea where to find the treacle well. Some said the well was in the Looking Glass maze, but moved around so that you would only get more and more lost if you ever tried to find it. Some said that only the most desperate of souls could ever find the treacle well. But most, like the cobbler, said it didn't exist at all.

The Caterpillar grunted. "Your joke was not charming."

"I wasn't meaning to be."

"What did you mean?"

Cath hesitated. "Only that . . . yes, we would have clootie dumplings?"

The Caterpillar peered at her a long, long moment, before sticking the hookah back into his mouth.

"Right," she muttered. "Thank you for all

of your help."

Turning, she grabbed Mary Ann's elbow and dragged her back outside, exiting to the sound of a few sleepy snorts from the bell.

Mary Ann was tying knots into her bonnet strings before they'd gone a dozen steps. "It's rather a miracle he's stayed in business this long, isn't it?"

"Indeed," said Cath, but she was already forgetting about the grumpy old cobbler. "Do you suppose the Duke would entertain the idea of leasing the building to us?"

"It's difficult to say," said Mary Ann. "I hope he would make the decision as a businessman should, based on our solid business plan and financial projections."

Cath shook her head. "No one thinks like that other than you, Mary Ann. I do think the Duke likes me well enough, as much as he likes anyone. But he also knows that I'm a nobleman's daughter who is supposed to be looking for a husband, not looking into storefronts. He might think it's a conflict of values to enter into a business arrangement with me." She cast her eyes upward, finding it too easy to imagine the Duke's haughty snort.

"Unless we have your father's permission."

"Yes. Unless that."

Nerves twisted in Cath's stomach, as they did every time she thought of broaching the subject with her parents. That was where the dream and reality refused to mix, as distinct as oil and water. No matter how many times she tried to imagine the conversation with her parents and what she would say to persuade them that her bakery was worth investing in, or at the least, worth giving permission for . . . they never said yes. Not even in her fantasies.

She was still the daughter of a marquess.

But she could push forward without them for now, for a little while longer still.

"We'll have our answer soon enough, though." She popped open the parasol as they headed back toward their carriage. "We're going to call on the Duke this afternoon."

The Most Noble Pygmalion Warthog, Duke of Tuskany, lived in a fine brick house upon a rolling-hill estate. The roof sported half a dozen chimneys, the drive was lined with apple trees, and the air carried the sweet smell of hay, though Catherine wasn't sure where it was coming from. She and Mary Ann left the footman to wait in the carriage again while they approached the house. Cath held a calling card; Mary Ann a box of miniature cakes that Cath had been saving in the icebox for just such an occasion.

A housekeeper opened the door.

"Good day," said Catherine, holding out the card. "Is His Grace at home?"

The housekeeper seemed momentarily baffled, as if the receiving of guests was an uncommon event — and perhaps it was for the Duke. "I — I will have to check," she stammered, taking the card and leaving them on the doorstep as she disappeared inside.

Minutes later, the housekeeper returned and ushered them into a parlor with a bowl of red apples on a sideboard and an array of cozy, if dated, furniture. Cath took a seat, leaving Mary Ann — in this outing, her dutiful lady's maid — to stand.

"Would you care for some tea?" asked the housekeeper. Her eyes were shining now, her uncertainty at the front door replaced with an anxious sort of delight. She seemed eager to please what Catherine could assume were very rare guests.

"That would be lovely, thank you."

The housekeeper bustled off. The door had just closed behind her when a second door opened, admitting the Duke.

He wore a velvet smoking jacket and held Catherine's calling card in one hoof. He looked at Catherine, then Mary Ann, and his stiff shoulders dropped a tiny bit as if in disappointment.

Catherine stood and curtsied. "Good day, Your Grace."

"Lady Pinkerton. What a surprise this is." He gestured for her to sit again and claimed a chair opposite her, folding one leg on top of the other.

"It had been too long since I'd come to call on you. I hope this is a good time."

"As good as any." He set her card in a silver bowl beside him. The bowl was similar to the one in the foyer at Rock Turtle Cove Manor, meant for collecting calling cards — except their bowl was often full, while this one had previously been empty. "When Miss Chortle delivered your card, I thought perhaps you might have . . . er, company with you."

"Company?" She listed her head. "Oh — my mother generally pays her own calls these days, but I've no doubt she'll be calling on you soon."

His flat nose twitched. "Your mother. Yes. How are the Marquess and Marchioness?"

"Quite well, thank you. And how is" — she hesitated — "your estate?"

"Quite . . ." He, also, hesitated. ". . . lonely, if one is to be honest." He followed the statement with a smile that kept pace with a grimace, and something in the look tugged at Catherine's heart. It made her want to pity him, but then, he was the one who was the ever-constant wallflower at the King's parties, who never so much as deigned to dance and was always the first to remove himself from a conversation.

Still, how much of his "aloof-like" behavior was snobbery, and how much was shyness? She wondered that she'd never considered it before.

"Would your maid care to sit?" the Duke asked before Catherine could think of anything polite to say in return.

Mary Ann had just lowered herself onto the edge of a small sofa when the housekeeper returned, carrying a tray with a steaming teapot and a plate of scones. Her hands were trembling as she poured the tea and her twinkling eyes darted between Catherine and the Duke so often that she spilled, twice. The Duke, frowning around his tusks, thanked her and ushered her away, adding the milk and sugar himself. As he bent over the tray, Cath caught sight of a bandage on his neck, stained dark with dried blood.

She gasped. "Are you injured, Your Grace?"

He glanced up at her, then dipped his head in embarrassment. "Just a scratch, I assure you. A war wound from the King's ball."

"Oh! Is that from the Jabberwock?"

"It is. Would you care for a cup?" This he offered to Mary Ann, who gratefully accepted.

"I'm sorry you were hurt," said Catherine.

"And I," he said, "am glad it was me and not one of the more delicate guests." He grinned cheekily and Cath couldn't help but return the look, though she wasn't sure she understood it.

Though her curiosity lingered, she didn't want to pry for more information on such a traumatic experience, so Catherine spent a moment searching for some other topic of conversation. "I worry that our visit is causing your housekeeper too much trouble. She seemed a bit shaken."

"No, no, not at all." The Duke handed her a cup and saucer. "We don't entertain much here, and . . . er, I think she might have you mistaken for someone else." His pinkish cheeks turned a darker shade and he looked away. "Would you care for a scone?"

"Thank you." Catherine set the treat on her saucer. Her curiosity was piqued now.

She wondered who the housekeeper had been expecting, or hoping for, but it was no business of hers and, besides, she had not come for idle chitchat — even if she was beginning to feel that such a motive would not have been unwelcome.

Her cup clinked against the saucer. "Mary Ann and I stopped in to Mr. Caterpillar's shop earlier today," she began. "I was surprised to hear that he's moving to a different storefront soon. The cobbler seems like such a permanent fixture of the neighborhood."

"Ah yes. You may be aware that Mr. Caterpillar is a tenant of mine? I will be sad to see him go."

"Do you have plans on what to do with the storefront once he's gone?"

"Not yet, no." The Duke cleared his throat. "This seems like a dull turn of conversation for young ladies. Perhaps you'd prefer to talk of other things, like . . . erm." He stared into his tea.

"Hair ribbons?" Cath suggested.

The Duke grimaced. "I'm not very educated on that topic, I'm afraid."

"Neither am I." Cath picked up the little triangle scone. "I am rather educated on baked treats, though. Do you know that baking is a hobby of mine?" She put the scone to her mouth.

"I do, Lady Pinkerton. I had the pleasure of tasting your strawberry —"

Catherine jerked forward, coughing. A chunk of scone landed in her cup with a splatter.

The scone had been wooden-dry and tasted like a mouthful of black pepper.

"What" — she stammered — "is in those — s-sco-*achoo*!" The sneeze racked her entire body and was followed by three more in quick succession. Tea spilled over the rim of her cup.

"I apologize!" the Duke said, passing a handkerchief to Mary Ann who handed it to Catherine, but the sneezing seemed to have stopped. "I should have warned you."

Cath rubbed at her nose with the handkerchief — the tip was still tingling, but the raw-pepper taste in her mouth was beginning to dissolve. "Warned me?" she said, her voice squeaky from her pinched nose. "Why — Your Grace, I think your cook is trying to kill us."

He rubbed his hooves together, his small ears flat against his head. "Oh no, Lady Pinkerton, I assure you that isn't it. It's just my cook. She's fond of pepper."

Cath accepted the new, hastily prepared cup of tea that Mary Ann handed to her and was glad to wash away as much of the peppered taste as she could. She coughed again. "Lord Warthog, your cook does know that there are other ingredients, doesn't she? And that pepper is not generally found in scones at all?"

He shrugged helplessly. "I tried to change her ways, but, well, you get used to it after a while. Sort of dulls your ability to taste much of anything."

She took another swig of tea. "That's terrible. Why haven't you fired her?"

The Duke's eyes widened. "Fire her? For being a terrible cook? What cruelty."

"But . . . she's a cook."

"Yes. And cook she does." He squirmed. "Just not well."

Catherine cleared her throat again. "I see. Well. Thank you for your hospitality, at least." She set the new teacup on the table beside the horrid scone.

The Duke shrank, any sign of confidence that he'd had at the start of this visit dissolving. "Are you leaving so soon?" He sounded miserable at the prospect.

"It was not my intention," said Catherine. "If it isn't too forward of me, I actually had meant to ask a . . . a favor of you."

His small eyes got smaller. "What sort of favor?"

"Nothing untoward, I assure you. But as I said before, I'm fond of baking. *Really* baking." She eyed the scones with distaste. "I like to think I'm quite good at it, and I never use pepper at all, I assure you." She smiled in an attempt to lighten what had become an awkward conversation. She nodded to Mary Ann, who stood and handed the box to the Duke. "These are some miniature cakes I made. They're for you to keep. I hope you'll enjoy them." She hesitated. "In fact, I hope your senses aren't so dulled that you can still taste them."

"I . . . that's very kind, Lady Pinkerton," said the Duke, opening the box and eyeing the cakes, not with gratitude, but suspicion. "But what are these for?"

"That's precisely my reason for calling. I've been thinking how Hearts could use a nice quality bakery and I thought, well, why shouldn't I open one? Which led me to thinking of the storefront Mr. Caterpillar is vacating and if you might be interested in leasing the storefront to me?" She kept her tone light and confident, but when she had finished, the Duke's expression had darkened. She brightened her own smile to compensate. "What do you think?"

"I see," he said, shutting the lid on the box and setting it on the table beside him.

"So this is not a social call, after all." He sighed, and the sound was devastating. Cath felt Mary Ann flinch beside her.

"That isn't so," Cath stammered. "I've been meaning to call on you for weeks and just —"

"It's all right, Lady Pinkerton. You needn't go on. I understand that I'm not much for popularity and your calling cards are doubtlessly wanted elsewhere."

Her chest tightened. "I'm sorry to have offended you."

He waved away her apology and, after a moment, sat straighter in his chair. His expression shifted into that cold exterior she knew from countless balls. His voice, when he spoke, carried a stiffness that had been missing before. "Is the Marquess aware of your plans?"

She thought to lie, but saw no point in it. "No, not yet."

He rubbed at his hanging jowl. "I have great respect for your father. I would not wish to insult him by being party to a business venture he does not approve of."

"I understand. I intend to speak with him about it soon, but thought it might be beneficial to have a storefront first. To better convey my plans to him."

Mary Ann leaned forward. "This request

is contingent upon a rental agreement that puts fair market value upon the storefront and a full inspection of the property —"

Cath pinched Mary Ann's leg, silencing her, but the Duke was nodding. Almost, but not quite, smiling at her interruption.

"But of course," he said. "That is smart business." He tossed a peppery scone into his mouth. A crumb stuck to his lower lip. He wouldn't look at Catherine and he had nearly finished his tea before he spoke again. "I will keep you under consideration for the storefront, once Mr. Caterpillar has moved out."

Cath's entire body lifted. "Oh, thank —"

"But I, too, have a favor to ask, Lady Pinkerton."

Her gratitude caught in her throat, right beside the still-scratching pepper. She swallowed it back down and hoped something mighty that he was about to ask for a lifetime supply of fresh-baked, pepper-free scones.

"Of course," she said. "What can I do for you?"

The veil of his confidence once again slipped and, if he hadn't been so very pig-like, Catherine would have thought he looked rather sheepish. "You are friends with . . ." His tusks bobbed as he gulped.

". . . Lady Mearle, are you not?"

She stared at him. *Friends* was not the most accurate depiction of her relationship with Margaret Mearle, but — "Yes. Yes, she and I are quite good friends."

"Do you think it might be possible for you to, er, if it isn't asking too much, might you . . . put in a fond word for me?"

She cocked her head to the side. "With . . . Lady Mearle?"

"Indeed. You see, I . . ." He flushed, and his lips turned into a brief, awkward smile. "I rather fancy her."

Catherine blinked. "Lady *Margaret* Mearle?"

The Duke might have seen the disbelief on her face, but he was too busy gazing at the wall. "I know. It's absurd of me to think I might be worthy of such a dear creature, or that she could ever share my feelings. But it's just . . . she's the jammiest bit of jam, isn't she? So very clever. And righteous. And so very, very . . ." He swooned. "Pink."

He dared to glance at her.

Catherine snapped her mouth shut and tried to look sympathetic.

Appeased, he looked away again. "But I can't even bring myself to speak to her. I can't imagine what she thinks of me."

Gnawing at the inside of her cheek, Cath

thought of all the snide comments Margaret had made about the Duke over the years, mostly regarding how stuck-up and arrogant he was. Traits that she, too, had seen in him, but no longer seemed fair.

It was difficult to imagine. She could not recall Lord Warthog, the perpetual bachelor, ever showing favor to a lady, just as she could not recall any man showing interest in the intolerable, unattractive Margaret Mearle.

Yet — here it was. Pudding and pie, right before her eyes.

She tried to smile, hoping to ease the desperation scrawled across the Duke's face. "I would be happy to put in a fond word for you, Your Grace."

Chapter 10

The days leading up to the tea party were agony. Catherine was filled with dread at what would happen when she saw the King again. Her mother was anxious too, though they were hoping for very different results from the meeting.

It felt like trickery of the worst sort to be making a batch of macarons with the intention of capturing the King's heart when Cath had no interest in capturing it at all. Nevertheless, she was glad for an excuse to spend a day in the kitchen, where she didn't have to worry about being ordered to go practice some useless skill, like embroidery.

Oh, if only, if only the King were fickle. If only he'd been so embarrassed by her disappearance that he wouldn't dare attempt it again or, at the least, he would have the sense to propose in private this time.

Although that thought, too, made her shudder.

Despite her growing trepidation, as the tea party approached, Cath also started to become fidgety with impatience. She tried to deny it, even to herself, but she was looking forward to the afternoon. Not for the King, or the lawn games, and not even for the mini cakes and sandwiches.

She was anticipating another encounter with the court joker.

Having had no more sightings in her dreams, she was longing to see him again, fantasizing over every potential facet of their next encounter. She wanted to witness another buoyant smile, to be the source of his easy laughter, to feel the brush of his fingers on the nape of her neck.

She paused, lifting the pastry bag away from the baking sheet, where fifteen piped disks of batter were waiting to be baked into almond meringue cookies. Her skin had a new flush to it that wasn't from the oven, and her hands had begun to tremble — unacceptable for such a delicate task.

She shut her eyes and tamped the thoughts back down, as she did every time they drifted in the direction of illicit caresses. Her mother would implode if she knew Cath was having such improper thoughts about the King's Joker.

The King, for goodness' sake. The one she

was supposed to dreaming about.

Her nerves were in tatters over it all.

Setting down the pastry bag, she swore that she would not allow herself to be carried away during the tea party. She was a lady, and he was a novelty. If she should see him again — which was unlikely in itself — she would entertain only civilized conversation. None of these flirtations that had carried her away before. There could be nothing improper at all.

Though she was curious to know if she would feel as drawn to the Joker again upon a second meeting, there was a part of her that hoped she wouldn't. Because what options were given to her even if she did feel it again? Her parents would never allow a courtship with him. She still hadn't decided what she was going to do about the King. And besides, she was supposed to be focusing on how she could persuade her parents to let her have the bakery, the one dream that had consumed her more than all the others . . . until the lemon tree, at least.

"Good graciousness, what is that delightful aroma?"

She jumped back from the counter. Cheshire — or rather, Cheshire's head — had filled up the cuckoo clock's face on the wall, the hands pointing at his left ear and whiskers, indicating it was just past two o'clock in the afternoon.

"Hello, Cheshire." She frowned. "You better not have just eaten that cuckoo bird."

He disappeared in a puff before reappearing, fully formed, on the high windowsill above the counter. The orange tint from the pumpkin pasties had faded from his fur. "I've done no such thing," he said, "although I am presently determining how many of *those* I can eat when your back is turned without your noticing."

She eyed him suspiciously.

"Oh, fine. I suppose I don't care if you notice or not."

"They are for the King."

Cheshire rolled his eyes — the pupils bouncing around like a child's bouncing ball. "They are always for the King."

Grinning, she picked up the pastry bag, wiped a drip of excess batter on a dishtowel, and resumed her piping. "I meant to thank you for causing the distraction at the ball the other night. Your timing was perfect."

"Most things that I do are."

"Were the guests quite upset over it all?"

"Lady Mearle did not seem receptive to the distraction."

"No, I meant about me leaving. Does everyone know that I was the one the King intended to . . ." She gulped. ". . . to propose to?"

"I don't think it's become widely assumed yet, though only because most people are so very horrid at paying attention."

She let out a slow breath, finished piping the last cookie, and thwapped the baking sheet on the counter to level them.

"Besides," Cheshire said, smiling wide as ever, "the King's failed proposal was overshadowed by the horrors that came afterward. I trust you heard news of the Jabberwock?"

She dabbed a sleeve across her damp brow. "I did. I suppose I shouldn't be thinking about some stupid proposal after what happened. I wasn't even sure I believed that Jabberwocky existed until now."

"It is a dangerous thing to unbelieve something only because it frightens you."

Cath popped the sheet into the oven. "But how long has it been since one was seen here?"

"Since long before you or I were born." His grin never faltered, making for an eerie foil to a dark topic. "Perhaps it has been here all along, lying in wait. Or perhaps it came in through the Looking Glass, though it seems an unlikely venture. I doubt we shall ever know the truth of it, but we do know that the beast is here now, and I don't suppose we've heard the last of its brutality."

Cath swallowed down the bitter taste in her mouth. "What are we going to do about it?"

"We? I have no intentions of doing anything at all."

"Fine, not you, then. But someone has to do something. The King should appoint a knight to go after it, like in the old legends."

Cheshire made a guttural sound in his throat. "Know you of any knights here in Hearts?"

She pondered this. The closest thing they had were the Club guards at the castle, and she doubted any of them would fare much better than the Diamond courtiers had.

"Someone has to do something," she repeated, though most of her fire had turned to smoke.

"Yes, and that something shall be to ignore such a horrible incident and go on pretending nothing has happened at all." Cheshire licked his paw and dragged it along his whiskers. "As is our way."

Cath's gut had tightened. She knew he was right — though she had never before witnessed something so awful, she knew everyone would be willing to pretend it away rather than upset their pleasant lives.

"What about those poor courtiers?" she murmured. "What is to become of them?"

Cheshire's grin began to slip, just — the — tiniest — bit. "They have already been found, dear Catherine. Two shreds of card-stock were discovered outside the Nowhere Forest yesterday morning."

She recoiled from him. "No . . . maybe it wasn't . . . ?"

"It was them. Part of a diamond was visible on one of the shreds."

She grimaced and turned away, squeezing her eyes tight. She felt suddenly childish and small. Chastised, though no one had chastised her but herself. Two days spent dreading a run-in with the King and day-dreaming over the Joker, and all the while, two courtiers were dead, and a monster on the loose.

"I called on the Duke of Tuskany yesterday," she said. "He had a wound from the Jabberwock. Was anyone else hurt?"

"I don't believe so, and quite lucky that. It was very nearly Lady Margaret Mearle."

"What do you mean?"

"When the great beast crashed through the window, it seemed — why, I hate to sound self-absorbed, but it seemed as though it were heading for *me.* And I was still on top of the girl's head, you see. So I vanished . . . as prompted by instinct, not at all cowardice, I assure you."

"Naturally."

"I came to on the other side of the ballroom just in time to see Lord Warthog launch himself in between Lady Mearle and the beast."

Her jaw fell open. "How heroic!"

"Fascinating, isn't it, how often *heroic* and *foolish* turn out to be one and the same. That beast had claws like carving knives and nearly took off the Duke's head. He's most lucky it was only a surface wound, I daresay." He scratched behind one ear. "Rather pigheaded he can be."

"But the Jabberwock didn't kill him."

"No. It turned its attention toward the feasting table and the two courtiers standing beside it. Grabbed them and took off, flew right over the balcony. It all happened very of-a-sudden."

She slumped against the baker's table. "I never dreamed such a thing could happen here."

Cheshire's yellow eyes slitted as he held her gaze for one beat, two. Then he began to unravel from the tip of his tail, a slow unwinding of his stripes. "These things do not happen in dreams, dear girl," he said, vanishing up to his neck. "They happen only in nightmares."

His head spiraled and he was gone.

Chapter 11

The moment Cath stepped through the garden arbor onto the sweeping green lawn of Heart Castle, she was searching for him. She couldn't help it, try as she might. Her eyes skimmed over the guests, hunting for a three-pointed jester's hat amid the bonnets and wide-brimmed sun hats. Her entire body was bating its breath, waiting for the moment she would see him — should he even be present. Did jokers attend garden parties? She didn't know.

She felt like an idiot, curtsying to the lords and barons, ladies and countesses, all the while letting her attention scurry off to each new arrival, each glimpse of black amid the colorful clothing of the nobility. She knew she should be looking for the King. Her mother had been adamant that Catherine make herself known to the King immediately upon arrival. She was to give him the delicate rose-flavored macarons that were tucked into her skirt pocket and she was not to leave his side until either the party was over or she had a gem on her finger.

To Cath's relief, as she made one complete turn around the lawn, the King was nowhere in sight.

To her disappointment, neither was Jest.

Stupid dreams. Stupid fantasies. Stupid lemon tree and white roses and —

What if he didn't come at all? It felt like it would be a wasted outing in her prettiest day dress. She hadn't realized until that moment that she'd chosen it specifically for him.

"My dear Catherine, how appropriately attired you are today."

She swiveled around to see Margaret Mearle gamboling across the grass, clutching two battledore rackets in her hands. She was dressed all in sunflower-yellow and on her head was a fascinator that looked like an enormous yellow rosebud waiting to bloom.

Catherine cocked her head. There was something different about Margaret today. Something difficult to place. If Cath hadn't known better, she would have thought that today, in that hat, in this light, Margaret looked almost . . .

Well, not pretty. But unoffensive to the

eyes, at the least.

Perhaps she was seeing her in a new light, knowing how fond the Duke was of her.

"Good day, Lady Margaret," she said, curtsying.

"Good enough, one supposes," said Margaret, "though unwarranted optimism is unwise for one who wishes to eschew disappointment. Nevertheless, I do hope it shall be a better day than the ball, at the least. Have you heard of my trauma?" She clutched the rackets against her chest.

"Oh yes, I heard all about the Jabberwock attack. I can only imagine how horrifying it was! I'm so glad to see you unharmed." Catherine, upon saying it, realized that it was true.

But Margaret only huffed. "Yes, yes, quite horrifying, but before *that,* have you heard tell what your awful cat did?"

"My . . . cat? You mean Cheshire? I wouldn't call him mine, precisely."

"Nevertheless, he is a nuisance that should not be suffered among civilized society. I hope you left him at home today."

Cath cocked her head, feigning ignorance. "What has he done?"

"Oh dear, I find it difficult to believe that word has not yet reached your ears. It was dreadful. The mongrel appeared from nowhere, in that uncanny way he does, and plopped right down on my head." She shuddered.

"I'm sure Cheshire meant no harm. I actually think he's rather fond of you."

Margaret pouted. "I hope not. My one solace is that everyone was distracted by the Jabberwock and that has overshadowed my torment — ah, my mortification!"

"Yes, we can hope." Catherine wrung her wrists and buried a remark about the poor Diamond courtiers. "Is it true, do you know, that the King also made mention of a . . . a bride at the ball?"

"He was about to propose before all turned chaotic. You did miss much that night, Lady Catherine."

"My loss, to be sure. And has there been much speculation as to who it might be?"

"I wouldn't know. I'm not one to gossip. Gossiping always leads to spoiled milk."

"Of course. That's a very good rule to live by." Cath was nodding sagely when she spotted Lord Warthog taking a turn around the lawn with the Dowager Countess Wontuthry. The Countess had her hand on the Duke's elbow, the other gripping a cane that kept sinking into the soft grass. She was speaking fervently on some topic, but the Duke's gaze was darting from Catherine to

Margaret to the ground and back to Margaret. His jowled face was warped with anxiety.

Clearing her throat, Catherine leaned closer to Margaret, like a conspirator. "Tell me more about the Jabberwock attack," she whispered. "Were you very frightened?"

"Oh! Must we speak of it?" Margaret placed a hand to her brow. "I feel faint at the memory. Did you know — that beast broke through the windows and headed straight for me! I cannot be sure why. One is made to wonder if a creature with such wicked propensities might not be naturally drawn to one of goodness and pristine moral values, such as myself."

"Er, yes," said Catherine. "One is made to wonder."

"Indeed, and the nightmares shall haunt me unto my deathbed. Even now I see its jaws when I shut my eyes, still hear the click-clacking of its enormous claws."

Catherine gripped her elbow for support. "Yes, but . . . you were rescued, were you not? I heard the Duke was very heroic. Is it true that he threw himself in between you and the beast?"

Margaret sniffed. "More like he couldn't get out of the way fast enough. That man has all the grace of a wild boar."

She squinted. "Actually, I think wild boars can be quite quick and athletic . . ."

"Oh! There he is! Wave, quickly, or he'll think we've been talking about him." With a look that was as much grimace as smile, Margaret wiggled her fingers at the Duke and the Countess.

The Duke immediately looked away, ducking his large chin behind a green cravat.

Margaret grunted. "Such arrogance."

"I'm beginning to think he might just be shy . . ."

"We mustn't encourage such ill behavior, Catherine. That is just like paying the cart in carrots before the horse gets his gift."

Cath tried to puzzle this out for a moment, but quickly gave up. "How I do wish I could find fault with your wisdom, Margaret."

Margaret scoffed. "Why — I daresay the Countess is flirting with him! What a vile woman."

"I'm not sure —"

"I could grab on to any man's arm, too, if I wanted to pretend to have a crooked spine."

"To be fair, she *does* have a crooked spine."

"Yes, and evidently a desire to add to her wealth. Can you imagine, curtsying to Her

Ladyship, the Dutch Countess Wontuthry? Or the Counting Duchess of Tuskany? Who needs that many syllables, anyway?"

"It seems to me that he's just helping an old lady across the lawn."

Margaret glowered. "You are observant as a toadstool, Lady Pinkerton."

Cath scrambled to right the teetering ship of their conversation. "Well, even if the Countess were flirting, I think the Duke is actually taken with —"

"Oh no. Now they're coming this way." Margaret turned her back on them. "Let's look as though we're caught in a game of Battledore and Shuttlecock so they won't pester us." Margaret thrust the extra racket into Catherine's hand.

"Won't that be rude?"

Ignoring her, Margaret hustled a fair distance away and threw up the shuttlecock — a needle-nosed hummingbird — striking it in Catherine's direction. Instinctively, Cath dove to hit it back, but missed. The hummingbird stuck nose-first into the sod.

"Sorry, dearest Catherine!" Margaret preened, loud enough to be heard halfway across the lawn. "You really must take more time to practice."

Stooping, Catherine pried the bird out of the grass. Its jittery wings buzzed. She glanced up at Margaret, who was adamantly not looking at the Duke, while the Duke, standing not far away, had eyes only for her, now that he was in no danger of being found out.

The Countess continued to prattle on beside him, oblivious to his wandering attention.

"Come on, Catherine," Margaret urged. "Hit it back."

Sighing, Cath tossed the bird into the air and batted it toward Margaret. They made it through three passes, Margaret growing more competitive with every hit. Though Catherine would never have considered herself athletic, she was in better shape than her competitor, who was soon wheezing with the effort, her face blotchy and scrunched in concentration. But her lack of skill was made up for in determination, and on her third hit, she sent the bird flying over Catherine's head. Cath ducked and swiveled to follow its path through the sky — straight toward an enormous jet-black raven.

Catherine gasped.

The hummingbird froze mid-flight and backed up fast on its fluttering wings. It hesitated a moment, not knowing what else to do, then turned and flew off toward the hedge maze.

Catherine did not care. Her heart was in her throat, her eyes scouring the crowd. Dresses and waistcoats, top hats and bonnets.

She spotted him amid the tables where the ladies were fanning themselves and sipping at their tea and beaming at the Joker as he strummed a mandolin. Above them, the Raven cawed, and Jest glanced up, still strumming. The Raven soared down and settled on his shoulder.

He hardly seemed to notice at first. Then, as Catherine stared as openly as a child at her first parade, Jest glanced toward her.

His eyes connected with hers in an instant, as if he'd known just where she was.

As if he'd been watching her for some while, and waiting for her to notice.

Even from so far a distance, she thought she detected a faint smile shot her way.

All sensation left her body. No more soft grass beneath her feet. No more racket clutched between her hands. No more hair clinging to the back of her damp neck.

The moment answered one question, at least. She felt as drawn to him as ever, though whether it was mere attraction or some other, stronger force, she had no way of knowing, and no previous experience to draw from.

Jest looked away. The connection snapped and Catherine dragged in a long breath, grateful to be rescued from her own lack of subtlety.

The look had been just long enough to fan the flames of her curiosity, and short enough to put none of them out.

His audience was growing fast. Even some of the Spade gardeners had stopped working to listen to the Joker's music. Catherine realized with a jolt that her mother was among them, beaming as large as anyone.

The song ended, the notes reaching Catherine over the expanse of lawn, followed by the delighted cooing and clapping of the crowd.

Jest tucked the mandolin against his side and bowed. The Raven took flight again, soaring off in the direction of the herb garden.

"Catherine! You look like a buffoon. What are you staring at?"

"Oh — oh!" She faced Margaret again, clawing her fingernails into the racket's netting. "I was distracted by . . . by the Raven. Did you see it? It appears that the, uh — the Joker is over . . . Oh, my. Margaret, what is happening to your hat?"

Margaret's face lit up and she reached

tentative fingers toward her fascinator. "What is it doing? Tell me."

"It's . . . blooming," said Cath, as the rosebud that was as big as Margaret's head began to open — the yellow petals curling open to reveal a lush flower, the hue deepening to rich gold at its center. The edges of the petals glimmered, as if dipped in sugar crystals, and the softest, most wonderful fragrance drifted toward Cath's nose.

"My, that is a fine hat you're wearing, Lady Margaret."

They spun to see the Countess, who had spoken, and the Duke, who was blushing at his hooves, standing not far away.

Margaret's enthusiasm fizzled as she stuck her nose into the air. "Thank you," she said, rather unkindly.

"Did you by chance get it at that new hat shop outside the Crossroads?" the Countess asked. "I've heard much about it these past weeks and have been meaning to make a trip there myself, though with my old age it's hard to get around much unless I have a strapping young man to assist me." She grinned, as if she'd said something wicked, and curled her fingers into the crook of the Duke's elbow.

"That is indeed where I got it." The confession seemed strained. Margaret's shoulders stiffened beside her ear. "That is to say . . . naturally, that pride and . . . the sin of arrogance . . . it requires willpower to . . . to doff the vanity that such attention-grabbing-ness might . . . otherwise . . . prevail upon oneself . . ." She gulped. "Amen."

"Amen," Cath, the Duke, and the Countess recited.

Cath cleared her throat. "I believe what Lady Margaret means to say is that 'Once a goldfish, forever a goldfish.' "

The Duke dared to glance up, his small dark eyes captivated by Margaret and her unfurled hat. Despite her haughtiness and upturned nose, with Lord Warthog ogling her in such a way and her hat sitting aromatically atop her head, it once again became possible to imagine her as not-unattractive.

"Forever a goldfish," breathed the Duke. "I could not agree more."

"It's nice to see young ladies taking up their exercise," said the Countess, gesturing her cane toward the battledore rackets. "I was just telling the Duke that this tea party is already much improved over the black-and-white ball. I should like to see the King maintain such high standards of guests.

None of that — riffraff that was about before."

"Oh yes," Margaret said. "Like that awful Cheshire Cat. What is a feline like that doing at a royal ball, with all the vanishing and unvanishing and sitting on people's heads. It isn't natural."

"Such is an insult to proper ladies and gentlemen." The Countess planted her cane back into the grass. "Not to mention Mr. and Mrs. Peter." She made a face akin to a child trying their first bite of cooked spinach. "Dreadful folk. I'll be pleased to never cross their paths again."

"What we can be grateful for," interrupted Catherine, folding her hands over the battledore racket, "is that you were present, Your Grace. Margaret was just telling me about your courageous sacrifice — throwing yourself in between her and the Jabberwock in order to protect a fair maiden! And I see you still bear the wound to prove it." She gestured at the bandage peeking above the Duke's cravat, then held the racket against her chest. "It's like something from a story. So romantic! Margaret, don't you think the Duke was very brave?"

She was met with a brooding glare from Margaret and was glad the Duke was too busy blushing again to notice.

A new voice intruded into their circle, deep and witty and tumbling with laughter. "I certainly hope," said the Joker, "that this won't be the standard of romance by which all men in the Kingdom of Hearts shall be held to."

Catherine whipped her head so quickly to the side she near gave herself a neck crick. The Joker was tipping his bell-tinged hat to the Duke. "You run a difficult competition, Lord Duke."

"Well, I wouldn't . . . ," the Duke stammered, his snout twitching. "Th-that is to say, any man would have . . . Lady Mearle was in danger, and I . . . it wasn't anything spectacular, I assure you . . ."

"He's humble too?" said Jest, raising an eyebrow and looking at Catherine, Margaret, and the Countess in turn. "Which of you three ladies is he trying so hard to impress?"

Biting the inside of her cheek, Catherine subtly nodded toward Margaret.

"Ah." If Jest questioned the Duke's choice, there was no sign of it as he rocked back on his heels.

The Countess batted her lashes, flattered to have been included as a potential romantic conquest. "All you young men these days fancy yourselves such charmers," she said, clearly charmed. "But I assure you, I won't be marrying again. Once in a lifetime was plenty enough for me."

"A loss to us all," said Jest, sweeping up the Countess's hand and kissing the back of it. She swooned some more.

"You must be the ever-wise Lady Mearle I've heard so much about," he said, giving a kiss to Margaret, and then — "And . . . the delightful Lady Pinkerton, if I'm not mistaken?" His attention found her again. The leather of his glove was warm and supple beneath her fingertips, and the slight graze of his lips on her knuckle was hardly worthy of the heat that climbed up her neck and onto her ears. There was a joke behind his kohl-lined eyes. A secret passing between the two of them.

"Enchanted, Mr. Joker," said Cath, glad when her voice didn't shake.

His grin brightened.

Lord Warthog straightened his waistcoat and squared his shoulders with renewed composure. "And what of you, Lady Mearle? I don't recall I've yet heard of your having any, erm . . . proposals?"

Cath flinched. Though she knew the Duke's intentions were anything but cruel, his sudden change of countenance made the hopeful question sound as though he were mocking her.

Which was, of course, precisely what Margaret heard.

Glowering, she snatched the battledore racket out of Catherine's hands. "I don't see that it's any business of yours. Or anyone else's for that matter. But if you must know, I consider myself above trivial matters such as courtships and flattery. I prefer to spend my hours improving my mind through an intense study of philosophy and stitching parables into the linings of my gowns. Now, if you'll excuse me, I'm going to go find my hummingbird." Adjusting the hat on her head, she marched off toward where the bird had fled, leaving a stricken Duke and oblivious Countess in her wake.

"Think I can guess the answer to your question," said Jest, joking, but not unkind. He handed the Duke a gracious smile. "Better luck next time, chap."

With a sigh, Lord Warthog tipped his hat to Catherine and led the Countess away, his interest in their conversation waning as soon as Margaret had gone.

"I apologize to have interrupted," said Jest, though he spoke quietly and it was difficult to hear him over the sudden galloping of her heart.

"You needn't apologize," she said. "I fear I was doing a disservice to the Duke, though I'd meant to help."

" 'Tis too often the way of good intentions. Is matchmaking a frequent hobby of yours, or is the Duke a rare and lucky beneficiary of your services?"

"So far, I'm afraid my services have been neither lucky nor beneficial, but it is in fact my first attempt. The Duke fancies Lady Mearle, but isn't adept at showing it, as you may have noticed. And so he and I are . . . trading favors." She shrugged. "It's complicated."

"So you deal in favors. That's good to know."

He grinned.

She grinned back.

"Speaking of favors," he said, with some hesitation, "I'd nearly forgotten. I was sent to summon you, Lady Pinkerton."

"Summon me?"

He clasped his hands behind his back in imitation of one of the royal squires. "His Majesty the King has requested a word with you."

CHAPTER 12

Catherine followed Jest with mounting trepidation. Her stomach was in knots over meeting the King, but she did her best to steel herself against what she assumed was his imminent proposal.

It was difficult to steel herself against it when she wasn't sure what her answer would be. Every time she imagined how miserable she would be upon accepting his proposal, it was followed by a vision of how delighted her parents would be. How very proud. Oh, how her mother would brag . . .

Her seesaw emotions were not helped by the casual whistling of the Joker who walked a pace ahead of her, or the narrow cut of his shoulders, or his elegantly long strides that made her blood rush for reasons she couldn't fathom.

Her head spun. Maybe she would faint again. She almost embraced the idea.

Jest led her into a courtyard that was surrounded by boxwoods and chiming bluebells. A fountain sat in its center and the King was walking around its edge like a tightrope walker, his arms outstretched for balance.

Jest cleared his throat. "Your Majesty, may I present Lady Catherine Pinkerton."

The King squealed with delight and hopped off the fountain.

Catherine curtsied, and cursed herself for not having fainted during the walk.

"Thank you, Jest, thank you. That will be all!" The King clapped his hands as Jest bowed once to him and once to Catherine. He seemed to hesitate as he met her eyes, as if he saw the pleading in her face. The chant of *please, please don't leave* that was running loops in her head.

His brow creased.

Bracing herself, Catherine looked away.

"I won't be far," said Jest, "should my presence be wanted."

Though it was said to the King, Catherine suspected he meant it for her. She did not look up again until she'd heard the faint thumping of his boots passing out of the courtyard.

She and the King were left alone in the romantic gardens. He was smiling at her like he'd just opened an unbirthday present and found it was precisely what he'd asked for.

"You wished to see me, Your Majesty?"

"I did, Lady Pinkerton."

A heavy, clouded silence followed before the King cleared his throat. "Don't the gardens look marvelous today? Listen to those bluebells, so in tune."

She listened. The bluebells' chime was beautiful, hitting all the right notes. The music did nothing to calm her.

The King offered her his arm, and she had no choice but to take it and allow him to lead her along the pathways, between geraniums and creeping ivy and heavy-headed dahlias. The King was so jovial, practically skipping beside her. She wanted to put her hands on his shoulders and order him to calm down, but she did her best to be amused by his enthusiasm instead. She listened while he gabbled on about which flowers the gardeners had chosen for the upcoming season and how his vintner was going to make elderberry wine this year and how very excited he was to attend the annual Turtle Days Festival that the Marquess and Marchioness were hosting, and would she be there — but of course she would, being their daughter — and would she dance the quadrille and was she eager to try her luck at the oyster hunt?

She listened with utmost politeness, but hardly heard any of it. The weight of the paper-wrapped macarons inside her pocket became an anchor dragging her down. She had baked them to ensure she was still in the King's good graces. She had baked them with the intention of compelling him into a marriage proposal.

Catherine had tried to leave them at home that morning, feigning forgetfulness, but her mother had had none of it.

She did not want to give them to the King. She did not want to encourage him.

Perhaps it wouldn't matter. He was going to ask for her hand anyway. Why else would he have had her escorted into the gardens?

She tried to breathe. This was better than the ballroom, at least. Better than being surrounded by every person she'd known in her life. Out here, she felt like she had a slim chance of saying no without dying of guilt as she said it.

They passed through an archway, around a cutting garden, beneath a trellis, while the King talked of everything and nothing. Catherine yawned. She wished she was still playing yard games with Margaret. She wished she was drinking tea and gossiping with her mother and her friends. She wished she would have thought to eat something when she first arrived — her stomach was going to begin gurgling any minute.

As they meandered into another courtyard, her eyes caught on Jest's dark motley again. As promised, he hadn't gone far, and he now crouched in the next garden before the Two of Spades, a young gardener who was watching the Joker with awe.

Jest was showing him a card trick.

Catherine's feet pulled her off the path without her noticing. She drifted toward the pair, watching as Jest took a pack of cards into his hands and fanned them up one arm, then flipped them with a gesture too quick to follow. The cards dominoed down to his elbow. He made them dance and skip, form a living chain between his fingers, spread out into the shapes of stars and hearts, before collapsing back into a deck of cards once again. Then he shot them all up into the air in a stream high as a water fountain and allowed them to rain down over their heads like red and black confetti.

The young gardener froze mid-laugh at the sound of a startling caw. The Raven swooped down from a nearby rose tree and caught a single card in his beak before landing on Jest's forearm. The bird cocked his head to one side, revealing the card he had caught.

It was the two of spades.

Jest gave it to the young card, who looked like he'd never been given anything half so special in his life.

"Do you like him?"

Cath jumped. She'd forgotten all about the King.

Heat flooded her cheeks. "N-no . . . I don't —"

"I think he's perfect."

She pressed her lips shut.

"I think he could be the best court joker this kingdom has ever seen, and that's including Canter Berry, the Comely Comedian."

Catherine had no idea who that was, but was glad to be able to let out a breath. Of course the King was asking her if she liked the Joker. His tricks and his jokes, his illusions and games.

Not the man.

And she didn't.

Like the man.

She barely knew him, after all.

She gulped.

"He's very . . . fun to watch," she confessed.

"Did you see his performance at the ball?"

She knotted her fingers together. "Yes, Your Majesty. It was spectacular."

"It was, wasn't it?" The King bounced. "Come, I shouldn't have sent him away so hastily. We'll have a bit of entertainment!"

"Wha— no!"

But the King was already pushing through the shrubbery. "Jest, oh, Jest!" he sing-songed.

Jest started. The Raven was allowing the young card to pet his wings, but as soon as they saw the King, the card threw himself onto his face out of respect and the bird took flight into the trees. The King did not seem to notice either of them.

Catherine lagged behind, tempted to hide behind the bushes.

"Another good day," said Jest, his kohl-lined eyes landing on Catherine, full of questions.

She straightened her spine, inch by inch, aware that she'd been slumping.

"We were just speaking of your performance the other night," said the King, rocking back and forth on the balls of his feet. "Lady Pinkerton is quite an admirer!"

Catherine flinched.

Jest glanced at her, not attempting to hide his amusement. "I'm flattered, Lady Pinkerton."

"Not too much, I hope."

His dimples stretched down either side of his face.

"Won't you entertain us?" said the King.

"Oh no, you don't have to." Catherine waved her hands. "I'm sure you have other guests . . . and for a mere crowd of two . . ." She trailed off.

Jest was peering at her like she'd offered him a challenge. "With great pleasure, Your Majesty," he said, not taking his attention from Catherine. "But first, perhaps it would be prudent to excuse the young squire." He rolled his fingers toward the Two of Spades, still prostrated on the ground.

The King blinked, as if he hadn't noticed the card was there. "Oh! Oh yes, yes, you're dismissed," he said, adjusting his crown.

The card hopped to his feet, bowed quickly, then ran out of the garden as fast as he could, clutching the card Jest had given him.

Unable to come up with a logical reason to excuse herself, Catherine let the King tug her down onto a stone bench. She kept a proper amount of space between them, yet her heart still fluttered like a bumblebee's wing. Did Jest know the King was planning to ask for her hand? Did he care?

"Do you have a preference on entertainment, Your Majesty?" Jest asked.

"No, no. Whatever the lady would like."

Cath could feel the King looking at her and she squeezed her hands in her lap, determined not to look back. "Surely you know your trade best. Whatever pleases you will no doubt please us as well."

He met her awkwardness with that relaxed, crooked grin of his, and slipped the deck of cards into his sleeve. "Nothing pleases me more than bringing a smile to the face of a lovely lady. But something tells me you will not make that task as easy as it was the eve of the ball."

She flushed.

"Oh, she thought you were spectacular at the ball," interjected the King. "She told me so."

"Did she?" said Jest, and he seemed truly surprised.

"I did," she confessed, "though now I'm wishing I would have chosen my words more carefully."

He chuckled. "It's my role to be spectacular. I shall do my best not to disappoint." Tipping off the black three-pointed hat, he reached inside and produced the silver flute she'd seen him playing in the gardens that night. His smile widened when he saw that she recognized it, and he whispered, "Try not to faint."

Cath crossed her arms, unbearably aware of the King at her side. Watching. Listening.

He was not a clever man, she reminded herself, for once glad that he was so dim. *He is not a clever man.*

Jest replaced his hat and lifted the flute to his mouth. He licked his lips, and Cath cursed herself for mimicking the action, glad that Jest's eyes were closed and he couldn't have noticed.

The music that followed was its own sort of magic.

The lilts and the skips, the dancing notes that swept over Catherine and the King and the hedges and the flowers. The bluebells stopped ringing so they could listen, the breeze stopped whistling, the finches stopped chittering. Catherine took in a breath and held it, feeling as though the flute's music were seeping into her skin, filling up every space in her body.

It wasn't a song she recognized. The notes were happy and sad all at once, and she imagined flowers blooming anew in the wet spring dirt, leaves unfurling for the first time on winter-ravaged boughs, the smell of rain in the air, and the feel of cool grass beneath her toes. The melody hinted at newness and rebirth and beauty and eternity . . .

. . . and by the time it was over, Cath had tears on her cheeks.

Jest lowered the flute and opened his eyes and Cath swiped away the tears, unable to look at him. She fished for a handkerchief from inside her pocket, her hand bumping against the forgotten package of macarons.

The King sniffled too, then began to applaud. "Bravo! Bravo, Jest!"

Jest bowed. "Your Majesty honors me."

The King's cheers were met with equal enthusiasm from all the creatures that had come to listen. Cath forced herself to look up once she'd finished dabbing at her eyes. She expected smugness, but what she saw was a hopeful question in his bright yellow eyes. It quickly turned into another grin, his *real* grin, she suspected. Whatever he'd seen in her face had satisfied.

The King was still clapping enthusiastically. "That was wonderful! Absolutely wonderful! Lady Pinkerton, wasn't that wonderful?"

She cleared her throat and conceded, "It was indeed. What is the song? This was the first I've heard it."

"I'm afraid I don't know, my lady," said Jest. "It came to me just now."

Her eyes widened. *Impossible.*

"Perhaps you are my muse," he added,

and the joking tone had returned. "I shall dedicate it to you, Lady Catherine Pinkerton, if it pleases."

The King squealed. "Oh yes, that's perfect! I shall have you play it again at our —" He cut off sharply.

Cath stiffened, clenching the handkerchief in one fist.

Jest's suspicious look returned.

The King fidgeted with the clasp of his velvet-lined cape, and his excitement was replaced with mumbled bashfulness. "At, er . . . the royal wedding."

Cath wished she could disappear down a rabbit hole.

"It would be my pleasure, Your Majesty," Jest said, with new tension in his voice. "I had heard rumors of an upcoming wedding. What a lucky joker I am, to have such a queen for whom to compose all manner of ballads and poetry."

Twisting the handkerchief in her lap, Cath forced herself to look at the King with as much ignorance as she could manage. "I wasn't aware you had chosen a bride, Your Majesty. I look forward to bestowing many congratulations on our future queen."

The King's round face was as red as the ruby heart in his crown. "Er — that is . . . well . . . I have not . . . exactly proposed yet, you see . . . but with you here, Lady Pinkerton —"

"Oh, how clever you are!" she said, cringing internally at the shrill in her tone. From the corner of her vision she could see that Jest had frozen, and the King, too, had a new wide-eyed visage. "It is so smart of you not to hurry. I'm sure the lady is most grateful."

The King gawped at her. "Er. Well, actually . . ."

"Nobody likes to be rushed into these things, after all. Courtships and marriage proposals should be taken slowly if they're to, er . . . result in mutual happiness. I find that men are too quick to ask for a lady's hand, not realizing that we prefer it to be a long . . . rather arduous process."

The King continued to stare at her.

"Of course. Lady Pinkerton is correct," said Jest, and his voice was measured and patient compared to Cath's desperation. She and the King swiveled their attention back to him.

"I am?" said Catherine.

"She is?" echoed the King.

"Absolutely, but you are a wise man to know it already." Jest threaded the flute between his belt and tunic.

"Er — yes. I mean, I am, naturally. Wise,

that is. But, er, what do you mean?"

"As Lady Pinkerton was saying, all ladies enjoy the dance of courtship, the rush of new love, the anticipation of a yet-unknown happiness." He hesitated, as if searching for the proper words, before continuing, "The courtship period is the foundation upon which a happy marriage will stand, and should not be hurried by any devoted lover — not even a king." Jest inclined his head. "But it seems you know all this, Your Majesty."

"Y-yes," stammered the King. He looked bewildered. "That's what I've always said. The courtship is the . . . the foundation . . ."

Cath's chest was expanding — with relief, with gratitude. Jest glanced at her and raised his eyebrows, as if in question. As if he was concerned that his involvement would not be appreciated.

But it was, more than she could express.

"The Joker has explained it perfectly," she said. "Wedding proposals, after all, should not come as a shock." She laughed, and hoped it didn't sound as frenzied to them as it did to her. "I can see that advice-giving is among your talents."

Jest's grin turned teasing. "I live to serve."

Suddenly, the King hopped to his feet. "I know," he said, beaming with renewed courage. “Let’s play croquet!”

“Croquet?” said Cath.

“Yes! Croquet! It is my best sport. I’m not much of a dancer, you see. And I can’t compose ballads or poetry. But . . . but the hedgehogs are fond of me.” He said it more like a question, and his eyes were shining when he looked at Cath. “You’ll see, Lady Pinkerton.”

He stomped off with purpose toward the croquet court, his fur-lined cloak fluttering behind him and his scepter held high.

Cath turned to Jest. If he shared any of her agitation, it didn’t show.

“Thank you,” she said.

“Whatever for?”

Before she could stammer out some response, he removed his hat and swooped it toward the retreating King.

“After you, my lady.”

CHAPTER 13

Catherine allowed her favorite hedgehog to sit on her shoulder, so long as it stayed calm and agreed not to poke her neck with its quills. Beside her, a flamingo stood with one stick-leg tucked up into its feathers. It had horrible shrimp breath and Cath kept trying to sidestep slowly away.

The King, Margaret Mearle, and Jack were all taking their turns simultaneously, making for a crowded court. Jest's hedgehog had rolled off grounds some time ago and Cath had lost sight of him over one of the rolling hills. Margaret's flamingo had the bone structure of a noodle and she wouldn't stop screaming and shaking the limp thing, so her progress had so far been painfully slow. Jack seemed only interested in trying to croquet everyone else's hedgehogs off course.

The King had started out the game well enough — his hedgehog was indeed fond of him — but his flamingo had since turned unpredictable. Catherine watched as he swung at his hedgehog for the third time in a row, and again his flamingo curled up its long neck at the last moment and missed the hedgehog entirely. The King let out an annoyed huff and shook his flamingo by its scrawny legs. "We practiced this, you foul fowl! You can't have stage fright *now.*"

"His poor Majesty," Catherine mused to herself.

The flamingo beside her rolled its beak a couple of times, and drawled, "Ah like yer pink dress."

Cath shot it a withering smile and tugged at her cotton eyelet dress, the same pale pink as the bird's feathers.

Flamingos were such stupid creatures.

Finally, on the fourth swing, the King smacked his hedgehog on the rump and it went flying over the croquet court, scampering just by the foot of the Six of Clubs without rolling beneath his arched back.

Balling his fists, the King stomped unhappily on the grass. "Useless thing!"

Cath, still on the sidelines, thought this boded well for her strategy. One of the guards had fallen asleep while in a backbend and she suspected he would make for an easy target if she got to him before he collapsed.

She turned her head and winked at her hedgehog. "Shall we?"

"Conspiring with the game pieces, I see," Jest said, startling her. She turned to see him leaning against a garden statue with his own flamingo draped over one shoulder. "I'm not sure that's allowed, Lady Pinkerton."

She smoothed down her skirt. The paper-wrapped macarons crinkled in her pocket. "Are you a sore loser, Mr. Joker?"

He cocked his head. "Am I losing, Lady Pinkerton?"

Shrugging, Cath scanned the lawn. "I'm not sure you're even still playing. Where has your hedgehog gotten off to?"

"Over there." He pointed his flamingo toward the corner of the court, where Margaret was attempting to croquet his hedgehog with hers, to rather no avail.

Her screams floated toward them — "YOU BLOODY BIRD, CAN'T YOU AIM STRAIGHT FOR ONCE?" She swung, and the flamingo's beak glanced off the hedgehog, sending it a fair few inches to the side of Jest's.

"Maybe you are winning," Catherine mused.

"I see that not every game piece is in play.

Won't you be joining us?"

"I'm waiting for the court to open up. I like to have a clear shot." Catherine scratched her hedgehog on its soft-tufted chin.

"Then I shall leave you to your plotting."

She was a little disappointed as Jest meandered back onto the court.

Margaret had made it to the next hoop, leaving Jest's hedgehog with a straight pathway. He wasted no time, just shook out the flamingo, lined up the hedgehog with the hoops, swirled the bird in one pinwheel and thunked the hedgehog with precision, sending it beneath two of the arched Clubs.

He had a noticeable swagger as he returned to Catherine's side a moment later, leaving his hedgehog where it had landed.

"Nice shot," she said.

"I confess, I am not the type of gentleman to blithely let a lady win."

She laughed — the sound so sharp it startled her hedgehog and one of its tines poked her beneath her ear. She ducked her head away. "A memory regarding corset laces has me questioning whether you're a gentleman at all, Mr. Joker."

He pressed a hand to his chest, feigning a wound. "At least, if I am to be a rake, I'll be an honest one. Whereas you, Lady Pinkerton, haven't been entirely forthright."

"What do you mean?"

"You had me convinced that you really had no idea the King was in love with you."

She flushed and stepped closer so she could lower her voice. "He is not in love with me."

He lifted an eyebrow. "I may look like a fool, but I assure you I'm not."

"He may wish to marry me, or think he does, but that is not the same thing as being in love."

His frown shifted. "I'll accede that point. But if you don't think he fancies you beyond what is required in a marriage of convenience, then you are as oblivious as Lady Mearle."

"Oh, look!" Cath interrupted. "Jack has just croqueted the King off the court. I'd best go take my shot."

"You're changing the subject."

"No, I'm playing croquet." She grabbed her bad-breathed flamingo and marched onto the court.

"Lady Pinkerton?"

She froze and glanced over her shoulder.

Jest had a gentle look, but it wasn't quite a smile. "I believe he honestly cares for you, as well as he can. You needn't be so humble about it. Doubtless, many of the present ladies would be delighted to catch the eye of our venerated sovereign."

She narrowed her eyes. "And you gave *me* a difficult time over playing matchmaker."

Her whole body felt stiff as she approached the start of the course. She saw that three of the Club arches had wandered off and were placing bets on the sidelines, but she hoped they would return by the time she needed them. The King was still chasing down his hedgehog. Margaret and Jack were nearly tied, with Jest still in the lead. As she stood at the start of the course, she spotted Jest returning to the game as well, some bounce missing from his step.

Catherine blew a lock of hair out of her face, frustrated with her behavior from the past few days. All those dreams, all those fantasies, all that time spent wandering in a giddy daze — all over what? A boy she'd barely met, hardly spoken to, and who, it was quite clear now, had not spent half as much time thinking about her. Who would just as soon see her married off to the King!

He was right. He may be the one dressed like a fool, but it seemed the title was reserved for her.

She noticed Jack stalking toward her, one fat fist strangling his flamingo's neck. His expression was dark and Cath stiffened before he could reach her.

"You haven't even started yet!" Jack accused. "What were you doing, talking to the Joker all this time? Are you playing or not?"

"It's no concern of yours who I talk to," she spat. "And I was just about to start my turn. If you'll step aside . . ."

Jack snarled and turned to look at the Joker with his good eye. Jest, however, was paying them no attention. "You think he's funny or some such?"

Cath rolled her eyes. "Well, I don't know, Jack. He is a joker."

"I think he's funny *looking.*" He faced her again. "And so are you, Lady Pinkerton!"

She waved her free hand exasperatedly. "Thank you for clarifying that. Could you kindly move so I can take my turn now?"

His face had gone red, but he didn't move. "Did you bring any sweets?"

Cath thought, briefly, of the macarons in her pocket, but shook her head. "Not this time, I'm afraid."

The Knave seemed caught momentarily between staying and going, like he wanted to say more but could think of nothing else worth saying.

Finally, he raspberried his tongue at her, then took off across the court at a quick jaunt.

Cath's shoulders dropped. Her weariness came on fast, her annoyance with Jest and the King and now Jack all burning in her veins. She was glad for the distraction of the game.

She took the hedgehog into her palm. "Let's get on with it, then," she said, setting him in front of the first hoop — the Nine of Clubs. The hedgehog curled himself into a ball.

Cath lifted the flamingo so they were eye to eye, and tried not to breathe in too deeply. "I propose a deal. You help me win this game, and the next time I come to the palace I'll bring you coconut shrimp cakes."

"Ah likes shrimp," said the flamingo.

"I can tell." Wrinkling her nose, Cath flipped the flamingo upside down and took hold of its legs. She lined its head with the hedgehog. Aimed. Swung.

The hedgehog galloped through the first two hoops, rounded smoothly to the right, over one hill, darted right by the King's retrieved hedgehog, swooped back to the left and beneath two more hoops and finally tumbled to a stop. He flopped onto his belly, grinning at Catherine.

She gave him an approving nod, feeling better already.

"Bravo, Lady Pinkerton!" said the King.

The audience that was watching from the sidelines started to cheer as well, having picked up on the King's preference.

"It's not who wins or loses!" Margaret shrieked. "It's how one stays the same!"

"Well said, Lady Mearle!" cheered the Duke, standing alone to the side of the crowd.

"No one asked you!" she yelled back.

Ignoring them all, Cath made her second shot, surpassing Jest on the court.

"Nice shot," he said, echoing her previous words back to her as she passed by.

She preened. "Why, thank you."

"Will you wish me luck on my next play?" he asked. "It seems I'll need it, if I'm to take the egg."

She glanced over her shoulder. "I will do no such thing."

He started walking backward toward his hedgehog. "You are a tough adversary."

Cath's eyes widened as his heels nearly collided with one of the in-play hedgehogs — Jack's, she thought — but even walking backward Jest knew when to hop over it. He chuckled at her surprise and turned away.

Shaking her head, Catherine yelled, "I hope your hedgehog goes into early hibernation!"

"All the easier to hit him," he called back.

Catherine's eye caught on a squat figure hurrying toward her. The King's face was rosy with excitement and a sheen of sweat had formed on his brow.

"Lady Pinkerton!" he said, dabbing at his forehead with the corner of his cloak. She considered offering him a handkerchief, but decided to pretend that he wasn't sweating instead. "Did you see?"

"Um . . ."

"My hedgehog went — *scheeew!* — right through three hoops." His hand gestures mimicked the roll and bounce of his last shot. "It was glorious! Didn't you think so?"

Cath resisted the urge to pat him on the head and offer him a biscuit for a job well done. "You were splendid, Your Majesty."

Beaming, the King turned to watch Jest take his shot. Cath glared at Jest's hedgehog, willing it to go off course.

"What were you and Jest talking about, anyhow?" asked the King.

"Oh. Uh — you, Your Majesty. And your phenomenal croquet —"

There was a *kathunk* as Jest sent his hedgehog rolling toward wide-open grass . . . at least it was wide open until all three of the absent Clubs raced over and threw themselves into arches just in time for the hedgehog to roll beneath them.

"— skills," Cath finished, glowering.

The King sighed, looking equally deflated. "Well, it does seem that I'm outmatched."

After three continuous swings, Jest had gotten his hedgehog nearly to the end of the course. One more half-decent play would hand him the win, for sure. He drifted leisurely toward his hedgehog, swinging the flamingo back and forth like a pendulum.

"Well done, Jest," called the King.

"Thank you muchly, Your Majesty."

Clenching her teeth, Cath hauled her flamingo toward her own hedgehog, a bout of stubborn determination burning through her limbs. Never had she considered herself a competitive person, but this — this was different.

This felt oddly personal.

After just one meeting, the Joker had infiltrated her dreams and overtaken her every waking thought. She'd even worked him into her bakery fantasy, though she would never admit that to anyone, especially now that she knew Jest would just as soon see her married to the King.

He was naught but a flirtatious louse, and she'd fallen deeper with every rakish smile. What a fine joke she must have made for his amusement.

How *dare* he?

She took up her place beside her hedgehog and surveyed the course. The hedgehog and flamingo both watched her, waiting, as she looked from the arched cards — a few of which had fallen flat in exhaustion while they waited — to the rover hoop, the final goal. To all the opposing hedgehogs scattered haphazardly around the course, their players chasing after them or screaming at their uncooperative flamingos.

To Jest, strolling across the grass.

She narrowed her eyes and widened her stance, lowering the flamingo's head to the ground. The hedgehog rolled up.

"If you fail me," she whispered to the flamingo, "I will wrap your neck around a tree trunk and tie it in a pretty pink bow and leave you there until one of the gardeners finds you."

The flamingo cautiously curled its neck to look at her from upside down. "Ah like purty pink bows."

She gave an annoyed shake and it straightened out again.

She pulled the flamingo back, pinned her eye to the hedgehog —

and swung
hard.

It was a picture-perfect croquet, knocking into Jest's hedgehog moments before he swung for it. Startled, Jest leaped back, and his hedgehog rolled right beneath his feet and bounded and bounced wildly off course.

He blinked up, meeting Cath's gaze across the lawn.

She grinned at him, pleased at Jest's flabbergasted expression, and gave her flamingo a twirl. She'd all but handed the win to the King.

"Well, dash it all," she said, feigning innocence.

Pleased, she strolled off the court and stuck her flamingo's feet into the soft dirt before heading toward the tables. With that excellent play, she felt she'd earned some cake and a nice cup of tea.

Chapter 14

"Why is there so much pepper in this soup?" the Marchioness complained, pushing back her bowl. "It's hardly edible."

"I'm sorry, my lady," said Abigail, whisking the offensive dish away. "It was a new recipe — I believe the Duke of Tuskany gave it to us, a specialty of his own cook's making."

The Marchioness wrinkled her nose. "It's a miracle he hasn't starved." She straightened the napkin in her lap while Catherine and her father sipped at their own soups without complaint.

Though, Catherine could admit, it was awful peppery, and starting to burn her throat.

"So, Catherine?" her mother said. "How did you find the tea party?"

Cath froze, her soup spoon lifted halfway to her mouth. She met her mother's anxious, hopeful grin with a nervous, innocent one of her own. "I found it to be rather like the last tea party, and the one before that," she lied, and choked down another spoonful. "Would you pass the salt, please?"

Mary Ann stepped forward to bring the salt to her so her parents wouldn't have to reach over the tureens and gravy boats.

"Perhaps so, but did you speak with His Majesty?"

"Oh. Um. Why, yes, I did. He and I took a turn around the gardens." She paused to ensure nothing she was about to relate would be condemning. "We crossed paths with the new court joker and he entertained us with a beautiful melody on his flute."

Silence. The grandfather clock that stood against the wall raised an arm to scratch beneath his gray mustache. Catherine glanced at him and wondered if the pepper was getting to the furniture.

"And?" her mother pressed.

"Oh, he's very talented." Cath leaned forward over her bowl. "Perhaps too talented, if you ask me. One might find it unnatural. To play the flute and the mandolin, and to know card tricks and magic tricks and riddles, and I hear tell he's even an adept juggler. It's enough to make the rest of us feel unaccomplished, and I don't think he needs to flaunt it all quite so much as he has, and after only two gatherings! Plus, there's something peculiar about that hat of his, don't you think? Something not quite . . ." She traced an invisible outline of the three-pointed hat with her spoon into the air. ". . . spatially accurate. I find it uncanny." She looked at her unimpressed mother and her confused father and realized she'd been rambling. She jammed the soup spoon into her mouth.

"Well," said her mother. "That's all . . . interesting. What happened after the Joker entertained you?"

She swallowed. "Oh. Then we played croquet."

"You and the Joker?"

"Y-yes. Well, and the King too. And a few others."

Her mother sagged with relief. "I hope you let him win."

Catherine was proud that it wasn't a lie when she said, "The King did win, as a matter of fact."

As the soup was taken away, Abigail came forward to carve slices from a roast set atop a bed of roasted squash.

Her mother's eyebrows rose. "And then?"

She thought. "And then . . . I had some cake. Though if we're to be honest, it was a little dry. Oh — and Jest came by and played his flute some more once the game was over. The show-off."

The melody had been beautiful, of course, and was still parading through her ears.

"Jest," said her mother, and hearing his name in her voice made Catherine startle.

"Sorry," she stammered. "That's the Joker. That's his name."

Her mother set her fork down on the table, so carefully that she might as well have thrown it. "What do we care about the Joker? Tell us about the King, Catherine. What did he say? What did he do? Did he try your macarons? Did he like them? Are you betrothed or not?"

Cath shrank away, all too aware of the rose macarons still heavy in her pocket. They were probably crushed to bits by now. She was grateful when her entree was set before her, giving her an excuse to look down. She dug a fork into a chunk of roasted squash. "I may have forgotten to give him the macarons," she confessed, stuffing the bite into her mouth.

She stiffened, surprised. Not any squash, but savory, buttery pumpkin, sprinkled with thyme leaves and, this time, just the right amount of pepper.

It was delicious. She shoveled a second bite into her mouth, wondering if they might all turn orange as Cheshire had. Which would be better than growing to the size of oak trees, which had happened once when their cook purchased a bad batch of acorn squash.

Her mother groaned, ignoring her own plate. "How this is wearing on my old nerves! To think I was so close to having my daughter engaged — and to the King himself!" She placed a hand to her chest. "It's more than my heart can take. All day I was waiting for that blare of trumpets, that announcement that the offer had been made and accepted, that I would live to see my daughter crowned a queen. But that announcement did not come, even though you took a turn with His Majesty through the gardens! And played croquet! And were serenaded! You can't mean to say the mood wasn't romantic. Unless . . . unless he has changed his mind. Oh dear, what will we do?"

Catherine met Mary Ann's gaze, and was rewarded with a confidante's smile, secretive but supportive. She smiled back, but covered it by sipping her wine.

"I don't know, Mother," she said, setting down the glass. "He didn't propose. I can't guess his reasons. Have you tried the pumpkin? It's fantastic. Abigail, please tell the chef that this pumpkin is fantastic."

"I will, my lady," said Abigail with a small curtsy. "I believe it came from Sir Peter's patch."

Cath stabbed another bite. "It's astonishing that such a horrid man can grow something so scrumptious."

"What are you on about?" screeched her mother. "Pumpkins! Sir Peter! We are talking about the King." She thumped her hand on the table. "And you may not be able to guess his reasons for not proposing today, but I certainly can. He has lost confidence in his choice of a bride, that is his reason. He heard you'd gotten ill at the ball and now he thinks you may be a sickly girl, and no man wants that. How can you have rushed off so soon?"

"To be fair, I did not know the King would be proposing, and you did insist on that very tight —"

"That is hardly an excuse. You know now. You knew today. I am marvelously disappointed, Catherine. I know you can do better than this."

Cath looked at her father, hoping for defense. "Is this how you feel too?"

He turned his head up, the slices of roast beef and pumpkin on his plate already three-quarters eaten. His expression, though bewildered at first, quickly softened, and he reached for Cath, settling his hand on her wrist.

"Of course, dear," he said. "You can do anything you put your mind to."

Cath sighed. "Thanks, Papa."

He gave her a loving pat before returning his attention to his plate. Shifting in her seat, Cath resigned herself to her mother's disappointment and focused on cutting her meat into very tiny pieces.

"I was so hopeful for those macarons too," the Marchioness continued. "I realize it isn't ladylike to slave away in the kitchen all day, but he does fancy your desserts and I thought, once he tastes them, he'll remember why he meant to propose in the first place. How could you have failed at such a simple task?" She scowled at Catherine's plate. "You've eaten enough now, Catherine."

Catherine looked up. At her mother's twisted mouth, at the top of her father's lowered head, at Mary Ann and Abigail pretending to not be listening. She set down her knife and fork. "Yes, Mother."

With a snap of her mother's fingers, the plates were taken away, even her father's, though he was still clutching his fork. He soon slumped with resignation.

Before the awkwardness could stretch on, the Marquess perked up. "I heard the most delightful tale at the party today," he said, dabbing his napkin at the corners of his mustache, "about a little girl who discovered an upward-falling rabbit hole just off the Crossroads, and when she started to climb, her body fell up and up and —"

"Not now, dear," said his wife. "Can't you see we're discussing our daughter's prospects?" Then she grumbled, "If she has any left at all, that is."

The Marquess deflated, and set his napkin on the table. "Of course, my dear. You always know just the right thing to talk about."

Catherine frowned. She would have liked to have heard the story.

Clucking her tongue, the Marchioness said, "No one ever warns you how exhausting it will be to have an eligible daughter. And now I have the festival to concern myself over. If this marriage ordeal was resolved I could better devote myself to it, as I have every other year, but as it is, my attention is being pulled into two separate directions. I shall never be able to focus on the festival now."

Mary Ann, Catherine saw, failed to refrain from an eye roll. Though the Marquess and

Marchioness hosted the Turtle Days Festival, it was the servants who did all the work.

"I'm sorry, Mama," Catherine said.

"It's even worse now that the whole kingdom is in a frenzy over this . . . this Jabberwock." She shuddered.

"It's terrifying," said Catherine, though her attention was wandering as a steaming bread pudding was set before her. It smelled of rich vanilla bean and custard. Mouth watering, she lifted her dessert spoon.

"Oh, good heavens, no," said her mother. "Don't be absurd, Catherine. You'll be mistaken for a walrus at the festival. Abigail, have this taken away."

Cath whimpered, gazing after the dessert as it was hastened off the table. She pressed her palm against her middle, feeling her stomach beneath the corset and wondering if her mother was right. Was she becoming a walrus? She did have an almost-constant yearning for sweets, but she only gave into it, well, maybe once or twice a day. That wasn't strange, was it? And she didn't feel any bigger, even if her corsets suggested differently.

She caught a sympathetic smile from Mary Ann as she filled the wineglasses around the table.

"Don't you have any thoughts on this at

all, Mr. Pinkerton?"

The Marquess was watching the dish of bread pudding disappear with the same sorrow Catherine felt. "About you sending away the dessert?" he said. "I do have a thought or two about it."

"Not that, you old man. Though *you're* where she gets it from, you know."

Cath bristled. "I am sitting right here."

Her mother batted the fact of her presence away. "I'm asking if you have any thoughts on the marriageability of your own daughter. The marriageability that is fading away as we sit here, sulking."

"I wouldn't be sulking if I were eating bread pudding," the Marquess muttered.

Her mother heaved a sigh. "We have had no other prospects, you know. No offers of courtship. Nothing!"

Cath licked her lips, and it sparked in her head that now was the time to tell them about the bakery. This very moment. She would have no better chance, not with both of them at her attention.

Now.

Ask them now.

She sat up straighter in her chair. "Actually, there is one prospect, Mama. One that I . . . I've been meaning to discuss with you both."

Mary Ann stiffened, but Cath tried not to look at her. Her presence would only make her more nervous.

"There is something I've been considering lately. Well, for quite some time, really. But I could use your assistance, and . . . support. And you did just say, Father, that I could do anything I put my mind to —"

"Out with it, child," said her mother, "we haven't got all evening."

"It . . . has to do with my hobby. My . . . baking."

Her mother threw her hands into the air. "Oh — your baking! That's what it is, you know. That's why none of the men want anything to do with you. Who's ever heard of a marquess's daughter that bakes, when she should be practicing embroidery or the pianoforte!"

Catherine cast a panicked look at Mary Ann, who had begun tying knots into her apron strings.

She turned back to her mother. "But . . . you just admitted this is half the reason the King liked me in the first place. He likes my desserts. Aren't you glad I have something I'm good at?"

Her mother guffawed, but her father was nodding. "I enjoy your desserts," he said. "Remember that rum cake you made for my birthday? With the raisins in it? You should make one of those again."

"Thank you, Father. I would love to."

"Don't encourage her."

"Mother, please. Listen for a moment, and . . . try not to cast hasty judgment."

The Marquess leaned forward, curious. The Marchioness grunted and folded her arms, but gave Cath her attention, at least. Mary Ann stood in the corner, silently counting off the knots she'd tied.

"You see," said Catherine, "there's this storefront in town that's set to become available. The cobbler's store, you know, on Main Street. And, well, I've been thinking, and —"

"Forgive the interruption, my lord."

Cath paused, turning to see Mr. Penguin, their butler, standing at the entrance to the dining room in his customary tuxedo.

"We have a visitor," he said.

"At this hour?" said the Marchioness, aghast. "Tell them to come back tomorrow."

"But, my lady," said Mr. Penguin, "it is the King."

CHAPTER 15

The dining room was still for a beat, two beats, three — before Cath's mother launched herself from the table.

"Whealagig! What are you waiting for? Get out there and greet him!"

"Er — right. Of course, darling." The Marquess tossed his napkin onto the table and followed Mr. Penguin to the parlor.

"We'll be right there! Do not let him leave!" The Marchioness rounded on Catherine, plucking some of her dark hair forward to hang in wavy locks over her shoulders. She pinched Cath's cheeks. Dipped a napkin corner into the nearest water glass and scrubbed at Catherine's mouth.

Catherine squirmed. "Stop it! What are you doing?"

"Making you presentable! The King is here!"

"Yes, but he hasn't asked for an audience with *me*."

"Of course he hasn't asked for an audience with you, but that's clearly why he's here!" Cupping Cath's face in both hands, her mother beamed. "Oh, my precious, precious girl! I'm so proud of you!"

Cath frowned. "Just a moment ago, you were —"

"Never mind a moment ago, the King is here now." Pulling away, her mother shooed at her with both hands. "Come along. To the parlor. Here, chew on this." She plucked a mint leaf from a bouquet on the sideboard and shoved it into Catherine's mouth.

"Mother," she said, chewing twice before pulling the mint leaf out. "I'm not going to *kiss* him."

"Oh, stop being such a pessimist."

Catherine blanched at the very idea of it.

She was bustled through the doors and past her father's library, into the main parlor where her father was standing with the King and the White Rabbit and two guards — the Five and Ten of Clubs — and . . .

Her heart leaped, but she silently chastised it until it sank back down again.

Jest stood at the back of the King's entourage in full black motley, his hands behind his back. Though he'd been inspecting a painted portrait of one of Catherine's distant ancestors, he straightened when

Catherine and her mother entered.

A drumbeat thumped against the inside of her rib cage. She barely had time to catch her breath before a trumpet blared through the room and she jumped.

Jest's yellow gaze fell to the floor.

The White Rabbit lowered the trumpet. "His Royal Majesty, the King of Hearts!"

"Your Majesty!" cried the Marchioness. Cath followed her mother into a curtsy, trying to gather her scattered composure. "Your visit honors us! Would you care for some tea? *Abigail! Bring the tea!*"

The King cleared his throat, smacking his fist against his sternum a few times. "Thank you warmly, Lady Pinkerton, but your husband already offered and I already declined the kindness. I do not wish to take up too much of your time." He was smiling, like usual, but it was an awkward, nervous smile, not the joyful one Cath was used to.

He would not look at her.

She felt sick to her stomach and was glad, for once, that her mother had sent the dessert away.

"Oh, but won't you at least sit, Your Majesty?" The Marchioness gestured at the nicest chair in the room — usually the Marquess's seat.

Whipping his red cloak behind him, the

King nodded gratefully and sat.

In unison, the Marquess and Marchioness sat on the sofa opposite him. Only when her mother reached up and yanked her down did it occur to Catherine to sit as well.

The guards stared at the wall, their club-tipped staffs held at their sides. The White Rabbit looked a little crestfallen that he hadn't been invited to sit too.

And Jest —

Mute and still and impossible for Cath to keep her eyes away from. Rake and flirt he may be, but against her better senses, she felt as drawn to him as ever. She stole glimpses of him again and again, like gathering unsatisfying crumbs in hopes they could be re-formed into a cake.

When the King did not immediately speak, Cath's mother leaned forward, beaming. "How we enjoyed your tea party this afternoon, Your Majesty. You indulge us so in this kingdom."

"Thank you, Lady Pinkerton. It was a splendid gathering." The King pushed the crown more securely onto his round head. He seemed to be preparing himself.

Catherine, stick straight and uncomfortable on the edge of the sofa's cushion, prepared herself as well.

He would ask for her hand.

Her father would agree.

Her mother would agree.

That was as far as her thoughts would go.

No, she must imagine it all. It was happening. It was here.

The King would ask for her hand.

Her father would agree.

Her mother would agree.

And she . . .

She would say no.

The silent promise to herself made her dizzy, but she remembered the determination she'd felt during the croquet game and tried to summon it again.

She would be a picture of politeness, of course. She would deny his proposal with as much grace as possible. She would be obliging and flattered and humbled and she would explain to him that she did not feel suited to the role of queen. She would say there was certainly a better choice, and though her gratitude for his attentions was limitless, she could not in good conscience accept him —

No, no, no.

She was wrong, and she hated the knowing of it.

With her father there, and her mother, and the dear, sweet King of Hearts, and all their hopeful eyes focused on her . . . she knew that she would undoubtedly say yes.

She stopped looking at Jest. Her eyes were suddenly repelled by him. His presence in the room was painful, suffocating.

"I quite enjoyed a game of croquet with Lady Pinkerton at the party," said the King.

"Oh yes, she was just telling us all about it," said the Marchioness. "She enjoyed herself as well. Didn't you, Catherine?"

She gulped. "Yes, Mother."

"She is a remarkably skilled croquetesse." The King giggled. "Why, one look from her and the hedgehogs just go — *woop!* — right where she means for them to go!" He kept giggling.

Cath's parents giggled along, though she could tell her father wasn't sure what was so amusing.

"We're very proud of her," said the Marchioness. "She is accomplished in so many ways, between the croquet, and the baking." Her eyes landed on Catherine, full of motherly adoration.

Cath looked away and caught sight of Mary Ann's pale blue eyes through the cracked door. The maid flashed an encouraging smile.

"Lady Pinkerton and I also, uh, had an enlightening conversation with my new court joker. Do you remember?" The King met her eye for the first time, and between his uneasiness and the mention of the Joker, Cath found herself caught in a mortifying blush that was sure to be misinterpreted.

Her mother elbowed her father.

"Yes, Your Majesty," she said. "I do remember."

"Oh yes, very good. He, uh . . . Jest, that is, has given me some thoughtful advice, for which I'm quite grateful, and I've been . . . thinking, and . . . well." The King pulled the fur collar of his cloak away from his throat. "I have a very important question for you, Lady Pinkerton. And . . . and Lord and Lady Pinkerton, of course."

The Marchioness grabbed her husband's wrist.

"We are your humble servants," said the Marquess. "What can we do for you, Your Majesty?"

Cath sank into the sofa. Good-bye, bakery. Good-bye, the smell of fresh-baked bread in the morning. Good-bye, flour-dusted aprons.

The King wiggled. His feet kicked against the chair. "I have called on you tonight with the purpose of . . . of . . ." A bead of sweat slipped down his temple. Cath followed it with her eyes until the King rubbed it away with the edge of his cloak. Then he started to speak, fast, like he was issuing an important declaration that had been rehearsed a hundred times. ". . . of asking for the honor of entering into a courtship with Lady Catherine Pinkerton."

Then he burped.

Just a little burp, out of nervousness, or perhaps even nausea.

Catherine, delirious with anxiety, choked back a snort.

Behind the King, Jest flinched, and the small action returned Cath's attention to him.

He found her in the room.

She couldn't tell if he was amused or embarrassed for the King, but it was quick to fade, whatever it was. Jest seemed to change as he looked at her. His body lengthening to full height, his shoulders tugging backward, his eyes searching hers.

Cath didn't know what he was looking for, or what he found. She felt half crazed, delusional with a wish that she was anywhere but here.

"A courtship?" said the Marchioness.

Cath yanked her gaze away from Jest. Her thoughts started to spin, her subconscious dissecting the King's words.

Courtship. That *is* what he said.

The King was asking to court her, precisely as Jest had advised.

He was not proposing.

Relief rushed through her, fast as a rising tide through the whistling cove.

She placed a hand over her thundering heart and looked at her mother, whose mouth was hanging open.

"Well," the Marquess blustered, "you honor us, Your Majesty. I —" He turned to his wife, as if searching for permission to respond.

Shutting her mouth, she kicked his ankle.

"I — uh, give my hearty blessing to such a courtship, but of course the decision lies with my daughter. Catherine? What say you?"

The room fell quiet.

The King, terrified but hopeful.

Her mother, pale with anxiety.

Her father, patient and curious.

Mary Ann, inching the door open so she wouldn't miss a word.

The White Rabbit, eyeing an expensive vase with yearning.

And Jest. Unreadable. Waiting, along with the others, for her to speak.

"I . . . am flattered, Your Majesty."

"Of course you're flattered, child." Her mother kicked *her* this time. "But don't leave His Majesty waiting for an answer.

What say you to this most kind and generous offer?"

Courtship. No obligations. No commitments. Not yet.

And, possibly, time to persuade the King that he did not really wish to marry her at all.

It didn't feel like she'd been given a choice, not a real choice in the matter — but it didn't seem so entirely dreadful, either.

"Thank you, Your Majesty," she said, already exhausted at the prospect. "It would be an honor to be courted by you."

CHAPTER 16

Catherine was trembling by the time she retreated to her bedroom, dizzy with the King's visit. Mary Ann had started a fire some hours ago, and the room was filled with a pleasant warmth that Cath couldn't enjoy. She sank into her vanity chair with a groan.

She was officially courting the King.

Or, rather, the King was courting her.

And soon all the kingdom would know about it.

A knock startled her, but it was only Mary Ann. She shut the door and fell against it. "Cath!"

Catherine held up a hand before Mary Ann could say more. "If you should dare to congratulate me, I will never speak to you again."

Mary Ann hesitated, and Cath could see her thoughts rearranging inside her head. "You're . . . unhappy?"

"Yes, I'm unhappy. Remember before when I said I didn't want to marry him, that I didn't want to be queen? I meant it!"

Mary Ann slumped, crestfallen.

"Oh, don't look like that. It is a great honor. I suppose."

"Maybe the courtship will change your mind?"

"I'm hoping it will change *his* mind." She rubbed her temple. "I have no idea what I'll do if he proposes. When he proposes."

"Oh, Cath . . ." Mary Ann crossed the room to wrap her in a sideways hug. "It will be all right. You're not married yet. You can still say no."

"Can I? And risk my mother's tyranny and disappointment for the rest of my life?"

"It's your life, not hers."

Catherine sighed. "I don't know how I've let it get this far already. I wanted to say no, but Mother and Father were right there, looking so eager, and the King looked so desperate, and I just . . . I didn't know what else to do. Now everything is more boggled up than before."

"Yes, but nothing that can't still be made right." Mary Ann smoothed down her hair. "Shall I bring up some tea to calm your nerves? Or — perhaps some of that bread pudding?"

Cath's heart lightened. "Could you? Oh, but help me take down my hair first. I feel like I've had these pins in for a week."

She turned so Mary Ann could begin pulling out the pins and her eyes alighted on the diamond-paned window. A single white rose rested on the outside sill.

She stifled a gasp.

Mary Ann was talking, but Cath didn't hear a word. Her hair cascaded, layer by layer, across her shoulders.

She averted her gaze from the flower, her heart beginning to pound. "Do you think I'm being silly?" she asked. "About the King?"

"We can't choose where our affections lie," said Mary Ann. She set the hairpins on the vanity and began turning down the bed linens, careful to avoid the thorny rose branches that were still wrapped around the bedposts. Cath's mother had decided to leave it for a time, in hopes that it would keep any further dream-plants away. "For what it's worth, though, I think the King is . . . a sweet man. And his affection for you is more than apparent."

Cath watched Mary Ann work, though it was torture to keep her eyes away from the window. Already she was thinking she'd only imagined the rose, but she dared not look again for fear it would catch Mary Ann's attention too.

Which was peculiar, this instinct to keep it a secret. Never in her life had she hidden anything from Mary Ann. But the rose felt like a whispered message, a hushed glance across a crowded room. Something precious and not to be shared. Something that she didn't think practical Mary Ann would understand.

"I've changed my mind about the bread pudding, and the tea. I have no appetite."

Mary Ann glanced up from fluffing her pillow. "Are you ill?"

Catherine laughed, the sound strained and high-pitched. "Not at all, just needing a moment of peace. I might stay up and read for a while. I'm not tired. You needn't bother with all that."

"Oh. Would you like me to stay? We could play a game, or —"

"No, no. Thank you. I . . . I'd like to be alone. I think I need to sort through everything that's happened."

Mary Ann's face softened. "Of course. Good night, Cath." She left the room, shutting the door behind her.

Catherine fought the whirlwind of nerves in her stomach as she listened to the sound of Mary Ann's footfalls receding down the hall. To the creaking of the house around her.

She forced herself to face the window.

She hadn't imagined it. One perfect white rose on a long stem had been laid atop the windowsill so that the flower was framed by the harlequin-shaped leading.

She approached the window with a racing pulse and lifted the sash. Careful of the thorns, she took the flower between her fingers.

The night air carried a citrus scent, and looking out, she saw that the lemon tree that had been replanted beneath her window had already grown up to this second story, its dark boughs full of yellow fruit. She scanned the branches, then down to the lawn and garden, but the nighttime produced only shadows.

Another glance upward, and this time she spotted tiny black eyes. She reeled back, dropping the rose at her feet.

The Raven inclined his head. Or, she thought he did. His inky feathers were almost invisible in the darkness.

"Hello again," she said, shivering in the night air.

"Good eve, fair lady, your forgiveness we implore, to come so brashly tapping, tapping at your chamber door."

"Oh, well, this isn't exactly my chamber door. More like a window, actually."

The Raven bobbed his head. "I made some alterations for the sake of the rhyme."

"I see. Well — good evening, fair Raven, my forgiveness I bestow, for this uncanny meeting outside of my window."

A boisterous laugh startled Catherine, sending her heart into her throat.

In his black motley, he was nearly impossible to see in the shadows, perched in the crook of a tree branch. He looked mysterious and elegant, his gold eyes glinting in the light of her bedroom's fire.

"That was impressive, wasn't it, Raven?" Jest said. "The lady is a natural poet."

"What are you doing here?" asked Catherine. "I thought you left with the King."

"He had no further need of me tonight, so I took my leave. I thought I could take a walk, look around. I'm still new to these parts."

"But you're not walking. You're climbing trees."

"It's still exercise."

Catherine leaned farther out the window. "The courtship was your idea, wasn't it?"

His smile faded and in the darkness he looked almost uncomfortable. "I hope I haven't overstepped, my lady. But it seemed, from your reaction at the party today, that you would prefer a proposal of courtship to a proposal of marriage."

She pressed her lips.

"Although it would also seem," Jest continued, his voice sympathetic, "that you don't particularly want either one."

"You must think I'm a fool to even consider rejecting him."

"My lady, I am a professional fool. I can say with certainty that you do not have the makings of one."

She smirked. "Then that's a relief."

"Is it? Have you something against fools?"

"Not at all. Only, if I were as natural at foolishness as I am at poetry, I might try to take your position from you, and you seem so very well suited to it."

His body shifted — a melting of his muscles — and she realized that he was relaxing. She hadn't seen the tension in his body until it was gone. "It does seem to suit me," he said, "though I daresay the hat would look better on you." He shook his head, just enough to make the bells jingle.

Their smiles met each other across the darkness, tentative and a bit shy.

The moment was shattered by footsteps in the hall. Cath gasped and spun around, her pulse racing — but the steps continued on. Probably her father, retreating to his library for the evening.

She let out a slow breath, feeling the hard thump of her heart beneath her fingertips.

Turning back, she saw that Jest hadn't moved from his perch, although his body was taut again.

"Well," she said, trying to keep her voice light, though it trembled a little, "it seems that whether or not I wanted a courtship, I now have one. Thank you for your . . . involvement, but you should probably leave, before someone sees you." She reached for the window sash.

"Wait!" Jest slipped off his bough, skipping across a few branches until he was arm's reach from her. He made it look as simple as walking on flat ground. "Is there someone else?"

She paused. "I beg your pardon?"

"Are you in love with someone else?"

She stiffened, bewildered. "Why would you ask me that?"

"I thought maybe that's why you're opposed to the King. I thought you might have already given your heart away to someone else, but maybe . . . maybe it's someone your parents wouldn't be so quick to approve of."

She started to shake her head. "No, there

isn't anyone else."

"You're sure?"

She was surprised at the dart of annoyance that stuck in her ribs. "If I had given my heart to someone else, I surely think I would know of it."

His shoulders sloped downward, though his hands were still securing him to an overhead branch. He looked almost relieved, but also confused. "Of course you would."

"Don't misunderstand me," said Catherine. "I am fond of the King. I just . . ."

"You don't have to explain it to me, Lady Pinkerton. I'll admit I've grown fond of the King myself, though I haven't known him long. Nevertheless, I think I understand you."

It was a kindness, saying it, when Catherine felt wholly treasonous at her lack of affection for the King.

"I'm fond of you too, I think."

She laughed at the unexpected compliment. Or what she thought might be a compliment. It didn't seem romantic enough to qualify as a confession. "Me?"

"Yes. You're different from the other lords and ladies here. I'm sure that any other girl would have screamed and started throwing rocks at me if I showed up at *her* bedroom window."

"I don't keep a very large supply of rocks up here." A sudden bout of heat rushed up her throat, realizing that he was right. There was a boy at her window. At night. They were alone — excepting his Raven friend, at least. She frowned. "Though if you're insinuating that I might have questionable morals, you are sadly mistaken."

His eyes widened. "That's not —" He paused, and suddenly started to chuckle. "It was intended as a kindness, I assure you."

She crossed her arms over her chest. "Either way, I think you're wrong. I'm not different. I'm . . ."

He waited.

She swallowed, hard, a twitch starting in her cheek. "What do you mean by that, anyway? Calling me *different.*"

"It's true. I knew it from the moment I saw you twirling at the ball, your arms raised as if you hadn't a care in all the world."

She blinked.

"Of all those ladies and all those gentlemen, you were the only one who twirled."

"You saw that?"

"In that gown, it would have been difficult not to."

She wrinkled her nose. "My mother chose it. She thought it would be my engagement ball. I honestly had no idea."

"I see that now." He squinted at her and opened his mouth once to speak, but closed it again.

Catherine swallowed. "You shouldn't be here."

"I'm not entirely sure that's true." He lowered himself on the branch, like a cat ready to spring. "Lady Pinkerton, have you ever been to a real tea party?"

"Oh, countless."

"No, my lady, not like at the castle today. I mean, a real one."

The question crystallized between them as Catherine shifted through all the parties, galas, gatherings she'd attended over the years, and she couldn't fathom what he meant.

"I . . . I suppose I'm not sure."

He smiled, a little mischievously. "Would you like to?"

Chapter 17

She ducked into the washroom under the guise of tying back her hair. Her heart was dancing as she combed back the long locks and knotted a ribbon at the nape of her neck. She didn't know what she was thinking. Perhaps she'd gone raving mad.

She shoved the doubts aside. She couldn't change her mind now. Or rather, she could, but she knew that she wouldn't.

It was only for one night. She would do this once. To see, to experience, to make her own choice.

She pinched her cheeks, dabbed rose water on her wrists, and was at the window again before her nerves could overtake her.

Jest was still in the tree boughs, playing with his deck of cards. Raven was cleaning his feathers. Noticing her, Jest perked up and slid the cards back into some secret pocket.

"Are you ready?" he asked, his whole face

lighting up in a way that filled her with warmth and sugar.

"I'm not sure this is a good idea."

"That's because it's most likely a very bad idea."

With one easy movement, he stepped across to her windowsill and hopped down into her bedroom.

A certain amount of shock skittered down her spine. There was a man in her bedroom — unchaperoned. Unsupervised.

In secret.

She said nothing of this nature, only took half a step away from him. Her heel brushed against the white rose she'd dropped.

Jest took off his hat and turned it upside down. "This is going to work," he said, reaching into the hat. "But it's going to require a certain amount of faith."

He pulled his hand out, revealing a black lace parasol with an ivory handle. He popped it open above their heads.

"What are we doing with that?"

"You'll see." He set the hat back on his head, stepped back onto the windowsill, and held his free hand toward her.

After a count of three, during which she determined that she had lost her wits, Cath placed her hand into his and allowed him to pull her up beside him.

"You're not going to scream, are you?"

She didn't bother trying to hide her terror when she met his gaze.

Frowning, Jest ducked his face closer and released her hand so he could instead grasp her elbow. "You're not going to *faint,* are you?"

She shook her head, though it had no confidence behind it. She risked a glance at the ground, two stories below.

"Lady Pinkerton," he said warningly.

She looked up again and moved her trembling hands toward his tunic. "I wonder if it would be terribly inappropriate for me to hold on to you."

"I think you'd better, anyway."

She nodded once and wrapped her arms around his shoulders, burying her face into his chest. She clutched him as one might a buoy in the sea.

Jest stiffened and wrapped his free arm around her waist.

There was a moment of suspension around them. She could feel his heart beating near to hers, and his breath in her hair. Something about him seemed crafted for her, and that thought made her face flame, like she was standing too close to a fire.

"All right then," he said, and she wondered whether it was her imagination that made him seem suddenly nervous. "No screaming."

She pressed her lips together.

Jest took a step off the windowsill, pulling her along with him.

A scream clawed up her throat but was captured and muffled against her clenched teeth. There was a sudden swoop, her stomach flipping inside her, and a drop — but a gradual one. Shaking, she peeled her eyes open. She turned her head so she could see beyond Jest's shoulder, to the brick and window trim of her house as they drifted to the ground.

It was over too soon.

They hit the ground easily. She did not, could not release him until her legs regained their strength, but he didn't complain. His grip didn't loosen until hers did, but he also didn't try to keep her once she pulled away.

As Catherine gaped up toward her bedroom window, glowing with firelight, Jest returned the parasol to his hat.

"How will I get back up?"

"Don't worry," he said, sliding a gloved hand into hers, in a way that seemed almost more intimate than their recent embrace. She didn't pull away, although she knew she should. "I have a trick for that too, Lady Catherine."

"In your hat?"

He chuckled. "My hat isn't the only magical thing about me."

She smirked, feeling bolder outside the confines of her home. "I'm well aware," she said. "Impossible is your specialty."

His face brightened with that true smile again. He whistled and she heard the flap of bird's wings overhead. Raven appeared from the shadows and perched on Jest's shoulder as he tugged Catherine toward the road.

"Where's the nearest Crossroads?" he asked.

"Under the little bridge over the creek."

Once they stepped off the lawn, Jest released her hand, and Cath attempted to hide her disappointment even from herself. He did, however, offer his elbow, which she accepted, folding her fingers around his arm and surprised to find more muscle there than his lithe frame would suggest.

It was a short walk to the bridge that crossed over Squeaky Creek, where a set of steps branched off the road and led down to the embankment. Cath took the lead, guiding them to the shore and pointing at a green-painted door that was built into the bridge's foundation.

Jest tipped his hat and held the door for her.

The Crossroads was an intersection that connected all corners of the kingdom. A long, low hall lined with doors and archways, windows and stairwells. The floor was made of black-and-white-checkerboard tiles and the walls jutted off in every direction. The shape was constantly shifting. Some of the walls were made of dirt, with tree roots growing through them. Others were covered in fine gilt wallpaper. Still others were made of glass, and water could be seen pressing on them from the other side, like a fishbowl.

Jest led Cath to a hollow tree trunk with an opening that looked like it had been cut out by a hatchet. He took her hand again and pulled her through.

On the other side, Cath found herself on a dirt pathway that was succumbing to moss. Trees towered overhead and through the close-grown trunks Cath saw a spot of golden light. This was the direction Jest headed, picking his way along the shadowed path.

The forest opened into a meadow and the source of the light was revealed — a small traveling shop. It had a canvas roof and rickety wagon wheels and a hitch on the front that no longer had any horses or mules attached to pull it. A round door was on the back of the shop with a sign above it that read, in flourishing gold script:

Hatta's Marvelous Millinery
Fine Hats and Headdresses for Distinguished Ladies and Gentlemen

Cath tilted her head to one side, brow furrowing. "We're going to a . . . hat shop?"

"The finest hat shop," Jest corrected. "And I assure you, the Hatter throws the maddest tea parties this side of the Looking Glass." He paused. "Probably on either side of the Looking Glass, now I think about it."

Anxiety was fast seeping into Cath's thoughts. She started to laugh, questioning how she'd come to be here. "I'm not sure I want to go to a *mad* tea party."

Jest winked at her. "Trust me, my lady. You do."

Stepping up to the back of the shop, he pulled open the door.

Chapter 18

Cath froze on the threshold, overwhelmed with the scent of herbal tea and the painful noise of an off-key duet. The millinery was easily eight times as large on the inside as it was on the out. A fire crackled in a corner fireplace and the walls were covered with hooks and shelves that displayed an assortment of elaborate headdresses. Top hats and bowlers, bonnets and coronets, straw hats and tall, pointed dunce caps. There were hats covered in living wildflowers and hats blooming with peacock feathers and hats fluttering with the wings of dozens of vibrant dragonflies, some of them occasionally giving off a puff of flame and smoke.

As Catherine stared, Raven abandoned Jest's shoulder and swooped inside. The wind from his feathers beat against her hair and — for but a moment — his shadow elongated across the shop's wooden floor. Cath's heart stuttered as she remembered the ominous shadow that had followed her over the castle lawn. The hooded figure, the raised ax.

She blinked, and the chill was gone. Just a bird, now settling on a ceramic bust of a clown with its silly, grinning face painted with black diamonds.

Jest drew Catherine toward the long table that stretched down the center of the hat shop. The surface was draped in bright-colored scarves of various textures and cluttered with teapots and cups and cream and sugar dishes and spoons of silver and gold and porcelain. The chairs around the table were just as mismatched — from wingbacks to schoolhouse benches to ottomans to a sweet little rocker. At the far end of the table was a chair that was luxurious enough for the King himself to have sat upon.

The occupants of the table were equally assorted. A Porcupine stabbed at a plate of scones with one of his quills; a Bloodhound spoke in hushed tones with a petite gray-haired woman who was working at knitting needles in between sips of tea; two Goldfish swam figure eights around each other inside a fishbowl filled with tea-stained water; a Dormouse dozed inside the mane of a Lion who was singing low to himself in vocal warm-up; a Parrot argued with a Cockatoo;

a Bumblebee skimmed a newspaper; a Boa Constrictor tuned a fiddle; a Chameleon squinted in concentration as she attempted to match the exact pattern of her upholstered chair; a Turtle dunked half of his cucumber sandwich into his cup.

The noisy whooperups at the center of it all were a March Hare, who stood on top of the table, and a Squirrel perched on his head. They each wore ridiculous floral bonnets, though holes had been added to allow their ears to poke through. Together they were the source of the very loud and rather obnoxious duet that had first pierced Cath's eardrums. The song was about starfish and stardust, though they both seemed too hoarse and confused to get any of the words straight, and they were horribly murdering the tune. Catherine cringed as the song dragged onward.

With one hand on her elbow, Jest guided Catherine around the table, toward the man who was occupying the throne at the far end. He was exquisitely dressed, with plum coattails and a crimson silk cravat. One finger skimmed idly along the brim of a matching purple top hat. Though he was young, his hair was silver-white, with a few choppy locks tumbling around his ears and the rest tied with a velvet ribbon at the nape of his neck.

He was slouched and apparently bored, feet set up beside a half-empty cup of tea.

Then his attention landed on Jest and turned lively, a grin fast to brighten his face. He swung his feet off the table.

"Well, well, if it isn't our star performer, returned from the world of gallantry and riches." He stood and gave Jest a quick embrace, before pulling away and grasping him by the shoulders. His smile had turned to scrutiny.

"Don't seem much changed," he mused, shutting one eye at a time to complete his inspection. "A bit scrawnier perhaps. Don't they feed you in that fancy castle of yours?" He pinched Jest's cheek, but was pushed away.

"Like a cow for slaughter," Jest said, "but I'm also forced to work for my pay. A novel idea to you, I know."

"A horrific waste of talent is what I call that." The Hatter — for Cath assumed this must be him — grimaced suddenly and cast his gaze toward the Hare and Squirrel on the table. "That's enough! I can't take any more." Grabbing a cane that had been propped against his chair, he whapped the handle of a spoon, which flicked a cashew from a bowl of nuts and sent it soaring right into the Hare's open mouth.

The Hare froze. A sudden silence fell over the tea parlor. The Hare pounded on his sternum — choking. His red eyes bugged. Catherine tensed.

The Boa Constrictor slithered onto the table, encircled the Hare's body, and squeezed. The cashew sailed out of his mouth and kersplatted into the Turtle's teacup.

Catherine watched, appalled, but the rest of the tea party guests had already taken back up with their conversations and tea drinking. She seemed to have been the only one concerned.

"What have you dragged in with you, Jest?"

She started. The Hatter's inspection had turned to her. His eyes, she noticed, were the color of soft violets, and his features equally delicate. He was very handsome, while simultaneously striking her as very pretty.

"Lady Catherine, this is my dear friend, Hatta. Hatta, Lady Catherine Pinkerton."

"Enchanted." She dropped into a curtsy.

Hatta tipped his hat, but didn't smile. "Pinkerton. A relation to the Marquess?"

"He is my father."

A robust laugh burst from his mouth. "A

true lady, then." He shot Jest a look that held layers of meaning Cath felt ill-equipped to interpret. "Or does that only go so far as her satin shift?"

Heat rushed into Cath's cheeks, but Jest did not rise to the bait. His tone was cold as he responded, "She is indeed a lady, as we are gentlemen. Do not force me to duel with you for her honor."

"A duel! Gracious, no. A hat-off, perhaps, but never a duel." His scrutiny slipped down Cath's dress, and she had the distinct feeling that he was estimating how many shillings the material had cost. "Any consort of Jest's is a friend of mine. Welcome to my hat shop."

"Thank you."

"And this is my long-time accomplice, Sir Haigha," said the Hatter, lifting his cane to the Hare as he came scrambling off the table.

"Sir Hare?" asked Catherine.

"Haigha," said the March Hare. "Rhymes with *mayor,* but spelled with a *g.*"

She stared, not sure how *Hare* could be spelled with a *g.* Before she could ask again, Jest settled a hand on her shoulder and whispered, "I'll spell it for you later."

She curtsied again.

Hatta slid his gaze back to the table and

scanned the occupants. The Bumblebee had turned his newspaper into three origami sailing boats and most of the guests were watching them chase one another around a teacup that was the size of a punch bowl. The Lion and the old lady were placing bets on which boats would sink first while the Turtle dumped sugar on the sails to sink them faster.

Hatta pounded the end of his cane on the floor three times, then swirled it through the air. "Everyone, move down! Make room for our joker and his lady. And who's up next?"

Chants of *move down, move down* echoed around the table as they pushed back their chairs and spent a topsy-turvy moment flitting to new seats. Sitting, testing, jumping and bounding, over the table and under, hopscotching between the chairs, stumbling into one another's laps and on top of one another's shoulders and some of the smaller animals finding a cozy spot inside an empty teacup. Only Hatta's throne was left out of the chair swapping, until finally everyone had settled down again, leaving the two seats on either side of their host open for Jest and Catherine.

Feeling like this was all a game she didn't know the rules to, Cath went to sit down.

"No, my lady, you'll want to be over here." Jest rounded to the seat on Hatta's left side and pulled it out for her.

Hatta snorted and tipped his hat up with his cane, watching Catherine as she sank straight-backed into the offered seat and smoothed her skirt around her legs. "Jest isn't confident you can hold your own among us rabble and hooligans."

Jest glowered. As he passed behind Hatta's throne, he leaned toward his ear. "She is our guest. I did not bring her here to entertain you."

Catherine folded her hands into her lap and tried to be pleasant.

"Wrong, Jest," Hatta said, his knowing smirk never leaving her. "Everyone is here to entertain me."

"Well then. Allow me."

Jest snapped the top hat from Hatta's head, holding it aloft as Hatta tried to grab it back. Jest was already chuckling and stepping up onto his chair, then onto the table. The cups and saucers rattled as his boots clomped against the wood.

With a disgruntled sigh that didn't hide the tilt at the corners of his lips, Hatta threw his heels back onto the tabletop and picked up his tea.

Catherine caught sight of Raven, still atop

the clown's bust, almost a part of the shadows. He angled his head to watch Jest's parade across the table.

The room hushed. Anticipation scrambled up Catherine's spine and she leaned forward, her fingers crushed together in her lap.

Stepping around the mess of dishes, Jest came to stand at the table's center. He held the top hat so everyone could see. Then, with a twist of his wrists, he sent the hat into a blurring spin and dropped his hands away. The hat continued to levitate in the air.

Catherine bit her lip, hardly daring to blink.

Tapping his fist against his chest, Jest cleared his throat. Then, to Catherine's surprise, he began to sing.

"Twinkle, twinkle . . . little bat."

Her lips twitched at the familiar lullaby, though Jest had slowed down the cadence so the song was more like a serenade. His voice was confident, yet quiet. Strong, but not overpowering.

"How I wonder what you're" — he tapped a finger onto the brim of the spinning hat so it flipped top to bottom — *"at."*

A flurry of bats burst upward. Catherine ducked as they swarmed through the room.

Their squeaks filled the shop with bedlam, their wings close enough to tease Cath's hair without touching her skin.

Jest's voice cut through the ruckus. *"Up above the world, so high . . ."*

The bats turned into a cyclone, encircling the room so the table was in the eye of a living storm. The cyclone began to tighten, closing in around Jest. Soon, he could no longer be seen beyond the mass of beating, squealing, pressing bodies. Tighter and tighter.

Catherine's chest constricted as the tornado of bats turned as one and streamed toward an open window — leaving behind Hatta's top hat sitting crookedly against a teapot, and no sign of Jest.

Her heart was pounding. Whispers began to pass up and down the table. Guests checked under the table and beneath the top hat and even in the teapots, but Jest had vanished.

"The nerve of him, to abandon you thus. At my mercy, no less."

She glanced at Hatta.

Setting his teacup on its saucer, he winked at her. "Jest has always had a weakness for riddles."

Brushing back the hair that had been tossed around by the bats, Cath did her best not to show how nervous the Hatter made her. "Have you known each other a long time?"

"Many years, love. I would try to count how many, but I'm so far into Time's debt, I would doubtlessly count them wrong."

She furrowed her brow. "Is that a riddle?"

"If you wish it to be."

Unsure how to respond, Cath reached for a teacup, but found it filled with mother-of-pearl buttons. She set it back. "Jest told a riddle at the ball," she said. "It was, 'Why is a raven like a writing desk?' "

The Hatter guffawed, throwing his head back. "Not that one! Sometimes I wonder if he's even trying."

"I didn't realize it was an old riddle. No one at the ball seemed to know it, and we were all amused by the answer."

"With due respect, my lady, the gentry are not known for their inability to be amused."

She supposed he was right — for the King most of all. But the way Hatta said it made it sound like a fault that should be shameful, and she wasn't sure if she agreed.

"Tell me, which answer did he give?" asked Hatta.

"Pardon?"

"Why is a raven like a writing desk?"

"Oh — because they each produce a few

notes, though they tend to be very flat." She was proud of herself for remembering, so caught in the performance had she been. "He covered the ballroom in confetti. Little paper notes, all with charming designs."

Hatta twirled the cane. "I always preferred the answer: because they both have quills dipped in ink."

Cath was surprised to find that the riddle, which had seemed impossible to answer when she'd first heard it, could have two such fitting solutions. She glanced at Raven, who had buried his face beneath one black wing, apparently asleep.

"That answer would have made quite a mess of the ballroom," she said.

Hatta stirred a spoonful of sugar into his cup, the spoon clinking loud against the ceramic. "I suppose you're right. I've been working on a riddle myself of late. Would you like to hear it?"

"Very much so."

He tapped the spoon on the cup's rim and set it on the saucer. "When pleased, I beat like a drum. When sad, I break like glass. Once stolen, I can never be taken back. What am I?"

She thought for a long moment before venturing, "A heart?"

Hatta's eyes warmed. "Very acute, Lady

Pinkerton."

"It's very good," she said, "although I wonder whether it wouldn't be more accurate to say, 'Once *given,* I can never be taken back.' "

"That would imply we give our hearts away willingly, and I am not sure that is the case. Perhaps we should ask Jest when he returns. I daresay he's the expert." He pulled a gold pocket watch from his waistcoat. "He doesn't usually disappear this long. Perhaps he was already tired of your company."

Cath bristled, sure now that he was trying to provoke her, though she couldn't imagine why. Clenching her fists beneath the table, she scanned the guests again. Most had gone back to their conversations. " 'Twinkle, Twinkle' is a lullaby," she said. "Not a riddle."

"How does it end? I can't remember."

She hummed through the song again. ". . . *like a tea tray in the sky.*"

Hatta snapped his fingers. "Haigha! Tea tray! Sky!"

The Hare, who had removed the floral bonnet, peeled back his enormous ears and gawked at Hatta. Then he hopped up from the table fast as a gunshot and grabbed a tea tray, dumping off a pile of crustless sandwiches, and rushed to an open window. Within moments, all the other guests — excepting Catherine and Hatta — had tossed aside their chairs and teacups to gather around him.

Catherine craned her head, thinking it wouldn't be ladylike to be jostled in with all those strangers . . .

"Oh, hogswaddle," she muttered, pushing away from the table and joining the crowd at the window.

Haigha tossed the tea tray — it spun out into the forest and disappeared into the night.

They waited.

Somewhere outside, they heard the clatter of the tea tray falling through tree boughs and thumping back down to the ground.

Breaths were held.

No one spoke.

The Dormouse yawned and shifted in the Lion's mane, turning to curl up on his other side.

"What are you all looking for?"

Catherine spun back to the table.

Jest was sitting to Hatta's right, holding a half-eaten biscuit in one hand and a teacup in the other.

The crowd cheered, whistles filling the shop.

With his gaze on Catherine, Jest smiled, and Cath's heart joined it. She tried to keep the humor from her face as she planted her hands on her hips and faced him across the table. "Hatta was right," she reprimanded. "It was terribly rude to abandon me so."

Jest licked a crumb from the corner of his mouth. "I knew you'd figure it out."

The Hatter grunted, taking his top hat back from the Boa Constrictor, who had fetched it from the table's center. "Let's not make a prodigy of the lady, when all she did was recite a child's lullaby." Grabbing his cane, he smacked it three times on the floor and yelled, "Who out of you lousy bunch wants to follow our joker? *Move down!*"

CHAPTER 19

The Hatter's tea party was not so much a tea party as a circus. Chairs were constantly swapped and shifted, and whichever guest ended up on Hatta's right was deemed the next performer. In turn, each guest would stand up, select one of the vibrant head-pieces from the surrounding walls, and proceed to entertain the others however they saw fit. The Parrot and the Cockatoo performed a comedy routine about a mime and a mimic. The Lion sang a perfect alto solo from a renowned opera. The gray-haired woman sat cross-legged on top of the table and drilled out an impressive drum solo using her knitting needles and an assortment of upturned dishes. The young Turtle recited a love sonnet with a warbling voice and shy, stammering words — once during his recitation, he glanced at Catherine and blushed deep green and was unable to look at her again for the rest of the night.

Maybe there was something in the tea — which she deemed the most delicious tea she'd ever tasted once she finally got a cup — because once Catherine relaxed, she found that she couldn't stop laughing and cheering and tapping her toes beneath the table. She learned that Hatta was prone to ordering everyone around, though most of his guests paid his orders little attention. She learned that the Dormouse used to be the liveliest one of the group, but he'd gone into hibernation a year and a half ago and had yet to come out of it. She learned that Jest felt guilty about his bat trick tangling up her hair, he confessed as he smoothed back a curl and sent goose bumps down her skin.

Flustered, she batted him away.

Each time they moved, Jest stayed at Cath's side, helping her navigate around the flurry of activity, coaxing her away from the performer's chair. It was a relief to not be forced into the center of attention, yet Catherine couldn't help racking her brain for some talent she could impress them with. A fantasy crept into her head of wowing them all, of being even more awe-inspiring than Jest with his illusions and tricks. But how? She could not sing or dance or juggle. She was not an entertainer.

She was only a lady.

When everyone had performed and Hatta again commanded them to move down, Jest was first to move toward the performance seat and keep Catherine free of it.

Before he could sit, though, Hatta smacked his cane over the chair's arms. "Patience, my friend. I don't believe we've had the pleasure of seeing anything from your lady yet." Hatta slid his haughty gaze to Catherine.

Jest nudged the cane away. "She's here to enjoy our hospitality, not have you turn her into a spectacle."

Catherine held Hatta's look, refusing to fidget.

Jest rolled his eyes and turned back to Catherine. "Don't let him bully you. I'm happy to perform in your stead if you'd like."

"It's only a little stingy," Hatta interrupted. "To take and take for your own entertainment, and offer none of yourself." His words dripped with disapproval.

Jest glared at Hatta, then turned back to her and whispered, "It isn't like that. There's no shame in asking someone else to perform for you, especially at your first tea party." He held out his hand.

She knew he was trying to alleviate the

pressure Hatta was putting on her, but she felt a bit of a sting. Right or not, how could he be so sure that she had nothing to contribute?

She studied his hand, slender fingers that weren't as smooth as hers, yet not as rough as a gardener's or servant's, either. She liked the way he had called it her first tea party, insinuating there might be more to come.

"I'll do it," she heard herself saying, from very far away.

A grin spread over Hatta's face, but she couldn't tell whether it was encouraging or taunting. "The lady is next!" he bellowed before she could change her mind, then swept his hand toward the hats on the wall. "Choose a hat, my lady. You'll find that it helps."

"Helps how?" She tried to look casual as she strolled down the wall of bonnets and top hats, netted veils and silk turbans.

"Think of it like wearing a costume. Or . . . perhaps to you, a very fine gown." Hatta ran his fingers along the brim of his own top hat. "A finely crafted hat makes a person . . . bolder."

Cath wasn't sure she agreed. Her very fine gowns had done little to make her feel any bolder in the past, but everyone else had worn a hat while they performed, so who was she to argue? The crowd waited to see what she would choose, but Cath knew she was only stalling for time as she fingered a gold clasp here and an ostrich plume there.

She must have some talent. Any talent that wouldn't embarrass her.

Most of the hats were far more extravagant than those she was used to. Her favorite so far had been a breathtaking pink-and-green-striped carousel, complete with nickering ponies that galloped around and around. But it had been worn by the Lion during his operatic performance, and she noticed with some disappointment that he had yet to take it off.

"Might I suggest one of the red ones?" said Hatta.

She startled and looked back at him. "Why red?"

He gave her a one-shouldered shrug. "It would suit your skin tone, beloved. How about that one, there?"

She followed his gesture to a wide-brimmed flop hat, its multitude of frills and gathers done in wine-red silk and ornamented with sprigs of white and yellow poppies. Cath wrinkled her nose. It was a beautiful hat, but not at all what she would choose for herself.

However, beside it was a white cooking

bonnet tied with a wide black ribbon. Catherine snatched it off its wooden peg and put it on her head before she could second-guess herself.

"Ah, a hat for making unconventional decisions." Hatta narrowed his eyes. "Interesting choice."

When she dared to look at Jest, he seemed indifferent to the hat. He again offered her a hand.

Cath tightened the black ribbon beneath her chin and accepted his assistance as she stepped onto a chair, then up onto the table.

While she had been making her decision, the hat shop had fallen quiet, a stark difference from the chaos she'd grown used to. The guests watched her, hushed in curiosity.

Cath was curious herself. Her hands had begun to tremble.

She found a spot amid the chipped saucers and overturned biscuits and inhaled a long breath, glancing around at the waiting faces. Slitted snake eyes and double-lidded lizard eyes and bulging fish eyes all stared back at her. The hem of her skirt collected spilled tea and crumbs.

"Sing a song, lovely lady!" suggested the Lion, as the carousel ponies pranced above his mane. "Sing us a ballad of old!"

"No, dance for us. Perhaps a ballet?"
"Can she serve tea like a geisha?"
"Paint with her toes?"
"Do a cartwheel?"
"Tell our fortunes?"
"Tie a knot in a cherry stem with her tongue?"
"Don't be a ninny — that's impossible!"
"Catherine."
She turned and realized she was still holding Jest's hand. He smiled, but it carried some concern. "You don't have to do this."
She wondered whether he was embarrassed for her, or for himself — for bringing her. A lady. A member of the gentry. Someone with soft hands and a head full of emptiness. Someone who was not mad enough to belong at the Hatter's tea parties.
She yanked her hand away and faced the Hatter. His heels were on the table again, his fingers fiddling with his cravat.
Her father was known throughout Hearts as a great storyteller, a gift that had been passed down through her family over generations and yet had somehow skipped her over. Now Catherine struggled to remember one of his tales. The ones that could enchant a school of wayward fish. The ones that could make the clouds cry and bring moun-

tains to their knees.

"Once . . . once upon a time . . . ," she started, but had to stop when the words caught in her throat.

She rubbed her damp palms on her skirt — and discovered a crackling lump in her pocket.

Her heart flipped.

"There was . . . there was a girl. She was the daughter of a marquess."

The corners of Hatta's mouth tilted downward.

"Though she was raised to be a lady," Cath said, turning away and scanning the enraptured guests — or at least, guests who were waiting and willing to be enraptured, "and taught all the things a lady ought to be taught, she was only good at one thing. It was not a big thing, or an important thing, or even a ladylike thing, but it was what she really loved to do."

She slid her hand into her pocket and pulled out the package of macarons. The wax paper had crinkled throughout the day, though the twine bow securing it had held. Around the table, the guests tilted forward.

"I . . ." She hesitated. "I make confections, you see."

"Did she say *confessions*?" the old lady murmured. "Oh dear. I fear I have done a lot worth confessing this year."

Cath smiled. "No, *confections.*" She opened the wax paper, revealing five rose macarons, a little crumbled around the edges, but otherwise intact.

A silence descended onto the table.

"Unconventional indeed," Hatta drawled, brow drawn with suspicion. "But what do they do?"

Catherine didn't retract her hand. "They don't do anything. They won't make you smaller, or larger. But . . . I do hope they might make you happier. These were meant to be a gift for the King himself, but I . . . I was distracted today. I forgot to give them to him."

She dared not look at Jest.

"A gift for the King?" Hatta said. "That does sound promising." He waved his cane at Haigha, who reached up and took the macarons out of Cath's palm. Her breath left her in a rush, relieved to have them gone. She was still shaking with nerves.

Haigha laid the macarons out on a plate and, one by one, cut the sandwiched meringues as neatly as he could. They crumbled and squished under the knife. The crowd gathered close, watching as the buttercream filling oozed and stuck to the paper.

Feeling a tug at her skirt, Catherine turned to see Jest holding his hand toward her again. She allowed him to pull her down from the table.

"You made those?" he whispered.

"Of course I did," she said, and couldn't help adding, "and as you'll see, Hatta isn't the only one here who can make marvelous things."

His lips quirked. His eyes had a new intensity, like he was trying to figure out a riddle.

The pieces of macaron were passed around the table, and even offered to Raven sitting darkly on his bust, though he huffed and turned his head away. Catherine and Jest were given the last two bites, leaving a pool of flaky almond meringue crumbs and smeared buttercream behind.

Hatta stood and raised his piece into the air. "A toast to Lady Pinkerton, the finest lady to ever grace our table."

Cheers resounded throughout the shop, but died out as they started to eat.

Catherine listened to the licking of fingers and sucking of teeth.

Jest's eyes settled on her again, shining like candlelight, a finger caught between his lips. He blinked in surprise.

Cath beamed and placed her own sample

on her tongue. The macaron was sweet and decadent and smooth, with just a tiny crunch from the meringue, and a subtle floral moment from the distilled rose water, all melting together into one perfect bite.

She listened to the gasps, the moans, the crinkle of parchment paper as someone scooped up the buttercream that had gotten missed.

This was why she enjoyed baking. A good dessert could make her feel like she'd created joy at the tips of her fingers. Suddenly, the people around the table were no longer strangers. They were friends and confidantes, and she was sharing with them her magic.

"Well done, Lady Pinkerton," buzzed the Bumblebee. Then there was a round of *huzzahs* bouncing up and down the table. In the renewed chaos, the Dormouse awoke and looked sleepily around the room. Someone had left a crumb on his plate, which he popped into his mouth without hesitation. He chewed and swallowed, grinned dreamily, and returned to his nap still licking his lips.

The Hatter alone was not cheering. Rather, he had tilted back in his chair and covered his face with his hat.

Cath's elation received a momentary

chink. A notch of rejection.

But then Hatta lowered the hat and she saw that he was smiling, and his smile was heart-thumpingly open, honest, beautiful. His lavender eyes sparkled as they found her, then shifted to Jest.

"Fine. Fine!" he said, holding a hand up in surrender. "I suppose I will allow her to stay."

Cath dipped into a curtsy, still flushed with success. "You are too gracious, Hat—"

The shop suddenly rocked. She slipped, toppling into Jest, whose arms encircled her.

The guests gasped and scrambled to gain their balance. Something clomped on the roof, followed by scratching, like talons scrabbling for purchase. The shop rocked again, sending an array of dishes over one side of the table, tea and cookies splattering onto the floor.

An ear-bleeding screech made the hair stand on the back of Cath's neck.

Jest glanced up, drawing Cath's attention toward Raven. The clown bust he stood upon had changed, the jovial grin turning down into a mockery of fear.

Raven tilted his head, as if his black eyes could see right through the beams of the ceiling, and recited in his somber cadence, " 'Tis the nightmare of the borogoves, the terror of the slithy toves. Though long believed a myth by all, the Jabberwock has come to call within our peaceful grove."

Chapter 20

Jest turned to Hatta. "We must make a run for the Crossroads. The beast will be too large to follow us through."

Cath gaped up at him, her heart squeezing tight. "You mean for us to go outside?" She turned toward Hatta, whose face was drawn, his jaw set. "Wouldn't it be more prudent to stay put and wait for the beast to tire? Surely it will get bored and leave if it can't get to us."

A window at the back of the shop shattered. The Porcupine and the Bloodhound scrambled away from the scattering glass.

Two clawed fingers pushed through the destroyed window. The remaining glass shards scraped over the scaled skin as the fingers writhed and searched for a way inside, drawing charcoal-colored blood from the wounds.

Cath shuddered and pressed herself into

Jest's arms. "It can't get to us here . . . can it?"

"These walls are but wood and nails, Lady Pinkerton," Hatta said, his voice low. "The Jabberwock may not fit through the door, but it can doubtlessly open a new one."

Her mouth dried.

The claw disappeared from the window. The shop rocked and trembled again as the monster paced to the other side of the roof. Searching. Through a gap in a set of drapes, Cath saw a slithering tail flick past.

Fear wrapped around her, encasing her limbs in stone.

She was going to die. Here, among strangers, in the middle of the night. She would be a feast for the Jabberwock, and her parents and Mary Ann would never know what had become of her.

A sudden gust through the chimney extinguished the fire that had been blazing in the corner hearth. The air filled with the smell of smoke and embers.

Hatta, the only one still sitting, pushed himself back from the table, the legs of his imitation throne scratching against the floorboards. He grabbed his cane and pressed his hat onto his head before surveying his guests. His attention landed on Jest.

"Think of it like being at home, mate," he

said. "Haigha and I will go out first to distract the enemy with a clear target. You and Raven helm us on the sides. Protect the others while they run for the Crossroads." His gaze slipped down to Cath and he seemed, briefly, to find something amusing in their situation. "As always, we must protect the Queen."

Jest flinched, his fingers digging into her arms.

A deep voice rumbled across the table. "I will bring up the rear."

Cath turned toward the Lion, who stood regal and imposing in the dim candlelight, his orange mane haloed around him, although the look was diminished by the carousel hat clopping around his head. His tail flicked as he scanned the other creatures, all smaller than he was. "I will not enter the Crossroads until we all are safe."

Hatta tipped his hat. "You are a brave soldier."

Overhead, the Jabberwock screamed again. It was followed by the sound of splintering wood and creaking nails. The walls trembled.

"Everyone into position," Hatta yelled. "Prepare to run for the Crossroads entrance. We must move as one."

Jest pulled back, gripping Cath's shoulders. His brow was drawn with fear and apology, but she stopped him before he could speak.

"It was my choice to come," she whispered. "You couldn't have known this would happen."

A muscle twitched in his jaw. "I will get you home safely."

She nodded and, despite the fear coursing through her veins, she trusted him. "Impossible is your specialty."

His eyes softened, barely covering his distress. "So it is."

"Are we ready?" asked Hatta. He had moved toward the door, ready to pull it open. Haigha stood opposite him, his large ears quivering.

Cath glanced around. The old lady had climbed onto the Bloodhound's back, gripping her knitting needles like daggers. The Squirrel had taken hold of the fishbowl, with the two Goldfish cowering beneath an overturned sugar dish that had fallen inside. The Boa Constrictor had the snoozing Dormouse cradled in his jaw. The Parrot and Cockatoo were ready to take flight; the Chameleon had colored himself to match the grass and wildflowers of the meadow outside; the Bumblebee was brandishing his stinger; the Porcupine had puffed up his barbed quills; and the Turtle had drawn his head into his shell.

The sight of them, who had been so merry and carefree minutes before, filled Cath with dread.

"Run fast," Jest whispered against her ear. "Head straight to the Crossroads and try to stay near the middle of the group if you can — it will be safest."

"Why?" she said. "My life has no more value than anyone else's."

Jest's eyes darkened and she thought he would refute, but he seemed to reconsider. Finally, he said, "Just hurry, and don't look back. I'll be right behind you."

Cath swallowed and nodded.

His hands fell from her shoulders. Raven swooped toward them and propped himself on Jest's shoulder.

With the bird's ink-black feathers and Jest's ink-black motley, they looked like shadows come to life.

"On the count of three," said Hatta.

More scratches across the rooftop. Another scream from the monster outside.

"One."

Jest pressed Cath forward, urging her to stand with the others. Though her legs were shaking, she willed them to be strong as she placed herself between the Porcupine and the Bloodhound. The gray-haired lady met her eyes and gave a nod that was perhaps meant to be comforting, though to Cath it seemed like a look passed between soldiers being sent onto a battlefield.

"Two."

Something cracked like splitting timber — the roof being ripped from its trusses.

At the back of the group, the Lion growled.

"Three!"

Hatta yanked open the door and he and Haigha charged forward, leaping clear of the wooden steps. Their feet thumped onto the grass outside and they took off in opposite directions — Haigha bounding full-speed toward the Crossroads, his powerful hind legs propelling him fast over the meadow, while Hatta took off toward the nearby tree cover. He propped his hat on the tip of his cane and extended it overhead.

The shop erupted into chaos. The animals rushed out the door in a tight pack. Cath gripped her skirt and hardly realized she'd started running until there was soft ground under her feet. Ahead, she could see Haigha waving to them from the brush, coaxing them toward the entrance of the Crossroads.

A shriek rattled the meadow, followed by the beat of thunderous wings. Cath imagined the Jabberwock launching itself off the rooftop of the traveling shop and diving toward them from the sky, but she dared not look back.

The monster's scream was met with the caw of a raven — no, two ravens — and a thrumming, rumbling roar from the Lion, and Hatta yelling something she couldn't make out.

Cath was already out of breath, her legs shaking so hard she thought they would collapse before she reached the brush. But they didn't. She bounded onto the pathway only a few steps behind the Bloodhound and felt an instant sense of safety from the tree cover.

Haigha stood beside a tree trunk, ushering them through the Crossroads doorway. The door was narrow, though, and after their rush from the hat shop, they had bottlenecked to a standstill.

The Squirrel and Goldfish disappeared into the shadows. The Boa Constrictor slithered through. The Bloodhound leaped across the threshold, carrying his charge to safety.

A whimper made Cath glance back.

The Turtle had frozen, not quite to the end of the clearing, and withdrawn all of his limbs into his shell. She could hear his sobs echoing from inside.

A shadow soared over him and the grasses bent back under the beat of the monster's wings.

Cath shrank down into the shrubs, her heart throbbing, and dared to look up at the beast that had once haunted her nightmares. Talons long as butcher knives. Slithery, writhing neck. Burning embers in its eyes. The creature was made of inky shadows and fire and muscles trapped beneath taut, scaly skin.

Two birds were flocking around it, circling its head, trying to keep it distracted from the creatures below. Diving, clawing, then darting out of reach.

Raven . . . and Jest.

Hatta was standing on the far side of the clearing, his hat still perched on his cane and eyes wild. Whatever distraction he'd first offered, he'd been forgotten now.

"Get up!" the Lion yelled, pounding on the Turtle's shell with his paw. "You're almost there. You must keep moving!"

"I'm . . . too . . . slow," the Turtle cried. "I'll never . . . m-make it!"

"You must try!" said the Lion.

"My lady!"

Cath glanced back. Haigha was waving to her from the doorway, his red eyes large with horror. Everyone else had gone through. "Come now, quick!"

She swallowed.

Overhead, the Jabberwock shrieked. It sounded hungry. It sounded *ravenous.*

It dropped down and perched again on the shop, which swayed on its rickety wheels. Even in the darkness Cath could see the destruction it had wreaked upon the roof.

Something slipped over her eyes and Cath shoved it back. She'd forgotten about the chef's hat, the one she'd chosen from Hatta's wall. A hat for making unconventional decisions.

She took in a deep breath and searched the ground. She grabbed a long stick.

"My lady!" Haigha screamed again, but Cath ignored him as she launched herself out of the brush, charging toward the Lion and the Turtle.

The Jabberwock cried and Cath knew it had spotted her racing across the meadow.

"No!" Hatta yelled. "Over here!"

A bird cawed.

The Lion's eyes widened in panic as Cath planted herself behind the Turtle. She angled the stick beneath his shell and jabbed him, hard.

The Turtle yelped in pain and bucked

forward, scrabbling at the ground.

"Move, move, move!" Cath yelled, poking him again and again, urging him along to a chorus of whimpers and yelps. He reached the path. His flippers treaded against the brush.

"Lady!" Haigha screamed.

The scream of the Jabberwock shredded her ears. Heart in her throat, Cath spun around, gripping the stick like a sword, just in time to see the shadow of the beast soaring toward her.

Every limb tightened and she could see its neck outstretched and its fangs bared and its tongue lolling toward her —

A blur of orange flashed in her vision, mixed with a ferocious roar and a whinny of tiny horses. The Lion threw himself in front of Catherine, one massive paw lifted as if he would bat the Jabberwock out of the sky.

The monster screamed and pulled its head back, shifting so that its massive talons were extended toward them.

Cath heard the moment of impact. Flesh and bone and soft ground and a cry of pain and beating wings and a triumphant screech — and then the Jabberwock flew upward again. Its prey was caught in its claws, the tuft of the Lion's tail dangling in the air behind it.

Chapter 21

Cath was still staring after the Jabberwock, the stick clutched in her shaking hands, when a shadow of feathers and bells dropped from the sky. Jest grabbed her shoulders. His gloves carried the memory of soft quills before they were leather once more.

"Are you all right?" he asked, breathless.

"N-no," she stammered. Her eyes were full of the horizon and the memory of the Lion's body, all grace and muscle, so quickly taken. So easily defeated.

Hatta was there too, then, in the corner of her vision. "Come," he ordered, shoving the two of them toward the forest. "Let's get to safety, in case the beast comes back."

"The Lion . . ." Cath's voice cracked with a sob.

"I know," said Hatta. "I saw."

Hatta ushered her past Haigha, whose eyes were glistening with tears. She heard

Raven's wings beating behind them. She spotted the Turtle's shell past the Crossroads door. Everyone was waiting for them on the other side, clustered together on the black-and-white tiles. Their frightened eyes began to turn away when they realized that one of their party had been lost.

The Crossroads felt too quiet, too ordinary, too safe after the horrors of the glen.

"He's gone," Cath stammered. "He . . . he saved me."

"He was a king among beasts," said Jest. It sounded like a memoriam.

"He was indeed," said Hatta. "Some might call that a checkmate."

Cath put up no argument when Jest offered to take her home. Though there was a sense of protection in the Crossroads, with its mismatched doors and access to all corners of the kingdom, as soon as they stepped onto the shores of Squeaky Creek, Cath felt the same terror wash over her.

Hearts was not safe. The Jabberwock was real and it was here and they were not safe.

"My lady," said Jest, his voice heavy. They had hardly spoken once the other guests had scattered and headed for their own homes. Even Raven had seemed happy to abandon them, flying off into some unknown corner of Hearts. "I am so very, very sorry. I put you in danger. I —"

"You had no control over the Jabberwock." She stopped and turned to face him. The creek burbled behind her. "Did you?"

Their hands were intertwined and had been the entire walk, but it didn't seem as romantic as it had when they had left her home earlier that evening. Rather, there was a need pulsing through her fingertips. For touch. For security. She felt safe with him there, whether or not it was warranted.

"If not for me," said Jest, "you would have been safe in your bed, and wouldn't have had to witness something so dreadful."

She looked down at their fingers. Hers so pale against the black leather of his glove.

"Perhaps tomorrow, when my senses are clear, I will feel that the whole night was a mistake. But I don't feel that way now." She took in a long breath and raised her eyes again. "Monsters notwithstanding, I enjoyed my first real tea party."

A ghost smile flickered at the corners of his mouth. "And I enjoyed taking you to one. Monsters notwithstanding."

"Then let us not end our night with talk of dreadful things," she said, and though there was a sting of guilt at her words — how could she dismiss what had become of the brave and gallant Lion? — it was refreshing to think back on the music and the hats and the tea that had come before.

"As it pleases you, my lady," said Jest, and he, too, seemed willing to think of more pleasant things. He tugged her up the bank of the creek. "I didn't have a chance to compliment your performance. The macarons were marvelous, just as you said."

She pressed her lips against a proud smile and shrugged. "Why, thank you, Sir Joker."

"Where did you learn to bake?"

She considered the question. Baking had been a part of her life for so long, it was difficult remembering a time when she hadn't enjoyed digging her fingers into a bowl of cake batter or warm, rising dough. "Our cook started teaching me when I was a child, but mostly I taught myself, using what recipe books I could find, and experimenting from there. I like the idea of taking ingredients that are unappetizing on their own — chalky flour and oily egg whites and bitter dark chocolate — and making something irresistible with them. This might sound mad, but sometimes it feels as though the ingredients are speaking to me." She flushed. "Which must be nonsense."

"I rather enjoy nonsense. What else can you make?"

"Most anything once I've seen a recipe for it. Pies. Tarts. Biscuits. Seed cakes, even — do you think Mr. Raven would care for one of those? I noticed he didn't seem tempted by the macarons . . ." She hesitated and cast a suspicious look at Jest from the corner of her eye. "Or, would *you* like a seed cake? I'm not yet certain whether you're more man or bird."

Jest laughed. "Unfortunately, if Raven were to sample your seed cakes and find that he enjoyed them, it might ruin his impeccable ability to brood." One of his fingertips traced the back of Cath's hand. "As for me, I trust I would like most anything you made, if the macarons are any indication."

She risked a bashful glance at him. Jest returned the look, before continuing, "The King mentioned some tarts you brought to the ball. I didn't give it much thought at the time — I'd assumed your cook had been the one to make them, but now . . . I understand why he's so drawn to you. You aren't only talented, but . . . do you know, you're extra beautiful when you talk about baking. You know you're good at it, and that knowledge lights you up."

Cath's defenses shivered and she had to look away, flattered and flustered and . . .

Newly miserable.

She hadn't thought of the King all night, what with Jest and the party and . . . and what had come afterward.

He was no longer simply the King, though. He was her suitor.

Now that the evening was at its end, no longer full of potential and impossibilities, her decisions seemed unbearably foolish. What could she be thinking, sneaking about with the court joker? Her parents would be mortified if they found out. Her reputation would be ruined.

"It's only a silly hobby," she muttered as they turned onto the drive of Rock Turtle Cove Manor. Her heels were loud on the cobblestones, so she tried to stay on her toes. Jest, on the other hand, walked like falling snowflakes. "It's nice to be good at something, though. It's not what my parents wanted me to be good at, but it is something." She sighed. "Whereas you seem to be good at everything."

"Not everything," he said. "Would you believe I've never so much as held an egg-beater?"

"Scandalous!"

He grinned at her, and she was surprised at how much she wanted to tell him about the bakery she and Mary Ann were going to open. The desire to bring him into her fantasy was fast and fervent, maybe even to tell him of how she'd begun to dream of him being a part of it all. But she and Mary Ann hadn't told anyone about their plans, other than the Duke, which had been necessary, and to tell Jest felt like it would have been a betrayal of her oldest friendship. That alone held her tongue.

"You don't have to walk me all the way to the house," she said, realizing that her feet were dragging more with every step.

"Stuff and nonsense. After the night we've had, I couldn't imagine deserting you before you've been seen safely to your door. Or, window."

Catherine was unwilling to argue. They cut across the grass, damp and soft from dew. Morning dew? The whole night had been whiled away, yet it seemed as if she had just left.

Her gaze traced the boughs of the lemon tree to her bedroom window. The glass was black as pitch. The hearth fire had burned down hours ago.

"I suppose now you're going to grow wings and fly us up there?"

"Unfortunately my wings come only in one size, and they wouldn't be helpful in this circumstance." His jaw clenched, his yellow eyes raw with uncertainty. "You asked if I was man or bird, Lady Pinkerton, but I'm neither." He drew in a long breath and turned to face her fully. "I'm a Rook, as is Raven."

She tilted her head. "Isn't a rook a type of bird?"

"In Hearts, perhaps." His fingers tightened around hers. "But in Chess, we are protectors of the White Queen."

She held his gaze, trying to puzzle through his words, unsure if this was another riddle. "Chess?"

His head shifted in what could have been a nod. "That's where Raven and I come from."

"Chess." The word was little more than a breath now, spoken with awe. Chess. The Land of the Red and White Queendoms.

She had never known anyone from Chess. There were rumors that one could travel between the two lands, but there was a maze that no one knew how to get to, and a doorway said to be guarded by fate itself.

But such rumors could all be fairy tales as far as she knew.

"If you're a protector of the White Queen," she said, "whatever are you doing here?"

"It's . . . complicated." He seemed to be fighting with an explanation. "The Queen sent us here on a mission of sorts. One that could determine the fate of Chess. One that could end the war between her and the Red Queen, a war that is as old as Time himself."

Cath gaped at him, wondering how there ever could have been a time when she had looked at this man and seen only a joker — all pranks and magic.

He was from Chess.

He was on a mission that could end a war.

He was the protector of a queen.

Her heart suddenly twisted, and she was surprised at how much it hurt. "Then how long will you be in Hearts?" she asked, not caring how the unexpected sorrow showed in her question.

Jest's eyes widened with surprise, then softened. He settled his free hand onto their entwined fingers, encasing hers completely. "I don't know. Once our mission is complete . . . perhaps I'll have a reason to come back, and to stay."

"Won't . . ." Her voice caught and she had to clear her throat to continue. "Won't your queen need you?"

"She appointed some replacement Rooks in our absence." His gaze shifted to some spot over Cath's shoulder and he frowned. "Bizarre little men, the Tweedles. Always fighting over a rattle, but . . . I suppose they fit the role well enough. Maybe she won't need me anymore, or Raven." He looked back and said, with more hesitation, "If I had a reason to stay, that is."

"Naturally." Her lips had dried and she licked them instinctively.

Jest inhaled and dropped her hand, taking half a step back. He rubbed the back of his neck. "I apologize, Lady Pinkerton. I've kept you out too long."

"No, I . . ." She folded her hands against her stomach, wondering how her fingers had gotten so cold so quickly. "Thank you for telling me your story. I promise your secret will be safe with me." She hesitated. "Or at least, I think it's a secret. Does the King know?"

"No one knows. Only you, and Raven of course, and Hatta and Haigha."

Her eyes widened. "Are they from Chess too?"

Jest rocked on his heels. "Of a sort, but their secrets are not mine to tell."

She nodded in understanding, although her curiosity gnawed at her insides.

"Anyhow, being the protecting sort, my job won't be finished until you're returned to your chambers." Jest took off his three-pointed hat and set it on her head. "Hold that, if you would."

"I should have known the hat would play a role."

"Actually, it just gets in the way. Besides, I was right. It does look better on you." Reaching overhead, Jest grabbed on to a low-hanging branch and pulled himself into the tree. Catherine backed up to peer into the shadows. He was pleasant to watch, so nimble and fast.

Crouching on a low bough, he held his hand toward her. "Now give me your hand."

She traced the limbs of the tree up to her window, apprehensive. "Have you run out of magic?"

"Some things, like climbing trees, are best done without. Your hand, my lady."

She twisted her mouth to one side. "You don't understand. I'm not . . . like you."

His hand started to sag. "Like me?"

"Graceful. Strong."

Jest's expression warmed.

"You might be surprised how often I'm compared to a walrus, actually. And walruses do not climb trees."

At this, his growing smile vanished. He hesitated, momentarily speechless, before retracting his hand. "Of all the nonsense I've heard tonight, that's the worst of it. But suit yourself." He straddled the tree branch, his boots kicking at the air. "Go ahead and use the front door, if you prefer. I'll wait here."

Cath pressed the hat down tighter to her head and scanned the tree branches again. She considered his proposal and could already hear the loud squeak of the front door that she'd been hearing all her life.

Huffing, she held her arms up toward him.

His grin returned and he shifted into a more stable position.

A flash of panic flickered through Cath's mind as he latched on to her wrists — what if she was too heavy for him to lift? — but moments later Jest was pulling her up without any apparent difficulty. He waited until he was sure she had her footing and one hand clasped around a branch before he let go.

The climb was easier than she expected, though Jest was doing most of the work. He instructed her where to place her hands, which branches to grab hold of, how best to leverage her weight. It felt like being a child again, scrambling through the trees, make believing she had been born into a family of chimpanzees. She had to stifle her laughter so she wouldn't wake anyone in the house.

Her bedroom window was still open. Jest stepped inside before turning to help her over the gap. It was the most daring part, trusting that her legs could span the distance, and she had to hold her breath until her toes were on the windowsill and Jest's hands were on her waist, pulling her across.

Catherine gasped and fell into him, hat bells jingling. Jest's arms encircled her and he turned, catching her mid-fall. Cath found herself hanging in his arms, her fingers digging into his shoulders, one foot still on the windowsill and the other scraping against the carpet. Her heartbeat danced between them and a tea-drunk giggle threatened to intrude into the chilly quiet of the morning.

Jest was grinning, and though it was too dark to see the color of his eyes, she could picture exactly what shade they were.

Gulping, she removed the hat and returned it to Jest's head. "Thank you," she murmured, hoping he knew it wasn't just for helping her up the tree and through the window. Hoping he knew it was for everything. The thrills, the laughs, the secrets he'd shared. The night may have had moments of panic and terror, but it had also been an entire night when she didn't have to be the daughter of a marquess.

He didn't set her down. Didn't let her go. "When will I see you again?" he whispered.

A tickle erupted in her stomach.

He wanted to see her again.

Happiness coursed to the ends of her limbs.

She could be his reason to stay in Hearts. She *wanted* to be.

But with that thought, the gut-deep ache of her situation returned full force.

In Hearts, he was not a Rook. He was a court joker, and she was being courted by the King.

Cath planted both feet on the floor and extricated herself from his hold. He didn't try to stop her — perhaps the worst disappointment of all.

She propped herself against a rose-covered bedpost, her legs still shaky. "We can't," she said, before amending, "I can't."

His dimples faded.

She tried again. "Tonight was . . ." *Magnificent. Marvelous. Magical.*

But also horrible and dangerous.

"Tonight can't happen again."

His half smile quirked, more sardonic this time. "I know. That is the way of Time."

She shook her head. "I'm sorry. You should go." She was painfully aware of how easily their voices could carry through the walls. Soon Mary Ann would come to light the fire and fill the washbasin. Jest had to leave, and he couldn't ever come back to her window again, and she could never admit to anyone this night had happened.

She had been to a real tea party. She had made friends who weren't in the gentry. She had narrowly escaped death and watched the poor Lion being carried away into the night.

But she could never speak of these things. She, too, had a secret now to keep.

"Perhaps I'll see you at the Turtle Days Festival?" said Jest. "If not more of His Majesty's garden parties."

His tone was light, but it felt forced. Clinging to optimism.

Cath shrugged, growing more tense by the moment. "I'll be at the festival. It's my family's festival, after all."

Surprised, Jest glanced around the room, taking in the elaborate crown moldings and silver candlesticks and tapestried bed curtains.

"That's right," he murmured. "You're the daughter of the Marquess."

As if he'd forgotten.

"It's tradition that I start the dancing. I'll be dancing the lobster quadrille. I expect . . . I expect I'll be dancing with the King." She stuck out her tongue in distaste.

Jest's expression brightened. "As I expect I'll be performing for him."

He stuck his tongue out to mimic her.

One of her embarrassing snorts escaped, unwilled, and Catherine buried her face in her hands.

"What if . . . ," Jest started.

She lowered her hands. He had taken a step closer to her.

"You dance your lobster quadrille, and I'll juggle some clams, and we'll both pretend to be hidden away in a secret sea cave, where we don't have to think about courtships or royal missions or anything but ourselves."

"That does sound lovely," she said, struggling to remember why this was a bad idea. Everything about him was a bad idea, and yet . . .

"Then I will see you at the festival?"

She started to shake her head, to be firm in her stance that this, whatever *this* was, could not continue past this night, this morning, this very moment. "Jest . . ."

His eyebrows lifted and he looked pleased at the intimacy of his name. No Misters, no Sirs.

"You should go," she stammered.

As if she'd summoned them, footsteps sounded outside her door.

Cath spun around. The knob jiggled.

There was a soft thump behind her and

the crackle of leaves.
She glanced back and Jest was gone.

CHAPTER 22

The door opened and Mary Ann was there, her maid uniform silhouetted in the hallway light, along with a pail filled with kindling and long fireplace matches.

Mary Ann took two steps inside, heading for the fireplace on her silent servant's feet — until she spotted Catherine standing in the light of the open window.

Mary Ann screamed.

The pail dropped to the floor and toppled over with a clamor, matches scattering across the carpet.

"It's all right! It's just me!" Catherine rushed forward, waving her arms.

Mary Ann placed a hand against her mouth and stumbled against the door frame. "Cath! Goodness! What are you — good heavens, my bones jumped right out of my skin! I thought you were the Jabberwock, climbing in through the window!"

Cath shuddered as memories of the monster cascaded over her. She tried to shake them off.

"Do I look like a monster to you?" Scurrying past her, Cath glanced down the hallway and, seeing that no alarm had yet been raised from her parents' rooms, shut the door.

"What were you doing by the window?" Mary Ann said, her voice warbling. "It's freezing in here. You'll catch your death! And . . . what are you wearing? Are you dressed?"

"Hush, Mary Ann. You'll wake the whole house, if you haven't already."

Dropping to the floor, Mary Ann started scooping up the fallen contents of her pail, while Cath bustled back to the nightstand and lit an oil lamp.

Even after righting the pail, Mary Ann stayed on her knees with her hand pressed to her chest. Cath felt bad for scaring her, but also glad that she hadn't been Abigail.

"What are you doing out of bed at this hour?" Mary Ann finally asked, the hysteria gone from her voice.

"I was — I thought I heard something. Outside."

Mary Ann's eyes widened again. She stood and crossed to the window. "And you act like I'm a frightened child. It really might have been the Jabberwock, you know." She stuck her head outside and scanned the shadowed trees. "Or maybe a raccoon bandit — sneaky little things."

"Perhaps," Catherine muttered, wondering whether Jest was still out there, sneaking.

Mary Ann shut the window, then turned and eyed Catherine's dress. It was the same she'd worn to the King's garden party the day before, but the hem was now stained with tea and wet with dew and her knees were muddied where she'd scrambled through the brush to try to save the Turtle. Glancing down, Cath noticed a waxy leaf caught in the lace cuff of her sleeve. She plucked it off. Chewed her lip. Met Mary Ann's stare again.

"You heard something?" Mary Ann drawled, suddenly skeptical. "Perhaps you were having another dream."

"Perhaps?"

Mary Ann crossed her arms.

Starting to shiver, Cath hugged herself tight. "It really is quite crisp in here . . ."

It was another long, awkward moment before Mary Ann drew herself up to full height and walked with agonizing slowness toward the fireplace. Her suspicious gaze lingered on Catherine the whole time.

Cath swallowed. "Thank you, Mary Ann."

She picked at the climbing roses, listening as Mary Ann removed the fireplace grate and set up the kindling. Within minutes, a fire had sparked and taken hold.

Cath spotted the single long-stemmed rose that Jest had left on her windowsill, now forgotten on the floor. The petals were already fading. She wondered whether Mary Ann had noticed it too, and whether she'd written it off as another figment from one of Cath's dreams.

Gnawing on the inside of her cheek, she looked back at her dearest friend. The fire's orange-gold glow flickered over Mary Ann's face. Her jaw was set in annoyance, and Cath felt a twinge of guilt.

She padded to the hearth and knelt down beside Mary Ann.

"I lied," she said.

Mary Ann's lips tightened as she used the poker and wrought-iron tongs to shift the wood around in the flames.

"I didn't hear anything outside. I wasn't going to investigate some mystery." She took in a long, slow breath, filled with the scent of char and smoke, and let her memory travel back to the beginning.

A sharp glee began in the pit of her stomach and crawled its way up through her chest and burst as a smile across her mouth. She wrapped her arms around herself, trying to contain the giddiness that threatened to burst out of her.

Mary Ann was watching her now, her irritation replaced with confusion. "Cath?"

"Oh, Mary Ann," she whispered, afraid that to speak would be to wake and find that it was all another dream. "I've had such a night. I hardly know where to begin."

"At the beginning would be advisable."

Catherine looked back, past the curtains and the walls and the Crossroads, to a little hat shop filled with revelry and song . . . and also a glen where nightmares had come to life.

She shook her head. She didn't want to frighten Mary Ann with the truth of all that. She would tell her only the joyous things, so she wouldn't have to worry.

"I was invited to a tea party." She felt like she was holding a soap bubble in her palms, afraid to say too much, too quickly, or she would frighten it away.

"A tea party? With . . . the King?" Mary Ann ventured.

Catherine groaned. "No. Good gracious, no. I don't want to think about the King."

"Then who?"

"The court joker." She scrunched her

shoulders, protecting her heart. "I went to a tea party with the court joker."

The silence that followed was punctuated by the popping of wood and a tower of kindling collapsing on itself, sending a flurry of sparks up the flue. Catherine stayed hunched over, bracing herself against whatever reaction Mary Ann might have — disbelief or disappointment or a fierce scolding.

"The Joker?"

"His name is Jest."

"You mean to say . . . I don't . . . Did you go by yourself?"

Cath laughed again and sat back up, beaming at Mary Ann for a long moment, before melting back onto the ground. She spread her arms out across the carpet and kicked her shoes off so her cold toes could enjoy the fire's heat. She traced the shadows on the ceiling tiles and wondered when was the last time she'd lain on the floor. It wasn't proper. It wasn't done by young ladies.

But this viewpoint seemed just right for recounting her story.

She told Mary Ann everything — at least, everything she dared. Fainting in the gardens. Playing croquet. The rose and the rhyming Raven and the marvelous millinery.

The Hatter and his guests. Jest and the dreams and his lemon-yellow eyes.

She did not tell her about the Jabberwock and the brave Lion.

She did not tell her that Jest was a Rook for the White Queen, or that he was on a secret mission that could end a war, or that she hoped maybe she would be his reason to come back to Hearts when it was done.

When she was finished, it felt as though her heart had outgrown her body. It was the size of the house now. The size of the entire kingdom.

But Mary Ann was not sharing her smile. She was making a grid of matches on the floor, her brow drawn.

With that look, all of Cath's happiness started to crumble. She knew that look. She could bet that it was the same look she'd given to Jest when he'd stood here in this very bedroom and asked if he would see her at the Turtle Days Festival.

No matter how spectacular the night had been, it could not happen again.

Catherine propped herself up on her elbows. "I know what you're thinking, and I know you're right. The King has asked for a courtship and I've agreed to it. I would be ruined if anyone knew about tonight and I . . . It won't happen again. I'm not a fool.

Or . . . I'm going to stop being a fool. Tonight. Now."

"That isn't what I was thinking at all," Mary Ann said. "Although you're right. This would cause such a scandal — an embarrassment not only to you, but to the Marquess and the entire household."

Cath looked away.

"But what I was really thinking was that you talk about him like . . . like you talk about a piece of decadent chocolate cake."

A honk of a laugh escaped Cath before she could help it. "He is not a piece of cake!"

"No, but I can tell you're already anticipating the time you'll see him again, and you're flushed and smiling the same way you do when you're perfectly satisfied. And . . . your mother would forbid them both."

Cath swallowed, her spirits dampened.

"It's a shame you can't feel this way about the King."

"I can't."

"I know."

Cath sighed. "It won't matter. I can't do anything until this courtship is resolved." She shook her head. "And nothing has changed. It was just a single night, one fun night. I wanted to know what it was like to be . . . someone else, for once." Reaching over, she took hold of Mary Ann's hand, and pulled her down to lie on the carpet beside her. Even after all these years she was surprised to feel the calluses on her friend's palm. "What's most important is that everyone who was there tonight will be avid patrons of our bakery. They loved the macarons, every one of them. So that's what I need to be focusing on now, and that's plenty enough to be thinking about without kings and jokers and tea parties getting into the mix."

Her statement was followed by a stretched-thin quiet, before Mary Ann turned her head and gave Cath's hand a gentle squeeze. "It may be true that you can't be a baker and a lady, or a baker and a queen . . . but there is no rule that you can't be a baker and a wife. If you truly are fond of the Joker, perhaps it isn't so hopeless after all." Her brows furrowed. "That is . . . if he would still want you, if you were no longer the heir to Rock Turtle Cove."

"For shame, Mary Ann! Do you mean to say that his interest could lie more in my dowry and title, when I'm so utterly charming?" Cath said it as a joke, though there was also a sting of naïveté in the back of her thoughts. How had it not occurred to her that her family's wealth could, indeed, be his motivation?

No, she couldn't believe it. He seemed to like her. Truly, honestly like her. He had even implied that she could be reason enough for him to stay in Hearts . . . but he also knew she was being courted by His Majesty. He knew there were people who believed she was going to be the next Queen of Hearts.

And still he had dared to ask to see her again.

Did he want her, or did he want something from her?

She shook her head, shoving the thoughts away. Jest had shared a great secret with her. What reason did she have to doubt him?

"I mean to say," amended Mary Ann, "that I do not know him. And despite how willingly you've gone gallivanting about with him after dark, I am not convinced that you know him, either."

Cath hummed, thinking of the dream. His dimpled smile, receding farther and farther away. The hollowness in her chest. Her hands reaching after him, trying to take back what he had stolen, but he was always out of reach.

"You're right," she said. "I suppose I don't know him very well at all."

A Joker. A Rook. A mystery.

Perhaps she didn't know him, but she was more certain than ever that she desperately wanted to.

Chapter 23

The days that followed were among the most torturous Cath had ever known.

It became habit to check her window for white roses and peer into the tree boughs for black ravens, but there was no sign of Jest or his companion. Jest did not try to steal her away for another midnight rendezvous. Nor did he come to her door and ask to speak to her father and make a case for why he should be allowed to court her.

Which was, of course, a good thing — practically speaking. And yet she couldn't stopper the fantasies of him doing just that, and her father somehow, miraculously, impossibly agreeing to it.

The King's courtship, on the other hand, had begun in earnest, and the courtship meant constant nagging from her mother. Why hadn't His Majesty invited Catherine to another gathering? Why wasn't Catherine doing more to put herself in his path? When was he going to propose? What flowers should they choose for the bridal bouquet? On and on and on.

"Another delivery for Lady Catherine," said Mr. Penguin. Their butler was dwarfed by a humongous flower arrangement, with only his webbed feet and black coattails visible beneath.

Cath sighed and set down the book she'd been reading. A week ago she would have looked at the flowers with hope — were they from Jest? Was he thinking about her half as much as she was thinking about him?

But the gifts never were from Jest, and one look at the bouquet of red roses, red carnations, and red dahlias confirmed that this was another gift from her doting suitor.

Their courtship, thus far, had been undemanding, though mostly because Cath was avoiding him. She had dismissed a number of requests for chaperoned walks through the palace gardens, trips to the opera, and invitations to tea. As far as the King knew, she had been afflicted with a week-long headache, and she was hoping he would soon deem her too sickly to pursue further.

Her beau (as her mother called him) had made up for their lack of companionship through a constant stream of gifts. Each one filled Catherine with dread, knowing the

King could not have bestowed such generosity on anyone less grateful. Her mother, on the other hand, was delighted with each delivery.

She received cakes and pies and tarts from the palace pastry chefs, and Cath did her best not to be too critical of them . . . on the rare occasions when her mother actually let her sample the desserts at all. She received diamond earrings and ruby brooches and golden pendants, all decorated with the crown's signature hearts, as if the King's intentions weren't obvious enough. She received fine silk gloves and music boxes and even a curled lock of prickly white hair tied with a red velvet ribbon. That particularly appalling gift had even come with a poem:

> Roses are red, violets are blue,
> I would even trim my mustache for you!

She had memorized the short stanza against her will and the words had nauseated her on multiple occasions since.

Worst of all were the gifts beneath which she could envision Jest's involvement. The occasional poem that warmed her soul. The letters that touched her on a deeper level. The words that she could imagine uttered in Jest's voice, perhaps even penned by his hand . . . yet always, at their end, signed by the King.

She knew the King was seeking Jest's advice on this courtship and each of these cards was a needle in her heart. She found herself poring over those words, imagining Jest crafting them with her in mind, and pretended that he meant every word.

A painful, bittersweet reality. Jest was wooing her, but only in the name of the King.

"Our house is beginning to smell like a florist," she muttered, taking the linen card out of the newest bouquet.

"Would you like me to put it with the others, Lady Catherine?"

"Please. Thank you, Mr. Penguin." The butler left, taking the flower arrangement down to her mother's sitting room, where the only person who appreciated the bouquet could admire it.

Breaking the wax seal, Cath unfolded the letter. She kept hoping, with each new delivery, that this would be the letter in which the King would apologize and confess their courtship was not up to expectations and he was forced to end their arrangement.

She should not have allowed such optimism.

At least it wasn't one of the letters that

made her tremble, lifting off the page in Jest's voice. This one was entirely His Majesty.

To my dearest, darlingest Sweetling —

Your eyes are like ripe green apples sprinkled with cinnamon. Your skin shimmers like buttercream frosting. Your lips are a ripe raspberry. Your hair is dark chocolate melted on the castle drawbridge on a very hot day. You smell better than a loaf of fresh bread in the morning. You are more beautiful than a birthday cake. You are sweeter than ~~vanilla honey~~ vanilla and honey mixed together. With sugar on top.

Yours most ardently, with all my gushingest, ooziest admiration —

The King's signature and postscripts were in a different penmanship. This had been the case with most of the cards he'd sent. She pictured Jest, quill in hand as the King dictated the letter. Flinching from the overwrought prose, politely biting his tongue.

The King of Hearts

(Not that there are any other kings around. Especially kings that call you their Sweetling.

At least, I hope not!)

(Tee-hee-hee!)

P.S. Can I have some more tarts?

Gagging, Cath tumbled onto the divan and slid the letter into the pages of her book, hoping it would be forgotten there ever after, when a second note fell from the envelope's folds — a piece of white parchment printed with a red heart. It reminded her of the slip of confetti she'd caught in the ballroom, what seemed like ages ago.

Her heart skipped when she turned it over. The note was written in the same flourishing penmanship as the King's letter.

Dear Lady Pinkerton,

Let us fault His Majesty not for his good intentions, but only for his inability to put such longing into words. For certain your charm would turn even the most articulate of men into bumbling fools. I will beg you to think kindly on our wretched attempts to flatter one whose praises could only be spelled out in the poetry of ocean waves and the song of distant thunder.

Yours,
A most humble Joker

P.S. Can I have some more macarons?

Cath laughed, her cheeks warming. She slipped the note back into the envelope and shut the book, hiding both letters between its pages.

"You aren't going to respond to your sovereign?"

She startled, but it was only Cheshire, lounging on the windowsill overhead. She released a slow breath. "Must you always sneak up on me like that?"

"Don't flatter yourself, Lady Catherine. I sneak up on everyone like that." Lifting a back leg, Cheshire began to clean himself in an inappropriately cat-like manner.

Catherine rolled her eyes and settled into the divan again, shuffling the book pages to try and find her spot. "No, I do not intend to respond to my sovereign's letter. I am trying not to encourage his attentions as much as can be helped."

"Has that proved to be an effective technique?"

"Not terribly, but I am determined."

"It seems that so is he. What are you reading?" His exuberant smile appeared above Catherine's knee and his striped tail flicked out, lifting the book so he could see the cover. She snarled at him, but he pretended not to notice. "*Gullible's Travels?* Never heard of it."

Cath snapped the book shut — the cat barely got his tail out in time. "Are you here for a reason, Cheshire?"

"Why, yes, I would enjoy a cup of tea. I take mine with lots of cream, and no tea. Thank you."

With another sigh, Cath set down the book and headed to the kitchen. Cheshire was there waiting for her when she arrived and started to purr when she pulled a bottle of cream from the icebox.

"How is the royal courtship progressing?"

"This is the extent of it. He sends me gifts, I give them to my mother."

"How romantic." Cheshire lifted the saucer in both paws and downed the cream in a single swallow.

Catherine leaned against the counter and waited for Cheshire to finish licking his lips. "I have no need of romance," she said, before adding, quieter, "at least, not from the King."

"Yes, I've heard that you may have other prospects, though I would not have expected *you* to be thus charmed."

She stiffened. "What do you mean?"

"I had a delightful spot of milk with Haigha yesterday — he's a Hare, and mad as march, but he did recall a lovely girl in attendance at the Hatter's most recent tea party, a guest of none other than the court joker. Would you believe she had with her the most delectable macarons he had ever enjoyed? Now, who, pray tell, could he have been referring to?"

For a heartbeat, Cath thought to deny everything, but Cheshire was not the sort worth denying. Gossipmonger though he might be, he was also dedicated to obtaining reliable sources for his rumor mill.

"You won't tell anyone, will you?"

Cheshire dug a claw in between his front teeth, as if worried he might have some cream stuck there. "Who would I tell?"

"Everyone. You would tell everyone, but I'm asking you not to. Please, Cheshire. My parents —"

"Would be devastated, and the King too. The Joker would likely lose his employment, and your reputation, along with any hopes you have for a proper match, would be ruined."

"I don't care about my reputation, but I don't want to hurt my parents, or the King, or . . . or Jest."

"You should care about your reputation. You know how people are. No matter how tasty your desserts, none of our lords or ladies would deign to shop at a bakery run by a fallen woman."

She shrank away. "Cheshire. Please."

"Don't give me those puppy-dog eyes. You know how I despise puppy dogs. I won't tell anyone, though I can't make promises for the rest of the party guests. I only came to make sure you were unscathed."

She shuddered. "Haigha must have told you about the Jabberwock then."

"Yes, my dear. And the brave sacrifice of the Lion, that most noble of felines."

Cath shut her eyes against the sorrow that hit her every time she remembered the Lion's final moments. His defiant roar. His golden body braced between her and the monster.

"The Jabberwock must be stopped," she said. "First the courtiers, and now this. Surely the King is doing something?"

"Oh yes, the King is quite busy these days. Penning love letters and such."

She let out a frustrated noise. "These attacks aren't going to stop on their own. Isn't there anything we can do?"

"I don't care for that royal *we,* but I'll advise *you* to avoid any more late-night excursions. Though the loss of the Lion is tragic, I did not know him personally. Whereas you, Lady Catherine, I might actually feel compelled to miss."

"That's sweet, Cheshire. I promise to be

more careful. No more tea parties." She gulped. "And no more jokers. At least, not until I've come to a decision with the King."

Cheshire stared at her with his slitted eyes and too-many teeth.

"What?"

"You really are taken with him, aren't you?"

"I'm sure I don't know what you mean. I'm already in a courtship, you know."

"But is the King the one you wish to be courting?"

"It doesn't seem to matter what I wish." She returned the cream to the icebox. "Not who I wish to be courting, not what I wish for my future to hold."

"You have the chance to be a queen, Catherine. What else is there?"

"Oh, Cheshire, not you too. I don't want to be the Queen of Hearts. I don't understand how I'm the only one who doesn't see the appeal of it."

"But if you were the Queen, perhaps you could have your cake and eat it too."

She cocked her head. "What's the point of having cake if you can't eat it?"

"I'm only saying that you might be the King's wife, but who is to say you couldn't also have more clandestine relations with the Joker?"

Her jaw fell open and she stormed across the kitchen in a blink. "You naughty feline! How dare you suggest such a thing!" She swiped at the cat, but he disappeared and her hand met only air. Her face was strawberry red when she spun around and saw Cheshire floating above the pan rack.

"Calm yourself, dear, it was only a suggestion." He punctuated the statement with a yawn.

"It was a crude one, and I won't tolerate such an insult again." She fisted her hands on her hips. "If I am to be a wife, I will be an honest one." She cast her eyes toward the ceiling. "And you misunderstand me entirely, Cheshire. My opposition to the King is not only because I'm . . . because I may be . . . as you say, just a bit taken with the Joker . . ."

"Obviously."

"I'll beg you to not repeat it." She scowled. "My opposition is because queens do not start bakeries. And that is what I wish, what you know I have always wished."

"Ah, yes, the infamous bakery, the most wondrous bakery in all of Hearts." Cheshire's whiskers twitched. "The one that, if I'm not mistaken, is no closer to reality now than it was when you first started talking about it, how many years ago?"

She clenched her jaw. "It is closer to reality. We are closer every day."

"The Marquess has given his blessing, then?"

She turned away, the blush still burning her cheeks, and carried Cheshire's empty saucer to the pile of dishes left from that morning's breakfast. "He will," she insisted, her back to the cat, "once I ask him."

"Keep telling yourself that. You might soon start to believe it."

Frowning, she rubbed her hands on a dishcloth.

"By-the-bye, I have another piece of news I thought would interest you and that maid of yours."

She faced Cheshire again. He had begun to vanish, leaving his bulbous head floating over the pots. A moment later, one disconnected paw appeared in front of Cath's face with a sharp claw punctured through a piece of weathered parchment. A poster.

She snagged the paper away and smoothed it on the baker's table. She sniffed. "Believe it or not, Cheshire, I was already aware of the upcoming Turtle Days Festival."

"But have you seen the schedule of events?"

She scanned the list, from the dreaded lobster quadrille to a battledore tournament to eight-legged races to . . .

She gasped. "A baking contest?"

"The first annual." Cheshire's paw vanished again to, Cath guessed, reconnect with the rest of his invisible body. "Please tell me you'll make a tuna tart for the contest. *Please, please, please.*"

"Do you know what the prizes are?"

"First place wins a blue ribbon."

"Is that all?"

"Is that *all*? Ribbons are lovely, you know. Not quite as nice as a ball of yarn, but nothing to snub."

She gnawed at her lower lip.

"Oh — I suppose there was something about a purse. Twenty gold crowns, if I'm not mistaken."

"Twenty!" Her heart sped up.

With twenty gold crowns in her possession, she wouldn't have to sell her dowry. She wouldn't need a loan or permission from her parents . . .

The recognition alone would be worthwhile. A big blue ribbon hanging in the bakery's front window, and a plaque —

GRAND WINNER
OF THE FIRST ANNUAL

"I, for one, am devastated that I wasn't invited to be a judge."

"Maybe if you didn't keep requesting tuna tarts." She folded the poster and tucked it into her dress pocket. "I wonder what I'll make. Maybe an apple pie or a berry trifle or . . . oh! I know. I'll make something with pumpkin. They're so trendy these days, and just the right season for it." She tapped a finger against her lip. "Who are the judges?"

"Let me think. Jack was one, I seem to recall."

"Ugh, not the Knave. He hates me."

Cheshire's eyes widened. "Are you sure?"

"He tells me every time he sees me."

The cat made a vague noise in his throat, and Cath wondered how he could, having no throat at the moment. "If you say so. Also judging are the Duke of Tuskany and that shoemaker, Mr. Caterpillar."

"That old curmudgeon? It's amazing he can taste anything the way he smokes that hookah all the time."

"Be that as it may. Who else? Oh, a representative of the turtles, of course. Some friend of Haigha's and the Gryphon. You may have met him at the party?"

"I did. Sweet young turtle. I quite liked him, and he was fond of my macarons."

"And the last judge, in a lucky twist, is already one of your biggest fans."

"Oh?"

"In fact, he may be your biggest fan. Well . . . he may actually be one of your smallest fans, but let us not hold that against his superior judgment skills."

Her enthusiasm began to wilt. "No."

"Yes."

Cath wilted. Of course it would be the King. Of course it would be the one person she was most determined to avoid.

Chapter 24

"I do not want to be here," Mary Ann whispered as the footman helped them from the carriage.

Cath's gaze swept to the top of the black iron gate before them, all curled bars and jagged-teeth finials. Jack-O'-Lanterns were staked along the top of the gate, their grotesquely carved faces staring down at the road, strings of their internal pulp stuck to the bars underneath.

On the opposite side of the gate, acres of dark mud were spotted with vines and leaves and gourds — most were goldish-orange, but others were ghost-white or yellow-green or speckled with crimson. There were pumpkins as small as Catherine's ear and some the size of the carriage. There were smooth pumpkins and warted pumpkins, fat pumpkins and narrow, caved-in pumpkins that lay like beached whales in the mud. Fog had rolled in from the nearby forest, covering the ground in misty gray. Though Catherine was wearing her heaviest shawl, she felt chilled to the bone as she looked out onto the gloomy patch.

"I'm beginning to have second thoughts myself," she confessed.

"Let's leave," Mary Ann prodded, latching on to Catherine's doubts with renewed enthusiasm. "We'll get pumpkins at the market like everyone else. They'll probably be more cost effective anyway. Or, better yet, let's not make a pumpkin dessert at all. Why not something with peaches? Everyone likes peaches."

"Pumpkins are seasonal right now and seasonal desserts are always best. And they do say that Sir Peter's sugar pie pumpkins are the sweetest in the kingdom."

"Fine, but — why not currants? Currants are seasonal. Or apples? You make a fine apple crumble . . ."

Catherine chewed on her lower lip. "I do make a fine apple crumble," she agreed. Sighed. Roughly shook her head. "We're being silly. We're here, and I've already chosen a recipe, and we might as well get this over with. He's a farmer, isn't he? He'll be glad for our business."

"Are you sure? It's not very welcoming."

Mary Ann eyed the piked Jack-O'-Lanterns. "In fact, he could really use a business adviser."

"Too bad your expertise is already spoken for. Come on, we'll be in and out in the flutter of a hummingbird's wing." Cath inched closer to the gate. She could see a small cottage situated to the north side of the patch, with a curl of smoke coming out of the chimney and firelight flickering through the windows. "They seem to be home."

The gate squeaked on its reluctant hinges as she pushed it open.

"Oh, fine," Mary Ann muttered. "Wait one moment while I grab my bonnet." She rushed back to the carriage.

Knotting her hands together, Catherine stepped onto the path that bordered the pumpkin patch. She inhaled the smell of fresh-churned dirt and growing things, but beneath the freshness was also something akin to mold and rot. She grimaced. It was impossible to imagine anything pleasant coming from this land, but the rumors about Peter's famed pumpkins were unmistakable.

Great baking began with exceptional ingredients. And she needed to win this contest.

"I feel like we're trespassing," Mary Ann said, shutting the gate behind them.

Cath turned, about to agree, but stopped short. Mary Ann's bonnet was one she'd never seen before. Simple but beautiful, made of crisp blue-dyed muslin that matched Mary Ann's eyes. It was tied with a sunflower-yellow ribbon.

"You have a new bonnet."

"Yes, I bought it yesterday. At Hatta's Marvelous Millinery." Mary Ann looped the ribbons into a bow.

Cath's eyes widened. "You didn't!" she said, trying to imagine Mary Ann browsing through the shop where she'd drank tea and stood on the table and cowered from a monster attack.

"What?" said Mary Ann, grinning cheekily. "I simply had to see it after you told me about the tea party. Besides, it's hardly your secret to keep. All the town's gossip has been about the extraordinary new hat shop. Now there's a man who knows how to market to his customers. What do you think?"

"It's . . . lovely," Cath answered. "You're lovely in it."

Mary Ann shrugged modestly. "It's by no means the most elaborate piece that was on display, but the moment I saw it I felt like it was just right. Wearing it makes me feel almost . . ." She hesitated a long moment. Too long.

"What?" Cath prodded.

Mary Ann looked away. "Whimsical," she murmured.

It took Catherine a moment to realize her friend was blushing.

Mary Ann never blushed.

"Whimsical," Cath repeated.

"It's silly, I know. But you're always dreaming of roses and lemon trees, and the Marquess has such a grand imagination when it comes to the stories he tells, and even Cheshire is passionate over tuna and cream. Whereas, to me, life is all numbers and logic. Profit and loss. Practical and safe. I thought it might be nice to let myself just . . . dream. For once." She fidgeted with a yellow ribbon. "With this hat, it seems possible. Why" — her eyes brightened — "this morning, I even had a fantasy that I'd single-handedly balanced the budget for the royal treasury, and all of Hearts saw me as a hero."

Cath shook her head, baffled. "Had some villain knocked the budgie off balance?"

"Never mind that. It was the hero part that was important. All my life, I never dreamed I could be anything but a maid, just plain old me."

"Oh, Mary Ann." Cath pulled her into an embrace. "I never knew you felt that way. I would share all my dreams with you if I could."

"I know, Cath. And you do. You share the most important dream with me . . . our dream."

Cath smiled. "Yes, and this is the beginning of it. These pumpkins, this baking contest, and those twenty gold crowns. Of course, I'll need my brilliant business partner to tell me what to do with those crowns once we have them. I would be sure to make horrible decisions if left to my own devices."

"You would," said Mary Ann, without apology. "But have no fear. The bonnet doesn't seem to affect my head for basic mathematics."

"Good. Then let's go find the best pumpkins in this patch, shall we?"

They picked their way toward the cottage, their boots squishing into the ankle-deep mud. To their right, they passed a picket fence — or what had once been a picket fence — though now it looked more like a series of uneven, half-rotted wooden boards with crackled, peeling paint. It surrounded a smaller patch, set off from the farm's main acreage, bearing signs of recent destruction and still smelling of smoke. Charred vines piled on top of one another, blackened stumps that may have once been pumpkins, blistered paint where flame had touched the fence boards. This corner of the patch looked abandoned.

The dirt path turned to loose gravel and weeds as they approached the cottage. Their footsteps crunched in the eerie quiet.

Cath plastered on a friendly smile and knocked on the door. They waited, their shoulders pressed together for warmth, but the only noise inside was the pop and crackle of a lonely fireplace. Catherine knocked again, harder, but was met with more silence.

After a third knock, she began to wonder if Peter Peter and his wife weren't home after all. She took a step back and searched the windows, but they were hung with a mesh of pumpkin vines.

"I suppose they're not home," Mary Ann said, sagging with relief.

Catherine scanned the patch. The pumpkins were like baubles disappearing into the fog. She had half a mind to grab a few and run.

"Do you hear that?" said Mary Ann.

Catherine cocked her head and listened.

A faint noise — sawing, she thought, the back-and-forth grate of teeth ripping through wood.

"Let's go see." She ducked away from the cottage door.

"Must we?" Mary Ann whined, but she followed Cath anyhow, through a tangle of vines that had overgrown their row and crossed over the mud-squelching path.

Rounding to the back of the cottage, Cath spotted a pair of lanterns flickering off the limbs of the encroaching forest, silhouetting the shells of two enormous pumpkins.

They were the biggest pumpkins she'd ever seen. Their severed stems were the width of tree trunks and their orange flesh reached the same height as the cottage's roof. The pumpkin farthest from them had even been carved to look like a building of sorts, with tiny square windows cut from its flesh and an iron pipe sticking out through the ceiling that could have been a chimney.

Peter Peter was standing on a rickety ladder against the second pumpkin, pushing a saw back and forth through its shell. He was dressed in filthy overalls and sweating, every muscle straining as he pushed the saw in and out, out and in. Watery orange liquid oozed from the cut and dripped down the pumpkin's side.

Afraid to startle him, Catherine and Mary Ann waited until he'd finished the cut. Hanging the saw from a hook on the ladder, he pushed at the pumpkin's shell, forcing a tall, thin piece of flesh into the gourd. It left a window barely wider than Catherine's hand. Inside she could see the stringy guts and seeds dangling from the pumpkin's ceiling. The smell of fresh-cut squash rolled over them.

Covering her mouth, Catherine coughed.

Peter turned so fast he nearly slipped off the ladder, but caught himself on a vine that hung down the pumpkin's side.

"What're you doing here?" he barked.

"Good day, Sir Peter," said Catherine, curtsying. "We're so sorry to bother you, but I was hoping I might be able to purchase some of your famed sugar pie pumpkins. I'm entering the baking contest at tomorrow's Turtle Days Festival and I have my heart set on making a spiced pumpkin cake."

Peter glared at them and Cath had the horrible vision of him sawing them both into pieces.

She shuddered. Mary Ann glanced sideways at her, and Catherine brightened her smile to hide the horrifying thoughts in her head.

Grabbing the saw, Peter scrambled so fast to the ground Catherine was surprised he didn't send the ladder flopping into the mud. His eyes darted between them with a discomforting intensity, a barely restrained madness. Catherine and Mary Ann both drew startled steps backward.

"I didn't ask you here! You're not welcome, and I'm not about to do business with entitled, condescending trollops like you, what think you're better than me, no matter I been knighted by the King himself, right as anyone. You want a sugar pie pumpkin, you can grow it yourself, get your own pretty hands all dirtied up for once."

Heart hammering, Catherine stumbled back another step, pulling Mary Ann with her. Her eyes kept darting to the saw and its rusted teeth.

"I . . . I'll beg of you," Mary Ann stammered, looking almost bricky with her newfound heroism, "not to speak of m-my lady in such a —"

Catherine tightened her grip on Mary Ann's elbow, silencing her. Mary Ann seemed relieved to be silenced. "I am sorry to have intruded on your privacy, *sir,* but if I've shown less than a tablespoon of respect for you, it's because of the shameful attitude with which you conduct yourself." Though her legs felt weak, Catherine held her ground, refusing to be cowed by ill manners. "I was under the impression that this pumpkin patch was open for business and if you'll behave with decency, I do wish to be a patron of yours."

Peter bared his teeth at her, which did cow her somewhat.

"I — I don't wish to take up too much of your time, but I am willing to pay your price if you'll just show me where the sugar pie pumpkins are. We could harvest our own —"

She was cut off by a loud thump. She jumped and glanced past Peter, to the pumpkin already carved with slitted windows. The thump was followed by scratching, nails carving into rotting wood. The sound reminded her of Cheshire sharpening his claws on her mother's finest upholstery.

Beside her, Mary Ann squeaked.

"What was that?" Cath asked.

"What's *what*?" Peter said, though Cath was certain he must have heard it too. His question was followed by a breathy snort from the pumpkin shell, like a horse struggling against its bit.

"Is there something . . . ?" Catherine took a step toward the pumpkin, but Peter put himself in her path. He was as big and unmovable as a boulder.

"Were my uneducated words not clear enough for all your fancy learning?" he said. "I do believe I told you to get off my land."

"But —"

"Catherine." Mary Ann tugged at her elbow. "He doesn't want our business. Let's just go."

Cath ground her teeth, meeting Peter's glare with one of her own, part of her wanting to shake off Mary Ann and slap this man for his crude behavior, the other part of her grateful for Mary Ann's intrusion and a reason to leave.

She glanced once more at the large pumpkin, which had fallen silent. She allowed the tiniest of respectful nods. "I'm sorry to have bothered you. Please give Lady Peter my regards."

"I'll give her no such thing," he growled, but Catherine pretended not to hear him as she and Mary Ann began picking their way back along the gravel path, pebbles and beetles scattering in their wake.

It was not until they had turned the cottage corner again that Mary Ann let out a strained breath. She took to tying knots into her new bonnet's yellow ribbons. "That's the last time I let you drag me here," she said. "The very last time."

"That won't be a problem. What a horrible, horrible man. And that strange noise — what could it have been?"

"An animal of some sort, I'd guess," said Mary Ann, shaking her head. "With those windows cut into it, the pumpkin reminded me of a cage. But why would anyone keep a pet inside a giant pumpkin?"

They passed by the scorched picket fence and Cath's eye caught on a spot of orange amid the wreckage. She came to a halt.

Mary Ann turned back. "What?"

"I think I saw . . ." She hesitated. "Wait here."

The fence was short enough that she could climb over it when she lifted her skirts.

"Cath!" Mary Ann glanced back toward the cottage. "What are you doing?"

"One moment." She picked her way through the squishing mud and scattered ashes, the coils of burnt vines. A pile of brush was in the corner, vines and leaves hacked to pieces. They all but crumbled in her hand as she pushed them to the side, uncovering the small orange pumpkin that had caught her eye.

A sugar pie pumpkin, with bright, unblemished skin and not a wart in sight. It was a beautiful, dazzling survivor amid the destruction.

Beaming, she dug the kitchen knife from her boot — she'd come prepared to harvest her own in case Peter proved less than helpful — and hacked away the sturdy green vine that tethered the pumpkin to its smashed kindred.

Cradling the dirt-smudged pumpkin against her dress, Catherine picked her way back through the ashes and hauled herself over the fence.

"Are you mad?" Mary Ann asked. "He'll kill us if he notices it missing."

"He won't notice. This patch was obviously meant to be destroyed. And look." She held the pumpkin up in the dim light breaking through the fog. "It's perfe— ow!" Something hard and sharp jabbed her through the thin sole of her boot. "What was that?"

Mary Ann leaned over, bracing herself on her knees, and picked something out of the mud with a slurp. Whatever Cath had stepped on, it was small, small enough to fit into Mary Ann's palm.

She held it aloft. "A . . . pony?"

Cath inched closer, trying to keep the weight off her throbbing foot. Her eyes widened. The tiny pony was run through with a metal peg, hints of gold paint visible beneath the filth. “A carousel pony,” she murmured, unable to meet Mary Ann’s eye. For she recognized it, sure as salt.

It was from the Lion’s carousel hat, the one he’d been wearing the night of the Hatter’s tea party. The one he’d been wearing when the Jabberwock had carried him into the night.

Chapter 25

Catherine awoke the morning of the festival with dried cake batter under her nails and a smear of frosting discovered behind one ear. It had been well after midnight by the time her spiced pumpkin cake had cooled enough to be frosted.

Though she was anxious about the contest, she wasn't afraid. She and Mary Ann had done a test run with a pumpkin from the market, and that first cake had been exactly what she'd hoped it would be — moist and rich, with hints of nutmeg and brown sugar mixed together with sweet roasted pumpkin that melted lusciously in the mouth, all layered with velvety, decadent cream cheese frosting and — on a whim — she had topped it off with shreds of toasted coconut, adding a hint of crunch and extra sweetness.

She'd been pleased with the trial cake and, after making a few minor adjustments, she was confident that the final product would be even more extraordinary.

Catherine could not wait to see the judges' faces when they tried it. Even the King's.

She didn't have to wear a formal gown, as the festival took place on the sandy, rocky beach and she would most likely be cold and wet by the end of it. But as her family was hosting the annual celebration, she was still expected to don a corset and a full-skirted wool dress that her mother picked out, emerald green and showing more décolletage than she would have liked. She did her best to hide it with a crocheted lace wrap that clung to her neck and shoulders, fastened with an amber medallion. When Catherine saw her reflection, she couldn't help but think of Jest, and how the amber brooch was almost the same color as his eyes.

The festival was well underway when Catherine and her parents arrived. Their carriage stopped at the top of the white cliffs, with the festival laid out on the shore below. Enormous tents cluttered the beach, their canvas walls painted in harlequin diamonds and stripes and plaids, their pennant flags snapping in the wind. Within the tents were pottery and paintings, pearl necklaces and windup toys, crocheted stockings and hand-stitched books that would forever have pages curled from the salty air.

From atop the cliffs she spied the beluga whale a cappella quartet harmonizing on the beach, and a sizeable crowd awaiting the start of the first seahorse race, and an octopus face-painter industriously painting eight faces at once. Then there were the tents that held Catherine's favorite part of the festival: carnival food. She could already smell the oil and garlic and applewood smoke. Her stomach rumbled. She'd intentionally skipped breakfast in anticipation of her most beloved festival treats — a savory meat pie, cinnamon-roasted pecans, and a soft sticky bun, the type that melted on her tongue and coated her lips in honey and crushed walnuts.

It was a treacherous climb down the steps that led to the beach, made more so as Catherine kept scanning the crowds below rather than keeping her focus on the path. Her eye skipped over the lobsters and crabs and starfish and walruses and dodo birds and flamingos and frogs and salamanders and pigeons. She was looking only at the people. She was looking for a black tunic and a tri-pointed jester's hat. She was listening for the telltale jingle of tiny bells. She was expecting a crowd circled around a performer, mesmerized and awed by some breathtaking spectacle.

But she reached the sandy shore without seeing any sign of Jest. In fact, she had not seen the King, either. Perhaps they would arrive together.

The Marquess and Marchioness wandered off to greet their high-society guests, leaving Catherine to explore the tents. She bought her meat pie first, hoping it would settle some of her nerves. Success — the moment she broke apart the flaky crust and breathed in the cloud of seasoned steam, she did feel calmer. A euphoric, drool-inducing calm.

It was a brisk, gray day on the beach, the wind catching at her shawl, but none of the creatures of Hearts seemed anything but jolly. The Marchioness had been a bundle of fears the day before. Word had spread fast after Catherine had told Cheshire about finding the pony from the Lion's hat, and a search party was sent to scour the areas surrounding the farm for any more signs of the Lion or the Jabberwock, but they'd found nothing. A theory was posed that the Jabberwock might be sheltering itself inside the Nowhere Forest, and the pony had fallen as the monster carried the Lion over the pumpkin patch.

With tales of the Jabberwock renewed, the

Marchioness had worried that people would stay locked up in their homes during the festival, but her concerns seemed unfounded. The crowd bustled and thrived. Catherine smiled her way through the familiar faces, but her mind was distracted, her eyes always searching for the one person she wanted to see.

None of the usual jewels and baubles held any interest to her, though her purse was jangling with coins her father had spared her that morning. Even the spice shop, with its exotic aromas and unusual ingredients, did not capture her enthusiasm as it usually did.

Wishing for a distraction, she headed for the largest tent, where the contest would be held. Mary Ann had brought the cake with her when she and the other servants had come to finish last-minute preparations, and Catherine hadn't seen her creation since the night before.

In the grandstand tent, the chairs were empty but for a few geese resting their wings after the long migration to make it to the festival on time. Catherine passed through the rows and up to the case that held the entries, and there, on the second shelf, three desserts from the left, sat her spiced pumpkin cake, the icing scalloped on the sides and woven like a basket on top. A tiny white ghost pumpkin was settled into the snowdrifts of toasted coconut — Mary Ann's idea.

She scanned their competition. It was mostly an assortment of fruit pies, a chocolate torte, two dessert puddings, and a small cake with EAT ME spelled out in currants on top. None were so pretty as hers, but that meant nothing for their taste.

"I believe in you, little cake," she whispered to her creation. "I believe you're the best." She hesitated. "I believe *we're* the best."

Feeling more anxious than comforted, she hurried from the tent. She had just turned down the main row of shops, her sweet tooth awakened and dreaming of those cinnamon-roasted nuts, when someone grabbed the brim of her bonnet and pulled it off her head. The ribbon caught on her chin and it fell, hanging down her back.

She spun around as another, heavier hat was placed on her head.

Hatta stepped back and crossed his arms, looking not at her but at the hat now atop her head. He looked too refined for the damp, dirty surroundings, done up in a formal-cut navy suit and an orange-and-purple-striped waistcoat. His white hair peeked out from a matching orange-and-purple top hat. A candy stick dangled from his thoughtfully down-turned mouth.

"Hello again," said Cath.

He tipped his hat to her, swirling the candy stick around to the other side of his lips. "Milady."

Catherine reached up for the wide brim of the hat he had set on her head, but he stopped her. "Ah-ah," he said, taking hold of her hand and sweeping her up the steps. "There's a mirror back here."

She realized with a start that she was in the Hatter's shop, the same rickety traveling wagon she'd seen in the forest, with the hand-lettered sign over the door: HATTA'S MARVELOUS MILLINERY. She couldn't imagine how she hadn't spotted it earlier among the tents.

One window, she noticed, was still broken from the Jabberwock's attack, now boarded over with uneven planks and iron nails.

Like before, the shop was larger on the inside than the out, but now the long table and mismatched chairs were gone, replaced with an assortment of display cases and hat stands and mannequin heads, two of which were having a discussion about fashionable cameo necklaces. The collection of hats had multiplied. There were top hats with ear holes cut out for bunny rabbits. There were waterproof hats for dolphins and sunbathing hats for lizards and acorn-stashing hats for squirrels. There were veils made from ostrich feathers and modest bonnets encrusted in rhinestones and one netted hat that would have draped over a person's body like an enormous birdcage.

Beyond the bizarre and unexpected, there were also simple things, lovely things. Dainty coronets done up in gold and pearls. Wide-brimmed garden hats covered in soft moss and chiming bluebells. Silk headdresses ornamented with intricately spun spiderwebs.

As Catherine passed, admiring them all, Hatta reached for the tie of her bonnet and pulled it off her neck. She spotted a standing mirror in the corner, shining with the light of a lantern on the wall.

Crossing the room, she stood before the mirror and promptly started to laugh.

The Hatter had made for her a replica of a rose macaron. Two meringue cookies were made from cream-colored muslin and speckled with pink sparkles, and the sweet buttercream filling was constructed from layer upon layer of gathered lace.

It was ridiculous and unflattering in every way. Cath loved it immediately.

"Good heavens, Hatta. And here I thought you didn't like me."

"My gifts by their nature do not equal affection, milady." In the mirror, she saw him scowl. "Rather, let us say that I was inspired by your performance."

She turned to face him. "So you don't like me?"

"I like you well enough." His purple eyes glinted. "I like you better when you're wearing one of my hats. What do you think?"

She looked at her reflection and couldn't help but laugh again. "It's like nothing I've ever worn before." Reaching up, she squeezed the bottom cookie and found that it was soft and squishable. "I'm quite fond of it, actually."

"Good. It's yours."

"No, no, I couldn't —" She pulled the hat off her head, surprised at how light it was, despite its girth.

Hatta scoffed. "I said it's yours, so it's yours. You can't give it back once it's been given. Now put it back on before your head gets cold. I hate to see bare heads."

"If you insist." She resisted a smile as she settled the macaron hat back onto her head. Remembering the coins in her purse, she asked, "Can I at least pay you for it?"

"Now you're just being rude. Consider it

an apology, Lady Pinkerton, for the way my humble gala ended in such terror. I usually seek to send my guests home without first endangering their lives."

"Surely the attack was not your fault."

He held her gaze a long moment, before replying, "I am glad to see that you made it home safely, Lady Pinkerton."

"As I did. Thank you for the gift, Hatta. It will be cherished." She glanced at the mirror one more time. It was impossible not to grin. "There has been a lot of talk about your creations lately. It seems you're earning a grand reputation."

"Reputations are fickle. Profits are not."

She smirked. "That's something my maid would say." Cath turned to face him. "It's an impressive feat, is all I meant, to become so popular so quickly. Your hats are marvelous indeed."

"I appreciate the compliment. I daresay Hearts was without a proper hatter for far too long."

"Perhaps you're right." Cath glanced around at the hats and headdresses that lined the walls. A rainbow of colors, a kaleidoscope of styles, a jamboree of textures. Every one of them seemed half magical. "I vaguely recall one other fine hatter, years ago, when I was just a child. My mother purchased from him regularly. I wonder whatever became of him."

"He went mad," said Hatta, with hardly a pause. "Then he killed himself. With a brim tolliker if my memory serves."

She turned back to gape at him. Hatta was watching her, but his expression was unreadable.

"Haven't you ever heard the saying, 'mad as a hatter'?" he asked. "It's an unfortunate family trait, one that's been passed down for generations."

Her lips pursed into a surprised O, but Cath couldn't form a question or an apology, though both lingered on her tongue.

Finally, Hatta tsked her. "Don't stand there looking so tragic, love. My father, and his father, and so many fathers back that one could never count them all. Every one a fine, gentlemanly hatter, and every one mad as march. But" — his mouth curved into a sly smile — "I know a secret they didn't know, so perhaps my fate isn't as hopeless."

Cath forced her mouth shut. Now that he had reminded her of the story, she could recall the tale of the hatter who had killed himself so many years ago. Why — Hatta must have been just a boy. But, like all tragedies in Hearts, it had been hushed and swept away, never to be spoken of again.

Her confusion increased when she thought of Jest's tale. She had assumed Hatta was from Chess too, but how could he be from Chess and Hearts both?

"May I know the secret?" she asked.

He looked appalled to have been asked. "You do know that telling a secret destroys its secrecy, don't you?"

"I figured as much." She wondered, faintly, if there really was a secret at all, or if telling himself so was a part of his inherited madness.

Was he mad already? She couldn't help inspecting him, newly speculative and curious. He didn't seem mad. No more mad than anyone else she knew. No more mad than she was herself.

They were all a *little* mad, if one was to be forthright.

"Well," she said, trying to push her thoughts back toward civilized conversation, "I'm glad to see your hat shop doing so well. I'm wishing the best for you."

"Wishes have value, Lady Pinkerton. You have my gratitude." He tipped his hat toward her. "If it isn't presumptuous of me, might I suggest wearing the macaron during the baking contest? I trust you're a participant."

"Oh — I am, actually."

"Good." He leaned closer. "Have you ever noticed how attraction is a subjective thing, difficult to capture in headwear, but *charisma,* now, that is more universal. I think I've accomplished something spectacular. One might even say you look irresistible right now, not unlike the treat that inspired the hat." He winked, though Cath wasn't sure what the wink meant.

"I'm not sure I had noticed that," she confessed.

He shrugged. "Others will, I assure you."

His statement was punctuated by a trumpet blaring from the beach, reminding Cath that she was still at her family's festival, and she still had the role of the Marquess's daughter to play.

Her dread returned tenfold. "Forgive me, but I must go dance the lobster quadrille."

"Ah yes." Hatta drifted his hand through the air. "Obligations rest heavy on the shoulders of nobility."

She couldn't tell whether he was insulting her or not. "Heavier than you might think. Thank you again for the gift."

"Will you wear it during the dancing also? I'm sure you'll be at the very center of attention, and a businessman couldn't complain over the attention."

Cath pulled the hat more firmly onto her head. "Hatta, I'm not sure I shall ever take it off."

He bowed. "Then off you go. And please, if you happen to see His Majesty, I hope you'll give him my regards."

She stumbled halfway to the door. "His Majesty?"

Hatta's violet eyes glinted. "The King of Hearts, love? I thought you knew him, but as you look so surprised, I must have been mistaken." He held his hands out in supplication. "Nevertheless, your path is more likely to cross with him than is mine, and I wouldn't complain of a kind reference put forth to our sovereign." His smile turned wry. "After all, I am a man of ambitions, Lady Pinkerton."

Chapter 26

The day had warmed, tempting the festival guests down to the shore with its foaming waves and rocky outcroppings. Knowing that she was already too late to join the opening ceremonies, Cath did her best to dodge in between the conch shells that stood twice her height on the damp shore and the swarms of people as they drifted toward the beach, leaving the vibrant tents with their flapping pennants behind.

She noticed an inordinate number of guests wearing Hatta's creations. It was easy to spot them in the crowd, with their elegant shapes and peculiar embellishments. She recalled Mary Ann telling her how popular his hats were becoming, but she hadn't been ready to believe it. It had seemed, at the time, that Hatta's Marvelous Millinery was *her* discovery, her special memory, but word had spread fast through the fashionable circles of Hearts.

On the constructed platform on the center-most beach, her father, the Marquess, was already halfway through telling the story of how the first Turtle Days Festival had come to be. Catherine loved the story, and loved even more the way her father told it. She was sad that she had missed hearing it from the beginning.

The legend was that her many-greats-grandmother, when she was young and beautiful and poor, had one day led a troupe of dancing turtles and lobsters into the throne room of the then King and Queen of Hearts. Under the girl's guidance, the creatures had danced a ballet that was awkward and preposterous, yet the girl's narration of the dance turned it into something spectacular. The dance told the story of a lobster and a turtle who fell deeply in love despite the impossibility of such a match. They battled through numerous trials and obstacles to be together, finally claiming their eternity of joy.

Her grandmother's telling of the story was so honest and heartfelt that, by its end, the dance had driven both the King and Queen to tears. They cried so hard that the throne room flooded and overflowed from the cliffs, and that was how Rock Turtle Cove came to be.

In her delight, the Queen granted the girl a mansion and the title of Marchioness.

From then on, that gift of storytelling had been passed through every generation that grew up in the manor off Rock Turtle Cove, and the talent had entertained countless kings and queens who sat on the throne. Cath's father was no exception. When Cath was a child, her father had told her stories every night as she lay in bed. Stories of faraway lands and mythical creatures, daring adventures and happy endings. As she grew, she had tried to replicate her father's skill. She practiced with her dolls first, and Mr. and Mrs. Snail in the garden, and Cheshire. She thought for sure that she, too, would be an amazing storyteller, as all her family before her.

The first time she'd told one of her stories to her father, he cried. Not because her tale was so poignant, but because Cath's telling of it was so ghastly.

The misery of her father's disappointment had haunted her for two long years, until the morning she'd stumbled down into the kitchen and watched their cook prepare a sweet potato pie, and Cath discovered a new passion.

"— the tale of Marchioness Pinkerton, may she rest ever in a piece of cake," her father was proclaiming from the stage, his voice flowing over the shore as easily as the crashing waves, and holding the crowd in raptures, "began to spread throughout the kingdom. Men and creatures alike came from far and wide to hear the Marchioness recount the story of the turtle and the lobster. Their forbidden romance. Their impossible match. The love that resulted in an age of peace between all the creatures of the land and sea."

Catherine glanced around, unsurprised to find tears glistening in the eyes of those beside her. She had cried at this tale so often as a child that sometimes just hearing the word *lobster* made her feel soft and pliant on the inside.

Not today, though. Today she heard *lobster* and knew that the opening dance was coming. Her dread deepened.

"As the people of the kingdom arrived in droves, a unity formed among those who had heard the Marchioness tell her tale of woe and wonder, and a nightly celebration began among those who had made an encampment on the beaches of Rock Turtle Cove. There was singing and dancing and revelry and bonfires, every night! The people shared with one another their food and their stories, and a great companionship thrived."

Cath heard a sniffle beside her and looked down. She startled upon recognizing the Turtle from Hatta's tea party, wearing the same bowler hat he'd worn at the party, embellished with a green satin ribbon. Tears were flowing from his eyes.

Cath dug a handkerchief from her purse and handed it to the young thing, who thanked her and pulled his head back into his shell, leaving the hat perched on top. His disappearance was soon followed by a nose-emptying honk.

She wanted to lean closer and whisper to him that she was glad he was all right, glad that he'd made it to the Crossroads that night when the Jabberwock had attacked, but he seemed already distraught enough to go about reminding him of such horrors.

"As the years passed," her father went on, "the Marchioness decided to honor the gathering on the beaches of Rock Turtle Cove, and she declared a day of celebration, a day in which all of Hearts' creatures were invited to remember the love of two unlikely beasts, and the happiness their love brought to the kingdom."

As her father finished, the crowd applauded. The Turtle appeared again and tried to pass Cath's handkerchief back to her, but she smiled and suggested he keep it — just in case he needed it again.

She braced herself for what was to come next, her throat as dry as if she'd eaten a handful of sand. She paced her breaths, trying to calm her jitters.

"Here to dance the lobster quadrille, our first dance of the day, I present to you all my darling, my dear, my joy — my daughter, Catherine."

Cath stepped out of the crowd. Excitement thrummed around her, but she did her best not to look at any of the faces she passed. Once she'd climbed onto the driftwood stage, her father held up his hands for silence. "Please clear the beach so the dancing can commence! Participating dancers, you may take your places!"

The audience pulled back, making way for the dancers, though most of the sea creatures needed no prompting as they hastened to their places. The orchestra, too, was already set up against the cliffs. That left only the jellyfish to be cleared away, and a team of walruses were there in seconds, shovels in hand, to make quick work of the job.

Catherine loved the festival and the story, but as traditions went, she hated this one. Her mother had passed the responsibility on to Catherine when she was eleven years old, and, as with every year, she and her partner would be the only humans among the seals and crabs and dolphins.

Catherine did not despise dancing, but she did despise being first, being watched, being judged. She was always sure that she was one dance step away from making a dunce of herself. She could still recall how her stomach had tied into knots that first year. How her palms had sweat, despite the cold. It seemed worse every year, especially as her body had matured and she'd been forced to dance with potential suitors, rather than the sweet-meaning gentlemen of the court who laughed like kindly grandfathers as they swung her through the air.

Only a handful of jellyfish remained on the beach when she felt the faint tickle of a fingertip tracing the back of her wrist.

Cath jumped and spun around, but Jest had already pulled back. His attention dropped as he pulled black gloves onto his hands. "Good day, Lady Pinkerton," he said, too casual. He was dressed in his usual motley, the black heart dripping from the kohl around his eyes. If it hadn't been for the faintest hint of redness in his cheeks she would have thought she'd imagined the touch, but she knew she hadn't. Her entire arm was still tingling.

"Good day, Sir Joker," she said, suddenly breathless.

The corners of his mouth twitched and he met her gaze, before his eyes skipped up to the macaron hat. "I take it you've been to see Hatta."

She reached up to give the hat a squeeze, liking the lightness of it more and more as the soft insides contoured to her head. "He's very clever."

"He certainly likes to think so." Jest inhaled sharply, and she noticed that his eyes were troubled, still looking at the hat. "Did he say what it does?"

"The hat? I'm not sure it does anything." She listed her head to the side, but the hat was snug enough that it didn't shift. "Unless you are going to teach me the trick with the White Rabbit."

He was shaking his head, but it was a subtle movement. "Hatta's creations are far from ordinary. And you look . . ." He hesitated.

Cath raised her eyebrows and watched his Adam's apple bob.

"Today, you seem rather . . ."

She folded her hands patiently in front of her skirt. She could see him biting back his words. Considering and reconsidering before, finally, he said, "You are a pleasure to look on, is all, Lady Pinkerton." He pointed his chin past Catherine's shoulder, disappointment clouding his expression. "As your beau will no doubt tell you as well."

"My b— oh."

Catherine heard the King first, his giggles loud over the chatter of the audience, and her dread returned. She turned to see the King of Hearts bobbling across the sandy dance floor.

Her pulse galloped. She had not been in the King's presence since he'd asked to court her. She wanted to turn and run, but she had already been spotted. The King scurried toward her and pulled himself up onto the stage.

"Good day to the most pretty, precious, and p- . . . p- . . ."

"Provisional?" Jest supplied.

"Provisional lady in all the land!" Then the King hesitated, not sure if the description was fitting or not.

Cath cast the Joker a cool look. He grinned.

The King shook his uncertainty away. "I must say, that is a very fine hat you're wearing, Lady Pinkerton. Why, you look almost good enough to eat — *my sweet*!" His face was full of blushes and frivolity, and all the horrible lines of poetry written into his cards over the past week came whirring back through Catherine's head.

She curtsied and tried to be flattered. "You're too kind, Your Majesty. Are you enjoying the festival?"

"I am indeed!" He jigged in place, his face all joyful anticipation. "It's all very good fun. Just what the kingdom needed, I daresay."

She inclined her head. "It is nice to have some merriment during these dark times. I'm sure you've heard that the Jabberwock attacks have continued." A shiver caught hold of her shoulders as she thought of the little carousel pony in the pumpkin patch. "And his latest victim, a courageous Lion —"

The King held up his hands, backing away as if *she* were the monster. "Please, I beg of you, my darling, let's not speak of it. I break out in hives every time that horrid creature is mentioned." He pulled away the collar of his cloak to reveal a newly developing rash.

Cath frowned. "But you are doing something about it, aren't you? I've thought that perhaps you should hire a knight or a monster slayer. In the stories, there was always some brave soul that volunteered to slay the Jabberwock, and that seemed to go rather well, judging from all the ballads that came out of it. Well, I suppose it didn't go very well for the Jabberwock, but all things considered —"

"Oh, oh!" The King clapped. "The lobster quadrille is about to begin! I've been eager for it all morning!"

Cath paused. "Yes, any moment now, I suspect."

The King was sweating profusely, not meeting her eyes. She recognized shame in his expression, but it only annoyed her. Silly or not, clever or not, he was the King of Hearts. He should be doing something about the Jabberwock, shouldn't he?

She sighed. "I take it you'll be watching the quadrille, Your Majesty?"

"I wouldn't miss it," he said, only too happy to look at her now that she wasn't pressuring him about the attacks. His eyes glittered.

She envied the ostriches, wishing she could bury her head beneath the sand.

When she didn't say anything more, the King's expression turned halfway pleading. "Have you yet . . . chosen a dance partner? For the quadrille?"

Guilt scratched at her. Cath felt as heavy with it as if her dress had been soaked through with seawater. Jest's presence lingered in the corner of her eyes, as tempting as fresh vanilla ice cream, but she did her best to ignore him.

"Not yet, Your Majesty."

His eyes brightened again.

And for a moment — just a moment — Catherine imagined turning to Jest and holding her hand out to him and asking if he would do her the honor of dancing the lobster quadrille.

She pictured her parents' baffled expressions, the surprised murmur of the crowd, Jest's sure hands on her waist, and she bit her tongue against a burble of glee.

"Your Majesty, good day! What a profound pleasure this is."

The fantasy crumbled away as her mother nudged in between her and the King.

She recoiled.

"Good day, Lady Pinkerton!"

They shared the requisite greetings, her mother's curtsy far grander than Catherine's had been. Catherine inspected her own feet, knowing that to look up would be to look at Jest — his magnetism was stronger by the moment.

"My darling Catherine, we are ready for the dancing to begin."

She peered up at her mother's fervent,

impatient face.

"Have you chosen a partner, my sweet daughter?"

She shook her head. "No, Mother. Not yet."

"Well then." Her mother's eyes were sharp. "We'd better make a choice, hadn't we? We don't want to keep everyone waiting." The Marchioness clasped her fingers beneath her bosom while Catherine worked her fists into the heavy wool of her skirt. Her mother's eyes widened at her, lacking subtlety.

Catherine inhaled and met the gaze of the King. His hopefulness was painful to look at, though, and her eyes skipped upward to Jest.

Jest. The court joker. Who seemed to be *laughing* at her.

Well — not literally, but his lips were pressed in an attempt to contain the laughter that was so very obvious behind his twitching mouth.

Indignation flared behind her sternum. Jest knew that the King desperately wanted to be asked. He knew that the Marchioness desperately wanted Cath to ask him. He knew that Cath was equally as desperate not to.

Once again, it seemed her palpable discomfort was a source of amusement to him.

Lifting her chin, Cath turned back to the King, then promptly lowered her chin once more to meet his eye. "Your Majesty," she said, "would you do me the great honor of being my dancing partner for the lobster quadrille?"

The King squealed. "Oh, yes, yes, I would be *delighted,* Lady Catherine. I do enjoy a quadrille, I must say!"

With some relief at the decision being made, for what it was worth, she threaded her arm through the King's elbow.

Before they could leave the platform, Jest craned his head toward her and whispered, "He means well, Lady Pinkerton."

She stared at him, long enough to see that his amusement had vanished, taking his confidence with it. In that moment, he looked vulnerable and maybe even disappointed, though he tried to smile. Tried to be encouraging.

"Enjoy your quadrille," he said, with a tip of his hat.

Her gut sank.

Once again, she had chosen the King. It was her choice. It may not have felt that way, but it was.

There was no taking it back, but . . .

"Oh, I won't be dancing the lobster quadrille," she whispered back. "I'm going to be in a secret sea cave. Remember?"

His eyes brightened, but she turned away before she could see whether he remembered his promise or not. Those hushed words spoken when he'd been standing in her room at the end of an impossible night.

She would dance her lobster quadrille. He would juggle his clams. And all the while they would pretend that they were hidden away in a secret sea cave, concerned with no one but themselves.

She was sure all the world would have noticed the longing in her face, except all the world was focused on her hand locked inside the crook of the King's elbow.

They reached the dual lines of sea creatures, already partnered with their lobsters. The King was far too exuberant to notice how distracted Cath was.

What would have happened if she had asked Jest to dance instead?

What would happen if she chose him?

Was such a choice truly outside the realm of possibility, or did it only seem that way because such a choice had never presented itself before?

She was as empty as a marionette as the dance began, her body leading her through the steps. They advanced, they retreated.

Her skirt twisted around her ankles. Her heels sank into the sand. The King's hands were soggy in hers and the wind was burning her cheeks, and all around her lobsters were being tossed out to sea and their partners were diving in after them. Everyone was laughing and splashing and turning somersaults along with the music. Even the King, caught up in the moment, charged out into the surf, wading halfway up to his calves. He turned back to her, laughing.

Catherine alone remained above the foam, her smile frozen. In her head, she was sequestered away in a sea cave somewhere. In her mind, it was Jest grinning at her, his dimples carved deep into his cheeks. He beckoned to her, and she went.

She knew, in that moment, that she would go to him, if only he asked. She would be his, if he wanted her.

"Oh no," she murmured, her smile thawing, falling, carried away with the undeniable, inevitable, impossible truth of it.

She was falling in love with him.

Chapter 27

The audience was fierce with applause as Catherine set her hand on top of the King's and they walked together up the beach. The King was soaking wet and a strand of seaweed was caught on the heel of his shoes and he could not have sounded any more delighted than if the entire festival had been a surprise unbirthday party thrown in his honor.

Catherine, her thoughts in turmoil, did her best to keep her eyes locked on the white overhanging cliffs so she wouldn't be tempted to seek out Jest in the crowd. She was sure that with one look at her, he would know the depth of her thoughts.

The orchestra leaped into a waltz and Catherine could feel the King gathering his courage to ask for another dance, and so she thanked him exuberantly for the quadrille and escaped into the crowd before he could find the words.

All around her, the festival's guests began to divide into couples and line up for the next dance. Cath avoided meeting anyone's eye, unwilling to be drawn into a conversation or another dance, to be captured in the endless turns and figures and trivial chatter until the festival ended and they all dispersed, afraid to be caught in the dark now that a monster was on the prowl.

She snapped from her thoughts to the sound of her own name roaring in her ears. The crowd had pushed in toward her. A dozen women were chattering about the rumors of her courtship, a dozen men were inquiring after her dance card and then backing away jokingly, pretending that they didn't want the King to take offense. Hands brushed her sleeves and smiles hovered Cheshire-like before her face. "Lady Catherine, how lovely you looked during the quadrille." "Quite the favorite with the King these days, aren't you, Lady Pinkerton?" "You looked beautiful out there — positively regal!" "Catherine —" "Catherine —" *"Catherine —"*

Lowering her head, she tried to shove her way through, begging to be allowed to pass. Her mind was spinning, tumbling, as the crowd thickened with congratulations and compliments and twittering praise. The grins of strangers who were too blind to see the frustration behind her pretty face and pretty clothes and pretty life —

A cloud of white smoke burst at her feet, filling the air around her with startled gasps. Catherine froze. Within moments the smoke was so thick she couldn't see her own hands outstretched before her.

Then there was a gloved hand in hers, fingers entwined, tugging her forward. *Jest.*

She followed without question, disconcerted at the press of confused bodies.

The smoke thinned as she was pulled up an embankment of craggly white stones, a narrow path tucked into an alcove beneath the cliffs. Jest glanced back to check that she was all right, before guiding them behind a wall of fallen boulders. Their surfaces sparkled with bits of quartz.

It was not as private as a sea cave, but it was serene and they were alone, at least for a time. Catherine, panting, was warm from her brow to her toes, but the shaded spot was comfortable and already her breaths were coming easier.

"Are you all right?" Jest said, cupping her hand and looking at her with the same concern he'd had when she'd awoken in the gardens.

She nodded. "Better already, thank you."

"I thought you were going to faint again. Have you eaten anything today?"

She gulped. "Y-yes. A meat pie, when I arrived this morning."

His mouth quirked. "Excellent choice."

The past few minutes faded away and once again Cath was standing on the surf, staring out into the sea, and realizing with sudden certainty that she was losing her heart to this fool.

She pulled her hand away and turned to peer through a crack in the rocks. On the beach, the smoke was clearing fast, leaving a fine mist over the baffled onlookers. The orchestra was still playing, though, and the confusion was giving way to another dance.

Jest brushed a lock of hair off her shoulder. "You don't enjoy dancing?"

She shut her eyes. His fingertips lingered on the bare skin of her neck and she couldn't resist leaning into them. "We can't all be great performers."

"Yet you are a lovely dancer." He was so close she could feel the heat coming from him, cutting through the chill of the wind. "Beside you, even the King looked half respectable. It's easy to see why he wants you for his queen."

Her stomach dropped. There was no bitterness in his tone. She wondered why.

Surely, if their roles were reversed and Jest was in the midst of courting another girl, it would have been shredding her to bits. Her emotions would have been lemon peel dragged across a grater.

She stepped away and opened her eyes, keeping her hands anchored to the glittering white stone. "You shouldn't touch me," she said, her voice strained around the rapid beating of her heart.

Jest leaned against the stone. "You're right. I'm sorry." She couldn't tell if he meant it.

Her heart tugged toward him. She wished that she hadn't pulled back. She wished that he had pulled her closer.

"Tell me, Sir Rook, did you behave this way with all the ladies in Chess too?"

"Which behavior are you referring to? My good manners, my charming witticisms, my beguiling charisma —"

"I was referring to your determination to make me blush, for no other purpose than to laugh at me later."

He blanched, then took a step closer. Cath could hear the creak of his leather boots. "I assure you that when I replay this conversation in my head later, it will not be in laughter."

Cath lowered her lashes, her insides fluttering. "I should get back. My parents will worry." She turned away.

"Wait?"

It was a question, not a demand, and so she waited. Stupid hope coursed through her veins.

"It isn't my place, of course . . ."

Gulping, she turned back. Jest had removed his gloves and was busy choking them in his fists. Though his expression was calm, his hands said otherwise.

"The King . . . ," he started, and Cath flinched, glad that Jest was too busy inspecting the gloves to notice. "He truly cares for you. I think he honestly means to make you happy."

She expected him to go on, but silence fell, and that seemed to be all he meant to say.

"Are you telling me to accept him?"

"No," he stammered. "I'm saying that if you did accept him, I would understand. I would be happy for you."

She clenched her fists. "How comforting that at least one of us would be."

Jest looked up at her again, his brow tight. "Something happened, down on the beach," he said, dropping the gloves onto a rock. "You came back from the quadrille looking like you'd seen a ghost."

"I don't know what you mean." She folded her arms protectively over her chest. "I entered a cake into the baking contest. I suppose I'm nervous about it."

A weak smile slipped over his features. "I can't believe that."

"What would you know about it? I can be nervous if I want to be."

He shrugged. "We both know you're going to win the contest."

"I do not either know it." She stood straighter. "I assume that I will win, yes, but that isn't the same thing. And I'll have you know that wasn't much of a compliment."

"It wasn't meant to be, but if it's a compliment you want . . ." His gaze softened. "You are stunning in that absurd hat. Absolutely, undeniably stunning. I trust that was Hatta's goal, but he can't know how well he accomplished it, else he would have deemed it improper to let you leave his hat shop so adorned." He hesitated and cleared his throat, looking almost shy. "That's what I wanted to say before."

She scoffed, but it was coupled with a quickened heartbeat. "You're infuriating."

"You're not the first to mention it." His momentary bashfulness turned to another maddening smile.

She squeezed her arms in tighter, still

shielding herself, or perhaps in an effort to keep from reaching out to him. "You act as though you know me, but you don't, not really. You don't know what I like, or what I want, or what I dream about . . ."

"You dream about me, if I'm not mistaken."

"I never should have told you that."

His eyes glinted.

"And all I know about you is that you sneak into girls' bedrooms in the middle of the night and you take their corset laces when they're unconscious and you seem to want me to accept the King but then you call me stunning or touch me when you shouldn't. And you're always laughing at me and you're on some secret mission from the White Queen but I haven't the faintest idea what that means and I can't tell what's real or what's an illusion and I — I have to get back." She pivoted away from him. "Thank you for rescuing me from that crowd, but I do have to get back."

"I can't stop thinking about you, either, Lady Pinkerton."

Without having gone a single step, she felt her feet digging into the sand. This time, she didn't dare turn around. She didn't have to. A moment later he slipped in front of her, not touching her this time, but close enough that he could have.

The look he gave her was already peeling back her layers of fortitude. How dare he look as though he were nervous or afraid, when she was the one with a gavel thumping inside her chest?

"That's not what I said at all," she breathed.

"I know, but I'm hoping it's what you meant." He licked his lips — a small, cruel movement that made her own lips tingle. "I can't stop thinking about you, Lady Catherine Pinkerton of Rock Turtle Cove. I've been trying, but it's useless. You've had me mesmerized from the first moment I saw you in that red dress, and I don't know what to do about it, other than to use every skill at my disposal to try and mesmerize you back."

The wind whistled through the rocks, the waves whispered on the beach, and Catherine had no response.

He let his attention drop to the ground, and she was able to almost-breathe again. Jest reached up to scratch his temple, but seemed surprised to find his three-pointed hat there, so he whisked it off and the bells jingled and his hair was matted and messy and when he wasn't looking directly at her he could pass as timid, though she found it hard to fathom.

Timid or arrogant, charming or infuriating, and Catherine was falling, falling, falling.

"His Majesty keeps coming to me for advice." He looked up again, misery in his expression. "He seems to think I'm an expert on how best to court you. What to say, what gifts to send." He hesitated. "Of course I help him, because . . . well, I have to. But also, I sometimes pretend that it's me, instead of him. I suggest he do the things that I would do, if I were . . . deserving of you."

Her heart drummed. "You mean, if you were nobility."

"I mean." He tried to smile, but it didn't reach his eyes. "I've been thinking about what you said, that there can be no more nights like . . . like the tea party. And you're right. I was a terrible cad to sneak you around like that, and I know the harm that could be done. Not only because of the Jabberwock, but . . . the dangers to your reputation, and your courtship, and . . . it was selfish of me."

"I hope you're not taking all the credit." Her voice held little of the fire she wanted it to. "I made the choice as well as you did."

"I accede your point."

Her fingers itched to reach out to him, to touch him. She refrained. "I swear to you, I'm not meaning to be fickle. I don't want to be in this courtship. It's just . . ." She laughed, a dismal sound. "I didn't think it would be so hard, but how does one reject a king? Not to mention my parents. My mother. Oh —" She groaned. "She wants it so much. She's so happy when she talks about the courtship, and I can't stand to think how disappointed she'll be." She squirmed and pulled her hands through her knotted hair, tugging it over her ears.

Disappointed did not begin to cover her parents' reactions if she were to reject the King, especially once she told them that she'd fallen in love with the court joker instead.

"I want to make them proud," she said, "but we have such different opinions on what my future should hold. It's as though . . . if I love them enough, surely I could learn to love the King too. I know that's how my mother sees it. She would think that I failed in this most simple of obligations. To be a good daughter who marries the King. Who makes them proud."

"You talk as if love is doled out like prizes at a festival. Surely they just want you to be happy."

"Of course they want me to be happy. They just think I'll be happy with the King, but I know they're wrong. I never could be. Which is why . . ." She squared her shoulders. "When he proposes, I won't — I cannot accept him. You must believe that."

He eyed her for a long, long moment, before he said, "I believe that *you* believe it."

She frowned. It was not the confidence she'd hoped for, but she couldn't blame him. Until now, she'd done little to dissuade the King's advances. "I can tell when the gifts and the poems are from you and not him."

He flashed a wry smile. "I should hope so."

She looked away. "Jest . . ."

"Lady Pinkerton."

She chewed the inside of her cheek, unable to find the words she wanted to tell him. Not sure that she was brave enough to tell him anything at all.

He edged closer. "I understand how much the King has to offer you, and how very little I have in comparison. I'll understand should you accept him."

"Jest —"

"Truly. He's the better choice in every way."

"Certainly not every way."

"Please don't give me false hope." His voice chipped, forcing her to meet his gaze again. Her pulse thundered. "I can't compete with a king, and I *won't* compete with the man who's given me employment, who's offered me a place in his court when he had no need to. I don't mean to make your choice more difficult than it already is. He's a good man. I believe he would do his best to be a good husband."

Catherine's mouth ran dry. A crack was burrowing through her chest, threatening to break her open.

"But," he said, his voice tender and low, "should you decide to refuse him . . ."

She blinked back the mist in her eyes.

"Then I hope it won't cause offense if I were to . . ." Jest hesitated. There was a new tension in his shoulders, an unexpected self-consciousness to the set of his brow. "To call on you. Or . . . your father."

"My father," she whispered.

"Do you think . . . is there any hope at all that he would entertain my request to court you? With every good intention a poor joker like myself could possibly have."

Her heart clamped. At the restrained hope in his voice. At the pleading in his eyes. At all the memories of her mother pushing her into the arms of the King.

"I don't know," she said. "Is Rook a very high rank in Chess?"

He pressed his lips and seemed to be considering the question. "Actually," he said, "it's on equal ranking to a marquess."

She straightened, surprised at this answer. And to think that all her parents would ever see when they looked at him was a lowly Joker.

"But," Jest said, perhaps seeing too much hope in her expression, "we are not in Chess."

"No, I know. If you asked to court me, I suppose my parents would be . . . well . . . they would probably be . . ."

"Mortified?" he suggested. "Insulted? Baffled that someone like me could be so bold as to think they would ever agree to such a match?"

Her breath shook as she inhaled. "Yes. All of that."

Another silence hung between them. She could not stand to meet his eyes, because if she did, she might lie to him. She might tell him that yes, there was a chance her parents would agree to the courtship. There was hope that her parents would accept him.

Or worse — she might tell him it didn't matter to her, when she knew that it did.

Jest sighed. "I figured as much. I suppose I'll have to find another way to make this impossibility possible." He chuckled, a rather hollow sound. "Perhaps I will enter the next pumpkin-eating contest and be knighted by the King."

Her cheek fluttered. "I wish you luck with such a noble conquest, Sir Jest."

"I sincerely hope you mean that, my lady."

Chapter 28

Cath's nerves were stretched taffy thin as she made her way back through the rows of snapping tents. This time, there was no excitement for the carnival food or pretty baubles. Her head was too full of Jest and the knowledge that she was a coward. Was she so afraid to disappoint her parents and the King, that she was willing to put their happiness before her own?

"Cath! There you are!" Mary Ann was rushing toward her, black skirt bunched up in both fists and hair tumbling from her blue-and-yellow bonnet. "I've been looking everywhere for you!"

"What's happened?" Cath glanced around and noticed, for the first time, how empty the beach felt.

"Nothing, yet. But the contest started ten minutes ago and they're going to get to your cake any minute, but you have to be present if you're to win!"

"Conte— ? Oh! The contest!"

Mary Ann shot her a disgruntled look. "You forgot?"

"No, of course not, I was just . . . I . . ."

Mary Ann grabbed her wrist. "You best not have. I've been dreaming about those twenty gold crowns all morning, imagining all that we can do with them to bring the bakery to life." Relaxing, she shot Cath a bright smile and pointed up at her bonnet. "I really do think there's something about this hat. Is yours from the Marvelous Millinery too? It's quite charming."

"Why, yes, it . . ." Catherine paused, one hand reaching for the squishy brim of her hat, the ridiculous macaron. She realized with a start that her mother, who should have thrown a fit at the impropriety of her daughter wearing such a garish thing, had said nothing. Had not even seemed to notice it.

What had Hatta said? Something about capturing charisma in headwear — but what did that mean?

She thought of Margaret Mearle at the King's tea party and how she looked almost pretty in her rosebud fastener. She thought of Mary Ann's burgeoning dreams. She thought of the chef's hat she'd picked off the hat shop walls, when Hatta had mentioned unconventional decisions, moments before she thought to offer her macarons as proof of her talent.

Cath's mouth twitched with delight, with the marvelousness of her discovery.

Hatta was selling exquisite, magical hats.

Mary Ann hauled Catherine into the grandstand tent. All of the seats were full, with countless more guests standing at the back. Five judges were seated at a draped table on the stage — the King and Knave of Hearts, the Duke of Tuskany, Mr. Caterpillar, and the Turtle that Cath had loaned her handkerchief to. Before each of them was a blue-frosted cupcake with raspberry-pink sugar crystals being dug into by the forkful. With the exception of the Turtle, that is, whose plate held only blue-frosted crumbs. Most of the sugar crystals had stuck to his pointed upper lip.

The White Rabbit stood at a podium on the side of the stage. Once all the judges had sampled the cupcakes, Mr. Rabbit bellowed, "The judges will give their scores for the berry berry cupcakes made by the Vine and Flower Society!"

Three potted plants had been set on the contestants' stand at the front, holding one another's leaves.

"Berry good!" yelled the King.

"Berry gone!" yelled the Turtle.

"Could have used some ground pepper on top," suggested the Duke, to which Catherine traded wary glances with Mary Ann, and Mary Ann mouthed back to her, *Pepper*?

Mr. Caterpillar removed the hookah from his mouth and blew a cloud of smoke across the table. The other judges coughed politely and leaned away.

Jack, the Knave, threw his fork down beside his cupcake, having tasted only a single bite. "Rubbish," he muttered.

The potted flowers bobbed their blossoming heads at one another — pleased with the judges' scores. Three footmen came forward to carry their planters off the stand, while another group of courtiers brought out the next dish — squares of right-side-up pineapple cake from Lady Margaret Mearle.

Margaret took her place on the competitor's platform and squared her already-rather-rectangular shoulders. From his seat at the judging table, the Duke's pink-tinged skin turned flaming red. He tried to smile at Margaret around his protruding tusks.

Margaret sneered and turned her chin haughtily away.

The Duke deflated.

Trying to still the fluttering in her stomach, Catherine looked out at the crowd and spotted her mother and father in the front row. They would have no idea that she'd submitted an entry into the contest, and she wasn't sure how they would react.

Behind her parents sat Peter Peter and his wife, whose pallor was only slightly improved from when Cath had last seen her, though her eyes remained glossy and ill-looking. She was staring hungrily at the case that held the contest desserts.

Cath peeled her gaze away before Sir Peter could notice her, hoping he wouldn't be suspicious over her spiced pumpkin cake. But why should he? He was by no means the only pumpkin grower in Hearts. He had no reason to suspect she'd stolen one from his patch.

She hoped.

Her eye drifted farther back and landed on Hatta himself. He loitered at the back of the tent, the ribbon from his top hat whipping in the wind from the beach. He noticed her, too, and cast a nod in her direction, indicating the macaron hat. But he turned away before she could return the nod, his whole demeanor changing. In a moment he'd dropped the broody stance and smiled his rare, friendly smile. Then Jest was there, too, squeezing Hatta's shoulder in greeting.

Her heart twinged, still too raw from their recent encounter.

The White Rabbit cleared his throat and Catherine forced her attention back to the stage. "What have the judges to say on Lady Mearle's entry?"

"Pineappley pleasant!" yelled the King.

"Pleasantly gone!" yelled the Turtle, scraping up the last bits of cake.

"Would be better upside down," said Jack, tipping back in his chair and staring at the tent's ceiling.

"Upside down is a fine way to be," agreed the Caterpillar. He had taken off one pair of house slippers and was pressing the bottoms of his bare feet into his cake. "I've spent quite a bit of time upside down myself."

After a nervous clearing of his throat and a scratching of his ear, the Duke said, "Well — I thought it was splendid. Just the perfect amount of pineapple and . . . turned upward-downside just the right way, if I do say so myself. Well done, Lady Mearle. I could not have asked for a more satisfying dessert!"

Catherine rolled her eyes, but Margaret had developed a tiny grin as she was ushered away from the contestants' stand.

"Next!" demanded the White Rabbit.

Cheshire's floating head appeared, and slices of a tuna tart were presented to the judges. Cath blanched and turned away. Her gaze latched back on to Jest.

He was watching her across the tent.

They both quickly looked down, and she hoped she wasn't the only one blushing.

"It's fishy fa-fabulous," stammered the King, his face looking a little green.

"Fabulously gone!" yelled the Turtle, revealing yet another empty plate.

The other three judges refused to try it, and within minutes of the tart being removed from the table, Cheshire was gobbling down his own creation offstage.

"Next up," said the Rabbit, "is a spiced pumpkin cake from Lady Catherine Pinkerton of Rock Turtle Cove."

Mary Ann's fingers laced through hers, squeezing tight.

"Come with me," Cath said, pulling her forward. "We'll win it together."

They marched between the rows of onlookers to take their spot at the front. Five slices of the cake were brought to the table. Cath risked a glance at her parents — her father's bushy eyebrows were raised in curiosity, while her mother was red-faced with borderline betrayal. Cath smiled weakly before facing the judges. The King was beaming at her, and the Turtle's face, too, lit up in recognition.

"The macaron girl!" he whispered excitedly.

Catherine tipped her macaron hat to him.

The Turtle leaned to the side, bumping into the Knave with his hard shell. "I've had her baking before," he said. "She's wondrous. And also brave . . . so very brave."

Her skin tingled. Though her most prominent memories of the Jabberwock attack revolved around the tragic loss of the Lion, she took a moment to be proud that the Turtle, at least, had been spared. She had helped save his life.

Not noticing her pleasure, or not caring, Jack snorted. His face turned cherry red. "*Wondrous* seems a bit excessive. She's adequate. Maybe. On a good day." His scowl deepened as he peered at Catherine and her hat. "Don't know what anyone sees in her, what with her delicious tarts, or her big doe eyes or unnaturally shiny hair." He folded his arms over his chest and turned his nose into the air. "Lady Pinkerton is highly overrated, if you ask me."

Mr. Rabbit cleared his throat. "We ask that the judges refrain from previous biases on the contestants."

Ducking his head, the Turtle shoveled his

first bite of pumpkin cake into his mouth, but the King was distracted, gazing starry-eyed at Catherine. She shuffled her feet.

Beside him, the Turtle moaned in sweets-filled ecstasy, his bowler hat tipping on his head. The other judges had just picked up their forks when the King pushed back his chair and stood.

"I cannot call myself an unbiased judge, your honorable Mr. Rabbit, our most thoughtful master of ceremonies!" His eyes glistened with barely contained joy.

Cath's stomach sank. She started to shake her head, but the King continued, "I am full of bias. I am the definition of bias! For this very pumpkin cake set before us was made by the ever-charming Lady Catherine Pinkerton, a girl that is someday to be my bride!"

Ice blew over Catherine's frame, freezing her feet to the platform, plastering her panicked smile onto her cheeks.

The King looked at her with pride that should not have belonged to him. "So you see, for any contest in which she is a participant, I will say to you, yes! She must be the winner! She wins it all, my heart, my joy!"

Catherine felt a hundred eyes boring into her, but she was petrified, unable to look away from the King.

This was a nightmare.

"What a queen you will make, Lady Pinkerton, cake baker and happiness maker! Oh, oh, somebody write that down! Jest — there you are! Write that down! I shall include it in my next poem!" The King clutched his stomach, overcome with a bevy of giggles.

The crowd stirred. Their whispers flooded the tent. Cath sensed her mother's overzealous glee. She could imagine how quickly the gossip would spread outward from this little festival on this little beach, like a pebble dropped into a pond.

Mortification washed over her.

I haven't said yes, she wanted to tell them all. *I haven't accepted him. I'm not his bride, despite what he says.*

She had opened her mouth, her body pulsing with denial, when a scream cut through the tent.

Chapter 29

Catherine swiveled, searching for the scream, as chaos erupted — chairs crashing, paws and wings scrambling away from someone, some*thing* . . .

Her attention fell on the Turtle, that adorable, most enthusiastic of judges. He had fallen off his chair behind the table, and if Jack hadn't accidentally tripped on the tablecloth in his haste to get away, yanking the cloth and all the cake-filled dishes away with him, Cath would not have been able to see the Turtle at all. As it was, he was on full view to the startled onlookers. Upended on his back, exposing the softer underside of his shell, his arms and legs flailing. He was still groaning and pressing his flippers to his stomach, his voice hoarse with pain, his eyes wide and frightened.

From her perch on the contestants' platform, Catherine had a perfect view of the Turtle when he began to change. His skin bubbled beneath the surface, shifting and undulating. Some of his scales sloughed away and new skin stretched along all four limbs. His screams turned gargled as his head, too, began to morph into something strange. Something horrid.

Cath pressed a hand over her mouth to keep from heaving. Someone suggested carrying the Turtle down to the sea so one of the Sturgeons could have a look at him, but nobody dared to touch the poor thing.

No one could look away, until the squashing and twisting of the Turtle's limbs gradually stilled and his screams dwindled into sobs. A puddle of tears had formed beneath his thrashing head.

The head that was no longer the head of a turtle.

The pointed beak and sunken eyes were gone, replaced with the contorted face of a baby calf, complete with flared pink nostrils and soft tawny fur.

Though his shell and belly and front flippers remained intact, the Turtle's lower legs were now hooves, and, with one last painful shudder from the creature, his reptilian tail stretched and curled and sprouted a tuft of fur on its end. His tail, too, was now that of a young cow.

"It's impossible," someone said, and the

word sent a chill down Catherine's spine.

The crowd could not stop gawking, though some of the children had been coaxed away from the horrific sight. The Turtle continued to cry enormous blubbering tears, still trying in vain to roll himself over, and it dawned on Catherine how vulnerable he was. Embarrassed and in pain for all the crowd to see, and having no idea what was becoming of him. Words formed beneath his sobs — *What happened? What's happening to me? What's going on? Help me, help, help . . .*

Unfreezing her legs, Catherine rushed forward. "Someone help him!" she cried, dropping to her knees to crawl beneath the table. She knelt at the Turtle's side and laid a hand on his leg, just above the new hoof. It was covered in a fine layer of fur and damp with sweat.

"You're going to be all right," she whispered. The Turtle continued to blubber nonsense and hiccups. "Or at least, mostly right. I hope. We're going to roll you over. Just hold still."

She looked up at the stunned faces. The King, pale and shocked, the Knave, disgusted, the Duke, looking on the verge of illness, and the Caterpillar, eyeing the Turtle like an unexpected result of a science experiment. The White Rabbit had fled from the stage and his pink eyes now peered over its edge. Mary Ann had removed her bonnet, maybe confused to see her dreams of the baking contest so quickly turned to a nightmare.

"Help me!" Cath yelled.

No one moved, and it was a startling sight that snagged her attention in the crowd. Two piercing eyes watching her from a livid face. Peter Peter's expression was twisted in fury, one lip peeled up to reveal gritting teeth. And he was looking straight at her.

Cath shrank back under the force of his loathing. She couldn't comprehend the fear that curdled in her gut as she glanced up at the judges' table and the five plates that had been set there.

Four untouched pieces of pumpkin spice cake — and one plate showing nothing but crumbs.

Bells jingled, mockingly cheerful, and the crowd parted to let Jest and Hatta through. They both looked as appalled as anyone, but concerned, too, as they climbed onto the stage and knelt beside the hysterical creature.

"It's all right, chap," said Hatta, picking up the bowler hat that had fallen off during the Turtle's transformation and tucking it under his arm. He laid his free hand on the creature's shell. "Calm yourself, now. It can't be as bad as all that."

But his creased brow and Jest's thin-pressed mouth said otherwise. The Turtle blubbered on and on.

They rolled the Turtle back onto his stomach, but the position was no longer natural, what with the hooves jutting from beneath his shell. Instead, with a gasp and a sob, the Turtle pushed himself onto two knobby legs, his flippers hanging dejectedly in front of him.

"I'm a turtle," he whimpered, looking down at the abomination he'd become. "I'm a real turtle. Y-you believe me, don't you?"

Catherine shivered. "Of course you are."

But it was a lie.

The poor creature was changed. Disfigured. She couldn't fathom how, but he had become a Mock Turtle, right before their eyes.

The festival that had begun with so much spirit and joy ended darkly with the memory of the Mock Turtle's sobs on everyone's minds and recent threats of the Jabberwock still plaguing them. Festivities that normally continued far into the night were over before dusk could fall. The baking contest was left uncompleted, a handful of entries still untasted and unjudged, but everyone having lost both their appetites and their sense of merriment. Cath could not bring herself to be selfish enough to ask about the prize.

She climbed into the carriage with her parents. The ride was suffocating. Catherine stared out the window, seeing again and again the furious expression on Sir Peter's face. She felt guilty, but not because she'd stolen a pumpkin from him. She couldn't help feeling responsible for what had happened, but how could that be?

It was only a pumpkin cake. And while she had heard of sweets that made a person shrink and mushrooms that made a person grow, she had never heard of anything disastrous happening as a result of a pumpkin.

With trembling fingers, Catherine reached up and pulled the macaron hat off her head, settling it on her lap. It no longer brought the delight it had hours before.

Her father sighed. He had not stopped sighing since they had left the beach.

"They're already calling it the *Mock* Turtle Festival," he said as the carriage rounded onto their drive. "It's a travesty. Soon they'll be calling me the Marquess of Mock Turtles."

"Don't be melodramatic," said her mother. "This whole catastrophe will be forgotten in a matter of days, you'll see."

But she seemed unconvinced of it herself, and the fact that she didn't mention the King once during the drive suggested to Catherine that she was more concerned than she wanted to let on.

The annual festival was their family's great contribution to the Kingdom of Hearts — in some ways, their place among the nobility rested on the festival's shoulders, and it had been their one notable distinction for generations.

Yet, knowing how much this could affect her family's reputation was barely a passing thought to Catherine. It was the poor Turtle who would suffer most of all, the pitiful, devastated thing.

As soon as they arrived home, Catherine escaped down to the kitchen. The fire had long gone out, so she kept her shawl tight around her shoulders.

Setting a lantern on one of the tables, she grabbed a stack of recipe books and laid them out before her. She began flipping through, scanning the names of dishes their cook had made for them over the years.

There were plenty of notes jotted in the margins — "Clarify the butter first or it will confuse the rest of the ingredients," or, "Don't let the tomatoes stew for too long as they're like to become bitter and resentful."

Finally she arrived at the recipe she was looking for.

Mock Turtle Soup.

She bent over the brittle, broth-stained pages and started to read.

> Begin with a medium-size mock turtle, *the recipe began.* Using a sharp butcher knife, remove the calf head. Mock turtles die slowly, so be aware that the head will continue to mewl and the body may try to crawl away for some minutes after decapitation. Once body is no longer mobile, submerge in a large pot of boiling water. Meat will naturally separate from the shell as it cooks. Remove the mock turtle from the water and peel away the skin and shell before —

Catherine slammed the book shut, her stomach roiling.

She would never eat mock turtle soup again.

Light footsteps thudded on the stairs and Cath turned to see Mary Ann descending the steps with a bundle of dirtied tablecloths in her arms. Her hair was disheveled and exhausted circles had appeared beneath her eyes.

Pushing the stool back, Cath went to hold open the bin of soiled laundry waiting to be washed.

"Are you all right?" she asked.

Mary Ann groaned. "That was a long, tiring day, even for me."

Cath pulled out one of the stools for her. "Were people talking about that poor Turtle after we left?"

Slumping onto the stool, Mary Ann untied her pretty bonnet and dropped it onto the counter. "It's all anyone would talk of. No one can fathom what caused it. They just kept saying over and over how awful it was." She sighed. "A mock turtle. What could cause such a thing?"

She thought again of Sir Peter. Of the one devoured piece of pumpkin cake.

"I don't know," she said, and started gathering up the recipe books again. Gnawing on her cheek, she turned back to see that Mary Ann had laid her head down on her arms. Normally she was the model of productivity. It was odd to see weariness catch up with her. "Would I be a horrible person to inquire about the winner of the baking contest?"

Mary Ann wheezed into her elbow. "We can be horrible people together. I keep wondering, too, but I couldn't bring myself to ask, even though I spotted Mr. Rabbit while we were tearing down the grandstand." She lifted her head enough to meet Cath's gaze. "They weren't able to finish the judging, so I don't see how they can award a winner. Probably the prize will go back into the treasury or be applied to some other celebration."

"I figured as much." Cath climbed onto the second stool, wishing she'd started a batch of bread rather than look up awful recipes. Kneading and pummeling the dough would have relaxed her.

Mary Ann's eyes had shut. "They say Mr. Caterpillar is almost moved out of his shop. It won't be long now . . ."

She didn't finish, nor did she have to. It wouldn't be long before someone else took up residence in their storefront, if they weren't ready to do it themselves.

"All right," Cath whispered, gathering her courage. "No more stalling. I have to ask my parents for the money, or permission to sell off my dowry. There's no other way around it."

"Oh, Cath." With a groan, Mary Ann

peeled her head off her elbow again. "I adore your optimism, I always have, but they're going to say no. You know it as well as I." Her mouth turned down and her thought seemed very far away as she added, "We'll have no bakery without financing, and no financing without an investor, and who would ever invest in a poor maid and the daughter of a marquess? Maybe it's time we realize this was never going to happen, and face our true destiny." She forced a smile in Catherine's direction. "At least, to be the maid to a queen is more than I ever would have expected when I was a young girl, so it isn't all that bad."

Gnashing her teeth, Catherine grabbed the blue bonnet and thrust it onto Mary Ann's head, cinching the yellow ribbon under her chin with a quick tug. "I won't tolerate such nonsense. If ever there was a time for dreaming, this is it, Mary Ann. Now, I am going to march up there and demand a word with my parents, and I need to know I have your full support behind me. So do you want to start a bakery together or not?"

Mary Ann opened her mouth to speak, hesitated, and seemed to mull over her thoughts for a moment. Her head began to sink between her shoulders, and her blue eyes misted with unshed tears. "I do, Cath. My head tells me it will never happen, but my heart —"

"Sometimes your heart is the only thing worth listening to." Cath peeled her shoulders back, preparing herself. "Who knows? Maybe they'll be so weary from the festival they'll have no fight left in them."

"*Your* mother, without any fight left in her? I wish you luck, Catherine, I truly do, but I also fear this day has already reached its limit on impossible things."

Chapter 30

The Marquess and Marchioness were drinking cordials in the library when Cath tapped at the door frame. They looked as exhausted as Mary Ann had, and though Cath knew their day had been spent entertaining and mingling more than the sort of labor Mary Ann and the servants had done, she still had a great deal of sympathy for them.

The Turtle Days Festival had been trying for everyone.

Despite Mary Ann's pessimism, Cath thought maybe her parents would be too upset to argue with her. Maybe they would be more receptive to her frightening new ideas when their long-held traditions had so recently collapsed around them.

She did feel guilty about hoping it was so.

"Retiring early?" her father asked when he saw her lingering in the doorway. "I don't blame you, child. Come give me a good-night kiss."

Cath forced her lips to smile and came forward to give her father a kiss on his wrinkled brow. "Actually," she said, pulling back, "I hoped I might have a moment to speak with you." She glanced at her mother, reclined on the sofa. She was still wearing her gown from the festival — the hem was caked with drying sand. "With both of you."

Her mother's face lifted, clearing away some of her tiredness, and she sat up with a grin. "Oh, Catherine. Of course we'll grant our consent — you needn't look so worried. But do sit and tell us everything. We could use some joy to finish this awful day."

Catherine's eyes widened, and astounding joy was just about to bubble over when she realized, of course, her mother was speaking of the King. "Thank you, Mother, but I wasn't . . ."

Her mother waved at the empty chair across from them. "Don't be shy, dearest. Your father and I have been waiting seventeen years for such good news, and it couldn't have come at a better time. We can hope that everyone will be so excited about the upcoming wedding they'll forget all about today's misfortune." She pressed a hand to her forehead, like trying to rub the memory out from her brow, before her eyes brightened again. "Did he propose during the quadrille? You looked so happy out there. Lovestruck, even, if I'm not mistaken. Naughty child, I can hardly believe you kept the secret from us for even a moment!"

Catherine gripped her hands together. "You misunderstand, Mother. The King hasn't proposed. He was speaking prematurely during the contest." The corner of her eye twitched. "To be honest, I'm irritated that he wasn't more careful with keeping our courtship an intimate affair."

Her mother frowned. "You aren't engaged?"

"No. I'm not." Cath perched herself on the edge of the wingback chair her mother had indicated. Its feathered wings tried to wrap around her but she shook them off. "There was something else I wished to discuss with you."

Her mother still looked confused. "Something other than the King?"

"I'm afraid the King does not occupy my thoughts nearly as much as he occupies yours, Mama."

Her mother stiffened, and Cath felt guilty for her sass, but her father's snort relieved it somewhat. He leaned forward, dwarfing his cordial glass in his enormous hands. "Go on, then. What's on your mind?"

"Well." She dug her fingertips into the

material of her skirt to keep from fidgeting. "You know that Mary Ann and I entered a cake into the contest today. The pumpkin spice cake that the judges were sampling just before . . ."

"Yes, we did notice," her mother said, eyes narrowing. "I understand the King is fond of your treats, but when will you realize it isn't proper to spend all your time in the kitchen — and to enter the contest! The daughter of the Marquess, entering a contest at the Marquess's own festival. Didn't you stop to think how that would look?"

"I wanted to win," she said. "I wanted the purse that was part of the grand prize."

Her father raised one thick eyebrow. "Whatever for? If you need money —"

"That's what I wanted to talk to you about. I do need money, because I . . . I want to open a bakery." She gulped, and spoke quieter when she realized that she was already getting flustered. "Mary Ann and I want to open a bakery."

Her parents gaped at her. Both speechless, for once.

She plowed on. "We've been talking about it for years. I know you don't think it's proper. I know you think it's a silly hobby, and one you barely approve of at that. But baking is what I love to do and I know our bakery would be the best in the kingdom. Mary Ann will be the perfect partner — she's good with numbers and she has wonderfully creative ideas for how to bring in customers. She calls it *marketing.* Plus, there's a storefront opening up on Main Street soon. Where the cobbler is now, you know. It's owned by the Duke, but I'm confident I can persuade him —"

"A bakery!" her mother roared, and Catherine jolted, wondering whether everything past her initial declaration had been wasted words. "Whatever do you want to open a bakery for? You're going to be Queen, Catherine!"

Her shoulders tensed. "The King has not proposed to me, nor have I accepted him."

Her mother tittered and flicked her fingers through the air. Appeased, just like that. Always halfway between irritation and amusement. "But he will. Besides, can you imagine? *You,* running a bakery? Why — you'd become an elephant! You can hardly control your sweet tooth as it is." She brushed her hands together, as if to clear them of such ludicrous talk. "Enough of that. Let's go to bed. It's late, and I think tomorrow will bring better things."

Catherine's chest was tightening. From her mother's accusation. From her dismissal. From the doubtful voice in her head that wondered whether her mother was right.

But also from anger.

She shifted her whole body to face her father, fixing her gaze on him as if her mother hadn't spoken. "I'm asking for your help. I never ask for anything, but I want this. I want this desperately. You don't even need to give me the money. I can use my dowry, with your permission."

"What?" Her mother again. "Your dowry! Absolutely not, I will never —"

The Marquess held up a hand and spoke, gently, "That is enough now, Idonia." To Cath's surprise, her mother clamped her mouth shut.

A tickle of hope stirred in her, but it didn't last long as her father's gaze turned pitying. "I'm glad you came to us about this, Catherine. But I must agree with your mother."

The Marchioness harrumphed and crossed her arms over her chest with a sturdy nod.

"But, Father —"

"Ladies are not meant to own businesses, and the heir to Rock Turtle Cove has much greater things in store for her future than a lifetime of being elbow deep in eggs and flour."

"Greater things according to whom? It's not my choice to become a wife. And it's certainly not my choice to become a queen. Those things are Mother's dreams, not mine."

"They are my dream too," said her father, and Cath flinched at the sternness in his tone. "They are *our* dream. For you. You're young, dear, and whatever you think now, we have only your happiness in mind. We know what's best."

She could feel the threat of frustrated tears tickling her nose, but she bit them back. "No — you think you know best, but you're wrong. This is what I want. This is what will make me happy."

Her mother threw a hand into the air, complete with a disgusted sound from the back of her throat, but her father's gaze was steady. In fact, Catherine could not remember her father ever looking so immovable. It was disconcerting, and her lip trembled at being the receiver of such a look.

"You don't understand what it is you're asking for. A life of labor. Long hours, the endless struggles that come with being the proprietor of your own —"

"How would you know?" she cried, swinging her arms around at the library's papered walls and collection of vintage books. "You were born into all of this. You know nothing about business ownership, whereas Mary Ann and I have been planning and researching for years. I know precisely what I'm asking. I don't care about inheriting your title. I don't care about being married off, to the King or anyone else. This is what I want, and it isn't fair for you to think that you know my heart better than I do."

"The answer is no, Catherine." Her father set down his cordial glass. His knuckles had gone white. "I will give you no money and you shall not touch your dowry unless it is in the process of giving it to a husband that your mother and I have approved. That is the end of this discussion."

Cath's vision blurred. She launched to her feet. "You won't even give me the courtesy of considering it?"

"I believe I just answered that question. Should you bring it up to me again, I will be forced to let go of Mary Ann's employment in this household."

She staggered back. Again, the chair's wings tried to comfort her and she blindly shoved them away. "What?"

"She is a maid, Catherine. Not a friend. Not a partner. Clearly she's been putting too many thoughts into your head and I will have none of it. Is that clear?"

She gawked at him, her jaw working but no words able to form.

"You're dismissed, Catherine."

With a spark of resentment, she slammed her mouth shut and clenched her fists at her sides. "Mary Ann may be a servant, but *I* am not. I can dismiss myself, thank you."

Turning on her heels, she marched from the room, slamming the door in her wake. Hot tears began to squeeze out of her eyes. Her thoughts screamed — a tirade of arguments, of insults, of childish tantrums pressing up against the inside of her skull.

In her head, she told her parents they were being unfair and old-fashioned. She told them she wasn't a child and she would make her own decisions. She told them she would find another way, with or without their blessing.

She was courageous and indignant and angry . . . but angry with herself most of all. Hadn't she known what they would say all along? Hadn't she expected this from the start? Isn't that why she'd avoided the conversation for so long?

She couldn't pretend this hadn't gone exactly as she'd expected, no matter how much she'd wished otherwise.

She was grateful to find her bedroom empty. She wasn't ready to talk to Mary

Ann about her failure. She couldn't stand the idea of crushing her friend's dreams, not when she was still so new to dreaming.

She needed a moment to compose herself. Maybe even to concoct a new plan. For this couldn't be the end of everything they'd longed for.

Her eyes fell on the macaron hat perched on a corner of her wardrobe. A flurry of emotions twisted inside her, all braiding together into one.

She was the best baker in Hearts and everyone who tasted her pastries knew it. Even Hatta was inspired enough to make her that bizarre hat after only a tiny bite.

Hatta, who made magical hats.

Hatta, whose business was thriving. Who had probably made more sales today at the festival than that miserable Mr. Caterpillar had made all year in his little shop on Main Street.

Sitting down at her desk, Catherine pulled out a sheet of parchment, unscrewed the cap to her inkwell, and considered her proposal.

CHAPTER 31

Hatta's Marvelous Millinery had returned to its spot in the forest meadow, the little ramshackle cart in the shadow of broad, leafy trees. But when Jest had brought Catherine before, the lane in between the Crossroads and the hat shop had been empty — abandoned in the dead of night in a secluded corner of the kingdom.

Not so anymore.

Catherine passed more than a dozen patrons of the shop on their way back to the Crossroads. Birds and mammals and reptiles, all with smiles on their faces and elaborate hats on their heads, some with servants dragging along in their wake, carrying yet more brightly papered hat boxes.

The Hatter's popularity was expanding like a hot-air balloon.

An OPEN sign hung on the shop door, crisp with newness. The window that the Jabberwock had broken had been replaced.

Cath entered without knocking. A pair of Owls were standing before a mirror, trying on different hats and hooting to themselves, but otherwise the shop was empty. It looked much as it had at the beach, only the long table was back, now covered with tools and supplies for shaping and felting and ornamenting a variety of headdresses. Not only shears and thread and ribbon and lace, but also the strange little ornamentations that Hatta was becoming known for: soft-worn chips of blue and green sea glass. Fish scales. Talons. Long, sharp teeth — she didn't know from what creatures. Assorted seashells. Still-sticky honeycomb. Dandelion tufts and huckleberry branches and white bark peeled from a birch tree.

There was a curtained doorway at the back that Catherine was sure hadn't been there the first two times she'd been in the shop. She approached it and knocked softly.

"You can pay the money tree out front for your purchases," came Hatta's tired-sounding reply.

Steeling herself, Catherine pulled aside the curtain, revealing a small, cluttered office and Hatta with his feet thrown up onto a desk.

"I am not here to make a purchase," she said.

His eyes lifted and there was a quick and deep down-turn of his mouth. "Lady Pinkerton," he drawled, "I wish I could say this is a pleasant surprise."

Catherine shouldered through the curtain. "Good day to you, too, Hatta. I didn't realize you'd gone back to disliking me."

"What do you want? I'm busy."

"Would you like me to come back later?"

"I wish you wouldn't."

A twitch started above her left eyebrow. "I'm not sure what I've done to earn your ire this time, but I've come with a proposal for you, Hatta."

He guffawed. "A proposal! My, my, you capricious thing. How many men do you intend to attach yourself to?"

Her shoulders tensed. "So it's the King's proclamation that has you turned against me?"

"I apologize, *Your Ladyship,*" he spat, "but you are not the Queen yet, and I have no time to entertain your whimsies. As you see, I'm working."

He did not at all look like he was working, but Cath bit back the accusation. "I am not engaged to the King, whatever you might think —"

He snorted.

"And even if I were, it would be no one's

business but mine and His Majesty's. You have no place to criticize."

"No one's business but yours and His Majesty's and the hapless chap that would twist himself into knots to impress you. But then, I suppose Jest willingly took the role of amusing plaything for the King's court, so why should you treat him any differently?"

Her heart throbbed. "Jest was there when the King asked to court me. I've kept nothing from him, so I don't see why you should take offense. Now, if you can stand to be civil for a moment, I came to speak with you about your business. I need only a minute of your time."

"You wouldn't believe how few minutes I have left to spare." Hatta swung his feet down from the desk. "Besides, my business is mine alone, Lady Pinkerton. I bid you good day."

She ground her teeth, trying to bury her growing annoyance. "As I said, I've come with a propo— proposition for you, and I believe a savvy businessman would hear me out."

His lavender eyes burned with more disdain than Catherine could ever recall having directed at her. "You could be offering me the King's crown itself and I would not wish to hear a word of it."

Red spots flickered in her vision. "I've done nothing to earn such disrespect."

"You are not playing by the correct rules!" he yelled, slamming his fist on his desk so hard Catherine jumped.

Hatta inhaled sharply and turned his face away. Reeling in his temper, or perhaps embarrassed that his madness — that hated family trait — was beginning to show.

Catherine swallowed and proceeded, more cautiously, "I did not realize we were playing a game, sir."

He took in a few long breaths before he said, "No, it is not a game. I spoke with little consideration for the reality of the situation." He cleared his throat and peered up at her again. Some of the anger had cleared from his face. "You are going to marry the King, Lady Pinkerton, and I shall wish you all the happiness in the world. I am only ashamed to have been party to your feigned interest in my friend. All those smiles and flirtations, and all the while you had your eye set on a crown? Quite the step up from a hat that jingles, I'll give you that."

"I am not —" She paused. Digging her nails into her palms, she continued, calmer, "I feigned nothing with Jest, but as I said, that is all between Jest and the King and me and has nothing at all to do with you."

"He is my oldest and dearest friend." Hatta glared at her, making Cath feel like a weed to be plucked. "I do not wish to see him hurt."

Her face was burning, self-loathing pulsing against her temple, when her eye fell on a bowler hat on the corner of Hatta's desk, wrapped with green ribbon. "What is that doing here?"

Hatta's gaze dropped and one eyebrow had shot up when he looked at her again. "In case you had not noticed, I make hats."

Shaking her head, she reached for the bowler cap, but Hatta batted her away. She frowned. "That's the Turtle's hat, the one he was wearing when he . . . when . . . during the festival."

"How observant you are."

She stared at him. Waiting.

He stared back.

Catherine lifted her chin. "Did this hat have something to do with the tragic thing that happened?"

"You'll have to be more specific."

"You know precisely what I'm talking about! Did this hat . . . Hatta, are your hats dangerous?"

"Dangerous! Bah!" His tone was scathing, harsh with ridicule. But a moment later he was marching around the desk and into the main showroom and shooing away the two Owls. Upon seeing the look in his eyes, they were quick to flutter out the door without complaint, and Hatta swung around the sign to read CLOSED. He slammed the door shut and stormed back to the office. Catherine had not moved.

"Am I right?" she continued. "Your hats . . . they change people, don't they?"

"You have no idea what you're speaking of." A careless flick of his fingers enraged Catherine further.

"Then explain it to me."

He chortled. "My, my. I cannot recall the last time I was thus ordered around. What a fine queen you will make."

"I am not going to be the Queen!" she yelled, and relished a spark of pride when the Hatter jumped at her raised voice. She continued with chilling composure, "The King has not proposed, but should he, I have every intention of rejecting him."

He gawked at her, disbelief written sharp across his features. "I don't believe that."

"Believe what you will, but stop changing the subject. These hats — Mary Ann's bonnet makes her capable of bigger dreams, and Margaret was certainly changed when she was wearing that rose, and now the

Turtle . . . that darling Turtle . . ."

"The Mock Turtle, you mean. Call him what he is."

"He was a real turtle before he put on that!" She gestured to the bowler hat. "How can you be so callous? If this was your doing —"

"The hat had nothing to do with his transformation. I only have it because he came to me this morning asking for my help. I tried my best to assist him, but he was beyond my reach. Wretched creature he's become, but not yet desperate enough."

"You were going to give him a different hat to change him back?"

He waved his arm through the air. "You misunderstand completely, but it's no business of yours."

"But your hats do change people. I've seen it with my own eyes. I've felt it. They're dangerous, Hatta. You have to stop!"

Their gazes warred with each other, a heady silence punctuated with the drum of Cath's heartbeat.

Hatta looked away first. Rounding back to his seat, he collapsed into it and folded his hands over his stomach. "My hats are not dangerous, and I will not have you spreading such damning rumors." His lips thinned. "But they are special. They are unique from any other hats found in the great Kingdom of Hearts, and as I told you before, I come from a long line of very fine hatters."

"I'm not interested in solicitations."

"You asked a question. I'm answering it."

"I wish you would do it in fewer words."

He smirked. "Yes. Fine. They change people. They *improve* them. But that does not mean this hat was at fault for the Mock Turtle. Satisfied?"

"Not at all. How are you doing it?"

"I don't do anything. I only make my creations from . . . unique materials."

"Unique in what way?"

He studied her for a long time and she began to doubt he would answer the question, before he finally said, "The materials with which my hats are crafted all come from the lands of the Red and White Queens."

A shiver skittered down her back. "Of course. You're from Chess, like Jest and Raven."

His eyes narrowed. "He told you that?"

"Yes. Because he trusts me." Her voice had an edge, and she could see the jolt of annoyance that flashed over Hatta's features.

His jaw tightened, but he seemed to make the conscious decision to not be riled. He leaned back and picked some lint from his waistcoat. "I'm sure he had his reasons for telling you as much. But I am from Hearts originally. Grew up in my father's hat shop before his untimely end encouraged me to search for my fate elsewhere, lest a similar fate find me. I found that fate in Chess."

"But . . . how? How did you find it?"

He shrugged. "A maze, a looking glass, a well . . . an abundance of desperation. It's not all that important. What is important is that my journey taught me how I could avoid the madness that's plagued my ancestors, and also how I could become the greatest hatter who has ever lived, on *either* side of the Looking Glass."

He examined his nails. "I met Jest there, and he introduced me to the White King and Haigha. I was poor and alone, but the King granted me a pawnship, and it was determined that Haigha and I would become his royal messengers, skirting the edges of the battlefield to run correspondence between the Red and White Queendoms. On our travels I collected materials to be turned into hats for the Queen upon my return. I gathered pebbles and flowers and bones and I began to develop my reputation. Not just as a pawn or a messenger, but a hatter. The finest of hatters."

"I don't understand," said Cath. "You went there to escape the fate of your father, so you wouldn't go mad. Why become a hatter again?"

He held up a finger. "That is the trick of it. You see, Time works differently in Chess." He pulled out his pocket watch and let it dangle like a pendulum over his desk. "Sometimes he moves forward and sometimes he moves backward, sometimes he goes fast or slow and sometimes he pauses altogether. But as long as I keep moving, as long as I am always moving in the opposite direction from Time, he can never find me, and I can never meet my fate."

His voice had a strange cadence to it, almost harmonizing with the quiet tick-ticking of the watch, and Cath wondered again if he was already mad, despite what he said.

She swallowed back these thoughts, determined to hear his story to the end. "But now you've come back to Hearts."

"So I have." He snapped his fist around the watch and dropped it back into his pocket. "Jest and Raven required a guide to help them across the Looking Glass, and the King and Queen needed a messenger to report back on their . . ." He hesitated.

"Mission," Cath supplied. "Jest told me

they're on a mission to stop a war."

His face turned briefly sour again. "And did he tell you what the mission is?"

She wished with all her heart that she could say yes, but he hadn't. She shook her head again.

"Thank goodness for that," he muttered, then sighed. "Anyhow, I was the only one who knew the way, so Haigha and I came along. I had not expected the happy discovery that awaited me here in my childhood home. This side of the Looking Glass, all those baubles were no longer simply pebbles and bones. They do not make regular hats."

"They're dangerous."

"They are *marvelous.* No longer does a hat complete an outfit — now it completes you. I am providing a great service to the people of Hearts and I am going to go down in history as the greatest hatter this kingdom has ever known, and as I can return to Chess whenever I wish, I will not need to lose my sanity for it."

"But what do they do?"

"Anything. Everything. They can make you a little braver, a little stronger, a little more charming or interesting or intelligent —"

"Or they might turn you into an ingredient for soup!" she bellowed. "You know your hats change people, so how can you be so sure this hat didn't change the Turtle?"

He rubbed his temple. "My reputation is the foundation on which this business is built. I would do nothing to harm that." He trailed his fingers over the ribbons and buttons and feathers scattered across the desk. "We can't all be so lucky as to be offered the hand of the King, after all."

She ignored the jab, scanning the table's accoutrements. His hats were quirky and whimsical and beautiful in their own strange ways. And now she knew they were more marvelous than even the sign outside proclaimed. Hatta would receive acclaim as a great hatter, and also an artist, but only if his reputation remained untarnished.

It wasn't unlike what she wanted to accomplish with her bakery. Though she didn't care to be wealthy, she did want to make a living on her craft. She wanted people to appreciate her not for a pretty face or a family title, but for what she could make with her own two hands.

"I apologize if I offended you, Hatta," she said, before she could change her mind. "I did not come here to argue with you. I came to make you a deal."

"Ah, yes. Your proposal."

Swallowing hard, Catherine reached into

her purse and pulled out the proposal she and Mary Ann had spent all night writing and revising. "You have my word that I won't tell anyone about Chess or the questionable properties of your hats. On two conditions."

He massaged the bridge of his nose, but didn't stop her.

"One: You must be sure your hats are safe to be worn, and stop selling them immediately if you find evidence to the contrary."

"A business with faulty merchandise does not flourish. I don't require your nagging to tell me this."

"Fine. But you might find my second request to be a little more unconventional." She took a step closer. "I want you to give me a loan."

He balked. "A loan? What — of money?"

"Yes. Businessman to business . . . woman. I'm starting a business of my own, but I require an investor."

He laughed, an enormous booming laugh. "I cannot wait to hear more."

She set the folded letter down on Hatta's desk, pressing it into the wood with the pad of her finger. "Enclosed in this letter you'll find my proposal for *Sweets and Tarts: The Most Wondrous Bakery in All of Hearts.*"

He grunted. "How quaint."

"You've tasted what I can make. Whatever your personal feelings toward me, I ask you to consider this as a businessman. People will come from all over the land to sample the richest cakes, the sweetest pies, the softest bread they've ever known."

He stared at her for a long time, his expression inscrutable. Finally, he said, "You plan to open a bakery."

"That is correct."

"And you want my help."

"I want a business loan. It's all lined out here — payments, interest, everything." She felt very smart saying it, and was glad she'd broken down and asked Mary Ann for help in drafting the proposal.

There was another long, long silence, before he said, "And tell me, Lady Pinkerton, does a queen have time to run a bakery?"

She bristled and answered, enunciating carefully, "I am not a queen."

"No," he said. "Not yet."

The twitch in her eyebrow worsened.

Pressing his own finger into the letter, Hatta pulled it toward him across the desk. But he didn't open it. "I admire your gumption more than I care to admit. You remind me something of myself."

She bristled.

"But no, I do not believe this would be a wise business decision, as I do not believe you will be successful in this endeavor."

It was like being slapped — so strong, so unapologetic the rejection. "How can you say that?"

"The macarons were impressive, but in your haste to blame me for the unfortunate incident at the festival, you have overlooked another possibility. Potentially incriminating evidence that others will not be so quick to dismiss. In fact, I wonder if you are so insistent on finding fault with me because *you* have something to hide?"

"I don't know what you're talking about."

"The Turtle — that poor, darling thing — had only moments before his transformation eaten an entire slice of your cake."

She froze.

Until she'd considered it might be the hat, this had been her fear, though she had hoped no one else would make such a connection. She hated to think he might be right — blaming his hats would mean she could stop questioning if she, herself, was involved.

Because it was only a cake. Only a spiced pumpkin cake.

"Of five judges," Hatta continued, "he was

the only judge to sample your dessert. Naturally, people are beginning to wonder if it wasn't your cake that resulted in his unfortunate change."

Her heart thumped. "I've cooked dozens — hundreds of cakes and never has anything like this happened before."

"It only takes one." Picking up Cath's letter, he started to shred it into linen strips, not even bothering to break the wax seal. Her jaw ached from clenching as she watched hours of careful planning ripped apart.

"Besides," Hatta said, tossing the shredded paper back at her. It wisped and fluttered and clung to the fabric of her gown. "I have a personal rule about not entering into business with spineless creatures. No snakes. No slippery eels. And worst of all, no fickle women. Play coy all you like, Lady Pinkerton. Cling to your belief in your own innocence. You know as well as I that you're going to break at least one heart before this is over, and I want nothing more to do with you."

Chapter 32

Catherine trudged through the back door, reeling with infuriation and insult. In the kitchen she nearly ran into Abigail as she bustled toward the stairs carrying a tray of cucumber sandwiches.

Abigail gasped. "Lady Catherine! Oh, thank heavens. Mary Ann was just called upstairs, and you'd best get up there, too, before the Marchioness works herself into a frenzy."

"Tea? This early?"

Abigail cocked her head, silently demanding that Catherine go on ahead, and fast.

Remembering her parents' threat to release Mary Ann, Catherine hung up her shawl and took the stairs two at a time. Normally her father took his tea in the library, but when she stepped onto the landing she heard voices coming from the front parlor, which was only used for entertaining guests.

The thought of entertaining anyone made her bones shudder.

She considered jotting up to her room and pretending she wasn't home, but before she could make a decision, her mother poked her head out of the room. Her face was contorted into a crazed grin. "Catherine! There you are! I thought I heard you come in, sweetest girl!"

Sweetest girl?

A new dread sank onto Catherine's shoulders. "I didn't think we were expecting guests. I'm not properly dressed for —"

Bustling forward, her mother smoothed back Cath's hair and picked at her dress collar, then nudged her toward the parlor. "Don't be silly, dear. We mustn't keep our guests waiting . . ."

"But —"

"Here she is, Your Majesty!" her mother bellowed, shoving Catherine through the doorway. "I found her loitering in the hallway, bashful thing!"

The King and the Marquess both jumped to their feet. Again, the King had brought with him the twitching White Rabbit, his guards, and Jest. Again Jest stood by the far window, his black motley and drooping hat silhouetted in the afternoon light. He stood at respectful attention, his hands linked behind his back, but this time he was pointedly staring at the wall rather than at her.

On the opposite side of the room, Mary Ann stopped pouring tea long enough to shoot Catherine a curious look. Cath couldn't hold it, too ashamed of her recent failure with Hatta.

The King clapped, a solo applause for Catherine's opportune entrance. "There she is, there she is!" he said. "And here I am — surprise!"

Cath forced a wobbly smile. "Good day, Your Majesty. To what do we owe this honor?"

"Ah, my beloved," said the King, beaming around the word and ignorant to Cath's grimace, "there is to be a spectacle most extraordinary at the Lobe Theater tonight — a special production of *King Cheer*, performed in my own honor! I was hoping . . ." He cleared his throat. "I hoped, with the permission of the Marquess, that you might agree to accompany me, my . . . my sweet." His hands knotted themselves together and his coyness would have been endearing if Cath hadn't been so reviled.

"My, that sounds splendid, Your Majesty," said the Marchioness. "Doesn't that sound splendid, Catherine?"

Her gaze darted to Jest, rather against her

will, but his expression was as blank as an undisturbed pond.

"I am flattered, Your Majesty, but I would require a chaperone for such an outing and I don't know that we can spare —"

"Take Mary Ann," said her mother. Mary Ann froze in the middle of pouring a spoonful of sugar into a cup. "Mary Ann, stop bothering with all that and go get changed. Snap, snap!" Her mother punctuated the words with snapping fingers and, with hardly a surprised glance at Catherine, Mary Ann had scurried from the room and the Marchioness had taken over the tea. "You, too, Catherine. Go make yourself presentable. The Lobe Theater is very nice, if I recall, though it's been years since Mr. Pinkerton took me there, isn't that right, Mr. Pinkerton?"

The Marquess grinned at her, all swoony eyes. "Oh yes, my love, I remember it well. You were ravishing that night, and I do believe I spent more time watching you than the show. *The Taming of the Stew,* wasn't it?"

The Marchioness tittered.

"But, Mother," started Catherine, "what about the Jabberwock? Surely it isn't yet safe to —"

Her mother's delight turned fast to a

frown. "Don't be daft, child. You'll be with the King! Surrounded by guards! No harm will come to you."

"But I've only just gotten home and I'm not —"

"Catherine. His Majesty has requested your presence at this most extraordinary spectacle. We will not disappoint him, will we?"

By which, Cath knew, she was asking if Catherine would dare to disappoint *her.*

She gave the slightest shake of her head.

"As I thought. Now run along and put on something proper." Her sunshine smile was back as she turned to the King again. "You did say that you take your tea with milk, isn't that so, Your Majesty?"

Gnawing on the inside of her cheek, Catherine turned toward the door. She dared one last look at Jest, but the only change was a tiny crease between his eyebrows. As if he sensed her attention on him, he sighed, slowly, but his focus stayed attached to the far wall.

As she headed up to change, Cath wondered which of them wanted to be there less.

The carriage ride proved to be even more awkward. With Catherine and Mary Ann taking up two spots in the King's barouche, the White Rabbit was forced to sit out with the footman and he looked so forlorn about it Cath almost suggested trading places with him.

In the end, she wished that she had, as she was left crammed into a tiny vestibule facing the King and Jest on the other bench.

Luckily, the King seemed oblivious to the discomfort around him. He jovially carried on a solo conversation with prattle about the palace gardens and how he wanted a tree house once some of the trees got big enough to support it.

Jest's eyes remained locked on the window, even though a curtain was pulled down over the view.

Cath found herself leaning into Mary Ann each time the King said something particularly annoying, and Mary Ann began doing the same, offering what silent empathy she could. Soon their shoulders were pressed so tight together Cath's fingers had started to tingle.

She was grateful when they arrived at the theater — an architectural marvel with seating that wrapped almost all the way around the stage, mimicking the shape of a human earlobe.

At the King's arrival, a hand of Diamond courtiers flattened themselves on their bellies, making a carpet that extended to the theater entrance, which was carved to look like two upright rabbit ears. The goggle-eyed footman assisted Cath and Mary Ann from the carriage.

Grabbing a scepter from the driver's seat, Jest led their group forward, hoisting the scepter high. Before he had gone into the theater, the great black raven swooped down from the sky and settled on top of the scepter like a perch. Jest didn't slow, but Raven did turn his head to glance back at Cath with his black, expressionless eyes. He dipped his beak toward Jest's ear and said something Cath couldn't hear. Jest shook his head sharply in response.

Catherine realized she was staring at him. She had hardly stopped staring at him since they'd left Rock Turtle Cove.

If Jest had looked at her once, she knew nothing of it.

The King, ever oblivious, offered his elbow and Cath took it, stifling her disappointment. Mary Ann followed behind, apologizing to the courtiers as she stepped across them.

The lobby was crowded with guests waiting to take their seats. Jest and Raven had already disappeared into the bustle as Catherine and the King entered and were met with bows and curtsies and so many congratulations they might already have been betrothed. Catherine did her best to look baffled when she received their well-wishes, earning plenty of baffled looks in return, but soon it became clear that she was losing this battle. After the King's proclamation at the festival, all of Hearts believed them engaged, and there seemed to be little Catherine could do to dissuade those rumors here, at a theater, on the King's arm.

Overnight her life had become a whirlpool, sucking her below the surface.

They greeted Margaret Mearle, who looked smug and unimpressed that Catherine was now a favorite of the King, and the Duke, who tried to hide his envy at the King's romantic success.

Cath realized she'd been so caught up in her own heart's matters, she'd pitifully failed the Duke. He had asked her to help him win Margaret's affections, but all she could think to do was to shake them both and order them to get over their pride and awkwardness before it was too late.

A hand suddenly grabbed Cath's wrist, pulling her free of the King. She spun and was surprised to find herself staring into the gaunt face of Lady Peter, who held her more tightly than Cath would have thought she had strength for.

"Do you have any more?" Lady Peter said before Cath could get off a greeting. She was whispering, but it was almost as loud as a yell in the crowded space.

Cath ducked her head closer, not sure she'd heard right. "Any more?"

Lady Peter nodded, her eyes wide and bloodshot. She cast her gaze around the lobby before tugging Cath closer. Their faces were mere inches away from each other now, and Cath could see the yellow tinge of the lady's teeth, the sharp edges of her cheekbones. There was a sheen of sweat on her upper lip.

"Tell me," Lady Peter said, pleading. "Please tell me you have more. I'll do anything, pay any amount —" Her voice broke. "That is, I haven't much money, but I can pay you in dirt and favors, or —"

"Lady Peter, please. I don't know what you're talking about."

Her voice dropped again. *"The cake."*

Catherine gaped. "Pardon?"

Lady Peter's mouth turned down with irritation and she dug into her dress pockets. It was, Cath realized, the same black muslin dress she'd worn at the King's black-and-white ball, and though it was practically rags compared to the gowns the other ladies wore, she wondered if it might be the finest dress Lady Peter owned.

The thought struck her with a dart of pity, and she wondered if it would seem terribly rude to give her one of her own dresses. She had plenty, though it would have to be taken in quite a lot to fit her, and Sir Peter hadn't seemed fond of charity . . .

Her thoughts halted when Lady Peter pulled her hand out of her pocket, revealing a sullied linen napkin. She peeled open the corners and in the center of the napkin were the remains of a slice of spiced pumpkin cake, so squashed that the cake and frosting had melded together into an almost unrecognizable lump.

A few crumbs started to tumble over the napkin's edge and Lady Peter gasped and leaned down, catching them in her mouth.

Her whole body was trembling as she peered up at Cath again and refolded the napkin over the cake, stashing it back into her pocket. "I took all what was uneaten after the festival, but this slice is all what's left. Please, you must have more. Tell me you have more."

Cath started to shake her head. "No, I . . . I'm sorry. I only made the one cake."

She saw no point in mentioning the test

cake she had made. Between her and Mary Ann, it hadn't lasted long.

Lady Peter's expression fell. Not into disappointment, but a crazed sort of anguish. She reached for Cath's wrists again, clamping on to both of them this time.

"But where did you get the pumpkin?"

Cath's lips parted. She hesitated.

She couldn't admit to the theft, not to the man's own wife.

"Please!" Lady Peter screeched. Cath gasped as her grip tightened, sure she was leaving bruises. "I'll die without it. Please."

Die?

Was she dying? She looked ill enough.

Cath stammered, "It was from your — your husband's pumpkin patch. I'm sorry. I shouldn't have taken it, but it looked abandoned and —"

"Liar!"

"Ow!" Cath yanked her hands away and looked down, bewildered, to see that Lady Peter's nails had left bloodied scratches on her arms. She stumbled backward, her previous sympathy eclipsed by shock.

"He destroyed them all," Lady Peter said. Her face was stricken and pale as bone. "Burned them, every last one. He doesn't understand how I need them, *need* them —"

A shadow loomed over them and Cath was almost relieved to see Sir Peter. He grabbed his wife's arm, turning from her to Cath with his terrible scowl. "What's this about?"

"Nothing," Lady Peter said quickly, withdrawing into the meek, trembling girl Cath remembered from the ball. "Only trying to make acquaintances, like you said . . ."

"Don't you bother with Lady Pinkerton. She thinks we're beneath her," he said, which Cath thought was unfair, even though she had seen little of them worth admiring. "The show is beginning."

Lady Peter didn't argue as he tugged her away, but her gaze did find Cath again. Pleading. Pleading.

As soon as they were gone, Catherine dragged in a deep breath. She rubbed her wrists, glad that the wounds weren't deep and had already stopped bleeding, though they stung something dreadful.

She scanned the crowd, dazed for a moment and unable to recall where she was or why she was there. She spotted the King having a conversation with the Dowager Countess Wontuthry — the King standing on a step so he could be at the Countess's height, even with her bent back.

It took Cath a long moment to remember

that she was here with the King. He was her beau. Many believed, her betrothed.

Only then did she realize that in her bewilderment she'd been looking for Jest.

Stomach sinking, she picked her way through the emptying lobby. The King lit up when he saw her and bid the Countess farewell before towing Cath up the steps. She followed him with mounting dread, down a lavish hallway artfully decorated with plaster molds of various hearing apparatuses — from tiny mouse ears to humongous, flopping elephant ears. Torch-like sconces cast warm fire-glow across the sculptures.

The King had a private box on the first balcony level — the kind that sacrificed a decent view of the stage in return for being seen by the rest of the theatergoers. The White Rabbit held back the velvet drapes.

Her heart leaped when she saw that Jest was there, waiting for them, a silent shadow against the rail. Raven was still perched on the scepter, cleaning his feathers.

But when Jest didn't so much as look up at their entrance, her heart plummeted back down again.

"Here we are, here we are!" the King said, ushering Cath toward the front row. She heard a sharp intake of breath from Jest as she was squeezed past him, his body drawing back to keep from touching her, and she had to tighten her own fists to keep from accidentally, purposely, brushing his hand.

She and the King sat in the front row while Mary Ann took a seat behind them. Jest and the Rabbit remained standing at the door. Cath locked her gaze on the stage and its closed curtain, eager for the show to begin so she could shut her eyes and imagine herself elsewhere.

"Can you see all right, Lady Pinkerton?" asked the King.

"Perfectly," she said, resisting the urge to ask if he required an extra cushion to lift him up.

"Do you want for anything? A glass of claret? Some cheese?"

"I'm fine, thank you, Your Majesty."

"Are you too warm? Here, Rabbit, take Lady Pinkerton's shawl —"

"No, thank you, Your Majesty."

The King hesitated, his face eager to please, before slowly settling back. After a moment, he leaned forward so far off the railing that Cath had a strange urge to push him over, though the thought made her feel wretched. This man, she reminded herself, was not at fault for anything that had happened.

She wished he hadn't made some assumptions, or made that mortifying announcement at the festival, but then, she was the one who had agreed to the courtship. She was the one who should never have let this carry on so long, not if she intended to reject him.

She had to reject him. She had to.

But thinking of it gave her a headache.

The King turned back to the Rabbit. "How long before the show begins?"

A rustling behind Catherine was followed by the ticking of a pocket watch — she wondered if it was the one Jest had given him at the ball, but she didn't turn to look.

"Five minutes, Your Majesty," came Mr. Rabbit's reply.

The King turned back, galloping his feet. "Jest, Lady Pinkerton and I are bored. Won't you amuse us?"

Cath's head snapped up. "That's not necessary. I'm not bored at all, in fact."

Jest looked at her — finally. She tried to smile, imagining they were accomplices in their understanding of the situation, but he flinched and turned away.

Withdrawing, Cath looked down at the mezzanine level. "I enjoy watching the people. Why — is that Mrs. Quail? I heard she had a nestful of eggs a few months ago but it seems they've all hatched. What a darling little family they make."

The King followed her gesture. "So it is!" He clasped his hands beneath his chin. "I just love when they're little, don't you? The cute little cherubs, with their itty-bitty beaks and plump little bodies."

He sighed and Catherine had to agree that the baby quails were adorable. She counted a baker's dozen of them, taking up an entire theater row.

"How many do you want?" asked the King, settling his elbows on the rail and dropping his chin into his palms.

She peered sideways at him. "Eggs? Or quails?"

"Children." His face had gone ruby red, but his eyes were dreamy when he glanced at Catherine through his lashes. "I want a full suit of ten someday."

Heat rushed up her neck, blooming across her cheeks. An impossible-to-ignore choking noise from Jest twisted like a knife in her stomach.

"I . . . suppose I haven't given it much thought," she said, followed by a painful gulp. It wasn't entirely true. She thought it might be nice to have a family someday.

But not with him. Dear Hearts, not with him.

Jest thumped his scepter so hard on the floor Cath felt it vibrating through her feet. Raven squawked and fluttered for a moment before settling down again.

Catherine and the King both turned.

"*I* could use some claret," Jest said, looking at the King as if he dared his sovereign to deny him such a request. "Can I bring the happy couple anything while I'm gone?"

Cath's heart pattered. "You're leaving?"

The rest of her question shrieked in her head. He was leaving her alone? With *him*?

She was surprised at how much it hurt. After all, Jest had told her he wouldn't compete with the King for her affections. He would stay out of it until she'd made her decision.

Every moment spent in their mutual presence made her feel like a spineless coward, but that didn't change the fact that she didn't want Jest to leave.

Coward, coward, coward.

The King started to bounce in his chair. "Aha! You see, Jest, she does wish for a spot of entertainment!"

"Oh no, that wasn't what I — heavens. It is rather warm in here, isn't it?"

Some of the tension in Jest's shoulders

drained away. "Allow me," he said, swooping forward and assisting her out of her shawl before she could take a breath. His gloved fingertips were tender against her shoulders. She shivered.

"I am of course happy to provide entertainment, if it pleases the lady," said Jest, hanging her shawl on a rack at the back of the theater box. "Perhaps I shall offer poetic waxations on the lady's buttercream frosting skin? Endless compliments on her hair like melted chocolate?"

Rather than be embarrassed at Jest quoting their "personal" correspondence, the King happily kicked his heels. "That was from one of the letters I sent you, remember? Jest only had to help with that one a little bit." He straightened the crown on his head. "I was awful hungry after writing it."

"Fine literature does work up an appetite." Jest was no longer trying to hide his ironic tone, but he seemed in no danger of the King picking up on his mockery.

Catherine squeezed the arm of her seat, her body still rotated to face Jest. Mary Ann watched from the corner, pretending to be invisible. "To be honest, it wasn't my favorite of the letters you sent. After all, I'm a lady, not a dessert."

Jest's cheek twitched. Cath didn't bother

to look at the King.

"In fact," she continued, "poetry and gifts may have their place, but I find I'm more keen on those acts of courtship that retain an element of foolishness, and hint at impossibilities."

A silence descended over their private booth. Jest's lips thinned. He stared back at her and squeezed his scepter. His eyes filled with quiet despair.

She'd said too much, and even if she'd said nothing at all, surely the truth of her emotions was scrawled across her face.

"My sweet," the King whispered. She grimaced and braced herself for what must be the end of this night, this nonexistent romance. She dared to face him, ready to accept his decision to call off their courtship. But she did not see a crushed spirit or annoyance or even confusion. She saw only joy in the King's eyes.

He took her hand. She jumped, her back stiffening.

"I feel the same way," he said, and looked as if he would cry. Her hand was a limp fish in his grip, but he held it like a precious gem.

"Er — Your Majesty —"

Behind them, Jest yanked off his jester's cap. The bells jingled. "I realize I haven't yet offered my congratulations on your engagement," he said, bowing. "You seem a most perfect match, and I wish you both the joy of a most contented heart."

Catherine tried to shake her head, her emotions in tatters.

The chandeliers dimmed and Jest settled his hat back on his head. "Enjoy the show. Your Majesty. Lady Pinkerton." He turned to the back row. "Miss Mary Ann."

Cath squeezed the arm of her chair and tried to convey to him how much she wanted him to stay, how she would give anything to be at his side, not the King's.

Jest tore his gaze away and swept from the theater box, Raven still perched on his scepter.

Miserable, she turned back to face the stage. Her hand was cold, but the King's was hot and damp. He didn't let go. She could catch glimpses of his pleased mug in the corner of her vision.

The curtain began to rise. An orchestra blared and the first act tumbled out onto the stage. The audience cheered, the King loudest of all.

Chapter 33

Catherine was weary, in her head, in her limbs, down to the toes pinched inside her finest boots. Her head was full of fantasies of going home and crawling beneath her covers and not coming out again until she'd achieved the longest sleep of her life. The wish was so powerful she wanted to weep from longing.

She could tell the performance was commendable, judging by the frequent gasps and cheers from the audience, but she could barely keep her stinging eyes open enough to enjoy the show, and the storyline muddled in her head by the second scene.

It was only when a fool appeared on the stage that she willed herself to pay attention. But it wasn't Jest, only an actor, done up in familiar black motley, doing cartwheels across the stage and spouting bawdy jokes that left the audience in hysterics. He poked fun of the King, he peeked up the skirts of the passing actresses, he wagged his hat until the jingle of the bells was all Cath could hear inside her head.

As the crowd broke into another bout of laughter, Cath launched to her feet. "I need to use the powder room."

The King took no notice as she inched past, too enthralled with the fake joker, but Mary Ann started to rise to come with her. Cath gestured for her to stay. "I'm fine. I'll be right back."

The stairs into the lobby echoed with her footsteps as she rushed down to the main level, gripping the banister to keep from tripping on her skirt. Only once her feet had hit the final step and she'd spun around the rail did she hear Jest's rumbling voice — followed by the higher-pitched, snooty tone of Margaret Mearle.

Catherine reeled back, ducking behind a pillar.

"— about as pigheaded as they come!" Margaret was saying.

"An apt description," agreed Jest, though he sounded tired, "but stubbornness is not always a flaw, particularly in matters of love."

Margaret guffawed. *"Love?"*

"Indeed, love, or so it seems from my perspective. You ought to see how his eyes follow you around a room. Small and beady they might be, but they overflow with affection, nevertheless." Jest cleared his throat. "The moral of that, of course, is that 'beauty is in the eye of the beholder.' "

"I've never heard such a moral, and as I'm sure you're well aware, I am most knowledgeable in the matter of morals."

"I think I read it in a book."

"Well." There was a long hesitation. "It is a decent sort of moral, I suppose."

"There was another too. Something about the depth of skin . . . not as apropos, I fear."

"He is both thick-skinned and thick-headed."

"Two of the Duke's finer qualities. I might also add that he's an impeccable dresser."

Margaret hummed, unconvinced.

"And brave," Jest added, "as showcased when he stood between you and the Jabberwock at the ball. And also loyal and compassionate, even to his servants — I hear he refuses to let go of his cook, though I'm told she's quite dreadful."

"But I don't understand it. He's always been so rude toward me. I've never felt so judged in all my life than when I'm in his presence, with that snooty look he gives everyone, and the way his nose turns up."

"Could it be, Lady Mearle, that you've

judged him unfairly? What you call rudeness might be nothing more than his inability to speak easily with a girl he admires."

"Do you really believe he feels this way?"

"He told me so himself, Lady Mearle. What reason would I have for leading you astray?"

"It just seems so . . . so sudden."

"I assure you it's been brewing for longer than you realize. Here, he asked that I give you this."

Catherine heard the crinkle of parchment.

"What is it?"

"An invitation to join him in his theater box tonight, if you'd care to, along with your chaperone, of course. He said he would leave a seat available, in hopes you might accept the invitation."

Margaret let out a delighted *oh.* The paper crisped some more. "I . . . well. I suppose it couldn't hurt . . . just for an evening . . . after all, I am not the sort of lady to dally about indecisively when faced with a man's well-intentioned admiration."

"I wouldn't dare suggest such a thing, Lady Mearle. I hope you'll enjoy the rest of the performance."

Catherine pressed herself to the pillar, inching around to its far side as she heard

Margaret's footsteps approaching. She ducked beneath the stair's banister as Margaret floated past, and was just letting out a breath when a flurry of feathers assaulted her face and a *caw* blared in her ears. Catherine stumbled away from the pillar, flattening herself against the wall and beating at the ferocious bird.

Raven twisted away and flew upward to alight on the sculptured bust of a stern-looking playwright.

"Raven!" Jest scolded. "That wasn't nice at all."

"No, no, I'm sure I deserved it," said Cath, trying to smooth back her hair. "I shouldn't have been eavesdropping."

Raven turned his head away, his beak stuck into the air, and it became clear that he now shared Hatta's low opinion of her. She was, after all, the charlatan who had played Jest for a fool while being courted by the King.

"Regardless, you didn't need to frighten her, Raven. You should apologize."

"Nevermore!" said the Raven.

"Raven!"

"It's all right. I'm the one who's sorry, for sneaking around so."

Cath stepped around the staircase and saw Jest leaning against a wall, holding his hat in one hand and the ebony scepter in the other. Half his hair was matted to his head and he looked like a vagabond who had claimed the theater for his own. If it weren't for the thumping drumbeat coming through the closed doors, the place would have felt abandoned but for them.

"Thank you for what you said to Margaret just now," she said. "You didn't have to help me."

He tugged the hat back on. "Let us imagine I did it not for you, but for true love." He shrugged. The gesture wasn't as nonchalant as she thought he intended it to be. "I had the honor of speaking to His Grace at the tea party — the *King's* tea party — and I believe he cares a great deal for Lady Mearle." His eyes narrowed as he glanced up the staircase where she had gone. "I'm not entirely sure why."

"It baffles me as well. But . . . what do you think will happen when she finds out the things you said weren't true? I think your intentions are commendable, but it might do more harm than good."

Jest cocked his head. "What makes you think I said anything that wasn't true?"

"Well, only that the Duke . . ." She hesitated. Brave. Loyal. Always impeccably dressed, though it was sometimes difficult to tell with his girth and awkwardness. Her brow knit together. "Would you believe I've known him nearly all my life? How is it possible that you have somehow come to know him better, so quickly?"

He turned his focus down to the scepter, idly rubbing his fingers along the polished-smooth orb. "You should go back to your seat, Lady Pinkerton. Go back to your beau."

"Please don't call him that."

"What shall I call him?"

"Just the King, if you would."

He wouldn't look at her. Though they stood a mere dozen paces away, it felt like miles and miles.

"Nothing has gone as I thought it would," he said, and she wondered whether he was speaking to her or himself, or even to Raven. "I thought this would all be much, much easier."

"Your mission?" she ventured, dropping her voice. "From the White Queen?"

Raven let out a surprised squawk, but Jest ignored him. Ignored her question too. "His Majesty is going to propose soon, you know. I almost expect him to do it tonight."

Grimacing, Cath glanced back up to the first tier, glad she wasn't up in that dark box, pretending to be enjoying herself. Waiting for the King to ask for her hand.

"If you're asking me whether or not my feelings have changed," she said, "they haven't."

"No, that much is clear." Jest scratched beneath the brim of his hat. "I'm sorry if I've been cold to you tonight. Even knowing you don't fancy him like that, seeing you with him makes me uncannily jealous."

Her heart skipped. "Does it?"

His expression turned wry as he finally looked at her. "That cannot possibly surprise you."

She tried not to sway too much from satisfaction.

Raven let out a disgusted choking noise and flew up into one of the chandeliers. He started cleaning himself, as if soiled.

"You should go back," said Jest. "In case anyone should come out here. We wouldn't want them. . . . It would seem . . ."

Her lips twitched. It was such an unusual thing for him to be out of words.

"You're right," she said, backing away from him. She drifted around the staircase banister, placed a hand on the rail, and looked up the long staircase. Her heart began to sink, like an anchor had been chained to it.

Back to the King. Back to her beau.

A cheer rumbled through the theater, drawing her attention to the closed doors.

"Lady Pinkerton?" said Jest.

She glanced back.

"Have you decided what you will say once he asks?"

Inside the theater, more cheers exploded, louder still. The Raven let out a shrill caw.

"Do you think I could possibly say yes?" she asked, for in this moment, it seemed impossible to her.

Jest was expressionless for a moment, before it turned to pain, the kohl creasing around his eyes. "I think you have to say yes," he whispered, and it sounded like he was pleading with her, but the words sent an arrow into her heart.

She took half a step toward him, but stopped again. "Why, Jest? Why do you keep doing this? You say you're jealous, or mesmerized, or that I could be your reason to stay in Hearts, yet in the very next breath you encourage me to accept the King. I don't understand you."

His expression was pained when he opened his mouth to speak again, but suddenly the building shook. Cath jolted, ducking at the distant crash of breaking glass.

A door burst off its hinges on the second floor. A wave of heat flooded the lobby, along with the smell of smoke.

Catherine reeled back but Jest was already beside her, catching her. She realized that what she'd thought were cheers were actually screams, and applause the stampede of feet.

Through the sizzling door, a creature burst onto the lobby's second level, all black skin and scales and dark, rabid eyes.

Cath froze.

It was the Jabberwock.

Chapter 34

A great shudder coursed through Catherine as she stared at the enormous beast. Though it had terrified her in the glen outside Hatta's shop, it had been too dark then to get a clear look at the beast. But now it towered over her, all claws and scales and rolling muscles. She could see the saliva clinging to its fangs. She could smell its rotted breath.

"Cath, back away, slowly," Jest whispered.

The beast fixed its burning eyes on them and hissed. Catherine stumbled back and Jest shifted, putting himself between them. "Run."

She gripped the railing, but her body wouldn't move. The Jabberwock crawled toward her on its massive limbs. Steam hissed from its nostrils.

With a gurgle in its throat, the Jabberwock leaped forward, jaw unhinged. Catherine screamed. Jest braced himself.

There was a screech and a storm of black

feathers. A drop of ink fell from the sky — Raven, fast as a dart, plunged his beak into one of the monster's ember eyes. The Jabberwock screeched and reared back on its hind legs. When it dropped back to the ground, the entire theater shook and Cath could see that one of the embers in its eyes had been extinguished. Charcoal-tinged blood leaked down the right side of its face.

With another roar, it swiped its claws toward the sky, but Raven was already out of reach, beating his wings against the theater's ceiling.

"Now! Go!" Jest yelled, holding his scepter like a weapon. He leaped onto the stair's balustrade and dashed toward the beast like running up a slanted tightrope. The scepter twirled. One leather boot pressed off a marble statue. He rolled in the air, landed on the back of the monster's long neck, and grabbed one of the spindly whiskers that grew from its head as if he were gripping a leash. Jest yanked the monster's head back. The Jabberwock screeched and bucked but Jest held firm.

Cath trembled, still rooted to the stair.

Raven darted again, aiming for the second eye, but the Jabberwock careened away, batting Raven back with a flailing claw.

"Cath! Run!"

She managed to tear her eyes away and spin around, but she had taken only a step when her toes caught on the voluminous fabric of her gown. Cath screamed and lurched, felt herself falling, crashing down the stairs in a tangle of satin and petticoats.

Her ankle snapped.

Her scream was lost in a torrent of shrieks and the thunder of footsteps. The lobby filled with guests fleeing the theater, surging down the staircase, lobbing themselves over the balcony rails, flooding toward the exit. Catherine curled into the pillow of her gown, her vision white with pain, and hoped not to be trampled.

"Pinkerton?"

She looked up through her cascade of tangled hair and spotted Jack a few feet away, his back pressed against the same pillar she'd hidden behind.

"Jack! Help me — my ankle — I think it's —" She swallowed back a sob.

Nostrils flared, Jack took a step toward her, but was halted by another piercing cry from the Jabberwock. He glanced up and paled. After a moment of indecision, he shook his head. "Not even you're worth it, Lady Pinkerton!" he yelled, before turning on his heels and bolting toward the exit along with the rest of the stampeding crowd.

"Jack! Come back here, you knave!"

But he was gone, lost in the chaos.

Locking her jaw, Catherine rolled onto her back, trying not to disturb her ankle. The sharp pain had turned to agony, but she didn't see any blood.

With stars sparking in the corners of her eyes, she dared to look up. Jest had his scepter hooked around the Jabberwock's neck and Raven's talons had left a series of claw marks between the beast's leathery wings.

Cath curled her fingers into her gown and thought of the stories she'd heard as a child. Fairy tales in which the beast was slain, its monstrous head cut clean from its shoulders like a gruesome trophy.

"Off with its head," she whispered to herself, tossing her gaze wildly around the lobby. There had to be a weapon — something sharper than Jest's polished-wood scepter. "We have to chop off its head."

She had spoken so quietly she could barely hear her own words in the turmoil, yet at that moment, Raven landed on the stair's railing and cocked his head, his fathomless eyes peering into her.

Jest grunted, his face contorted with the effort to control the Jabberwock. The beast suddenly hurled itself upward. Jest lost his grip and slipped back, struck by the monster's whipping tail.

He flipped in the air, landing on his feet with only a slight stumble.

The Jabberwock beat its great wings. All around the lobby, candle flames flickered and blew out.

But one of the monster's wings was off-kilter.

It was wounded.

Raven tore his focus from Catherine and soared upward, targeting the monster's remaining eye. With a snap of its jaws, the Jabberwock caught a tail feather in its mouth. Raven retreated with a cry.

The Jabberwock warbled in the air. It reached for a chandelier but missed and crumpled back toward the lobby's floor. What was left of the crowd scattered. The tiles cracked under the impact. The walls quaked.

The creature panted and gurgled. One burning eye darted around the destruction. A curl of steam spiraled from its nostrils.

It fixed its eye on Catherine again, like a predator singling out the weakest from the herd. Its tongue lolled as it shuddered itself up onto all four legs.

Cath pushed back, her palms slipping on her gown's fabric. She was tangled and trapped and the very idea of putting weight on her ankle brought hysteria clawing up her throat.

The beast lumbered toward her, great globs of saliva dripping from its teeth.

"No!" Jest yelled. "You're fighting me, you great smelly beast! Leave her alone!"

He launched himself off the mezzanine and swung down from a chandelier. The candles were still swinging, splattering wax on the floor, when he landed between the beast's wings. His brow was beaded with sweat, lines of kohl running down his cheeks, yet he managed to make it look like a choreographed dance.

It was like being at the circus. Cath could see it all in her pain-filled delirium. *For our next act, please welcome Jest and the Jubilant Jabberwock, best acrobatic team in all of Hearts!*

She started to laugh hysterically.

Raven puffed his wings, still watching her.

Raging and twisting, the Jabberwock tried to shake off the Joker again, but Jest latched on to the soft tissue where its wings met its back, his scepter raised to strike. Catherine didn't believe he could kill it with a wooden stick. Take out another eye, perhaps. Wound and maim, no doubt. But soon the Jabberwock's teeth would find Jest and end this act.

Feathered wings beat at her hair. She screamed and ducked away, but it was only Raven. He dropped to the ground beside her, his chest fluttering with quick breaths. He had Jest's hat in his talons, the bells silenced against the broken ground.

He fixed his eyes on her and nudged the hat forward.

Cath grabbed it. The fabric was worn and soft. It felt like an ancient thing, not a recent addition to a joker's motley. The bells twinkled as she thrust her arm inside.

No fabric lining, no worn seams. The inside of the hat was a void, deep and endless. She pressed her arm in up to her shoulder, her fingers reaching and stretching until they wrapped around something cool and hard.

She pulled her arm back and gasped.

She was gripping the handle of a sword.

No — the *Vorpal* Sword. She knew it to her bones. Its blade shone silver in the theater's warm light, its hilt encrusted with the teeth and bones of the creatures it had slain before.

She thought of the stories. The brave king who had sought the Jabberwock in the forest and slain it with the righteous Vorpal Sword.

She looked up. Jest was still clinging to the monster's back. He spotted her and his eyes widened. "Catherine — !"

The Jabberwock bucked. This time Jest was flung at the ground, landing on his side with a groan. His scepter skittered into the crowd, the few who were stuck by the theater doors, too afraid to make a run for the exit. They stood huddled in terrified groups, some fleeing back into the theater, others hunching into what safety the staircase could afford them.

The Jabberwock rounded on Catherine again, as if Jest had been nothing but a pestering gnat and she was the true target. Its next meal.

The beast saw the sword in her hand and froze.

The weapon warmed in her hand as if it, too, sensed its prey.

Catherine gulped and allowed herself one whimper of denial. One panicked moment of refusal in which she absolutely, positively, *was not* going to stand on her broken ankle and face this monster with an ancient, mythical weapon.

Then she clenched her jaw and yanked her skirt out from beneath her tangled limbs, ignoring the sound of ripping fabric. She stumbled onto her good leg first, pain jolting up her wounded ankle with each movement. With one hand gripping the sword, she used the other to brace herself on the staircase banister. Her breath had gone ragged, her skin clammy. She was already dizzy from the exertion required to stand.

But standing she was.

Exhaling, she released the handrail and put her weight onto her injured leg. She bit back a shriek, but refused to crumple. She wrapped both hands around the sword's handle and lifted the blade, ignoring the tremble of her arms.

The Jabberwock prowled closer, wary now. It sniffed, like it could smell the steel, or maybe the blood that had once coated it.

Another slow step closer, prowling on all fours.

Catherine tried to gulp but her scratchy throat rebelled.

Another step.

She imagined herself doing it. Swinging the sword as hard as she could. Chopping through sinew and spine. She imagined the creature's head rolling, thumping across the lobby.

She imagined it over and over and over again.

Off with its head.

The words churned through her thoughts.

The creature took another step. Then two.

A salty bead of sweat fell into her eye, stinging her. She blinked it away.

"Catherine . . ." Jest's voice was strained.

The Jabberwock watched her with its one burning coal of an eye, the blood still dribbling down its opposite cheek. Its mouth was open and she could see all of its teeth lined up along its huge jaws. Row upon row of fangs, so big that she wasn't sure it could close its mouth even if it wanted to.

She bared her own teeth.

Off with its head. Off with its head. Off with its —

The Jabberwock shuddered suddenly and turned away. It darted across the floor, claws scratching and scrabbling, and squeezed its wings against its back so it could fit through the doors that had been left open. The crisp twilight air shimmered over the empty streets.

On the outside steps, the Jabberwock spread its wings. The left one trembled at first, but with a snap, the beast lobbed its body into the air. A rush of air blew back into the theater and then the creature was gone, a shadow on the rooftops, its pained cries fading into the night.

Chapter 35

Catherine dropped the sword with an echoing clang.

Pain rushed through her all at once, a burning iron in her ankle, fire shooting through her bones. She wilted down into her dress. Her pulse was a hammer, her fingers hot with rushing blood.

Another gasp from the crowd. A frightened hesitation. No one knew what to do. It was clear they were all waiting for someone else to make a decision. To be the first to move.

A ruler, a leader, a king.

But the King of Hearts stood in their midst, as pale and whimpering as any of his subjects.

Cath realized she was crying. She could feel her nose dripping, but she didn't swipe at it. Let them see her blotchy skin and torn dress and the mucus that was to be expected after witnessing such a horror. Let them see.

Jest stumbled toward her, ignoring their audience. He had a limp, which was even more peculiar than the smeared mask of kohl.

"Catherine. *Catherine.*" He hovered over her, eyes bloodshot. "Where does it hurt? Is it your leg?"

She locked her jaw and nodded — though that slight movement sent her reeling with nausea. She collapsed onto her back and Jest disappeared from view, but she could feel him pushing up the hem of her dress — just a little. Just enough to see.

Cath started to laugh, shrill and hysterical. "Well now — that's hardly — proper," she stammered, choking, tears rolling into her tangled hair. "Oh, stuff and nonsense, it *hurts.*"

Jest touched her ankle and she screamed. The world turned swarmy and full of flashing light. The touch left her.

"L-L-Lady Pinkerton?"

She groaned. Her head fell to the side and she saw the King and the White Rabbit and Mary Ann stumbling down the stairs. Mary Ann was pale with fear, her apron balled up in both fists, her pretty new bonnet crooked on her head.

"Y-Your Majesty," she said. She wished they would all go away, leave her alone. She wished for unconsciousness. "The Jabberwock —"

That was as far as she got before another shot of pain had her reeling.

The King hurried down the rest of the stairs and knelt at her side, taking her hand into his. "You were stunning." He pulled a handkerchief from some fold of his garb, but rather than offer it to Catherine, he dabbed at his own glistening brow. Lifting his head, he peered around at the speechless, still-frozen crowd. "Behold! The treasure of my heart! The keeper of the Vorpal Sword! The most brave and b-b-*brilliant* Lady Catherine Pinkerton. Behold our future queen!"

"No," she murmured, but no one heard her over the applause. Her head lolled and she felt a tender hand supporting it. The soft pad of a thumb stroking the arch of her ear. "I'm not — the sword. It isn't . . ."

"Your Majesty," said Jest, his voice cutting through the cheers. "She's hurt. She needs help."

The King spun back. Panicked. "Oh. Er. Y-yes. Of course."

He looked at her ankle and greened.

Cath clenched her teeth, trying to sharpen her focus as her skull pounded. "If I am stunning — and brilliant — and brave" —

she swallowed a scream — "then you are *useless*!"

Jest froze. The King shrank back.

"The Jabberwock has been terrorizing us for weeks! And what have you done? What are you doing to stop it?"

Squeaking, the King ducked his head between the velvet folds of his cloak.

"You are the King! You have to do something!"

"Catherine." Jest settled a hand on her brow, smoothing back her wild hair. "Reserve your strength, Cath — Lady Pinkerton."

Mary Ann appeared over the King's shoulder, her expression bewildered until she saw Cath's ankle. She pressed a hand over her mouth. It was only momentary, before she steeled herself and turned to the King. "The pain is driving her mad, Your Majesty. Someone must take her to the Sturgeons. I'll call a carriage straightaway —"

"A c-carriage, yes," said the King, his head bobbing, his mustache twitching with each breath. His chest heaved and it seemed he might be sick, but he fought it back.

Cath was crying again, dizzy from the pain. "The beast must be stopped, before anyone else is hurt —"

"I'll take her," said Jest. "It will be faster."

Mary Ann hesitated. "Faster than a carriage?"

"Yes." He met Cath's gaze, his eyes tumultuous and vivid and too, too yellow. She saw him gulp before he added, "We're desperate enough."

Turning away, he grabbed the Vorpal Sword and thrust it back into his hat, which he yanked onto his head. The bells were too bright, too joyful, and they echoed sharply in Cath's ears.

Jest swooped his arms beneath her.

"Nonsense! You can't carry her the whole way!" cried Mary Ann.

"I assure you, I can," he said, and any further protests were drowned out by the roar of an earthquake beneath their feet, the crash and rumble of the theater floor suddenly erupting. Around them. Under them. A tower of stones thrust upward, trapping Jest and Catherine in its center. Her breath caught as she stared at the walls that cocooned them, where far, far above her she could see a jagged parapet and the theater chandeliers, getting farther and farther away. They were sinking, but for the rumble of the ground, it felt as though they weren't moving at all.

"How?" she breathed, sure she was hallucinating. "How are you . . . ?"

Jest's brows were drawn tight as he peered down at her face. "I'm a Rook," he said, as if this were answer enough. Then he whispered, "And I'm sorry for this."

He lifted her into his arms.

Agony crashed through her all at once, a red-hot poker jammed into her leg. She screamed —

Dizzy, throbbing, raw sparks shot up her limbs. Cath awoke crying and disoriented. The hard floor of the theater lobby was now soft, cool grass. She tasted salt on her tongue, felt the crumbly leftovers of tears on her cheeks.

She was surrounded by trees and shrubs that towered palatially above her. The world smelled of dirt and growing things, plus a hint of something sweet, like warm molasses and ginger biscuits.

She heard a creaking rope and grinding pulleys, but that could have been all the noise in the world. No birdsong, no crickets, no chattering voices.

Head drooping to the side, she squinted open her eyes.

She was in a meadow of sorts — the sharp blades of grass pressing into her temple. The world felt still — no breeze among the wildflowers, no birdsong chiming from the trees. Though it had been evening when they'd arrived at the theater, the light was reddish gold here, trapped between day and night.

Through her bleary lashes she spotted an ancient well in the glen's center, its stones worked through with moss and a family of mushrooms growing to one base. Jest stood beside it. His hat was on the ledge and his sleeves were pushed up past his elbows, revealing tan skin above his dark gloves. He pulled on the rope, lifting the water bucket one crank at a time. From how he groaned, it was clear that either the bucket was very heavy or the gears were very old or his arms were very, very tired.

He'd carried her here.

How far was that?

Cath had no idea where *here* was or how much time had passed.

Another shot of pain had her whole face tightening up. She whimpered.

"Almost there, Catherine," Jest said through his panting. He tied off the rope and she could hear the slop of liquid as he pried the bucket off the hook. "Here we are." He teetered toward her. Something spilled over the bucket's side and Cath could see years of buildup on the wood — something sticky and caramel colored. Not water.

"This isn't the beach," she said, trying to focus on something other than the pain. "You were supposed to take me —"

"This is better." He set the bucket beside her. "Much faster than the Sturgeons, I promise. Can you sit?"

Dizziness threatened her as Jest helped her sit and for the first time she saw her leg.

He had cut away her boot. The stocking, too, had been trimmed off at her calf, leaving her ankle bare. It hardly looked like her ankle at all. It was swollen and purple. Her foot was turned at an odd angle and there was a massive lump on one side — the bone, she suspected, just shy of pushing through the skin. She whimpered again. Seeing the reality of it made the pain flare up all over again.

"Here," said Jest, reaching for a wooden cup inside the bucket. The dark liquid squelched and sucked as he pulled it out, dribbling like honey down the sides. "Drink this."

"What is it?" she asked.

"Treacle."

"Treacle? That isn't —"

"Just drink it, Catherine." He sat beside her as she took the cup in her weak hands, her fingers sticking to the sides. Jest was so close his knee was pressed against her thigh, his hands ready to assist her if she needed it.

The treacle well — another impossible tale. A place where sweetened syrup bubbled up from the depths of the earth, containing mythical healing properties.

And Jest had found it. Jest knew where it was. How . . . ?

Her mind was too hazy to think. She drank, because she couldn't think of any reason not to, though drinking the treacle was a slow, thick process. Like slurping down spoonful after spoonful of the thickest, sweetest, richest syrup.

It was delicious.

Oh, what she wouldn't give to make a treacle-bourbon-pecan pie with it.

Or that clootie dumpling, just to prove to Mr. Caterpillar that he was wrong and the well did exist after all.

As the syrup filled her stomach, its warmth seeped into her body. It spread through her limbs, growing hotter, like her muscles had been set aflame. It was its own sort of pain, but nothing like her shattered ankle.

"It's working," said Jest.

She hardly felt it. The slow straightening of the joint, the shrinking of the lump, the gradual reduction of her swollen flesh.

She slumped forward as the pain became

bearable, then bordered on slight discomfort, then disappeared altogether.

Jest brushed a strand of hair off her brow. "How does it feel?"

She rubbed her ankle, gently at first, but growing bolder when there was no flare of pain. She imagined how distraught her mother would be to witness such a thing — her daughter rubbing her bare ankle while alone in a strange place with a strange man . . .

"Better, thank you."

"Good." This single, simple word was full of an ocean's worth of relief.

Jest stood and carried the bucket back to the well, replacing it on its hook. "Thank you," he said. "What do you ask for payment?"

A snicker echoed up from the bottom of the well, sending a chill of goose bumps along Cath's bare arms.

It was followed by a high, dreamy voice, like that of a little girl. She sang, *"Elsie wants the lady's boot, cut near in two. Tillie wants the lonely stocking, lost without a shoe. And I shall take an unspent kiss, as you've given far too few."*

Jest was expressionless but for a brief tightening of his jaw, then he nodded and returned to Cath's side. Without looking at her, he gathered up the destroyed boot and shredded stocking foot.

"Who's down there?" Cath whispered.

"The Sisters," he said, and she could sense the weight of the title. "We owe them payment for the treacle, but don't worry. They only ask for things we have no need of."

He carried the boot and stocking to the well and dropped them inside, though there was no splash down below. Then a tiny, pale hand attached to a bony wrist twisted up from the well. Jest bent over it and placed a kiss into the upward-turned palm.

The fingers curled into a fist the moment he pulled away and the hand disappeared back into the well, taking its prize with it. Cath thought she heard another low laugh, then silence.

Jest grabbed his hat and paced back to where Cath still sat on the wildflower meadow. He sighed and crouched down, almost at eye level, and this close she could see the weariness in his eyes and the exhausted set of his shoulders. Between fighting the Jabberwock and carrying her all the way here, she wondered he had strength to stay upright at all.

"Are you all right?" she asked.

A ghost smile fluttered over his mouth — but just one side, barely revealing his dimples. "Mostly right, my lady."

She grinned, briefly, at the memory of their first meeting, but with her thoughts no longer writhing with pain, questions were fast pouring into her. "How did we get here? There was . . . I remember a wall of stone, surrounding us . . ." Her thoughts were hazy. It felt more like a dream than reality.

"I am a Rook," Jest said. "I can travel faster than any carriage, so long as the path is straight."

She opened her mouth, but shut it again. She didn't understand, but she sensed he had been as clear as he could. So she started again, "The treacle well is real."

He nodded.

"Do you think . . . do you think it could help the Turtle?"

Jest looked surprised at the question, but gathered himself quickly. "Hatta already tried, but the poor creature wouldn't follow him here. He wasn't desperate enough."

"Desperate?" She faintly remembered Hatta saying something about desperation too.

"Yes. He was distraught and miserable, no doubt, but that isn't enough. I'm afraid he will forever be a Mock Turtle now." He rocked back on his heels and, as if afraid of what other questions Cath might be preparing, said, "If you think you're able to walk, I'll escort you home. Miss Mary Ann will be worried. No doubt, everyone will be by now."

She glanced around. "How much time has passed since we left the theater?"

"An hour or two, I think, but no timepiece will work here."

"That can't be right. It's near daylight."

Amusement glinted in his eyes. "Or it's near night. Never one or the other. At least, that's what Hatta told me. I've only been here once before, but it was the same then."

"Never day or night," she murmured, looking around at the gold-lit grasses. "How can it be?"

"I suspect Time has never set foot in this glen. Perhaps he isn't willing to pay whatever price the Sisters would demand." His voice lowered. "Or maybe he's never been desperate enough to find it."

Cath dug her bare toes into the soft grass. "And how did you find it? You and Hatta."

His shoulders slumped and, as if realizing that she was not about to leave, no matter how much time had or hadn't passed, he lowered himself to sit beside her. He peeled off his gloves and set them and the tri-pointed hat aside. "Only the desperate will ever find this place. Hatta found it when he was desperate not to meet the same fate as his father. I brought you here because you were in so much pain, and I was desperate to make it stop."

Her heart expanded, but she tried to squeeze it back into place. "And what about the first time you came here?"

He peered back at the well and stared at it for a long time — a very long time — before returning his attention to her. He looked like he'd lost an internal debate.

Finally, he said, "I was desperate to fulfill the request my queen had made of me, and the treacle well is between times and between lands." He dragged in a long breath. "We are standing at the doorway to Chess."

Chapter 36

Cath blinked. "You must be wrong, Jest."

He looked up at her, surprised, and she swooped her arm over the wildflowers. "We can't be standing at the doorway to Chess. We're sitting, after all."

This time, both cheeks dimpled. "So we are." He pointed at the wall of shrubs on the other side of the glen. They were, she realized, surrounded by a hedge on all sides, without any openings so far as she could tell. "You can't see it now, but this is the entrance to a great maze. If the Sisters allow it, the maze will open, and you can pass through to the Looking Glass. Beyond that . . ."

Cath searched the wall of green leaves and wild branches and pale wildflowers. She imagined it. The narrow corridors that wound back and forth, the living walls that played games on mind-weary travelers. In its very center, the Looking Glass, the door to —

"Chess," she said. "The Looking Glass leads to the lands of Chess."

He nodded. "The Red and White Queendoms."

She turned her focus back to him, inspecting his profile — sharp nose and smeared kohl and unruly dark hair. "Why are you here, Jest? Why did the White Queen send you?"

He grimaced and again faced away from her. "Please don't ask me that."

She leaned back, more intrigued than ever. "Why not?"

"Because things are different now. You've changed everything."

She twisted her lips to one side and pondered a while, before asking, "Do you mean I've changed your mission, or your thoughts toward it?"

"Both." He started picking at the grass, considering his words. He snapped the stem of a blue flower and twirled it between his fingers. "You live in a peaceful kingdom. Maybe Hearts has always been this way. But Chess is different. We're one country torn apart by two ruling families, and we've been trapped in this war since . . . forever, as far as I can tell. And whenever it seems that one side has finally won and the war should be over . . . it's as though Time resets and we start from the beginning. We do it all over again. Over and over. We're trapped in a forever war between the white and the red. I've watched so many die on the battlefield. I've taken so many lives myself — pawns of the Red Queen, mostly, only for them to be replaced by new soldiers and sent forward again. There's never any end to it."

"That sounds awful," Cath breathed.

Jest looked up at her, but didn't acknowledge her words. "I serve the White Queen. I always have. But she's rather like your King — bumbling, a little clumsy, sheepish at times and terrified of conflict. She isn't strong or brave . . ." He swallowed, hard, his nervous fingers tearing the soft leaves from the flower's stem. "I don't know if she can ever win this war. She doesn't have the fortitude we need to defeat the Red Queen, once and for all, and our King agrees. This mission, it was his idea." His focus returned to the flower, twisting the slender stem around his finger. "We were told that Hearts had a queen. We were told that she was a great ruler — fierce and passionate."

He hesitated again, his lips parted. He dropped the flower between his feet. "Raven and I were sent here to find her and . . .

and to steal her heart." He became so quiet Cath wasn't sure she'd heard correctly. Then he looked up and held her gaze, his expression full of torment. "I came here to steal *your* heart."

Cath's heart thumped at his words, almost fearfully, but she started to shake her head. "Hearts doesn't have a queen."

"I know. Time tricked us, I think, or maybe it was the Sisters that brought us here too soon. But there will be a Queen of Hearts soon, and . . . Catherine, I do think it's meant to be you. You're everything we hoped to find. You're fierce, and passionate, and brave —"

"Me? I can hardly stand up to my own mother!"

"You stood up to the Jabberwock."

Cath bit back her protests. She had been delirious and frantic. She had not felt brave or fierce, and she could remember the rush of relief she'd felt when the monster had run from her, rather than fight.

"Then there's the Vorpal Sword," Jest continued before she could form her thoughts. "It's been passed through the Chessian royal family, generation after generation. I don't know how it came to be in my hat, or how you managed to pull it out. Supposedly . . ." He trailed off, his shoulders falling again. "Supposedly, only one with royal blood can wield it."

Cath shook her head. No. *No.* That wasn't her future. That wasn't her fate. She wouldn't allow it.

"I am not a queen," she whispered, willing it to be true. "And I never will be. It's impossible."

Jest's eyes softened. "The White Queen once told me that there were days when she believed as many as six impossible things before breakfast."

Catherine's brow tensed. "But . . . that's what I said."

"I know." He licked his lips. "I knew it the moment I met you, Catherine. The moment I saw you, even. You are the one we came to find — no matter how you try to fight it."

She opened her mouth to refute again, to insist that she had no desire to wear the crown, that she would find a way to refuse the King — but she hesitated, as another thought trickled through her denials.

Her chest suddenly squeezed, forcing the air from her lungs.

"You've been trying to steal my heart."

A muscle twitched in his jaw and he looked away.

Mouth suddenly dry, Cath placed a hand to her collarbone, feeling the steady thumping beneath her skin. "Is that . . . has it all been for that? The tea party, the letters, what you said at the festival . . . all of it, no more than an attempt to steal my heart so you could take it back to your queen?"

"The easiest way to steal something," Jest murmured, "is for it to be given willingly."

She realized it was true. He would already have her heart if he had only asked for it. She would have been too willing to give it to him.

Instead, he was telling her the truth.

She sucked in a trembling breath. "Why haven't you taken it then? Surely you know . . . I'm sure you've realized . . ." Her words caught, the confession strangling her. She loved him. Or, she had loved him. She wanted to love him still, though now she wasn't sure if it had all been riddles and tricks.

Jest sounded miserable, and was still unwilling to look at her, when he said, "You are not yet the queen, and I was sent to take the heart of a queen."

Tears misted her eyes. "That's why you've been pushing me to marry the King, and all the while . . ." She sniffed and launched herself to her feet, glad there was no residual pain left from her ankle. She felt off balance, though, the bare toes of her foot pressing into the soft ground. She spun to face Jest, though she could see only the top of his head, his black hair hanging over his brow, his shoulders slumped and defeated. "How dare you? You made me believe you wanted a courtship. You pretended that you would choose to stay in Hearts, for *me.* My heart is not a game piece, to be played and discarded at will!"

He lifted his head at this, his golden eyes full of distress. "You're right. It isn't. But I have lived my life knowing that someday I would die in service to my queen, and everyone I've ever cared for would die, and it would mean nothing. Our sacrifices mean nothing, because it never ends and it never will end. I believed —" He dragged a hand through his hair, shaking his head. "I believed this was the only way to end the war. I still believe that."

She folded her arms over her chest. "I am sorry, then, Sir Joker or Rook or whatever you are. Your mission has failed. I will never be the Queen of Hearts."

His expression twisted. With agony. With hope. "I cannot tell you how much I want that to be true."

She frowned. "Why? Because you want to fail?"

"Because I don't want to hurt you." He

opened his hands, palms held toward her, pleading. "Don't you understand? My role has been compromised since that first night in the gardens. I don't want you to marry the King. And even if I could still somehow claim your heart, even after telling you how cruel and unfair I've treated you, I wouldn't be able to give it to the White Queen. Catherine, I don't want your heart to belong to anyone but me." He groaned and fell back onto the grass, covering his face with both hands. "It wasn't supposed to happen this way. Hatta and Raven saw what was happening even before I did. They tried to warn me, told me to protect my own heart, but it's too late now and I've ruined everything, and somehow, if it means saving you, I'm not even sure if I care."

She clenched her jaw, trying to hold on to her anger, her resentment. She took a step closer so she could stare down at him, scowling. "How do I know you aren't only saying these things now as part of another attempt to gain my trust?"

He chuckled, but there was no joy in it. His hands fell to his sides. He looked almost vulnerable lying beneath her. Her nerves tingled with the absurd and unwarranted fantasy of curling up beside him, tucking her body along his side, staying there forever.

"You don't," he said, propping himself up on his elbows. "Don't give your heart to me, Catherine. I don't deserve it. But . . ." His voice turned strained. "Don't give it to the King, either. He may deserve it even less."

"Does he?" she barked. "At least he has been nothing but honest with me."

"That's true. But I'm sure he doesn't feel as strongly as I do."

She held his gaze and let her breath out slowly, slowly, her crossed arms a shield between them. Finally she sat down again, draping her skirt over her crisscrossed legs. "You have nothing to fear, then. I am not going to marry the King. I am going to open a bakery."

Jest sat up and folded his long legs, facing her. "A bakery?"

"That's right. Mary Ann and I have been planning it for years, and we're close now to making our dream a reality." It was only a partial lie. Though her attempts had failed so far — no contest prize, no dowry money, no loan from Hatta — she now felt more certain than ever that she had to find a way. She would not allow fate to trick her out of this dream. "So you see, you've been wasting all your efforts on me. I suppose you will have to wait and see what other girl the King chooses, and set about charming her instead." She didn't bother to bury the sour note in her words. Jest flinched and she was surprised at how much the small motion pleased her.

"A bakery," he said again. "And your parents approve of this?"

"Of course not. But I'm not going to let that stop me. It's my life, after all."

"But . . . you would no longer be gentry. You would have to give up everything."

She glowered. "Don't imagine you can tell me anything I don't already know. I have given this much more consideration than you have."

His gaze turned intense, peering into her as if he expected to find a weakness in her plan. She seemed to have rendered him speechless.

When the silence had dragged on for so long Cath found herself in danger of telling him everything — the fight with her parents, the deal she'd struck with the Duke, even how she'd gone to Hatta for help, which, now, knowing his ulterior motives, seemed painfully naïve — Catherine instead straightened her spine and forced herself to say, "I would ask you to take me home then.

As you said, everyone will be worried, and I'm sure you must have much to do. Finding another heart to steal, stopping a war, and all of that."

She still did not move.

He didn't either.

Instead, Jest said, "Once you have your bakery" — as if long minutes hadn't dragged on since she'd made this confession to him — "and you're no longer in danger of . . . of me. Would there be any way . . ."

Her pulse began to flutter, but she tried to keep her expression blank. She waited, not daring to hope. Not even sure that she *should* hope.

Jest licked his lips. "I understand if you'll hate me forever, but if there were any way you could trust me again. No more lies, no more tricks . . ." His knuckles whitened, his fingertips pressing into his knees. Cath found herself staring at those hands. The lithe fingers, tight with tension, showing more than his face would allow, telling her more than his words.

She *was* hoping, still hoping, no matter if she should or not.

She cocked her head to the side, and though she wanted to be flippant, she couldn't. "Are you suggesting you would still want to court me, Sir Joker? A lowly baker, with no hope of being the queen?"

"More than anything in this world, Lady Pinkerton."

Her traitorous heart stuttered. "What of your mission?"

"If there is no queen, there is no mission."

"And if the King should marry someone else?"

"Another girl with a heart like yours? She doesn't exist, not here in Hearts. I'm sure of it."

Her brow knit together. "What of the White Queen? What of the war?"

Jest shrugged helplessly. "We could do nothing before and we can do nothing now." His shoulders sank. "Cath, there is nothing for me there. A never-ending war. Almost certain death. I'm not sure if I meant it before, but I mean it now. If I had a reason to stay in Hearts, I would. Hatta and Raven will probably hate me forever, or maybe they'll stay too, I don't know. But I would stay. For you. If you want me. If—"

"I want you."

Jest fell silent, his lips half formed around some new declaration.

Her breaths quickened. Her body hummed with nervous energy, renewed uncertainty, but there was no taking the words back, and she wasn't sure she wanted to.

"You have my heart, Jest. I don't know if you deserve it or not. I can't tell if you're a hero or a villain, but it doesn't seem to matter. Either way, my heart is yours."

He stared at her, his eyes wide, burning, stunned. Her heart continued to pound. Her words hung in the space between them.

Finally, Jest whispered, "Now that you've said that, you must promise me you will reject the King."

"I promise," she said, without hesitation.

Relief washed over him, then he was on his knees, reaching for her hands. She gave them willingly, and his lips were on her fingertips, brushing over each one. "Catherine," he said, breathing her name into her palms. "Dear Catherine. I have wanted to kiss you from the moment you awoke in that rose garden."

She licked her lips, a reflex, the result of a hundred daydreams. A hundred daydreams about him.

The glen was quiet but for the drum of her heart. Cath could imagine it. Everything about it. His lips, his arms. His body pressing her back onto the soft grass, the golden light of a timeless day cascading over them.

She curled her fingers over his. "Kiss me, then."

She offered no resistance when he pulled her to her knees, trapping their interlaced fingers between their bodies. His nose brushed against hers.

"My heart is yours," he whispered, sending a chill down her spine.

The corners of her lips lifted, in anticipation, in joy. "Do be careful, Sir Joker," she said, remembering Hatta's riddle. "A heart, once stolen, can never be taken back."

"I know," he said, and kissed her — soft, at first. "But I'm giving it to you willingly." Another kiss, hesitant, growing bolder. "Catherine," he murmured against her, "you taste like treacle."

Catherine grinned, delirious once more, and pulled him down onto the grass.

Chapter 37

Catherine was giddy when Jest's mysterious tower of stone deposited them into the Crossroads — arms linked, faces flushed, and lungs full of laughter. Her hair was a tangled mess, her toes were uncomfortably cold on her one bare foot, and Cath had not known before what happiness was. Her whole body was smiling. She felt that she could step off the checkered-tile floor and fly up, up, up if she wasn't careful.

They found the door to Rock Turtle Cove, and Jest opened it for her with an elaborate bow. "After you, my lady."

She curtsied. "Why thank you, good sir," she said, dancing through the door and out onto the riverbank. The bridge above them was sullen and quiet, the air still but for the chirping of crickets and the crackle of lightning bugs.

Jest shut the door beneath the bridge and followed her up to the path. She felt the tender brush of his fingertips against her lower back and the caress warmed her to her bones.

She smiled back at him and saw her contentment reflected in his face. It only took the gentlest of tugs before she was in his arms again.

No sooner had their lips touched than a warning caw darted down Catherine's spine. She gasped and swiveled her head, spotting Raven in the trees.

Jest grabbed her elbow. "Cath —"

The night's tranquility erupted with the sound of clanging armor and shouted commands.

Catherine cried out as Jest's hand was ripped away from her, leaving her skin burning. She turned in time to see the Two and Seven of Clubs forcing Jest onto his knees. A suit of palace guards spread out behind them, their clubs and javelins raised.

"What are you doing?" she screamed, wrapping her hands around Jest's upper arm. The guards held firm. "Let him go!"

"Catherine! Oh, thanks to goodness!"

She spun around. Her mother and father barreled out from behind a border of shrubs. The King, too, was there, and the sight of him made Cath's veins run cold moments before her mother wrapped her in a suffocating embrace. "Oh, my sweet girl! My darling child! You're home! You're safe!"

"Of course I'm safe. What is the meaning of this?"

"You needn't be frightened anymore." The Marchioness stroked her hair. "We heard all about the Jabberwock attack — much as I adore His Majesty I may never forgive his putting you in harm's way like that!" She said this with an element of cheekiness, knowing His Majesty was standing not far away and, of course, he was already forgiven. "They said you were injured and . . . and this wicked joker had taken you to the Sturgeons! We went there, your father and Mary Ann and I, but you were nowhere to be seen and no one had heard from you and the Sturgeons said you hadn't been to see them and all I could think was that you were helpless and afraid and hurt and this awful man had secreted you away and was doing something vile and awful and —"

She was sobbing, great big blubbering sobs that turned Cath's stomach with guilt.

A loud honk drew her attention over her mother's shoulder. Her father was blowing his nose into a handkerchief, his eyes red and sleepless.

She spotted Mary Ann and Abigail, too, loitering near the tree line. Both were pale and wide-eyed. Mary Ann looked relieved, her hands pressed against her stomach.

"Did he . . ." Her mother swallowed, hard. "Did he hurt you?"

"What? No!" Cath shook her head as her mother's words pieced together. She disentangled herself from her mother's embrace. "He didn't . . . it was nothing like that. This is all a misunderstanding." She spun back to the guards. "Let him go. He hasn't done anything!"

"It's all right now," said her father, stepping forward to brush back a strand of Cath's hair. "He's captured. You don't have to be afraid. His Majesty has ensured us this will never happen again."

Aghast, Catherine peered down at Jest. His lips were pressed thin, the only sign of emotion on his face. All signs of their previous euphoria were gone. His gaze, now cunning and sly, was darting from the King to the guards to Raven, perched somewhere overhead. He wasn't looking at her.

Nor was he looking particularly innocent.

Cath frowned and planted her hands on her hips. "You're all overreacting. Jest was helping me. He took me —" She hesitated, but only for a moment. "He took me to the treacle well. He knew where it was, and look! My leg is healed!" She lifted the hem of her dress.

"Catherine!" Her mother slapped her hand down and the hem fell, but not before Mary Ann's hand had flown to her mouth. She had seen the damage at the theater. She knew the miracle of it.

Cath dared to turn her focus on the King. Her suitor. She gulped, but guilt over her mussed hair and swollen lips was barely a gnat pestering at the back of her thoughts. "Your Majesty, please. You can't arrest him. He hasn't done anything wrong."

The King ducked his chin between the folds of his cloak. The crown started to slip on his head.

"Nothing wrong!" her mother barked, fluttering her arms. "He kidnapped you! Twice!"

Catherine's breath snagged.

"I can't imagine what spell this man has on you," her mother continued, "but to steal you away . . . once, directly from beneath the nose of your betrothed —"

He's not my betrothed.

"And even from our own house, your own chambers!" She wailed. She was crying again. Catherine's father scooped her into his arms, but she pushed him away, turning her wrath on Jest, who was still on his knees, held firm by the guards. "You wretch! You villain! *How dare you!*"

Jest held her gaze, his jaw twitching, his expression unreadable.

"Mama, stop it!" Catherine clung to her arm. "It isn't like that. He's . . . He . . ."

Her thoughts skidded to a stop.

Her parents knew. They knew he'd come to her chambers. They knew they'd sneaked away in the middle of the night.

Her eyes drifted back to Mary Ann, chest aching with betrayal.

Mary Ann stared back, her eyes watering and hands clasped. *I'm sorry,* she mouthed.

"We were expecting a demand for ransom," her father said, his voice gruff. "We didn't know if we would ever see you again."

"Yet here I am," Cath said, still reeling. "Not kidnapped. Not ransomed. I can explain everything."

"He stole you away from this very house!" her father bellowed. "Unchaperoned! Anything could have happened!"

"But nothing did happen —"

"You mean to tell me —" His voice had darkened. He was an ocean storm gathering on the horizon. "That my daughter, my angel, went with him willingly?"

Her cheeks flamed. "I . . . Father . . ."

"Did my daughter," he continued, speaking as if every word were a strain, "sneak out of my house in the middle of the night, alone, with the court joker, and attend a gathering of strangers and ruffians and who knows what sorts of creatures?"

Her ribs collapsed inward, pushing the air from her lungs. How many of her secrets had Mary Ann told?

This was her last chance, she knew. To deny it all. To blame Jest for everything, to pass the consequences onto his shoulders. To maintain her parents' perception of her forever.

She swallowed down the knowledge of how easy it would be.

And how impossible.

No, she could not betray him.

She squeezed her fists and opened her mouth, but it was a deeper voice that spoke.

"No."

They all spun to Jest. His chin was high, but his eyes downcast. He didn't look at Cath, or her parents, or the King. "She did not come with me willingly, though she might think it."

Her pulse sputtered. "Jest!"

The chattering insects had silenced and for a moment there was only the burble of the creek behind them. Jest looked up and met her stunned expression with something dark and determined. "I used a charm to persuade her to come with me. It was a trick."

"He's lying. That isn't —"

"Lady Pinkerton is innocent. She is not at fault for anything that's happened."

The Marchioness wilted with relief and gratitude, her faith in all the world restored.

"But, why?" stammered the King, his voice a squeak in the darkness. Cath could never recall seeing him so distraught, so unhappy, and the look of betrayal gave her a sharp sting of guilt. "Why would you do it, Jest?"

Jest fixed his eyes on the King, expressionless. "My loyalty belongs to the White King and Queen of Chess. I was sent to steal the heart of your queen and bring it back. I have been trying to woo her, so that her heart would be mine to take once you were married."

The King stumbled back, a hand over his chest as if Jest had stabbed him. "How could you do such a thing to Lady Pinkerton?"

Cath tensed. "Jest. Don't —"

"Hold your tongue, daughter of mine." Her father's firm hand landed on her shoulder. "It's clear that he still has you under some enchantment."

Jest's gaze skipped to her. "It's true. I have

been using every skill at my disposal to mesmerize her."

Goose bumps swept across her skin.

He had her heart, and she had his. Nothing could change that.

Nothing . . .

But he was making himself a villain. To her parents. To the King. To all of Hearts.

And what for? To save a reputation she cared less for by the minute?

Her mother nodded. "You see? He's confessed his crimes, with us all here to witness it. What fortune that we discovered this now, before it could go any further. Thank heavens Mary Ann came to her senses and thought to ask for help."

Catherine's insides writhed. Her eyes began to well with tears, but she blinked them back and turned to look at Mary Ann again. Her lifelong friend stood beneath a copse of trees, looking stricken and so very, very sorry.

A hard knot of anger tightened in the base of Catherine's stomach.

Following the look, her mother waved her hand at the maids. "Abigail, Mary Ann, go back to the house and draw a warm bath for Catherine. She's been through quite an ordeal tonight."

They dropped into fast curtsies.

"I'm so glad you're all right, Ca— Lady Catherine," Mary Ann said, her voice barely a breath before she followed Abigail toward the house.

Cath's anger twitched and grew. She was not right at all.

"I trust this criminal will be taken to a prison cell?" said the Marquess.

"He had better!" said the Marchioness. Some of her spittle landed on Jest's cheek, but he barely twitched. "For the safety of our daughter! I don't want him to be able to ensorcell anyone but prison rats from this day forward!"

"O-o-of course!" stammered the King, forcing himself into their circle. He was wringing his hands and Cath could see he was desperate to have this whole situation behind him. "I cannot begin to convey my remorse for . . . for all that's happened." His eyebrows bunched in the middle of his brow as he gestured toward Jest. "He just seemed so trustworthy."

Cath sneered. "You are all idiots."

"Catherine!" her mother snapped.

The Marquess placed an arm around his wife's shoulders. "Now, now, dearest. She's not herself, can't you see?"

Catherine crossed her arms over her chest. "Then who do you think I am?"

"Er, well." The King cleared his throat, changing the subject. "The Joker will be, er, dealt with." He tugged his collar away from his throat. "And then we shall forget any of this unpleasantness ever happened!"

Cath turned to Jest. He held the look, and there was something insistent in his gaze. Maybe he was telling her this was all for the best, but she refused to believe it.

Suddenly, the King started clapping, an impulsive, anxious sound. "Ah yes — that's what we'll do! Let's have a party!"

Catherine's attention swiveled back to him. "A party!"

"You were right what you said at the theater, my sweet," said the King, and Catherine cringed. "I am the King, and I must do something to make the people of Hearts feel safer. None of this Jabberwock and kidnapping nonsense. We'll have a great masquerade and then we'll all dance and eat and be quite merry, and we'll forget anything bad has ever happened, ever."

"That is a terrible idea!" Cath screeched. "Don't you remember? The Jabberwock attacked the last party you —"

Her anger was muffled by her mother's hand, slapped over her mouth. "Brilliant, Your Majesty. Positively brilliant!"

The King bounced on his toes, pleased

with her approval. "Tomorrow night, then! And — and —" He grew suddenly bashful, his cheeks reddening behind his curled mustache. "And perhaps I shall have a special announcement to make?" He waggled his eyebrows at Catherine, and if she hadn't been caught in her mother's firm grip, she would have screamed.

"Now then," the King chirped, "back to the castle we go. Bring the prisoner. That's all right, then, uppity-up."

The guards had begun to move into formation when Jest cleared his throat. "Actually, Your Majesty, if I might say one more thing?"

The clearing quieted. All eyes drifted to Jest. Wary, except for Cath, who was panicked and hopeful.

Any spite he'd had before was missing from his expression. All signs of discontent gone. He smiled at the King with an abundance of charm, and said, "You have been good to me, Your Majesty."

The King's chest lifted and he tugged on the fur trim of his cloak. "Ah — why, thank you, Jest."

"Which is why it pains me to have betrayed you so, and to now betray you again."

His yellow gaze found Cath, brimming with unspoken words.

Jest's body dissolved — a shadow, a flutter, a wisp of ink-dipped quills. Raven cawed and dropped down from the trees and two identical black birds stole away into the night.

Chapter 38

Catherine barely managed to smother her grin as she was coaxed back to the house — for her safety, they told her — while the King was ushered into a carriage and carted away and the guards set up a method for searching the perimeter and recapturing Jest.

"He will be found," the Marquess said, again and again, as Cath was loaded into the foyer of their home. "You needn't worry. I know he will be found."

"No, he won't," she said, gliding up the steps. "And I'm glad for it. You're all wrong about him."

"Halt right there, young miss," her mother barked, and Cath's obedient feet halted on the first landing. She turned back to her parents. Their relief had settled into some sort of frazzled frustration. There was a shadow on her father's brow, and a twitch at the corner of her mother's mouth. "I don't know what that boy has done to you," she said, planting her hands on her hips, "but it's over now and we are never to speak of him again. We shall go on as if none of this has happened, and you are to start showing some appreciation for all we've done for you, and some gratitude toward His Majesty!"

"Gratitude! What has he done to be grateful for?"

"He has preserved your honor, that's what! Any other man would have called off the courtship immediately after hearing that you were carried off, *twice,* in the arms of another man. His Majesty is doing you a great kindness, Catherine. You will respect that, and when you see him tomorrow, I expect you to reward such generosity."

"I do not want his generosity, or his kindness, or any other favors!"

Her mother sneered. "Then you are a fool."

"Good. I've become rather fond of fools."

"That is enough!" roared the Marquess.

Catherine clamped shut her lips, silenced by the rarity of her father's temper. His face had gone flaming red, and though he was in the foyer looking up at Catherine, the look made her feel as inconsequential as a stomped bug.

He spoke slowly, each word carefully measured. “You will not disgrace this family any more than you already have.”

Tears stung at Catherine’s eyes, fierce with shame and guilt. Never had her father looked at her like that, spoken to her like that.

Never had she seen such disappointment.

“You will do as your mother says,” he continued. “You will do your duty as our only daughter. You will not embarrass us again. And should His Majesty ask for your hand, you will accept.”

She started to shake her head. “You can’t force me to.”

“Force you?” her mother cried. “What is wrong with you, child? This is a gift! Though you’ve done nothing to deserve it.”

“You don’t understand,” Cath cried. “If you’d only met Jest under different circumstances . . . if you talked to him, you would see that he isn’t —”

Her father threw up his hands. “I will not listen to this. That boy has done enough harm for one night, and until you are thinking clearly and can begin to behave like the lady we raised you to be, this conversation is ended.” The Marquess tore off his coat and draped it on the rack beside the door. “You will do as we say, Catherine, or you will consider yourself no longer a member of this household."

Catherine clenched her jaw, tears pooling. Her thoughts were thrashing inside her head, clawing at the inside of her skull, but she kept her mouth shut tight.

Jest's confession had destroyed any credibility she might have had. There was nothing she could say to them now, no argument she could make to persuade them she was not under some enchantment — that Jest was not a villain.

That she loved him. She chose *him.*

Turning, she fled from the foyer before she dissolved into a tantrum-stricken child.

Rushing into her bedroom, she slammed the door and slumped against it. In the hallway, a painting fell off its hook and crashed to the floor with a muffled *Ouch!*

Leaning over, Cath gathered up her skirt, pressed her face into the fabric, and screamed as loud as she could.

"Catherine?"

She startled at the meek voice and peeled the skirt away. Mary Ann stood before her — her black-and-white uniform blurred in Cath's vision.

"I'm sorry," she stammered, before Cath could gather herself.

Cath swiped her palms over her eyes. "You

told them everything! How could you?"

"I had to. You don't know him, Cath. Nobody knows him, and I was so scared —"

"I do know him! I trust him! But you've ruined it. He's a wanted man now, a criminal. It's all over, and it's all because of you!"

"I thought you were in trouble. That sorcery he used to take you away from the theater — it was like nothing I've ever seen before. We were all so frightened, but still, I wanted to believe he was taking you to the beach, and when it turned out you hadn't gone there at all . . . I thought you were in danger. You've been gone for hours and the Jabberwock is still out there somewhere and I didn't know . . ."

Cath pushed herself away from the door and yanked it open. "I don't want to hear it. You had no right to tell them what you did."

"Cath —"

"Get out!"

"Wait, please. Listen to me, Catherine. I think I saw . . . when we were at the theater, I could have sworn —"

"I don't care!" Catherine shrieked. "I don't care what you think or what you saw. We had a plan, Mary Ann. We had a future, and now you've ruined it!" Tears began to streak fast down her cheeks. "I never want to see you again. You can go be a scullery maid for all I care!"

Without waiting for Mary Ann to leave, she turned and stomped into the washroom and locked the door behind her. With a sob, she slid down onto the tile floor and hugged her knees close, pushing her face into the folds of her skirt. She tried to recapture the feeling of the meadow and the wildflowers and Jest's arms and lips and how everything had felt so very, very right.

She couldn't fathom how, so quickly, it had all become so very, very wrong.

When Catherine awoke the next morning, a new shrub had sprouted from the posters of her bed. The room was scented with dirt and metal and sadness and she could see a blur of red blooms beyond her swollen eyelids.

The vines drooped along the canopy, the flowers dripped toward her quilts.

Hundreds and hundreds of small, delicate hearts surrounded her — all of them bleeding.

She reached up and touched a finger to the soft flesh of the nearest bud, gathering a single drop of warm blood on her fingertip. Each bleeding heart bloom was a delicate thing, beautiful and haunting.

She crushed the flower in her fist, relishing the wet smear in her palm.

Mary Ann never came to start a fire. Abigail never brought her breakfast. Catherine stayed in bed, undisturbed, well into the afternoon. She felt like a Jack-O'-Lantern hollowed out. She wondered if Jest had been found and taken to prison, but she knew he hadn't. He was too clever for them, too quick, too impossible.

Her eyes repeatedly drifted to the window, hoping to see a white rose sitting outside, beckoning to her. But there never was. Jest had not come back for her.

Never in her life had she felt so abandoned.

She imagined that Mary Ann had not betrayed her, and that her parents and the King had discovered nothing. She pretended that Jest would be there at the masquerade and she would walk straight up to him in his black motley and bell-twinkling hat and kiss him in front of everyone. Then she would announce the opening of her bakery, and she would leave the castle with her head held high and begin her new life with Jest at her side.

The dream was fickle, though. If it had ever been possible, it certainly wasn't now.

Jest was considered a criminal, and — as Cheshire had warned her — no one would ever be a patron at a bakery run by a fallen woman, no matter how delicious the treats. Even if they could clear Jest's name, they would forever be destitute and disgraced. They would have nothing.

It was past tea time when Cheshire appeared among the stems of the bleeding heart plant, his plump body curled in the corner of the bed's canopy.

Catherine stared up at him, unsurprised. She'd been expecting him all day. Surely the kingdom's greatest gossipmonger could not stay away.

"I thought you might like to know," Cheshire said, by way of greeting, "that everyone is talking about you and your escape from the dastardly joker. What a lucky, heroic thing you are."

"I thought you might like to know," she replied, "that it's all a bunch of hogswaddle. The Joker did not kidnap me."

She said it mildly, knowing it didn't matter what she said to Cheshire or anyone else. Most of them would go on believing whatever was most convenient, and right now, it was convenient to think that the King's bride, their future queen, had been taken against her will.

Cheshire scratched a gob of earwax from an ear with one claw. "I was worried you might say that. It isn't as good a story, you know, though I shall continue to be amused as all the King's horses and all the King's men scramble to find him again."

"They never will," she said, believing it a little less every time she said it.

After all, Hearts was not a large kingdom. Where could he go? Back to Chess?

Maybe so, but it was little consolation. It meant she would never see him again.

"His Majesty is beside himself with anxiety," Cheshire continued. "I don't think he has the faintest idea what to do with all this madness, between the Jabberwock and the Joker and a plot to steal the heart of his future queen . . . He is not accustomed to real treachery, is he?"

"All the more reason he should not be wasting his efforts on an innocent man, and what for? Because his pride has been wounded?"

"What pride?" Cheshire folded his paws. "Our King is an ignoble idiot."

A weak smile flittered over her lips. "So he is."

"Of course, ignoble idiocy seems to be an epidemic around these parts." Cheshire began to fade away. "So he shall not be alone."

He vanished at the same moment a tap came at her bedroom door. Abigail poked her head inside. "I'm sorry, Lady Catherine, but it's time to dress for the masquerade." She crept into the room like a timid mouse.

Catherine sighed and slid from her bed without argument.

The night was inevitable.

She made no fuss as her cheeks were pinched to bring back some of their color, and Abigail made no comment on how her complexion was drawn tight from all her crying.

"Oh, Lady Catherine," Abigail murmured. "It'll be all right. The King's a good man. You'll see."

Cath scowled and said nothing.

She was stuffed into a white crêpe dress striped with wide bands of burgundy, and a fine ivory mask covered in rhinestones. As Abigail went about tidying the discarded underpinnings, Catherine caught her own reflection in the mirror. She looked like a doll ready to be put on a shelf.

Then Abigail handed her the final touch.

A tiara, all diamonds and rubies. As it was settled onto her head, Catherine no longer thought she looked like a doll.

She looked like a queen.

Her lips parted, her breath escaping her.

She had promised Jest that she would reject the King. She had promised.

But that promise had been made by a girl who was still going to open a bakery with her best friend. That promise had been made by a girl who didn't care if she was a part of the gentry, so long as she could live out her days with the man she loved.

That promise had been made by a girl with a different fate altogether.

Her eyes narrowed and she reached up to adjust the tiara on her head.

Mary Ann had betrayed her secret. Jest had condemned himself forever.

But maybe it wasn't all for naught.

Cath lifted her chin and, for the first time, dared to imagine herself a queen.

Chapter 39

"Presenting the Most Honorable Whealagig T. Pinkerton, Marquess of Rock Turtle Cove," announced the White Rabbit, "accompanied by his wife, Lady Idonia Pinkerton, Marchioness of Rock Turtle Cove, and daughter, Lady Cath —"

Cath stuffed a rosebud-embroidered handkerchief into the Rabbit's mouth. He startled and peered up at her with wide eyes.

Already on the third step into the ballroom, her parents paused and glanced back. Cath flashed them a tight smile. "Go on," she said. "I think it will be more fitting for me to be announced separately." She turned her cool gaze back to the master of ceremonies. "As is befitting for the future Queen of Hearts, don't you think?"

The Marquess and Marchioness exchanged surprised but pleased looks before descending down the rest of the steps.

The Rabbit pulled out the handkerchief.

His expression flashed between irritation and complacency as he cleared his throat. "Of course, Lady Pinkerton, rightly so, indeed." He puffed up his chest in an attempt to reclaim his dignity and blew into his trumpet again. "Presenting Lady Catherine Pinkerton of Rock Turtle Cove!"

"Better," she said, and swooped down toward the floor, her shoulders peeled back. Though she could imagine how collected she must appear on the outside, her mouth tasted of stale fruitcake.

She did not make eye contact with any of the guests, glad that the bejeweled masks made it easy to pretend she didn't recognize the costumed guests surrounding her. A pair of skunks tried to approach her, and she suspected they were hoping to get into the good graces of their soon-to-be queen, toad-eaters that they were, but she glided away before a greeting could be uttered. She would not pretend that she wanted or needed the approval of the noble sycophants.

"Catherine!" A damp hand grasped her elbow, spinning her around.

Margaret Mearle dipped into a curtsy. Her mouth was pinched in a smile, her nose hidden behind a pale pink snout. "Have you heard the wonderful news?"

Cath found it impossible to smile back, despite Margaret's overjoyed expression. "I don't believe I have," she said, without much enthusiasm.

Margaret let out a dreamy sigh. "The Duke has asked for my father's permission to begin a courtship. With *me*!"

"I can hardly believe it to be so."

"And yet it is. We're to have our first chaperoned visit tomorrow afternoon. Oh, Lady Catherine, I'm full plumped up with satisfaction." Linking her arm with Cath's, she waved a fan over her flushed face. "The moral of that, of course, is that 'the caged canary does not eat from the hands of vipers.' "

Catherine tore her arm away and rounded on her. "Stuff and nonsense, Margaret."

Margaret blinked. "Pardon?"

"What does that even mean? 'The caged canary does not eat from the hands of vipers'? Vipers don't have hands. And would a canary truly prefer to be caged than take a risk on someone who might seem dangerous, but — but maybe they aren't dangerous at all. Maybe the viper only wants to share some birdseed! Did you think of that when you were concocting your ridiculous moral?"

Margaret stepped back. "Why — I don't

think you comprehend—"

"I comprehend well enough. Your so-called morals are nothing but an excuse to act better than the rest of us. To treat us as though we are not as clever or as righteous as you, when really, all you're doing is trying to hide your own insecurities! It's childish and contemptible and I've put up with it long enough."

Margaret's cheeks turned the same color as the strapped-on nose. "Why, I . . . that isn't fair. I've never . . ." She huffed. "This is unacceptable, Lady Pinkerton. I hoped that you, more than anyone, would be happy for me, but I see now that you've been harboring too much envy to be mollified. I suppose it's true that I've always held myself to a higher standard than you, but I've done my best to keep you in my good graces nevertheless. To try and raise you to my level, so you could see the error of your ways."

"Please. Spare me."

Margaret's eyes darted past her and widened. "Ah! Fair evening, my lord."

"To you as well, my lady."

Catherine turned to Lord Warthog, who had joined them, his small ears trembling with joy. He was wearing a snout to match Margaret's, though it hardly changed the look of his face at all.

She rolled her eyes in disgust.

"How do you do, Lady Pinkerton?" he asked.

"Not as well as some, it would seem."

"Lady Pinkerton," Margaret said through her teeth, "is out of sorts tonight."

"I am most sorry to hear that. I actually wondered if I might have a word with you, although" — he cleared his throat, and his voice softened — "only after Lady Mearle tells me whether she might have any openings left on her dance card?"

"Something tells me you'll have your pick of them," Catherine grumbled, but her low insult went ignored as Margaret and the Duke flirted and flustered until Margaret made some comment about powdering her nose and bustled away. The draped fabric of her gown swayed behind her as she marched into the flurry of coattails and petticoats, and the Duke watched as dopey eyed as a flamingo.

"Good riddance," Catherine cursed after her.

"Beg pardon, Lady Pinkerton?" said the Duke.

She sneered. "For shame, Your Grace! You should know better than to eavesdrop on a girl when she's grumbling to herself."

"Ah yes, I do apologize." The Duke rubbed at his jowl. "Please, finish your thoughts."

Catherine crossed her arms over her chest. Margaret was egotistical and wearisome, and for all his faults, the Duke could have done better for himself. But what business was it of hers?

None at all, perhaps, though it filled her with loathing. Margaret, of all people! Insidious, obnoxious Margaret was being courted by a man who adored her. There would be no hiding and no shame and everyone would bless them joyfully and wish upon them many snout-nosed children.

"Shall I speak now?"

She grunted. "Fine, go ahead."

"I am sorry to see you feeling so poorly, Lady Pinkerton," said the Duke. "I wanted to thank you. I'm not sure what involvement you might have had in turning Lady Mearle's affections toward me, but . . . well, a favor for a favor, I believe our deal was." He grinned around his tusks. "The storefront is vacant, now, if you weren't aware. I understand if you've no longer any interest, given the . . . the situation with the King . . ." His eyes twinkled and for a moment Catherine feared he might wink at her, but he didn't. "But should you still want to lease the building from me, I could hardly deny you anything."

Her jaw began to ache from grinding her teeth.

The storefront was hers.

Now, when she had no hope of a blessing from her parents, nor a shilling from her dowry, nor an ounce of respect from her peers if she dared to reject the King's proposal.

Now, when her friendship with Mary Ann was over.

"Is that all?"

The Duke frowned. "Why — yes, I suppose. Aren't you pleased?"

She forced an annoyed breath through her nostrils. "I am not, I'm afraid, though it's through no fault of your own." Forcing her tight shoulders to loosen, she pressed her hands into her heavy skirt. "Thank you, Your Grace, but I don't think you should reserve the storefront for me. There was never going to be any bakery, and there certainly isn't going to be one now. Please forget we ever spoke of it, and . . . go dance with your lady. She's already spent too many waltzes watching from the sidelines."

She left before she could feel the full sting of his happiness, but she had not gone far when a hand grabbed her forearm, squeezing so tight Catherine nearly choked. She tried to yank her hand away, but was tugged back against an iron-solid chest. A gruff voice growled into her ear, "What'd you do with it?"

Warm breath rolled over her, smelling of pumpkin.

Cath twisted around. Peter Peter was clutching her arm, his fingers pressing indentations into her flesh. There were purple-gray circles beneath his eyes and a deep gouge across one cheek, like someone had attacked him with a knife. Though the wound was healing, the sight of it made her stomach flip.

He was wearing muddied coveralls and no mask, as if he had no idea there were expectations around attending a royal masquerade.

"What'd you do with it?" he growled again.

"What are you — release me this instant!"

His grip tightened. "Answer me."

"I don't know what you're — ow! You know, you and your wife could stand to learn some manners when it comes to —"

He yanked her closer and Cath gasped, dwarfed by his hulking shoulders. Then, surprisingly, he did let go. She rubbed her arm, pulse racing.

"I don't know what that maid of yours saw or thought she saw," he said, his menacing voice barely carrying in the crush of music and laughter, "but I won't let you hurt her. I will see you made into worm food before I allow it. Now tell me what you've done with it."

"I don't know —" She started to shake her head, but stopped. Was this about the pumpkin she'd stolen? The cake she'd made, that his wife had been so desperate to eat? "I-I'm sorry," she sputtered. "I just used it to make a cake, just that one cake. I didn't think it would do any harm and it was just one little pumpkin, and you seemed . . . so *busy,* and I only wanted —"

His hand latched around her arm again and she yelped. "I already know about that," he growled. "I was there at the festival. I saw what happened to that Turtle, and now my wife —" He inhaled sharply, his nostrils flaring. "I don't know what you're playing at, but I'm not an idiot. The whole kingdom saw you with that sword. Now tell me what you've done with it!"

Her heart caught in her throat. "Sword? You mean — the Vorpal Sword?" Her thoughts roiled. "What does that have to do with pumpkin cake?"

His eyes flamed and he shook her again.

She hissed through her teeth, sure he was leaving bruises. "I will ruin you, Lady Pinkerton. Mark my words, if anything happens to her before I can fix this —"

"That is enough, Sir Peter!" Cath said, raising her voice when she remembered the role she'd sworn to play this evening. Everyone believed she was to be their future queen — surely she wouldn't stand to be spoken to in this way by a measly pumpkin farmer. "I demand that you release me at —"

"Pardon my intrusion." A voice as warm and soothing as melted chocolate slipped between them.

A shock jolted down Catherine's spine. She fell silent, her lips hanging open.

"If the lady's card isn't full," continued the voice, "might I request the honor of this next dance?"

Soft leather brushed against her upper arm. Her gaze fell, watching as a gloved hand pried Peter's fingers off her, one by one. She was afraid to look up. Afraid to meet the speaker of the voice and find she was wrong.

For he couldn't be here. Not even *his* bravado would have brought him here.

It was . . . impossible.

Chapter 40

Cath slowly turned her head and dared to peer up at — not a joker. A gentleman.

He wore a fine-cut suit, all in black, with long coattails and a satin cravat, a black top hat and a face mask covered in silky raven feathers. Only his eyes defied the darkness of his ensemble. Bright as sunshine, yellow as lemon tarts.

As soon as he'd freed her from Peter's grasp, he trailed the leather of his palmed glove over her bruised arm, like he wanted to rid her skin of Peter's grip. Goose bumps followed where he touched.

Peter forced himself between them and Jest's hand fell away. He was nearly a head shorter than the gigantic farmer, but there wasn't a hint of intimidation as he met Peter's glare.

"The lady and I," Peter growled, "were having a conversation. So why don't you mind your own —"

"That will be all, Sir Peter," Cath said, trying to channel her mother's domineering spirit. She noticed that people were watching them and had probably been watching since the moment Peter had accosted her. He was a sore thumb in their pristine world, after all.

But none of them had stepped forward to interrupt or defend her, no doubt hoping the drama would resolve itself.

"In fact, my dance card is quite empty," she said, louder still, and threaded her arm around Jest's elbow.

Jest tipped his hat to Peter and before there could be any argument, he was leading her onto the dance floor. Her heartbeat outpaced the music — still livid over Peter's treatment of her, and afraid that Jest would be recognized at any moment. But mostly she was exhilarated.

He was here. He had come for her.

The fool had come.

She turned to face him. Their hands linked together and a waltz began. Her feet knew the steps, though she barely heard the music.

They were dancing, in front of everyone.

There was no alarm from the crowd. No guards were sent to apprehend him. There were no whispered rumors of his presence.

In this ballroom full of masks, no one would know it was him. It was easy to believe that he was nobility, like any of them. Not an entertainer, or a fool, or a wanted man. He was as refined a gentleman as any guest.

They pressed their palms together and turned in a half circle and Jest took the opportunity to dip his head toward her. "You seem surprised, my lady."

She stifled a laugh and turned toward the next girl in line, twirled around, gripped loose hands with the lady's partner and found herself returned into Jest's waiting hands. "What are you doing here?" she whispered. "You're . . ."

He grinned. "A wanted man?"

She ducked beneath the raised hands of the next couple. Rotated back. Curtsied.

"Exactly," she said as her palm found Jest's again.

"Good," he said, his dimples showing, "I hoped you might still feel that way."

They finished the rest of the dance in silence, and by the end of it Cath knew she was wearing a silly, dazed expression, but she couldn't escape it. Jest leaned over her hand and pressed a kiss against her knuckle, and in that touch she felt a slip of paper being pressed into her palm.

He stepped away, watching as she looked down at the piece of crumpled confetti, just like those he had once scattered across the ballroom.

On it was printed a tiny red heart.

She wrapped her fingers around it and looked up again. She swallowed hard, bracing herself. "I'm going to accept the King's proposal."

Jest's face froze. They stood in agonizing silence, staring at each other for a long moment, too long, before the storm came into his gaze. He moved closer, his toes brushing against the hem of her gown. She had to tilt her head back to maintain eye contact.

"You promised," he growled. "You promised that you wouldn't."

"That was before you ruined any chance we might have had of being accepted — by my parents or the court or the entire kingdom. They all think you're a liar and a cheat. They all think you're a villain."

"I was trying to save your reputation," he whispered back at her. "Besides, you made it clear at the festival that a courtship between us would never be accepted, no matter what I did."

She licked her lips. His eyes followed the movement, creating a flutter in her stomach that was painful to ignore. "You're right, it wouldn't. Which is why I have to accept the King."

Hurt crossed his face, drawing deep wrinkles across his brow. "Catherine —"

"Then, when I give you my heart, it will truly be the heart of a queen."

He sucked in a breath and started to shake his head, but she plowed on.

"And you can take it back to Chess and end your war. That's what you came here for, isn't it?"

"But —"

She inched closer, letting herself be drawn into his shadow. "Maybe there is no amount of magic that could ever make this a possibility," she whispered against his jaw. He was trembling, but so slightly she could only tell when she stood so close. "If I am not to have happiness, let me at least have a purpose. Let me give you the heart of a queen."

She watched him swallow, feeling the faint warmth of his breath on her cheek.

Then she stepped back and turned away. His hand grabbed for hers but she pulled it out of reach and slipped into the swirl of masks and dancers.

Her heart was hammering. She wanted him to call out for her, to stop her, almost as much as she wanted him to let her do this while her courage held.

A trumpet blared across the ballroom. Over the heads of the gentry she could see the White Rabbit beside the throne. "Ladies and gentlemen, presenting His Royal Majesty, the King of Hearts!"

The crowd applauded and drew toward the dais. Cath crumpled the slip of paper in her fist and couldn't help looking back at Jest . . . but he was gone.

She spun in a circle, searching the feather-and-rhinestone masks for a black top hat and yellow eyes.

"Catherine."

Her mother's voice halted her stampeding thoughts. An arm fell around her shoulders and ushered her toward the stage.

"It's time," the Marchioness said, her voice light with joy. "Oh, my dear girl, it's happening, finally!" She shoved her way through the crowd. Catherine felt her body going numb with every step she took toward the King, who had started to make a speech, but she couldn't hear him. She couldn't feel the pinching of her mother's fingers. She didn't notice the curious faces watching her pass by.

It's time.

She was going to accept the King.

She was going to be the Queen of Hearts.

She looked back a few more times, but the crowd had closed in behind them and there was no sign of Jest. It was as if his being there had been nothing more than a dream.

Inhaling a deep breath, Cath tried not to be hurt. If they had more time, would he have tried harder to dissuade her from this plan? Would she have let him?

No. She wanted this. She wanted to give him what he had come for.

Her heart belonged to him either way, whether it was the heart of a baker or a queen. At least this way it could serve some purpose beyond her trivial life.

She began to feel like she was above it all, looking down on a stranger. Watching herself being shoved onto the platform. Seeing the guests applaud without sound and the King take one of her hands and pull her to the center of the stage. It was another girl standing pale and speechless. It was another girl sacrificing her happiness for something greater than herself.

Another girl accepting that some things were never meant to be.

Her heart shriveled to a prune.

"As you all know," the King was saying, bouncing on his toes, "our kingdom has faced some horrible things these past weeks, but it is my privilege to take your thoughts from these f-frightening times, and instead give us all cause to celebrate." He beamed. "This lady that stands before you has shown herself to be brave and gallant, and I —" His eyes glistened as he peered up at Catherine. He squeezed her hand. "I both admire and adore her."

Catherine fell back into her body with a jolt, and nothing was distant anymore. The air was stifling. She was choking on panic and disbelief. She ordered herself to be strong, but it was difficult when she could hardly believe this had become her reality.

Was it only yesterday Jest had taken her to the treacle well? Only yesterday when he had kissed her breathless?

"Lady Catherine Pinkerton of Rock Turtle Cove," the King said, all tenderness and joy. His voice magnified in her skull. He knelt before her. His fingers were clammy and thick. "Would you do me the great honor of becoming my wife and my queen?"

A delighted gasp burst from the crowd.

Tearing her attention away from the King, Catherine found herself staring at the people she had known all her life. They all looked so happy, so eager.

It was a startling realization to her that the King was right about this. He wanted to pretend the attacks weren't happening, that the Jabberwock wasn't a very real nightmare. He wanted his people to feel safe and happy in their beds at night, and to do that, he would take their minds off it with a proposal. A wedding. A new queen — a queen who had battled the Jabberwock and survived.

It was a coward's solution, but it was working.

She wondered what would become of Hearts after Jest claimed his prize. When her heart was given to him and taken back to Chess and this kingdom was left with a hollow husk of a queen instead.

She imagined they would all go about their lives and pretend nothing had changed. Pretend that all was well. Pretend, like they always did.

Chess needed her. Hearts did not.

She squared her shoulders and faced the King, who was still kneeling with her hand between his damp palms. His face jovial and honest. He did not deserve the ungrateful wife he was going to be trapped with.

She held his gaze and stretched a smile over her lips. "I will, Your Majesty."

Her words had barely left her when the crowd erupted into cheers. All around her, women dabbed the corners of their eyes with handkerchiefs, like they were witnessing something beautiful. Men tipped their hats. The orchestra started up with an enthusiastic song, deafening with celebration.

She sought out her parents. The Marquess stood at her mother's side, an arm around her shoulders. They both looked so delighted, so proud.

Cath felt like she didn't even know them.

Her gaze scanned the crowd, searching, searching, but she didn't see Jest. She wanted to know if he was as miserable as she was. She wanted to know if he understood why she was doing it. She wanted to know if he was grateful for her sacrifice, or angry that she had broken her promise.

The crowd began to swarm onto the stage. Women she hadn't spoken to in years grabbed her by the shoulders and pulled her into embraces, brushed kisses against her cheeks, adoringly pressed her hands. She heard the Dowager Countess Wontuthry making a bawdy joke about the wedding night, and a couple of the courtiers placing bets on when the kingdom would have its first prince or princess.

Congratulations whirred through her ears.

You are such a lucky girl . . .

The Marquess and Marchioness must be

overjoyed . . .

What a pretty queen you'll make . . .

She ran her hands down the sides of her stiff skirt, trying to rid them of the touch of so much unwanted kindness. This was her decision, she reminded herself. She had made her choice.

Someone called for a dance, and another cheer filled the ballroom. She and the King were ushered off the dais, down to the center of the dance floor. She found herself facing him, staring down at his curled mustache and twinkling eyes and a grin that could not have looked any happier.

"Oh, Lady Pinkerton, my decadent truffle," he said, tears gathering in his eyes. "You have made me the happiest of men!"

She felt the twist of guilt in her chest.

She was going to be ill.

How much longer could she keep up this feigned joy? She didn't think she would last the night, much less the rest of her life.

The orchestra started up again and the King reached for her hands. She shoved her derision down as far as she could and placed her palms into his.

But before the dance could begin, a crash echoed through the ballroom — the massive entry doors being thrown open and colliding with the quartz walls. A gust of wind blew in, extinguishing the chandeliers overhead in a single breath and casting the guests in blackness.

A swath of light from the open doors cut through the ballroom and two shadowy silhouettes stretched along with it, reaching almost to where Cath and the King stood. One silhouette she remembered from that first night in the gardens — a hooded man gripping an enormous curve-bladed ax.

The other shadow wore a three-pointed hat.

Jest stood in the doorway, once again in his joker's motley, his feathered mask replaced with the dark kohl and dripping heart. Raven was perched on his shoulder.

The King squeaked. "Jest?"

"Jest," Cath breathed in response, letting her hands fall out of his grip.

Though she could barely make out Jest's face in the darkness, she knew he was looking at her. Only at her.

"I know a way," he said, his voice calm and cutting through the stunned silence. "I know a way, Catherine. We can be together and save Chess and you can have your bakery, and all of it."

Her lips parted, almost not daring to hope.

"You would be giving up all of this," he said, gesturing at the ballroom and the masqueraders, "but I think you were already willing to do that." He paused and took in a hesitant breath. "I know another way, my lady."

"This . . . this man!" The Marchioness's high-pitched voice cut through the stillness. "He is the one who tricked my beloved daughter, who would make your future queen out to be a strumpet. He is deceitful and wicked and he must be stopped!" She stepped out of the crowd and waved her arms at the King. "Your Majesty, do something!"

"O-oh, yes! Guards! Guards!" the King wailed, pointing at the Clubs that lined the ballroom. "Capture him!"

It took another moment for the guards to shake off their befuddlement and begin to mobilize, their boots clomping against the tile.

Jest never took his attention from Cath. "What do you choose?" he whispered, and though he was so far away, she could hear him plainly. Hope and wanting, so much wanting.

The guards hoisted their weapons and moved toward him, pushing their way through the startled crowd.

"You," she whispered back to him, and though her voice barely reached even her own ears, she saw the brightness enter his eyes. "Over everything, I choose you."

He grinned and moved toward the stairs.

Cath grabbed her skirts and began to rush toward him, ignoring the startled cries of the crowd, her mother's shrieks, the guards' thundering footsteps. They would reach him before she did, though Jest was swooping down the steps. The guards changed directions. Aimed their spears.

Cath started to run. She could see the collision coming, and she didn't know if she could make it to him before the guards did, and the King was calling her name and her father was ordering her to stop and Raven was lifting off Jest's shoulder and soaring overhead.

Something sparked at her feet. Smoke thickened the air.

The guards drew up short.

Cath tripped, but Jest's arms were already around her, like feathers against her skin, carrying her away.

Chapter 41

"I'm sorry. I'm so sorry," she said, her voice muffled against Jest's shoulder, her arms like vises around his neck. She didn't know where he was taking her to. She could feel the evening air on her hot skin. She could hear his heavy breathing — he was running, with her and all her crinoline in his arms. "I thought I could do it. I thought I could marry him and give you what you want, but it's not what I want, Jest, you must know that —"

"It's all right, Cath. It's going to be all right."

He came to a stop and sank down to his knees, cradling her in his lap.

Untangling her arms, Catherine looked up. At her Joker. Her Rook. Cath pressed her hands against his face and saw it instantly. The openness in his eyes, the tenderness.

"I choose you," she repeated. The words

tasted like sugar.

His jaw twitched and with his free hand he grasped her fingers, keeping them pressed against his face. "Cath, you have to be sure." His voice was thick, practically choking. "Raven gave me the idea. I wouldn't have thought of it otherwise, and I . . . I don't think you're going to like what I have to say. It isn't too late. They already believe I have you under some spell, it would be easy to persuade them —"

"Wait." Cath's hands slid down his cheeks, reaching for the collar of his tunic instead. "You said we could be together. We can save Chess and I'll have my bakery and —"

He nodded. "It's true. I think it will work."

"You think?"

Tilting forward, Jest buried his face into her neck. He was shaking as hard as she was. "It won't be easy. And you can still change your mind. The King will still want you, I know he will, and I'll leave you be, you and your heart, I promise. I couldn't do it anyway, Cath. I couldn't take it from you."

His words dug into her chest. She stared past him, seeing the white rose tree where she'd seen him that first night. He'd brought her to the gardens.

They would be followed. Probably the

guards were already searching for them. She doubted it would take long for them to be found.

Stomach twisting, she shoved Jest away and scrambled out of his hold. She tried to stand but her legs were too weak and she collapsed back down to the grass. "You gave me a choice and I made it. How could you even suggest I change it now?"

Jest tried to string his hands through his hair but found his joker hat in the way. Ripping it off, he threw it on the ground. The bells clinked once, dejectedly, before falling silent. "Because you have to be sure. Because it will kill me if you come to regret this, to know that you gave up everything the King was offering and it was my fault."

The cold air stung her throat, but she couldn't stop gasping for breath. Clenching her jaw, she shoved him as hard as she could. Jest fell onto his side in the grass.

"You idiot. I don't want him or what he's offered me, and I never have. I don't want to be the stupid Queen!"

"I know. I know that, Cath. That's why you might regret this."

She gaped at him and started to shake her head. "It won't take them long to find us here. Just tell me. What was this idea Raven had?"

Jest glanced up and Cath startled upon spying Raven among the roses.

"There is a law in Chess," Jest said, drawing her attention back to him, "that a pawn who can make it through the enemy's territory, all the way to the border, can become a queen."

She frowned.

"Come back with me." Jest pushed himself back to his knees and wrapped Cath's hands in his. "We can get you to the border — Hatta, Raven, and I — and you can be a queen, and you can lead us to victory, Cath, I know it."

"But . . ." Her throat dried and it was a struggle to wet it again. "But you said . . . I could have my bakery, and . . ."

Jest chuckled, a warm sound that surprised her. His grip tightened. "That's just it. Once the war is over, the White Queen can take over again — we won't need two queens, after all — and you can be anything you want. And you and I —"

He was interrupted by the sound of marching in the direction of the castle. Cath tensed and looked back, spotting two rows of Club guards making their way down the steps. The Ace of Clubs stood at their helm, shouting orders to spread out and search the grounds.

Jest was staring at her when she faced him again. "I know you never wanted to be a queen," he said, apology lacing his voice.

A humorless laugh burbled out of her mouth. "It seems I was going to be a queen either way." She wriggled one hand out of his hold and traced the painted heart on his cheek with the pad of her thumb. "I love you, Jest. I want to be with you, any way I can."

His breath formed crystals on the air. Boots echoed, hitting the gravel paths. Overhead, Raven let out a warning caw.

Jest grabbed her suddenly, crushing his mouth against hers. Cath threw her arms around his neck, delighting in the way her heart expanded as if it could consume them both.

"I love you too," he whispered in the spaces between another kiss, and another. "I love you too."

It was impossible, and she absolutely believed it.

He was kissing her again when Raven coughed, loudly. "They are coming. We mustn't tarry any longer."

Cath and Jest looked up into the tree boughs.

"That didn't rhyme," said Cath.

"Who has the time?" Raven snapped.

"He's right, of course," said Jest, beaming. "Yet this interlude has been sublime." He grabbed his hat and pulled Cath to her feet.

With a nod from Jest, Raven swooped down to join them, just as Cath heard the first guards clomping through the rose gardens. No sooner had Raven landed on Jest's shoulder than the earth quaked and a tower of stone burst up from the ground, swallowing them back down.

Cath did not know if this magic could be called a tower, a tunnel, a bridge, or some other impossible passageway, but she was relieved when it deposited them into the meadow outside Hatta's shop. She was trembling, though Jest and Raven looked as though traveling through the earth was the most natural thing in the world.

"And to think," she gasped, pushing herself up onto wobbly legs, "I've been bothering with carriages all these years, when there was such a more reasonable way of traveling."

Jest was grinning as widely as ever as he laced his fingers with hers. "It's a favored trick of us Rooks," he said. "You get used to it."

She sniffed and straightened her gown.

"That remains to be seen."

They approached the Marvelous Millinery with their hands fiercely entwined. The windows of the traveling shop glowed warm and gold, but the forest was quiet.

Jest reached for the doorknob on the shop's round door but found himself holding a furry striped tail. A cat yowled.

Jest jumped away, bracing his body in front of Cath's.

Cheshire's head appeared next, grinning enormously despite the way his slitted eyes glared. He licked at his injured tail. "Well," he said, "that was uncouth."

"Cheshire, what are you doing here?" asked Catherine.

"Tending to my wounds. I fear he may have bruised me."

She fisted a hand on her hip. "I mean it, Cheshire. Have you been following us?"

He stopped licking and his tail vanished, leaving only his bulbous head hanging where there might have been a door knocker. "Following you? I was here first, dear girl."

Catherine lifted an eyebrow.

Cheshire's vivid smile widened even farther. "I heard a rumor that you had fled the masquerade in the arms of our most-wanted criminal. Well, our only wanted criminal. I wanted to see the truth of it for myself."

"And now you've seen it. Please move aside."

Cheshire's eyes narrowed, peering into the distance. "Is that bird friend or food?"

Cath and Jest glanced back. Raven had claimed a spot on a low-hanging tree bough. He puffed up his feathers until he was the same size as Cheshire. Or, the same size that Cheshire would have been had his entire body been visible.

"Friend," said Catherine, turning back. "What do you want?"

Cheshire's head turned upside down. "I suppose you haven't any idea what's been about this evening. Been awful preoccupied, what with your proposal and such and such. Do you want to hear about it?"

"Not particularly. I have a few preoccupations of my own, you may have noticed."

"It involves the pumpkin eater."

Her gut tightened. She'd all but forgotten how Sir Peter had accosted her earlier that evening. "Why would I have any interest in him?"

"And also Mary Ann. And even the Jabberwock. A zesty new rumor that might be even more scandalous than our King's bride running away with the Joker. I'm positively dying to tell someone" — his eyes turned to silver coins, like those placed upon the dead — "and you were the first person I thought who would want to know."

A chill scurried down her spine. She could sense Jest peering at her, could imagine his concern, his curiosity, but she shoved her own curiosity down into the pit of her stomach, right beside the angry pit where lay Mary Ann's betrayal.

"You were wrong. I don't want to know. Go bother someone else with your gossip and leave us alone, or I'll bruise much more than your tail."

The coins turned back into glowing eyes. "I see," he said, drawing out the words. "It appears I was incorrect about you, Lady Catherine. After all these years." His gaze shifted to Jest. "He's handsome enough, I suppose . . ." His ears and eyes and nose vanished then, leaving only his smile — hanging downside up so it became a frown without a body to tether it. "If one cares for that sort of thing."

Then he was gone.

Jest was still looking at her.

"It's fine," she said. "He won't tell anyone where we are." She didn't know if it was true, but she hoped they would be far gone before it mattered.

With the cat gone, Raven left his perch in

the trees and flew down to join them as Jest pulled open the door.

No longer a tea parlor, no longer a shop — the little room was a messy workspace, a hatter's studio. The long table was littered with ribbons, feathers, felt, buttons, needles, and thread. A dozen mannequin heads were lined up, wearing unfinished hats of varying styles, blinking bored eyes at the newcomers.

The Dormouse slept curled up on the table, wrapped in velvet ribbon like a present.

The March Hare was stringing different-colored buttons onto a thread and draping them around his neck like a pile of beaded necklaces. There were enough on him that they reminded Catherine of a noose.

Hatta sat on his throne, wearing his plum top hat, one leg strewn over the chair's arm and his chin propped up on his knuckles. An incomplete lady's hat sat on a mannequin's head before him, half done up with yellow rhinestones and half done up with seashells, but his eyes were on Jest and Catherine and Raven.

He scanned Jest's dark motley and smirked. "Still playing the part of the royal idiot, I see. Or maybe that's an effect of the girl who has you so neatly wrapped around her finger."

Jest tipped his hat, letting the bells tinkle around his face. "Everyone always underestimates the idiot."

Hatta waved his hand at them. "Come in, come in. Haigha, stop mucking with those buttons and put on a pot of tea."

"That won't be necessary. This isn't to be a long visit." Jest tugged Catherine around the table, like he was afraid to release her.

Hatta's eyes lingered on their entwined hands a beat longer than Cath thought necessary. "What's your hurry? If the rumors are true, the only place you have to be right now is His Majesty's prison." He squinted. "Speaking of His Majesty, does he know that you're about with his lady fair?"

Jest pulled out a chair for Catherine. She felt too anxious to sit, but she did anyway.

"The King proposed marriage to Catherine tonight," he said, claiming the chair between her and Hatta — what would once have been the performer's chair.

Hatta's eyes swept toward her and he lifted a teacup from a saucer, like a toast. The rim was stained with long-ago drips of tea, and she wondered how long it had been sitting there untouched. "Congratulations must be in order, Your Queenliness."

She scowled. "Are you congratulating me

or yourself? I know you wanted to see me become the Queen as much as anyone, though I now understand you didn't exactly have my best interests in mind."

There was a moment of silence, the cup hanging in the air. Then Hatta guffawed and slammed the cup back to the table. It was empty.

"If you know that, then you know I was not alone in the plot." He swung his leg off the arm of the chair and leaned toward them. "She is a rose, Jest. Lovely on the eyes, yes, but such thorns are not to be ignored. She belongs in a King's garden, not yours." As an afterthought, he tipped his head toward Catherine. "No offense meant, milady."

"None at all?" she deadpanned.

He shrugged, a flippant one-shouldered shrug that made her blood run hot.

"I love her, Hatta," said Jest. "I didn't mean to fall in love with her, but I did."

She squeezed his hand beneath the table.

Hatta slid his gaze back to Catherine. She returned it, though she felt as insignificant before him as she had the first time they'd met. There was little cruelty in his expression, though. More like a mild curiosity. Like he was trying to determine what it was Jest saw when he looked at her. "That *is* a problem, isn't it?"

"I love him too, if that's what you're wondering."

He shook his head. "Oh no, that much is plain to see." He ran a finger along his lower lip. "I suspect you didn't come here to allow me the privilege of sharing in your mutual happiness."

Jest removed his hat and tossed it amid the table's mess. "Cath is not going to marry the King and we are not going to steal her heart."

"I thought that might be where this was heading." Hatta cut a quick glance at the March Hare, who was watching them like a fascinating match of lawn tennis. "Prepare yourself, Haigha. It will not be any fun informing the White King that our dear Jest has failed."

"I have not failed." Jest cocked his head toward Raven. "Raven has reminded me of the law of promotion."

Hatta's eyes widened, almost imperceptibly. "Queening," he murmured. His gaze swooped to Cath, studying her with new intensity. "Why steal a queen's heart when you can steal the queen herself?"

"She isn't a queen yet," said Jest. "But she could be. It solves everything, Hatta."

Hatta sat back and shut his eyes, his brow

tight. "Not everything," he said, but it was whispered so low Cath thought he was speaking to himself. When he looked up again, he was shaking his head. "We are a parliament of idiots. A murder of fools."

"No," said Jest, his voice soft. "That would be an unkindness."

"So it would." Hatta sniffed, and glanced wryly at the March Hare again. "What say you, Haigha?"

Haigha was peering at Catherine, his nose twitching. "Are we sure she can do it?"

"That's a legitimate question." Hatta leaned forward. "Once we cross through the Looking Glass, you'll no longer be the daughter of a marquess, but a lowly pawn, like Haigha and me. If you fail to defeat the Red Queen, you are accepting many lifetimes of servitude. Are you willing to risk that, Lady Pinkerton?"

"She won't —" Jest started, but Cath interrupted him.

"I am willing to risk it. There's nothing left for me here."

Hatta looked at Jest. "It really would have been so much simpler to just stick to the plan."

"This couldn't be helped," said Jest.

"No, I suppose it couldn't." Rubbing his temple, Hatta once again glanced at the

March Hare. "So. Which of us is coming and which of us is going?"

Haigha's ears folded down and he sank deeper in his chair. "I went last time," he said, his voice warbling. "And by-the-bye, weren't you just saying you ought to go gather more hatting supplies? I mean, it isn't that I'm afraid or anything of that sort." He scratched his neck, looking very afraid indeed. "Just thinking of what's best for your business, that's what."

Hatta scoffed and nudged a teacup toward Haigha with the bottom of his cane. "Don't get all harried over it. I'll go." He let out a heavy sigh. "Time has been running short on this side of the Glass, anyhow."

Haigha wilted with relief, though he remained half hidden beneath the table, shivering.

"What are you afraid of?" Cath asked, frowning at what little she could see of Haigha's ears. "Haigha?"

His bloodshot eyes appeared again. He looked at Jest first, then Catherine.

"Nothing," he spat.

Hatta stood and began gathering his coat and gloves.

"The Sisters," said Jest. "When we came through before you were . . . you seemed uncomfortable around them."

"Uncomfortable?" Hatta barked and whapped his cane on the table. Haigha was hidden entirely beneath it now. "Do they make you uncomfortable, Haigha?"

"Not exactly." Haigha's voice floated up through the wood. "More like they make me want to drown myself in a pool of treacle."

"Why?" Cath glanced at Jest. "What's wrong with them?"

Jest shook his head. "They're a little odd, is all."

Haigha shuddered so hard beneath the table that the teacups shook.

"A little odd?" said Hatta. "You must have crossed over on one of their good days, dear Jest. I assure you, Haigha means what he says and says what he means." Adjusting his sleeves, Hatta fixed a smirk on Catherine. "But what can be done to avoid them? Nothing is what." He grabbed his cane and twirled it through the air. "Let you not say that you weren't warned."

Chapter 42

Hatta pushed his chair back from the table and stood, adjusting his top hat. "Are you sure you're desperate enough to come with us, Lady Pinkerton?" he said, eyeing her. "Are you sure you wouldn't prefer to stay here and live your days in luxury?"

She stood too, facing him over the scattered flowers and felts. "What is luxury if your life is a lie? I can never go back there. I belong with Jest now."

Hatta's eyelid twitched, but he turned away and approached the standing mirror Cath had once used to admire her macaron hat. He pulled it away from the shop's wall and swiveled it on creaky wheels. The back was the same. Another looking glass in a polished wooden frame, except —

Cath stepped around the table, her fingers trailing on the backs of the mismatched chairs.

The reflection no longer showed the hat

shop. It showed a glen of grasses and wildflowers and a treacle well glowing in the twilight.

"Step through, then," said Hatta, and his tone carried a warning. "The Sisters will know how desperate you truly are."

She glanced back at Jest, but he nodded encouragingly. There was no doubt in his expression, unlike Hatta's, and that bolstered her. She knew this decision, once made, could never be undone. But what choice was left to her?

She had meant what she said.

She no longer belonged in Hearts.

She would never see her parents again. Or Cheshire. Or Mary Ann. She wondered if she should leave them a note explaining where she'd gone. Maybe Raven would carry it back for her. But when she tried to think of what the note would say, all her thoughts turned bitter. Angry as she was with her parents, she didn't want that to be the last they ever heard from her. No — Hatta was a messenger who traversed between the Looking Glass regularly. When she was calm and happy in her new life, when she had saved Chess and she and Jest had their bakery . . . then she would send a letter to her parents and let them know she was all right.

Until then, she would let them worry. They were the ones who had threatened to disown *her,* after all.

There was no going back.

She was desperate, but she was also hopeful.

Gathering her voluminous skirt, Cath stepped up to the mirror, inhaled a deep breath, and stepped through.

She was back in the meadow, caged in by towering hedges on every side. The grass was speckled with crimson and gold and the sugar-molasses scent filled Cath's lungs.

No sooner had she stepped forward than she heard footsteps behind her — Jest and Hatta, with Raven perched on Jest's shoulder.

Hatta lifted an eyebrow and looked mildly surprised, perhaps that Cath was desperate enough after all. But all he said was, "Haven't anything for warmth, Lady Pinkerton?"

She glanced down at her ball gown and bare arms. "I was not expecting an adventure tonight, and my shawl was taken by the castle courtiers."

He grunted, as if this were a weak excuse, and brushed past her, moving toward the well.

Jest took hold of her hand. The bells on

his hat jingled extra loud in the stillness.

Hatta knocked his cane three times against the well's rocky ledge before leaning over and smiling into its black depths. "Hello, Tillie."

Two small hands appeared at the top of the well, followed by a child's gaunt face. She was ghostlike, not more than six years old, with white-silver hair that cascaded down her back and skin the color of milk thinned with water. Her eyes, in contrast, were coal black and far too big for her face.

"Where have you been, Hatta?" Tillie said, pulling herself onto the wall and perching there on her knees. She wore a white muslin dress that was covered in filth, as though . . . well, as though she'd just crawled out of a well. "We've missed you."

"I'm sorry, love. It's been a busy time. Are your sisters around?"

"They're at the bottom, racing boats made from two halves of a lady's boot." Tillie grinned. Both of her front teeth were missing. "Is that Jest? Ah, and Raven as well. How do you do?"

"Hello, Tillie," said Jest.

"Nevermore," greeted the Raven.

Tillie's gaze drifted to Catherine. "And you are the girl he brought before. The one he finally kissed and kissed."

Cath blushed, but no one seemed to notice.

Hatta cast his eyes upward. "I could have gone without that knowledge, love."

Tillie dropped her head to one shoulder and stared hard at Cath's skirt. "Your ankle is repaired."

"Yes. Thank you for the treacle," Catherine stammered.

"It is not *mine.*" Tillie held her gaze. "But then, it isn't yours, either, though pay for it you did." Her lips pulled upward, but the smile made no attempt to reach her impenetrable eyes. Cath wondered if that youthful face had ever seen a true smile.

She was unsettling. A child who carried the sorrow of an old crone.

"Tillie," said Hatta, "we need to get through the Looking Glass again. Will you open the maze for us?"

"The Looking Glass again, again," Tillie singsang. "How many times have you passed back and forth now, Hatta?"

"Too many to count, love. But this is important."

"You have said *that* too many times to count." She pouted. "Always one is coming and one is going but none are ever, ever staying. Won't you come down to the bottom and race boats with us a while? I'll fix you a cup of piping hot treacle."

"That's a kind offer, but I'll have to accept it another time. For now, we must get through the maze."

"All four of you?" Tillie asked.

Hatta nodded. "All four of us."

The child heaved a great, heavy sigh. "My sisters and I are ill, Hatta. We have been dying a long time, and must ask for payment to sustain us."

"I understand. What is the price for our passage?"

Tillie listed her head, her black eyes staring up at him as if she were in a trance. "Lacie wants a feather, black as blackest ink. Elsie wants three joker's bells that twinkle, *tink tink tink.* And I shall take your time, dear Hatta. Five minutes will do, I think."

Hatta glanced back at their group before asking, "Nothing from the lady?"

Tillie's hollow gaze fell on Cath and she had to force herself not to shy away. Slowly, the child shook her head. "She has nothing we want. Not yet."

Then she grinned again, that same eerie, gap-toothed smile.

Cath stood by silently while they made their payment. A tail feather from Raven and three bells torn from Jest's hat, all dropped into the well. Hatta went last, pulling out his pocket watch and turning the hand forward, five minutes. He didn't seem happy about it, but neither did he complain.

Tillie nodded once payment was made and vanished back into the well. Cath tensed, but there was no scream and no splash down below.

"You are running out of minutes, Hatta."

They turned. A new girl sat cross-legged on a fallen, moss-covered log. She was identical to Tillie, with the waxen skin and eerie dark eyes, only her silvery hair was cropped short like wild leaves.

"I know, Elsie," said Hatta. "You keep taking them from me."

She scrutinized him, unblinking, for a heartbeat too long, before she allowed a close-lipped smile. "How much longer will you run from Time?"

"For as long as I can."

A third voice sang, *"Time would never find you here."*

Cath spun again. The third girl stood beside the wall of hedges, again a mirror image of her sisters, although her shining hair had grown all the way to her ankles. Huge, bottomless eyes watched them across the glen.

A door was now set into the hedges behind

the third Sister, an enormous wooden structure with black iron hinges. Tillie stood beside it, digging her bare toes in the dirt and gripping its enormous handle.

"You could stay with us, you know," said the third girl.

Hatta shook his head. "I'm sorry, Lacie, but I can't."

"What about them?" asked Tillie, pointing her chin at Cath and Jest and Raven.

Cath was glad when Jest answered, as she didn't think she could speak. "I'm sorry, but we must go back to Chess. We have a role to play."

"Oh yes," said Elsie. "Two Rooks, a Pawn, and a Queen. That's how the riddle begins, but howsoever shall it end?" She started to laugh.

Cath shivered.

"We shall see what role you have to play," said Tillie.

"Once you reach the other side," added Lacie.

Tillie pulled open the ancient door. Its iron hinges creaked and the wood grated against the moss-covered stone. Cath could see nothing beyond but more hedges.

In unison, the Sisters murmured, "We will all greet fate, on the other side."

Cath took a hesitant step forward, with

Jest gripping her hand and Hatta a mere step away. As they approached the door, she saw that there were stairs on the other side, a short flight of crumbling stone steps that dropped down into another forest meadow. Overgrown hedges pushed in on either side, making the stairwell too narrow for her and Jest to walk side by side.

She followed Hatta through, lifting her skirt to keep from tripping on the uneven stones. Leaves clung to her hem. Shadows pushed in from the sides.

The moment they passed through, the massive door slammed shut, making Cath jump. Jest squeezed her shoulder and his presence alone warmed the chill from her bones.

They reached the bottom of the steps and Cath paused. Her brow furrowed.

She glanced back, but the stairs were gone. She was staring at the empty wall of an enormous hedge, with no doors and no exits.

She turned again, her heart pattering against her sternum. They were still in the same forest glen with the same treacle well.

But this time, the Three Sisters were already waiting.

Chapter 43

Elsie, Lacie, and Tillie sat on the edge of the well sipping from porcelain teacups. They still wore their plain white dresses, though the meadow seemed colder than before and Catherine thought they must be freezing in such flimsy fabric.

The oddest thing, though, was that the three girls were now wearing masks. An owl. A raccoon. A fox. The masks were tied to their heads with ribbons and only the girls' enormous eyes could be seen through circular cutouts — so black and fathomless it was like looking through the holes into nothing.

Catherine was grateful when Jest's hand found hers again, lacing their fingers together.

It was a strange thing, to stare across a peaceful forest glen at three little girls and feel that she'd stepped onto a battlefield.

"Hello," said Hatta, with a calmness that

was offset by his tense shoulders. "Tillie. Elsie. Lacie."

The girls did not move. They held their teacups in one hand and their saucers in the other, their pinkie fingers pointing at matching angles.

"We've been practicing," said the Owl.

"We've been drawing," said the Raccoon.

"We've seen many things," said the Fox.

They sipped their tea in unison.

"I have given you five minutes of my time," said Hatta. "Show us, so we might be on our way." It sounded like a script, like a tired conversation he'd recited too many times.

The Sisters were quiet for a while, their empty eyes gazing, before Lacie the Fox set down her teacup and stood. Her long hair clung to her calves as she stepped away from the well. The silvery ends were sticky with treacle.

Jest and Cath released each other's hands so Lacie could pass between, splitting them like an ax into a log. She reached the wall of hedges and pushed her hands into the brush. Grabbed and pulled.

The leaves and vines fell away, revealing a wall of stone. It was covered in drawings. Some were faded and smeared, while others still glistened from wet ink. The Fox stepped back and beckoned them to approach.

Cath stepped closer, scanning the array of drawings. A marigold. A mosquito. A menorah. A milk bottle. A branch of mistletoe. Mousetraps and mirrors and memory.

"See our new work?" said Lacie the Fox, gesturing to a group of drawings, and Cath noticed that she had Raven's quill tucked behind one ear, dripping ink down the back of her neck. Her fingers were smudged with recent ink as well, though Cath was sure they'd been clean before.

Catherine followed the girl's gesture and felt the blood drain from her body.

The drawing showed two men. One was on the ground, surrounded by a pool of darkness that she assumed was blood. His head had been severed clean from his body. A three-pointed joker's hat lay on the ground beside him.

The second man stood in the distance — enormous and cloaked in an executioner's hood. A bloodied ax was in his hand.

A memory darted through her thoughts. It was the same ominous shadow that had followed her across the castle's lawn on the night she met Jest. The shadow that always attached itself to Raven.

She recoiled, pressing a hand over her mouth. "Why?" she stammered, knowing that Jest was right beside her, alive and well, and Raven was his friend and would never hurt him. Or did she know that? The picture was detailed enough to insert a sliver of doubt into her thoughts. "Why would you draw something so terrible?"

"Cath . . ." Jest's voice was strained. He wasn't looking at the same drawing. Her gaze followed his and she saw —

Herself. Sitting on a throne, wearing the crown of the Queen of Hearts and gripping a heart-tipped scepter in one hand. Her expression was cold as stone.

Her mouth ran dry. "What is this?"

"It's . . . it's you," he said.

She shook her head. "They're just drawings. Terrible drawings."

Beneath that image was another, this one of Hatta. He sat at a long table scattered with broken teacups and cracked plates. Rather than surrounded by friends and music and laughter, the chairs around the table were empty. His hair was unkempt, his hat tilted to one side, dark circles beneath his eyes. His smile was crazed.

"Why would you show these to us?" Jest growled, his hands tightening into a fist.

The Fox folded her hands and recited,

One to be a murderer, the other to be martyred,

One to be a monarch, the other to go mad.

"That last one will be me," said Hatta. He'd taken off his top hat and was fiddling with the decorative ribbon. Cath didn't think he'd looked at the wall once. "Always the same fate, the same warning. As you'll see, I've not gone mad yet."

He said it as if this were proof that the drawings were nothing but harmless whimsies. Cath wanted to believe that, but Hatta seemed more shaken than he wanted to admit.

They were leaving Hearts, she told herself.

She couldn't become the Queen of Hearts once they were gone.

Maybe she would become a monarch — Jest wanted her to become the new White Queen after all. Maybe that's what the Sisters meant.

But there was no mistaking the crown topped with the heart finial in the drawing.

"Your future is written on stone, but not in it."

Catherine spun around. Elsie the Raccoon stood arm's reach away, the expressionless mask and hollow eyes peering up at her. Cath hadn't heard her approach.

"It's only an idle warning, then?"

"It is a truth," said the Raccoon. "But one of many."

"Many, many muchness," said Tillie the Owl, her voice like a sad trill. "Eeenie meenie miney mo."

"Choose a door, any door," Elsie continued. "They all lead to this truth. It is a fate, and fate is inevitable."

Catherine shook her head. "If they all lead to this, then how can we avoid it?"

Tillie tittered. "Time cannot follow you here, so he cannot follow you out. To put it most simply, you mustn't go through a door."

The Sisters all started to laugh, the sound shrill and bubbling. Cath hated the sound.

"Fine, we won't go through any doors," said Hatta. "May we go?"

"Patience, patience," said Elsie.

"Don't lose your head," said Tillie.

They turned their heads together and snickered.

"We drew your grandmother too, a long, long time ago," said Elsie the Raccoon, drawing closer to Cath's voluminous skirt. "The first Marchioness of Mock Turtles. Do you wish to see her?"

"You mean the Marchioness of Rock Turtle Cove," said Cath, and though she shook her head, she still followed to where Lacie was pointing and saw a drawing of a beautiful girl surrounded by turtles and lobsters. Her many-greats-grandmother, recognizable from a portrait that hung in her father's library.

How old were these girls? How long had they been here, drawing the future in the key of M?

"We have one minute still," said Tillie. Her sisters came to join her, all surrounding Cath and staring up at her. "Won't you tell us a story?"

She gulped. "I'm not a good storyteller like my father, or grandmother, or . . . I'm sorry. You'll be disappointed."

"Then we will tell it," said Tillie.

Elsie curtsied. "A gift to take with you through the Looking Glass."

"Another truth we've seen," added Lacie.

They began to recite in a haunting voice, like synchronized puppets:

Peter, Peter, pumpkin eater,
Had a wife but couldn't keep her;
He put her in a pumpkin shell
And there he kept her very well.
Peter, Peter, pumpkin eater,
Had a pet and couldn't feed her;
Caught a maid who had meant well —
What became of her, no one can tell.

Cath and Jest both clapped politely when

they had finished, though Cath was disturbed by the poem. She'd never heard the rhyme before, and thinking of Sir Peter tightened her stomach.

She looked at Hatta, who was still clutching the brim of his hat against his stomach. Tapping his fingers, impatient. She wondered if this happened every time he wanted to pass through the Looking Glass. If he gave up five minutes of his time to look at their drawings, listen to their tales, humor them as well as he could.

He wasn't humoring them much now, but then, Cath knew it would drag on her after a while too. It was difficult to be polite when you wanted to run away.

"Are you sure you wish to go?" asked Tillie the Owl, cocking her head to one side. Cath kept expecting the masks to take on expressions — to smile or cry — but there was nothing but blankness about them.

"Or do you wish to play?" said the Fox.

"We could fix you some warm treacle," added the Raccoon.

Jest shook his head. "We must go. But thank you for — for the poem, and for showing us your drawings."

"Fine," said the Raccoon, sounding put out by the refusal of their hospitality. "We'll open the maze for you. You'll want to go right. Right is always right. Except when left is right, naturally."

"Do you remember the way, Hatta?" asked the Owl.

Hatta tipped his hat to her. "Like the way to my own hat shop, Tillie."

Tillie cocked her head — like a real owl with her humongous eyes. "Your hat shop," she said, quite plainly, "is on wheels."

"Don't get lost, Hatta," warned Lacie the Fox.

"Don't lose yourself, Hatta," added Elsie from behind her Raccoon mask.

"Or anyone else," added Tillie with a secretive laugh. "Shall we draw you a map of the maze before you go?"

Hatta shook his head. "I know the way."

The girls nodded and spoke again in unison. "Farewell, then. So long. Good eve. *Murderer. Martyr. Monarch. Mad.*"

Cath shut her eyes, her skin writhing. She wanted to get away from them. She was suddenly as desperate to get away as she'd been to get here in the first place. She found Jest's hand and squeezed and was grateful when he squeezed back.

Then she heard the chirrup of three jingling joker's bells. She opened her eyes in surprise, but the girls and the bells were gone. The glen fell silent. Not a breath, not a breeze.

The wall that had held the girls' drawings was gone too, opened wide to reveal the entrance to a hedge maze, with walls that towered three times Cath's height.

Hatta let out a weary sigh. "Thank you, loves," he said, sounding truly grateful, as though he doubted each time if they would let him through or torment him forever. He approached the entrance to the maze without half as much bounce in his step as before. As he passed by Catherine, she heard him muttering beneath his breath, "Though if I go mad, we'll all know who's to blame for it."

Cath wanted to smile, but her nerves were still frazzled. She followed behind Hatta and, thinking it would not do to be impolite, she whispered to the empty glen, "Thank you very much."

Only once she had stepped past the first wall did a ghostly whisper, three girlish, ghoulish voices, brush across her earlobe.

"You are welcome," they said, "Your Majesty."

Chapter 44

The maze walls were made of entwined dead branches and tight-packed laurel leaves and the occasional bare spot of ancient stone wall. Catherine felt a sense of helplessness the moment they'd stepped through the entrance and peered down the first endless stretch. The maze continued in each direction as far as she could see, fading in a swirl of fog in the distance. The path itself was padded in a white-flowering ground cover that was soft and damp with dew.

"Well," said Jest, clearing his throat — the first sound to break the miserable silence that had engulfed them in the Sisters' absence. "That was not exactly like the first time you brought us to meet the Sisters."

"No? I've passed through so many times they all start to feel the same." Hatta smirked and started undoing the buttons of his coat. "What was their price before?"

"Raven gave them a recitation of a classic Chessian poem," said Jest, "and I gave them a lemon seed."

Cath startled, thinking of the lemon tree that had grown over her bed.

Mistaking her surprise, Jest gave her a nonchalant grin. "I'd had some lemon in my tea that day — the seed was stuck in my tooth. I'd been working at it all afternoon, but the moment they asked, it popped right out. I was glad to be rid of it."

Cath was still mulling over the lemon seed and the dream, wondering whether it could be a coincidence, when she felt the heavy wool being draped over her shoulders. She looked down, her free hand grabbing the lapel. The coat was impeccable, not a speck of lint on it.

She turned to face Hatta. "What is this for?"

"It is a long, damp walk, Lady Pinkerton. I do not wish for you to catch a cold." Hatta turned away and started walking down the maze's first wildflower-dotted path.

"Thank you," Cath said, somewhat uncertainly, as she and Jest hurried after him. She slipped her arms into the sleeves. The lining was silken and warm and smelled of herbal tea.

"Yes, that's kind of you, Hatta," added

Jest, who had no coat to offer her himself.

Hatta waved a hand at them without looking back. "I wish she'd taken a hat before we left the shop. How I find myself in the company of such an unadorned cranium, gallivanting about mazes and wells, is ever the mystery."

The corners of her lips twitched.

Jest offered his elbow and she took it gladly, the warmth of Hatta's coat and Jest's company driving back the chill the Sisters had given her.

They had not gone far when shadows began to close in around them, reminding her that it was still nighttime, despite the golden light of the meadow. Jest removed his hat — its new silence disconcerting — and found an oil lantern inside, already lit. It shed a welcome circle of light onto the maze walls and flickered in Raven's black eyes.

"Did they draw such horrible pictures when you came across the first time?" Cath asked as they traipsed after Hatta.

"They drew, yes, but I didn't think much of the drawings at the time." Jest pondered for a moment, one finger trailing over Cath's knuckles. "Do you remember what they were, Raven?"

Perched on his far shoulder, Raven ducked

his head to peer at Catherine around Jest's profile. "A merry-go-round was cast in ink, a monster sketched on stone, and a messenger who would go mad for mistakes he must atone."

"That's right," Jest mused, his voice turning low. He was no longer smiling as he stared ahead, watching Hatta pull farther away from them. "Hatta was the messenger. I remember that now."

Cath's feet stalled beneath her. "And they drew a monster, like the Jabberwock? And a merry-go-round? Like the hat the Lion was wearing when . . ."

Jest fixed his gaze on her, filling with the same thoughts, the same horrors.

If they were prophecies, those two at least had come true.

The Sisters' words spun through her head. *Murderer, martyr, monarch, mad . . .*

"Do not go through a door!" Hatta yelled back at them. He hadn't slowed his pace and was fast disappearing into the maze's shadows. "They gave us their warning, now we have only to heed it."

Cath shuddered and traded a concerned look with Jest, but it was too late to turn back now, and nothing had changed, besides. They were still going to Chess, and every step brought them closer to it.

They hurried after Hatta before he could desert them, the lantern's light skipping and swaying over the walls. Though there was nothing joyful about the maze, Hatta began to whistle, twirling his cane as if he were leading a marching band. The first turn was easy enough to find. A break in the hedges on their left. Hatta skipped and clicked his heels together as he turned beneath it.

Catherine, feeling no such glee, approached with more wariness. The hedges had grown together overhead, creating an arched doorway that looked as though it had been there for a thousand years.

"How long will it take to pass through the maze?" she asked.

"Why?" asked Hatta. "Are you late for an appointment?"

Jest frowned apologetically. "He's insufferable when he gets like this, but never mind him. When we came through before, the walk lasted most of the night." He glanced down. "If your shoes begin to hurt, I can carry you."

She shook her head, not wanting to be a burden on this journey. "I'll be fine. I only want to get through as quickly as possible."

Jest laced their fingers together and brought her hand to his mouth. The kiss was wistful, the touch a comfort — but his eyes were still shadowed when he looked up again, and she knew he was thinking of the drawings. His own headless apparition. The hooded figure standing over him, ax in hand. And her, the Queen of Hearts he'd once been sent to find.

She couldn't shake the memory, no matter how she wanted to. She would be grateful when this journey was over.

"Do tell me if you change your mind," he said. "After that spectacle at the well, I'm in the mood to be chivalrous."

"Are you?" she said, forcing her tone to be light. "Perhaps we'll have to find you a suit of armor." She reached up with her free hand and tugged on one of the points of Jest's hat. The lack of a jingling bell caught her off guard. "Do you think there might be one in here?"

Jest laughed. "We'll have to ask Hatta. He made it."

Cath looked ahead. Hatta was barely in the circle of their lantern's glow, still whistling, though she suspected he could hear every word they said. Maybe he was trying to ignore them, though.

"And what does it do? All of his hats do something, don't they?"

Jest's fingers tightened around hers. "I hope you won't be disappointed if I tell you that the hat is what makes me so impossible."

She raised an eyebrow at him, thinking of the way he kissed her, and the way he made her laugh, and how he had battled the Jabberwock to protect her. She smirked. "Perhaps that was the intention, but I can't believe that it's true."

He twisted his mouth to one side and nodded sullenly. "You're right. I suspect it's actually just a glorified storage closet."

After the dreary, dramatic evening they'd had, the joke was so unsuspected that Cath snorted in laughter before she could stop it. Up ahead, Hatta stopped whistling and glanced back at her in surprise.

Cath covered her mouth to stifle the laughter that followed and elbowed Jest hard in the side. He grunted, but only gripped her hand tighter.

"I mean it," he said. "You found the Vorpal Sword in there, after all. It wouldn't surprise me if there was a suit of armor."

She cast him a playful glare. "That isn't what I meant. I assure you it isn't the hat that makes you impossible, Sir Jest."

His eyes twinkled at her and their brightness was welcome after the haunted expression he'd had in the Sisters' meadow. Up ahead, Hatta started to whistle again, louder this time.

Jest ducked his head closer to Cath so she could hear him when he whispered, "I cannot tell you how I look forward to a lifetime at your side, and all the impossible things I'll have you believing in."

Cath's heart was beginning to patter when a disgruntled sound came from Jest's other side, startling her. She'd forgotten Raven was there.

"Such happiness I hope you'll make, but these flirtations I cannot take. I wish for you all the joy this darkened world can employ, but you're still giving me a stomachache." With a squawk, Raven tossed himself into the air and went to join Hatta instead.

Cath's cheeks flamed, but Jest only chuckled. "It's difficult to interpret him sometimes," he said, "but I think what Raven means to say is that he likes you."

They continued on, the lantern's ring flickering against the hedge branches. The glen's reddish glow had faded long ago, leaving them to make their way through the middle of the night. Jest's fingers, strong and lithe, stayed entwined with hers. Raven made himself comfortable atop Hatta's top hat, though Cath wondered why he didn't fly up above and look on ahead. He would have made an excellent guide, she thought.

But maybe not. Maybe there weren't enough words that rhymed with *right* and *left* for him to direct them all the way through to the end.

Besides, Hatta believed he knew the way, and he showed so little hesitation Cath had to believe him.

One hour became two, then three, then four. Cath couldn't imagine how anyone could have traversed this maze and remembered the way, but Hatta never seemed in doubt. Left and left and right and left again. Every straightaway looked exactly like the others, and though she looked for landmarks — an extra cluster of flowers here or a branch that stuck out there — there was nothing. She soon became convinced they were going in circles.

The night dragged on and grew cold. Cath pressed herself against Jest, seeking his warmth through the lining of Hatta's jacket. His arm wrapped around her shoulders, rubbing the wool sleeve to ward off her shivering.

She stumbled more than once. Her toes were cold as ice inside her boots. Her feet began to ache. She felt a blister forming on her left big toe from the rub of stockings and dress shoes.

Hatta's pace never slackened.

Her eyelids grew heavy and she wondered if she could fall asleep while walking. Or perhaps she was already asleep and this was another dream and she would wake up to find that the mansion at Rock Turtle Cove had been overgrown with laurel.

As their meanderings dragged on and began to seem endless, Jest tried to distract Cath with banter and jokes, flirtations and riddles. She did her best to be amused, and his attempts warmed her from the inside out, especially as his own weariness was showing around the edges of his composure.

At some point, even Hatta stopped whistling. Raven, it seemed, had fallen asleep on his hat.

Cath's adrenaline had fled. Her body dragged forward, step by stumbling step. She grew thirsty and her stomach rumbled. The night must be near its end, she thought, but the world remained pitch-black beyond the halo of the lantern.

Then, unexpectedly, something new.

Jest halted first and she drew to a stop beside him.

They stood together on a set of moss-covered steps that dropped down into a little glen. A glen full of wildflowers and the sudden golden glow of twilight.

In the center of the glen was a well, smelling of sweet, sticky treacle.

Hatta firmed his shoulders and inhaled a long breath. “Welcome to the beginning of the maze.”

There was a sullen pause, a heady silence, before Catherine shrieked, “The beginning? But we’ve been walking all night!”

“Or has the night just begun?” Hatta mused emptily, then he turned back and shot Cath a weary smile. “Worry not, love. I haven’t led you astray. Not yet.”

His gait was uncoordinated, heavy with exhaustion, as he approached the well. Cath and Jest followed, her hand tightening around his with every step.

Only once she stood over the well did she see that it was no longer a well at all, but a spiral staircase leading down, down, down into the earth.

Chapter 45

The walls of the well were dripping with treacle and Cath's heels kept sticking to the steps. The air carried that same sickly-sweet aroma. Normally Catherine would have been dreaming of treacle biscuits and treacle-nut cakes, but the smell was so encompassing it turned even her stomach with its syrupy thickness. She imagined it filling her lungs, drowning her.

After such a journey as they'd been on that night, she couldn't guess what would greet them at the bottom of the well. A treacle fountain? A sailboat made from her old boot? A fox, an owl, and a raccoon inviting them to tea?

She was not expecting to reach the bottom of the well and find herself in a circular room with a black-and-white-checkered floor and a small glass table at its center. The room was expansive and tidy and . . . familiar.

Catherine turned in a full circle.

They were in the Crossroads, the thoroughfare of Hearts, and they were surrounded by doors. Nothing but doors everywhere she turned.

Her palms started to sweat, her pulse roaring in her ears.

She paced the room's edges, sure there must be a mistake. There must be something she wasn't understanding. Through one enormous keyhole she could see the beaches at Rock Turtle Cove. Through a tinted peekaboo window she recognized Main Street — the cobbler's storefront now abandoned. One heart-shaped door, she knew, would lead to the drawbridge of Heart Castle.

Her heart sank. "This isn't Chess."

"Quite the riddle, isn't it?" said Hatta, leaning against the rail at the bottom of the stairs, one leg crossed in front of the other. "Choose a door, any door — they all lead to some horrible fate. Then they drop you down into a room full of doors." His voice was humorless.

Cath spun on him. "They dropped us back into Hearts. I thought you were taking us to Chess!"

He smiled at her, but it wasn't a kind look. "I said I would take you to the Looking

Glass, and so I have."

Catherine shook her head, her insides roiling with anger, with frustration, with exhaustion. All night they'd wandered. Humored those awful girls, looked at their awful drawings, listened to their awful poetry. Her stomach was empty, her feet were blistered, and her future was as uncertain now as it had been the moment she and Jest had run from the castle.

This was supposed to be a new start. Her and Jest, escaping into a new life together. And Hatta dared to taunt them.

"Cath," Jest said, quiet and calming. He settled his hands on her shoulders and pulled her away from Hatta. Perhaps she'd looked on the verge of murder to worry him so, though Hatta seemed unconcerned. "It's all right. Like he said, it's a riddle. The answer will seem obvious once we figure it out."

She grit her teeth and jabbed her finger at Hatta. "He already knows the answer! He's toying with us!"

"I'm making sure that you're worthy," said Hatta.

"Worthy of what?"

"Everything," Hatta snarled. "Life is made of sacrifices, Lady Pinkerton. I had to pass their test to enter the lands of Chess, and now you expect to go into Chess and be crowned a queen, without any trials? Why should it be so easy for you?"

"Sacrifices!" she screamed, not realizing she'd thrown herself at Hatta until she felt Jest holding her back. "I'm leaving everything! My home! My family! My whole life behind!"

"Because you have no other choice."

"No. Because I love Jest. I chose him. Who are you to judge me, to doubt me? Who are you to think you have any dominion over our lives?"

His grin turned wry. "Dear girl, I'm the man with the answer to the riddle."

She let out another outraged scream and leaped for him, but again Jest wrapped his arms around her and held her back. She found herself engulfed in his arms, feeling the loud thud of his heartbeat against her back.

"Fine," she snapped, planting her feet on the ground and forcing herself to take long, steady breaths. "We'll figure out this stupid riddle. Jest and I."

"You might recall that I did guide you through the maze. A little appreciation might be warranted."

She wriggled out of Jest's hold. "You've done nothing but lead us in circles."

She tore off Hatta's fine coat and threw it at his feet.

Hatta scowled. "You're welcome for that too."

Snorting, Cath peered back up the spiral staircase. There was a wooden trapdoor covering the top, blocking out any sign of the golden world above.

Another door. All doors.

"You didn't have to solve this puzzle when you came here?" she asked Jest.

He shook his head. "We met the Sisters and traveled the maze, and at the end of it — or, the beginning, whichever it may be — was a Looking Glass, like the one in Hatta's shop. We went through it and were here in the Crossroads, in Hearts. There was no riddle, and no warning about doors."

"Sometimes they make it easy, when they want you to succeed." Hatta sighed. "And sometimes they don't want you to leave. The Sisters are not selfless creatures."

Cath clenched her jaw and scanned the room again.

Raven had taken up a spot on the round table at the room's center, like a regal display piece. The table was made of solid glass — even the legs, so it seemed as if the bird were standing on air.

Beside him was a crystal bottle and a silver

hand mirror. Cath hadn't noticed either of them before.

She stepped forward and picked up the bottle. Tied to its neck was a paper tag scrawled with large letters.

DRINK ME

"What about this one?" Jest asked. He was on his knees, peering into a long black tunnel made of dirt. "It looks like a mole tunnel. That doesn't count as a door, does it?"

"I'm not sure," said Cath, holding up the bottle to show him, "but I suspect the answer has something to do with this."

Hatta said nothing.

Cath knew that, no matter how Hatta felt about her, he cared a great deal for Jest. She hoped that if they were on the brink of making a bad decision, he would stop them.

For now, though, she did her best to pretend he wasn't there.

She uncorked the bottle and sniffed it. "It isn't treacle," she said, sniffing again. There were hints of cherry and custard, pineapple and turkey, toffee and hot buttered toast. "Shrinking elixir. I'm sure of it."

Jest came to her side and read the tag. "I've heard of it," he said, "though we don't have any in Chess."

She chewed on her lower lip. If they drank the elixir in the bottle and it turned them small — what then? How would that help?

Her eye caught on the hand mirror and she gasped. "That's it!"

She picked up the mirror and held it up to her face. She looked, and looked deeply. A grin stretched across her lips. For in the glass, beyond her reflection, she saw a patchwork of rolling yellow hills and emerald forests and snowy purple mountains. *Chess.*

"The Looking Glass! It's only small on our side."

Jest wrapped his arm around her waist, beaming. "But the elixir will make us small so we can pass through."

Raven cocked his head. Hatta remained silent, even when Cath and Jest glanced at him for approval. He lifted an eyebrow — a silent challenge.

Jest deflated, just slightly. "Honestly, Hatta. Why are you acting this way? We're fulfilling the job we were sent to do, even if it is in a different manner than we expected. And there's no reason for us to stay here, anyway."

Hatta's frown deepened and Cath could tell that wasn't what he wanted to hear. But then his face softened into something that resembled a smile, albeit a sad one. "I wish for you all the joy this darkened world can employ," he said, quoting the Raven. His gaze shifted to Catherine. "That, and I expect to be repaid for my assistance in scones and tarts every time I come to visit."

She sagged, surprised at how quickly he could deflect her anger. "I hope you'll visit us often."

He grunted. No commitment. "I am always coming and going somewhere, love. That's the only way I'll stay ahead of Time, after all." He lifted his chin toward the table. "Go ahead, then. Somewhere there is a white crown waiting for its queen."

Cath and Jest faced each other, holding the bottle between them. His eyes were glowing. Her nerves were vibrating.

They'd made it.

The Looking Glass. Chess. A future, together.

"Don't drink it all now," Hatta reminded them as Cath lifted the bottle to her lips. "Raven and I will be following shortly after. Our fates were little better than yours, if you recall."

Murderer, martyr, monarch, mad.

Cath nodded and had just tipped the bottle against her lips when she heard a scream.

She froze and lowered the bottle.

Hatta grimaced, but he looked like he'd

been expecting this. The scream, Cath was certain, had come from the door behind him — an ominous wrought-iron gate. Heavy fog was creeping through the bars, entwining around Hatta's feet.

"What was that?" she asked, taking a hesitant step toward him.

Hatta shook his head. He didn't turn around. Didn't look.

"That," he said, his voice dripping with ire, "is your reason to stay."

Cath handed the bottle to Jest and approached the door, but Hatta moved himself in front of her. "Don't, Lady Pinkerton. Jest said you had no reason to stay, but he was wrong. There is always a reason to stay. Always a reason to go back. It's best not even to look, not even to guess. Turn around. Drink the elixir. Go through the Looking Glass and never look back."

She tried to peer around him, but Hatta grabbed her elbow, halting her. "But . . . that scream. It sounded familiar. I —"

"Remember the drawings. They will be your fate if you pass through this door. Murderer, martyr, monarch, mad. Remember?" Hatta did look on the verge of madness, his violet eyes shining with intensity.

She pressed her lips together. The scream echoed over and over in her skull.

“I’m not going to go through,” she said. “I just want to look.”

She pried her arm away and ducked around him, approaching the black gate. She wrapped her hands around the bars and peered through. The rolling fog brought goose bumps to her bare skin, or maybe it was the familiar sight that greeted her on the other side of those bars.

The pumpkin patch.

In the distance she could Sir Peter’s little cottage, and to her left were the two enormous pumpkins he’d been carving the day she and Mary Ann had come. Only now, one of the pumpkins was destroyed, great chunks of orange shell and moldy flesh scattered across the mud.

The second pumpkin had two tiny windows. They glowed with candlelight, a beacon in the fog.

A hand was reaching through one of those windows, struggling to find purchase on something, anything. Cath heard a woman’s voice crying. Pleading. *Please, let me out. Please!*

Horror wrapped around her body, freezing her to the core.

A moment later, the hand disappeared, replaced with a face in the window. Tear-stained cheeks. Frightened eyes. Confirming what Cath had feared.

It was Mary Ann.

The sound of grating metal dragged her attention to the other side of the pumpkin patch and she saw a figure shadowed against the backdrop of the forest. Though it was murky and dark, she knew it was Peter, focused on his work. It looked like he was sharpening a tool of some sort. Or a weapon.

She spun back toward the Crossroads. "Is this real? It isn't just an illusion, a trick?"

Hatta shut his eyes. "It's real," he whispered.

Her blood throbbed. "I have to go. I have to help her!"

"No." Hatta grabbed her wrist. "You have to go on through the Looking Glass. Remember what will become of you — of any of us!"

She peered at Jest, who looked as aghast as she felt.

She thought of the drawing. His crumpled body. The pool of blood. The hat lying limp beside his severed head.

Her attention darted to Raven. As always, he watched her. Silent. Waiting.

Could he really become a murderer? Could he really hurt Jest?

It was too much of a risk.

"You can't follow me," she said. "Not any of you."

Jest shook his head. "You're not going alone."

"I have to." She tore away from Hatta and reached for Jest's hand, squeezing it tight. "It will be all right. Those drawings — that's all they are. Odd little drawings from odd little girls."

"Cath —"

"I know. It's too much to risk your life, but I can go. I'll go and I'll save her, and then I'll find the well again. I'll find the Sisters. I'll come to Chess and find you. But I . . . I can't just leave her."

"Fine, but if you go, I go."

"No, Jest. If you're there, I won't be able to think of anything but that awful picture. I need to know you're safe." Her heart stammered. "Or — fine. You stay here and wait for me. Don't go through to Chess yet, just wait and stay safe and I'll come back. I will come back."

"I can't —"

She threw her arms around him and silenced him with a kiss, digging her hands into his hair. His hat tumbled off, landing on the tiled ground with dull thud. His arms drew her closer, melding their bodies together.

"You won't come back." Hatta's haunting words cut through the desperation in her body, the need for this kiss to not be their last, to not be good-bye.

She pried herself away and glared at Hatta. "Have *you* ever stayed after you heard the Sisters' prophecy?"

His lips thinned. "Never."

"Then how could you possibly know it's real? How could you possibly know what will or won't happen?" She turned back to Jest, unwilling to hear whatever excuse Hatta would make next. She lifted Jest's hand and pressed a kiss into his palm. "Stay here," she said. "Wait for me."

Pulling away, she faced the massive gate, wrapped her fingers around the bars, and pushed her way through.

Chapter 46

Her feet sank into the muddied ground of the pumpkin patch. Mist swirled around her, clinging to her skin. The patch felt like a place that had never known light or warmth. She wished she'd kept Hatta's coat, wished she hadn't let her emotions carry her away, even if he had been insufferable at the time.

To her left she could see the enormous pumpkin with its carved-bar windows. Mary Ann's cries had quieted, but Cath could still hear her sobs carrying over the otherwise-silent patch.

To her right was the cottage, this time without the smell of wood smoke and the welcoming light behind the windows. It seemed deserted.

She could no longer see Peter in the distance.

Picking up her skirts, Catherine trampled through the overgrown vines, hurrying toward the pumpkin where Mary Ann was being kept prisoner, casting terrified glances over her shoulder at every noise. The shrieking wind. The rustle of leaves. The squish and slurp of her nicest boots pulling from the mud.

The Sisters' refrain haunted her thoughts.

Peter, Peter, pumpkin eater,
Had a pet and couldn't feed her;
Caught a maid who had meant well —
What became of her, no one can tell.

She tripped suddenly and fell, sprawling into a mud puddle. Her hands sank to her wrists, filth coating the front of her dress. Cath sat panting for a moment, feeling the hectic thrum of blood in her veins. Her teeth chattered. Pushing back onto her knees, she glanced around again and tried to catch her breath.

Still no sign of Peter.

Then her eyes took in the uneven ground that had caused her to trip.

Catherine scurried backward, hoping her eyes were mistaken — but no. It was a footprint planted into the mud, the edges dried and cracked. It could have been days old, or weeks, undisturbed until Cath had tumbled into it.

A three-clawed footprint was pressed into the mud. The puncture of talons dug deep holes into the ground. Pumpkins and vines had been crushed beneath the weight of some enormous creature.

Heart galloping, Cath scrambled to her feet and wiped her hands as well as she could on her ruined gown.

Mary Ann's cries had dwindled to sniffs and wavering gasps.

Cath lifted her skirt and ran the rest of the way.

"Mary Ann," she whispered, throwing herself at the window with its pumpkin-flesh slats. "Mary Ann! It's me!"

The sniffling quieted and Mary Ann appeared at the window, her eyes bloodshot. "Cath?"

"Are you all right?"

Mary Ann pushed her hand through the bars, reaching for her. "It's Peter. He put me in here and he — he has" — her voice broke — "the Jabberwock."

Jabberwock.

Somehow, Cath had already known it. The beastly footprint. Peter's determination to have the Vorpal Sword from her. The tiny wooden horse from the Lion's hat.

Peter, Peter, pumpkin eater . . .

Cath shook her head to clear it of the

haunting melody. "How do I get you out of there?"

"There's a door in the roof that opens," said Mary Ann, pointing up.

Cath stepped back and paced around the pumpkin until she saw it, the jagged saw-cut that made a small square opening beside the pumpkin's prickly stem.

"Cath?" said Mary Ann, as Cath started looking around for some way to get up to the door. A ladder. She needed a ladder . . . or a saw to cut off the window's bars so Mary Ann could climb through.

"What is it?" she said, pressing her hand against the pumpkin's outer flesh. The wall must have been nearly a foot thick, but if she had a blade that was sharp enough . . .

"It's his wife."

She met Mary Ann's gaze through the window. "What?"

"The Jabberwock. It's Lady Peter. I saw her going into the powder room at the theater, looking like she was going to be ill, and then . . . the beast came out."

Cath frowned, thinking of the sickly woman who had been so very desperate for more pumpkin cake.

"Are you sure?"

Mary Ann nodded, her expression taut. "There was no one else in the powder room,

I'm sure of it. And also . . . the pumpkins . . ."

Cath shuddered. "The pumpkins," she breathed. Lady Peter had won a pumpkin-eating contest. And at the theater, she'd been so desperate for the cake that Cath had made, the cake that . . .

She swallowed, hard. "They changed the Turtle too."

Mary Ann whimpered, guilt mingling with her distress. "We shouldn't have stolen that pumpkin. It's our fault. I came here hoping to find a cure, or some evidence that I could take back to the King. Woman or Jabberwock, she has to be stopped."

"You came here alone?" Cath said. "What were you thinking?"

Mary Ann's blue eyes began to fill with tears. "I know. It isn't logical at all, but I thought . . . I thought maybe I would be a hero. I believed I could stop the Jabberwock. *Me.* Then I could ask the King for a favor and I thought . . . I thought I could get him to pardon your joker. Then maybe you would forgive me." Her voice dissolved into renewed sobs. "But Peter caught me and now he . . . he means to feed me to her, Cath. He's going to kill me."

"Oh, Mary Ann." Her gaze flitted up to the soiled bonnet on Mary Ann's head.

Hatta's bonnet. The one that turned logic into dreams.

Resentment shot through her, mixing with the fear and the panic and the need to get both of them away from her as quickly as possible.

"I forgive you. I do. But you need to be calm now. Take off that bonnet and try to be sensible, if you can. We need to find a way to get you out of there."

Mary Ann untied the bonnet and tore it off her head.

Cath gave the bars one good shake but if Mary Ann couldn't pull them open, she had no chance. "I need a ladder. Or something that can cut through these bars."

Sniffing, Mary Ann pointed toward the far corner of the pumpkin patch. "There was a shed on the other side of the cottage. There might be something there."

"Right. I'll be back."

"Be careful," Mary Ann cried as Cath turned away and started picking her way toward the darkened cottage. Her skin was covered in gooseflesh, her gown made heavy by the drying mud. Her gaze searched the patch in desperation, looking for any sign that Peter or the Jabberwock might be near.

A whisper drifted past her ears and she froze. Her pulse drummed as she turned in a full circle, searching.

The whisper came again and this time she was ready for it. The familiar poem turned her organs to ice.

Peter, Peter, pumpkin eater . . .

She forced down a gulp.

Had a wife but couldn't keep her . . .

She spun around again, her legs trembling. She wished she'd taken Jest's scepter or Hatta's cane, anything to use as a weapon.

He put her in a pumpkin shell, and there he kept her very well.

She turned again and spotted the destroyed shell of one of the enormous, house-sized pumpkins. It was the one she and Mary Ann had seen before, the one they'd heard the strange scratching from. Now the shell lay in gigantic pieces scattered across the pumpkin patch, as if some beast had destroyed it from the inside.

Some beast. Like the Jabberwock.

Cath pushed ahead. The sooner she got Mary Ann out of here, the sooner she could return to Jest and begin her new life far away from the Kingdom of Hearts.

"He'll take you too."

Cath yelped. The voices were louder now — right at her feet. She jumped back and looked down at a knee-high pumpkin that sat off the path. As she stared, its flesh peeled back, revealing two triangle eyes and a gap-toothed mouth.

"Run away," the pumpkin told her, still whispering, as the carved pupils of its eyes slid from side to side. "Run away."

"Run away before he finds you," warned another Jack-O'-Lantern two rows over.

"You . . . you're alive," she stammered.

"He'll kill you," said the first pumpkin, "to feed the insatiable Jabberwock."

"He killed our brothers, blaming us for what became of her."

"It wasn't our fault."

"It wasn't our fault."

"It was those other pumpkins. Those cruel pumpkins."

"The ones that came from the Looking Glass."

"They're to blame, but we'll all suffer for it."

"You should run away, run away with your human legs, run away . . ."

Cath hurried on, as much to get away from their nerve-tingling words as to heed their warnings. She thought of the Jack-O'-Lanterns spiked on the wrought-iron fence and bile rose in her throat. She choked it back down as she rounded the corner of the cottage.

No ladder. No saw. No ax.

But there was a woodshed, not much farther, the door ajar and black shadows spilling out. She lifted her skirts and jogged toward it, her eyes beginning to water with the suffocating presence of fear.

Something grabbed her and slammed her back against the cottage wall so hard the wind kicked out of her lungs. A scream died in her throat.

Peter hunched over her, eyes ablaze and a gleaming ax in his hand.

Chapter 47

"So you came back to finish it?" Peter growled, his lips curled back to show yellowing teeth. Cath recoiled at the smell of rotting pumpkin on his breath, but he held her firm against the cottage's side.

"I — I came for Mary Ann," she stammered, wishing she could have sounded courageous, but her words came out a squeaking rush. "P-please let us go. We don't wish you any harm . . . We just . . ."

"Where is it?" Peter said, ignoring her pleas as he thumped his big hands down Cath's hips, pressing down the voluminous fabric, searching. "Where's the sword?"

Cath squirmed against the wall. "I don't have it, I swear. I just want to get Mary Ann and leave, and you'll never see either of us again, I promise!"

"Give it to me!" Peter yelled, spittle flicking against Catherine's cheeks.

A black shape appeared in the corner of

her eyes, then a roar as Jest flung himself toward them and locked his scepter beneath Peter's chin. "Let her go!"

Whether it was the command or the scepter or mere surprise, Peter did release her. Cath slid down the wall, grasping at her bruised shoulder.

No. No, Jest couldn't be here.

The charcoal drawings flashed through her thoughts.

Peter was a head taller and twice the girth of Jest, and with a snarl he had grabbed the scepter with his free hand and tossed Jest over his shoulder.

But Jest — blithe, magical Jest — turned the movement into a cartwheel, landing easily on his feet.

Hope fluttered through Cath's rib cage, but then her eye caught on another shadowy figure. Someone large and unfamiliar, each step built upon a threat. It was a man, tall and lean and wearing a black hood that hung low, concealing his face. A leather belt was strapped over his black tunic, and tucked into it was a massive, curve-bladed ax.

The inked drawing. The hooded figure. The ax brandished over Jest's headless form.

Cath screamed. "Jest! Look out!"

Peter loped forward, preparing to swing his ax.

Jest ducked away. He glanced at the hooded figure stalking toward them. "It's all right, Cath," he panted, tumbling away from Peter again. "It's only Raven."

Her heart sputtered, and this did nothing to alleviate her panic. *Murderer, martyr . . .*

Jest snatched his scepter off the ground where Peter had thrown it and danced out of reach. It occurred to Cath that he was leading Peter away from her. Protecting her.

"He won't hurt you," Jest yelled again, his eyes glued to Peter. "He just looks threatening because, well . . ." He ducked. Spun. "He used to be an executioner for the White Queen."

She looked back at the hooded man. Watched as he set his enormous hand, cloaked in a leather glove, atop his ax's handle.

It was not *her* fate she was worried about.

She forced her feet to move away from the cottage wall and stumbled toward Raven, intercepting him before he could get too near to Jest, before he could interfere. Jest was quick and agile and clever. Peter was crazed and slow.

She had to believe that Jest would be okay. But if the Sisters' prophecy came true . . .

"Raven!" she cried, clutching his arm. She caught a glimpse of ink-black eyes glinting in the shadows of his hood. Otherwise, she could see nothing of his face or form. Just an empty hood, dark eyes peering out of dark nothingness.

"Raven," she said again. "Please — you have to help Mary Ann."

The hood shifted, and she felt, rather than saw, his attention latching on to her.

"Peter has her trapped in a pumpkin and I don't know how to get her out. But with your ax . . . you could . . . *Please,* Raven. He's going to feed her to the Jabberwock!"

His attention shifted to Jest. Pondering. Calculating.

"Raven," Cath whispered, desperate, "think of the Sisters' drawing. We can't let it come true. You shouldn't be here. Neither of you should have come back."

His chest and shoulders rose with a deep inhale, and the hood fluttered with a nod.

Cath slumped with relief. "She's behind the cottage."

He pulled his hood farther over his face and retreated, disappearing into the mist.

She turned back to the brawl. Jest was crouched on the ground, his face contorted and his hair matted to his forehead. His jester's hat had fallen off during the fight and now sat atop one of the Jack-O'-Lanterns. He was gripping the scepter, but it had been splintered in half, making for a pathetically short stick, while Peter still held his ax in both fists.

Jest looked like he was in pain — from what injury Cath couldn't tell — but he was also alert and composed. While Peter, larger and better armed, was panting heavily.

Cath's gaze dropped again to the hat. A single thought ricocheted through her head.

The sword.

"This isn't necessary," Jest said, disarmingly polite. "Let us go and you'll never see us again. We're only here for Mary Ann."

"You came to kill her!" Peter roared.

Jest frowned. "Who?"

With a battle cry, Peter rolled toward him and swung, but Jest dodged to the side and shot to his feet a safe distance away, holding the broken scepter like a shield.

"I won't let you touch her!" Peter yelled.

"We don't wish to harm anyone . . ."

Peter's back was turned to Cath. Her gaze attached to the three-pointed hat. She clenched her jaw, grabbed her muddied skirt in both fists, and ran.

The mud slopped and slurped, dragging her heels down, but she didn't stop. Her focus was on the hat and the weapon it might have inside it.

A sword. Jest had a better chance of defending himself with a sword . . .

A screech spiked in her head and Cath stumbled, throwing her hands over her ears. Dead leaves and withered vines fluttered beneath a massive pair of wings.

The Jabberwock crashed to the ground, blocking her path.

Cath staggered backward.

The beast curled its serpentine neck toward the sky and snorted, its nostrils steaming. *Her* nostrils steaming, Cath thought, picturing the frail woman. A victim of too many poisoned pumpkins.

The Jabberwock's right eye had healed over, sealing it forever shut, but the left was still an ember of coal. The beast tilted her head to the side, eyeing Cath as her massive claws scraped across the ground.

"Cath!" Jest screamed. Then, louder still, with an edge of hope — "Hatta!"

His yell was cut short by a thump and a groan. Cath's head swiveled around in time to see Jest collapse onto his side. The pumpkin Peter had thrown shattered on the ground beside him. Cath cried out, horrified. In the broken shell pieces she could see a single triangle eye.

Jest was all right. He had to be all right.

He was groaning, one hand pressed to his head. Cath took a step toward him but the Jabberwock snapped, sending her stumbling backward again.

She spotted Hatta now, running toward them at full speed, his colorful shirt too vibrant for the gloomy patch. His gaze flicked to the Jabberwock, to Jest, to Peter, more horrified with every heartbeat.

Peter spotted him and snarled. His grip tightened around the ax handle. *"You!"*

The Jabberwock prowled closer to Cath, tongue slithering between razor teeth, leaving a trail of saliva in the mud. Cath stumbled backward.

"Hatta," she said, her voice warbling. "Jest's hat. It might have the sword."

Hatta was shaking his head, as if denying that any of this were happening, as if wondering why he'd ever left the comfort of his hat shop. "We should not have come back," he murmured, but in the next moment he was sprinting toward the hat, scooping it into his hands.

The Jabberwock swiped at Catherine. She screamed and jumped away. One claw caught on her muddied gown, drawing a great tear across the front of the skirt and into the heavy petticoat, barely missing her knees. Catherine wondered whether she was lucky, or whether the beast liked to toy with its food before devouring it.

Hatta cursed, still digging through the hat. A pile of assorted joker's tricks grew around him. Bright juggling balls. A deck of cards. A bundle of scarves knotted together. Silver hoops. Fireworks and sparklers. Smoke bombs. A stuffed rabbit. A single white rose, its petals turning brittle. "It's not here!" He pulled out his arm and bunched the hat in his fist. "It has to be you!" His eyes pierced Catherine beneath the Jabberwock's outstretched wing. "It answers only to royalty, love."

"But I'm not —"

He threw the hat. It landed a couple of yards away. She couldn't get to it without edging closer to the Jabberwock.

"YOU!"

Peter's howl was so sharp and loud even the Jabberwock swiveled her head toward him.

Seizing her chance, Cath darted toward the hat. She snatched the hat off the ground and thrust her arm inside, still running. As before, her fingers curled around the bone-studded handle and the sword emerged, gleaming.

Cath halted and spun back to face the monster.

The Jabberwock snarled and hunkered her head in between muscled, scaly shoulders. She took a step back, her single burning eye studying the sword like a lifelong enemy.

Cath raised the weapon with both hands. It was heavy, but determination strengthened her arms. Resolve pumped through her veins.

The beast took another step away.

Cath dared to glance at Jest, afraid it was already too late, that she would see the vision from the drawings . . .

But no, he was alive, and had managed to get back to his feet. One hand was pressed to the side of his head. He seemed dazed. His feet kept stumbling out from beneath him as if he couldn't hold his balance. If he noticed Cath standing there with the Vorpal Sword, he showed no sign of recognition.

"How dare you show your face here?" Peter yelled. His face was flaming red, his nostrils flared with rage.

"Such a pleasure to see you again, as well," said Hatta, seemingly unsurprised that the pumpkin grower looked ready to tear him apart. "How is business?"

Peter swung the ax at the ground, disconnecting another Jack-O'-Lantern from its vine. With a guttural scream he lifted the pumpkin and heaved it in Hatta's direction.

Hatta ducked away. The pumpkin splintered against the ground.

"This is your doing," Peter said. "You and those damned seeds. They were cursed!"

Hatta's jaw tightened and Cath knew, without any idea what they were talking about, that Peter's accusation was not news to Hatta.

"You know each other," she said. Her arms were trembling and she allowed herself to lower the sword, just a few inches. The Jabberwock blew a puff of steam at her. "How do you know each other?"

"This devil brought me bad seeds," said Peter. "I didn't even want 'em, not knowing the quality, but he threw them away in my patch and now look what's happened. Look what you did to my wife!"

He pulled the ax from the mud and pointed it at the Jabberwock.

Hatta released a hearty guffaw. "You don't honestly expect us to believe that this . . . this creature . . ." He trailed off, his smile fading, his eyes widening as the Jabberwock looked back at him and her one eye blazed in recognition, not unlike how she had recognized the Vorpal Sword. "It can't be."

"You brought him seeds?" Cath stammered. "From Chess?"

The pumpkins.

The Mock Turtle.

The Jabberwock and Jest and the Vorpal Sword.

It all started on the other side of the Looking Glass.

And the connection between them?

Hatta.

This *was* Hatta's doing.

But Peter was the one who had captured Mary Ann. He was the one trying to keep a monster as a pet and feed it innocent lives.

"I'll kill you for what you've done to her!" Peter shouted. "I'll post your head on my gate!"

Cath's fists tightened around the sword.

"Stop this," said Jest, breathless. "Whatever Hatta's involvement, it was a mistake. How was he to know what the seeds would do? And this . . . this creature is no longer your wife, Sir Peter. I'm sorry, but you have to see that."

"Isn't she?"

It was Hatta arguing with him. Cath snarled, "Hatta!"

But he shrugged, his gaze scraping over the beast's scaly dark skin, wide-veined wings. "Is the Mock Turtle no longer the Turtle? How can we know Lady Peter isn't still inside the body of this beast?"

"She's been eating people!" Cath

screamed. "If she is still in there, she's a murderer!"

"You turned her into this," Peter said, swiveling his gaze back to her. "I destroyed those cursed pumpkins. She was getting better. But once she saw that cake she couldn't stop eating it. And now she won't change back. She's my wife, and you did this to her!"

"She's a monster!"

The Jabberwock reared back on her hind legs and sent a piercing scream into the sky. Her claws returned to the ground with a thump that rattled through Cath's teeth.

It happened fast.

The venom in the Jabberwock's eyes.

The way she reared her head back like a poisonous snake.

The way she opened her enormous mouth and Cath saw the light glinting off row after row of teeth.

The way she dove for Hatta.

The Sisters' voices were there, in Cath's head. *Murderer, martyr . . .*

Hatta stumbled back —

Pudding and pie, he was going to die.

A scream was ripped from Cath's throat and she charged forward, swinging the sword as hard as her arms would allow it.

The blade made one fast, clean cut. Easy

as slicing through a pat of butter.

The Jabberwock's head disconnected from her slithering neck. Her body crashed onto the rows of abandoned pumpkins. Her head dropped and thumped and rolled toward Hatta's feet, who leaped back with a cry. Dark blood splattered across the ground, like ink from a broken quill.

The world paused.

The fog swirled around them.

Peter's face slackened.

Cath stared at the sword edged with blood, her heart thud-thumping inside her chest. Stunned. Horrified. Relieved.

She had slain the Jabberwock.

She raised her eyes and sought out Jest. Air began to creep back into her lungs.

She had slain the Jabberwock. She had done it. The monster was dead. Hearts was saved.

It was over.

They would take Mary Ann to safety and leave Peter to mourn his wife. In the morning, Cath and Jest and Hatta and Raven would be far, far away from here, and none — not a single one of the Sisters' prophecies — had come true.

Jest watched her, bewildered and proud. His eyes began to refocus, though he was still weak from the fight.

In the stillness, Cath forced herself to look at Peter. His arms slumped. His face was twisted with anguish as he stared at the dead monster.

Cath's heart filled with unexpected sympathy. There was devastation written on the plains of his face. Agony flooding his eyes. He was a breath away from collapsing into the dirt and weeping over the body of the beast he had loved.

But the moment passed and he stayed standing. His upper lip curled. His eyes sparked.

He looked at Catherine.

With disgust. With *murder.*

She gulped and adjusted her hold on the sword.

Peter adjusted his hold on the ax.

He moved toward her. One step. Two. His muscles undulating, his body strung with tension.

"Please," Cath whispered. "This can end now. Just let us go."

To her surprise, Peter did hesitate. His attention caught on something in the distance and Cath dared a glance over her shoulder.

Raven was there, stalking toward them. Mary Ann, too, but she was an afterthought to Raven's ominous approach. The gleaming ax he held was like a mirror to Peter's.

His dark cloak whipped around his shoulders, the hood hung low over his brow. The White Queen's executioner, Jest had said.

He looked like a threat, or a promise.

He looked like justice.

Cath turned back and Peter's expression had changed again. Now there was fear and a shadow of indecision.

He looked once more at Catherine with a hatred so pure and transparent it sent a shock of terror through her. She could see his desperation. She sensed his resolve.

With a guttural scream, Peter turned and swung the ax.

It was over and done before Cath knew what was happening. In between the space of a gasp and a scream, there was the sound of blood splattering across the ground. Like ink from a broken quill.

Like a drawing made on stone.

Before she could make sense of it, Peter was running away. He had dropped the ax. He was gone, into the forest. There was the distant sound of flapping wings — Raven dissolving back into a bird and chasing after him. A flurry of black feathers. A cry of heartbreak and rage. Then, silence.

Cath held her breath.

She waited for the vision before her to turn into an illusion. One more magic trick.

The impossible made right again.

Because this was not real. This couldn't be. It was a nightmare she would soon wake from. It was a drawing done in ink, executed down to every horrific detail. It was . . .

Jest.

Mutilated. Severed. Dead.

She took one step forward and collapsed. The sword slipped from her fingers.

"Treacle," she breathed. Medicinal treacle. Life-giving treacle. "Bring him treacle. Go! Hurry! Treacle will . . . Treacle will . . ."

"No, love," came Hatta's ragged reply. "Nothing can save him."

"Don't say that!" She dug her hands into the mud, squeezing it through her fingers. "We have to save him! We have to — *Jest*!"

A hand brushed the hair back from her forehead, and Mary Ann's voice came to her, painfully gentle. "Cath . . ."

"Don't touch me!" she raged, tearing away from her. "I came back for *you*! If you hadn't come here, if you hadn't gotten yourself caught, then we wouldn't be here. This wouldn't be happening, but for you!"

Mary Ann drew back.

Cath ignored the look and tried to crawl forward, dragging her skirt through the mud. "There must be a way. Something we can do. Something in the hat that can save him, or . . . or . . . the Sisters. Fate. *Time*. There must be someone who can . . ."

Her hand fell into something that wasn't cold mud, but warm and wet. Something that felt real. Too real.

"It's impossible," she said. "He didn't do anything — he was innocent. He . . ." A sob lodged in her throat.

"You're right. He was innocent," Hatta said, so quiet she barely heard him. "Martyrs usually are."

Mary Ann pulled Cath away from the body and the growing pool of blood, wrapping her in an embrace. Cath barely felt her. Her breaths grew shorter. Her lips curled against her teeth. She peered over Mary Ann's shoulder, into the dark trees. At the place where Peter had run.

Her cries died in her throat and were buried there, suffocated by the fury that was even now pounding, shrieking, demanding to be released.

She would kill Peter.

She would find him and she would kill him.

She would have his head.

Chapter 48

Cath remembered little about how she got back to the manor at Rock Turtle Cove. Hatta carried her part of the way, though she screamed and clawed at him to let her be, to leave her with Jest. He had restrained her until she had exhausted herself and her throat was worn raw. Her head pounded with the need to find Peter, to destroy him.

A muscle was twitching in Cath's eye. Her fingers kept tightening, imagining themselves around Peter's throat. Squeezing. Squeezing.

When they arrived at the mansion, her parents took one look at the blood and the dirt and the shredded gown and her dead eyes and ushered them all inside.

Her anger simmered beneath her skin. She looked at no one. Said nothing. Sent them all away. When finally she was alone in her bedroom, she knelt at the window and pleaded with Time until her lips were chapped and her tongue was too dry to go on. Surely he could turn back the clock. Surely he had dominion over her fate.

She would spare the Jabberwock this time, if only Jest would live.

She would let the beast have Mary Ann, if only Jest would live.

She would listen to Hatta's warnings. She would turn away from Mary Ann's cries and escape into the Looking Glass. This time, she would not look back, if only Jest would live.

She would do anything. Marry any king. Wear any crown. Give her heart to anyone who asked for it. She would serve Time himself if he would bring Jest back to her.

Her agony turned to fury when Time refused to answer her. There was no this time, no next time, no time at all.

No amount of bargaining made any difference.

Jest was gone.

At some point that night, Raven tapped at her windowsill. Cath sprang forward to open it — but he had only come to tell her that Peter had gotten away.

Cath fell onto the carpet, the pain knocking into her all over again.

Her rage split her open.

The night passed and she became a wild

animal, raging and inexhaustible. When Abigail brought her tea, she threw the tray at the wall. When Mary Ann tried to draw a bath, she screamed and flailed. When her mother cried outside her bedroom door — too afraid to come inside — Cath snarled at her reflection and pretended not to hear her. She plotted Peter's demise. She swore on every grain of sand in the cove that she would avenge Jest's death.

It took almost two full days before she could cry and then, as if a levee had been broken, she couldn't stop.

Murderer, martyr, monarch, mad.

So far as she could tell, only one of the prophecies had come to pass.

Jest was martyred. Jest was dead. *Jest.*

Chapter 49

Shrill laughter and the rustle of branches jolted Catherine awake. Her eyes snapped open. Her nostrils flared at the onslaught of crisp citrus.

Her blankets had been kicked off in the night, likely due to another nightmare of monsters and murderers and merry-go-rounds, and she lay sprawled on her bed with cool sweat clinging to her skin. She stared up at the canopy and the waxy leaves that had grown up in the night. Green key-shaped fruits swayed overhead.

Her limbs felt heavy as she reached for one of the lower hanging fruits and snapped it from its branch. The tree rustled.

The key lime was almost as big as her hand. It must have been made for a very large lock.

More tittering drew her attention upward and she was met with a pair of black eyes through the foliage.

Cath bolted upward and snarled. “What do you want?”

Tillie pushed aside a branch so Catherine could see her narrow face and waxen hair, tangled with leaves from the tree. “We told you this would happen,” she said, in her eerie child’s voice. *“Murderer, martyr, monarch, mad.”*

Loathing kindled in her vision, red and burning. With a guttural scream, Cath threw the key at the girl as hard as she could.

Tillie ducked back. The fruit crashed through the tree branches and plopped somewhere on the carpet, harmless.

“That was not polite.”

Cath spun around, searching out the owner of the second voice. Elsie, with her messy cropped hair, was clinging to one of the bedposts.

A third girl appeared over the canopy, hanging upside down. Lacie’s long hair brushed against the pillows. “In fact,” she said, “that was not very queenly at all.”

“Get out!” Cath screamed. “It’s your fault he’s dead! You cursed us! *Get out!*”

The Three Sisters watched her, as calm as if she’d offered them a cup of tea.

“We did not swing the ax,” said Tillie.

“We did not kill the Jabberwock,” said Elsie.

"We did not go through that door," finished Lacie.

New tears sprung up in Catherine's eyes, steaming with hatred. "It was your prophecy. You killed him. You —" She sobbed. "Get out. Leave me alone."

Lacie began to swing from her knees, her long hair tickling Cath's shoulder. "We see many things," she said. "We know many fates. We have come to make you a deal."

Cath swiped at her eyes. For a moment, there was hope. Cruel, brittle hope. She hardly dared to breathe the words that formed on her tongue. "Can you . . . can you bring him back?"

The girls tittered as one, acting as though Cath had made a joke. Tillie shook her head and pushed aside the branches again, until her whole torso was hanging over the bed. There was a scratch on her cheek from one of the branches, and though it had started to bleed, she didn't seem to notice. The red blood was a strange contrast to her white skin and hollow black eyes. "We cannot bring back the martyr, but we can bring you something else you want."

Cath began to tremble. "What?"

"Vengeance," they spoke in unison.

"Peter Peter will never be found," said Elsie. "Your Raven is a murderer, but not a hunter, and no one is even looking for him anymore. The King wants it all to go away."

"But Peter Peter is desperate," said Lacie. "His wife is dead and his livelihood in tatters. He will come to us, looking to start a new life in Chess."

Tillie grinned, showing the gap in her teeth. "We can bring him to you, and let your justice be served."

Cath struggled to swallow, her mouth sticky and dry.

They could be right. Raven had lost track of him, and she knew the King was too pathetic to ever hunt down a killer and kidnapper.

She knew Mary Ann had concocted a story to explain what had happened that night, doing her best to save a reputation Catherine no longer cared for. She told everyone that she had uncovered the truth of Peter's crimes and gone to stop him and the Jabberwock, and Cath and Jest had come to rescue her.

In death, Jest was absolved of his crimes and made a hero.

That did not pardon Cath, though. She had still run from the castle moments after accepting the King's proposal. She had been whisked away by another man, in front of everyone. The King was mortified. He would just as soon pretend nothing had happened at all.

Cath had no such option. The truth belonged to her and she couldn't escape it and would never forget it.

Peter deserved punishment. He deserved death.

For the first time since she'd collapsed in the mud of the pumpkin patch, she felt her heart stir in her chest.

"What would you want from me?"

Lacie swung her body down and plopped onto the bed linens, crisscrossing her bone-thin legs. "We are ill. We have been dying for a long time. We require payments to sustain us."

Elsie spun around to the other side of the bedpost. "A heart could sustain us for a long time. A strong heart, full of passion and courage."

Tillie stretched forward and trailed a dirty fingernail across Cath's collarbone. "We want the heart of a queen."

Cath dodged away, pressing her fingers against her chest as goose bumps raced down her arms. "I am not a queen."

Tillie grinned again. "Not yet."

Then the Sisters recited the words that had too often echoed through Cath's skull — *"Murderer, martyr, monarch, mad."*

She shook her head. "Everyone thinks I'm hysterical and traumatized. The King will never have me now."

"Won't he?" Lacie plucked a key lime from the branches and offered it to Catherine on her tiny palms.

Cath stared at the fruit, unconvinced that these girls were blameless for what had happened. But they were right. They were not the ones who had swung the ax.

She looked around, meeting each of their fathomless gazes in turn. "You will bring Sir Peter to me? And his fate will be mine to decide?"

"Of course," Elsie said. "You will be the Queen, after all."

They all snickered.

Catherine locked her jaw and snatched the key lime away.

Shrill laughter and the rustle of branches jolted her awake. Her eyes snapped open. The Three Sisters were gone, but the tree remained, heavy green fruit drooping over her head.

Chapter 50

The royal footmen eyed her warily as she swept into the throne room. Even the candlesticks flickered in fear as she passed them, her head high as a swan's and her billowing black mourning gown fanned out behind her. She carried a box wrapped in red paper and tied with a red velvet bow.

The throne room was all ruby-encrusted chandeliers, pink gilt mirrors, and rose quartz pillars. There was no carpeted aisle, and each footstep echoed off the walls and up to the arched cathedral ceiling.

Her attention didn't stray from the King of Hearts, who was fidgeting on his throne, his fingers twitching with every thundering *clack-clack* of her heels.

Catherine knew how she must look in her head-to-toe black, including the black lace veil that partially covered her face. She had seen herself in the mirror before she left, pale as a ghost with crazed, bloodshot eyes.

She didn't care.

She knew the King. She knew how to get from him what she wanted.

The White Rabbit's voice trembled when he introduced her. "L-Lady Catherine Pinkerton of Rock Turtle Cove, requesting an audience with His Royal Majesty, the King of Hearts."

She waited a beat, before turning to the nearest member of the court — the Queen of Diamonds — and dropping the red-wrapped package into her hands. The woman gasped and barely caught it before the box smashed on the floor.

Turning back to the King, Catherine stretched her lips as far as she could and dipped into her finest curtsy. "Thank you for seeing me, Your Majesty."

"L-Lady Catherine. Good d-day," stammered the King. He scratched his ear. "We've had word of your unfortunate un-un-w-wellness. It's so good to see you . . . about."

"Your concern flatters me, Your Majesty."

The King leaned forward. "And w-what can I do for you, Lady Pinkerton?"

She stood as straight and sharp as a spade in her engulfing ebony dress.

"I came to apologize. My reaction to your marriage proposal was appalling. I hope you know it was a result of temporary madness, not any disregard for your proposal. You did me a great honor when you asked for my hand, and I did not respond as a lady ought to."

She finished her practiced speech with another upward turn of her lips.

The King cleared his throat. "Er — that's not necessary, Lady Pinkerton. Of course, your apology is h-heartily accepted." His mouth quivered. Still nervous. It was clear that he hoped Cath was done, now. That she would leave.

But she wasn't.

"Good." Her smile fell. "With that unpleasantness behind us, I would like to officially accept your proposal — again."

The blood drained from the King's face. "O-oh," he said. "Is that . . . is that so?" His eyes skittered toward the White Rabbit, as if the master of ceremonies might be able to respond for him.

Catherine had expected this. No man — not even a silly, empty-headed man — would wish to marry a girl after she'd rejected him. Humiliated him, even. A girl everyone was saying had gone quite ill in the head.

But the King was meek and spineless.

So she waited while the King searched the

faces of his courtiers and guards, looking for a way out. A way that did not include him having to reject her, for he was not the rejecting sort.

His expression slipped toward helpless. "Well. That's certainly . . . er." He cleared his throat again. "You see, Lady Pinkerton, the thing is — I . . . um."

"I understand, Your Majesty. I would not have expected to earn your favor again after the way I treated you. But I also know that you are a thoughtful, good-hearted man."

His cheeks reddened behind his curled beard and pointed mustache. "Well, I don't know if that's —"

"Which is why I brought you a gift. A symbol of my devotion." Her voice cracked, but she shoved the pain down, down, down. Turning to the Queen of Diamonds, she raised an eyebrow.

It took a moment for the startled woman to step forward, box in hand.

Catherine flicked her fingers toward the King.

Flushing, the woman dragged her feet up onto the dais and deposited the gift into the King's hands, before retreating back to her spot among the courtiers.

The King's face was tight with dread as he untied the ribbon and peeled the paper back. He moved as cautiously as if he had expected the present to combust in his lap.

He lifted the lid. Everyone in the throne room tilted forward — all but Catherine, who watched with empty eyes.

The King squeaked. "L-lime?"

"Key lime pie, Your Majesty. You told me once that key lime is the key to a king's heart, after all."

He licked his lips, eyes filling with hunger. Behind him, the Knave of Hearts surged upward on his toes, trying to see into the gift box with the same overflow of desire.

Cath lowered her lashes. "I believe we shall get on quite well, and I shall be proud to bestow upon you many such delicacies. I have always been fond of baking, you see."

Her chest quivered, but she clenched her jaw. Stayed strong. She knew he was crumbling. She knew she would win.

Down, down, down.

"Oh. Right," said the King. "You were — er." He gaped at Catherine, then at the pie. Licked his lips. "Many such delicacies . . . you say?"

"As many as you wish." She raised her chin. "As I see no cause for delay, I suggest we set the wedding for a fortnight."

His eyes widened. "A fortnight?"

She bobbed her head. "Your Majesty

makes a most excellent point. A single week would be much preferred."

He stuttered incoherently. The crowd was stirring, concerned glances passing through the courtiers and the guards.

"Very well, if you insist," said Catherine. "Three days hence will be as good a time as any." She turned to a young page — the Three of Diamonds — who was hiding behind a pillar. "Note that the royal wedding between the King of Hearts and the daughter of the Marquess of Rock Turtle Cove is to be held in three days hence. The entire kingdom is to be invited. Does that sound all right to you, Your Majesty?"

"I . . . I suppose . . ."

"Wonderful. I'm so pleased." She dropped into another curtsy.

The King wrapped his hand around the box containing the key to his heart and squeezed it against his middle. "Th-three days hence. I am — it is — I am honored, Lady Pinkerton."

Her lips twitched, more with derision than flattery. "I do believe the honor is meant to be mine."

Pivoting on her heels, she marched out of the throne room without looking back. She was glad when the aroma of sweet-sour lime finally faded behind her.

All during the carriage ride home she thought of the Sisters' drawing. Catherine upon her throne, wearing a queen's crown. She tried to recall the feeling of horror she'd had then. How adamantly she'd refused to believe it could ever come to pass.

Those emotions were far out of reach.

"I am the Queen of Hearts," she said to the empty carriage. Practicing. "I am the Queen of Hearts."

CHAPTER 51

The white rose tree was in full bloom. Catherine could see it from the castle chambers where she had been brought to make her final wedding preparations. Its flowers were like glowing white lanterns amid the green foliage of the gardens.

She couldn't take her eyes from it.

There was a coal burning in her chest. Her fury had grown since she'd seen the Sisters, since she'd accepted the King's proposal. Three days had been agony. She wanted it over. She wanted to be the Queen so the Sisters could fulfill their end of the agreement.

Raven was on her shoulder, his talons puncturing her skin through the fabric of her wedding gown. He had become her most constant companion, though they rarely spoke. He was the only one she had told about the deal she'd struck with the Three Sisters, and at first she had expected him to try and talk her out of it. Even when he didn't, it still took her a full day to realize he yearned for vengeance almost as much as she did.

Jest had been his friend, his comrade, his fellow Rook.

"Soon," she breathed — to Raven, and to herself. "Soon."

Raven said nothing, just dug his talons deeper. She didn't flinch, though she did wonder if there would be spots of blood left on the white brocade.

Behind her, the door opened. "Cath?" came Mary Ann's timid voice. "I've come to fix your hair."

Cath turned to her and nodded, before moving away from the window. She sat at the vanity.

Mary Ann waited a moment, as if expecting more of an invitation than that, before she sighed and padded across the carpet. Raven fluttered up the top of the vanity mirror.

Mary Ann worked in silence, pinning Cath's hair with expert fingers and working it through with pearls and red rosebuds.

"You don't have to do this."

Cath met Mary Ann's gaze in the glass.

"The King will let you out of the arrangement if you ask," the maid continued. "Tell him you've changed your mind."

"What then?" Cath asked. "I could be the Marchioness of Mock Turtles. Die a spinster, all alone with my half-invisible cat?"

Mary Ann paced in front of her and leaned against the vanity. "What about us? Our dream, our bakery?"

"My dream," Cath snapped. "It was my dream, and mine alone. It only became yours when a trickster hat fooled you into having an imagination."

Mary Ann flinched. "That isn't true. I always —"

"I haven't changed my mind." Catherine stood, tugging her skirt into place. "I am getting precisely what I want."

"A false, loveless marriage?"

Cath sought out her reflection. The face in the mirror was that of a corpse, bloodless and indifferent. But her dress was breathtaking, for those who had breath to take — a full-skirted gown bedecked in lace and ribbon. Red roses were embroidered across the bodice.

She felt nothing at all when she looked at her wedding gown, or imagined herself on the throne, or lying in the King's bed, or someday watching their full suit of ten children race across the croquet lawns.

Her future existed like a barren desert

with a single bright spot on the horizon. The one thing she wanted. The last thing in the world she craved.

Peter's head.

"Yes," she said, without emotion. "This is what I want."

Mary Ann's shoulders fell and Cath could see her biting back what she wanted to say. Finally she slinked away from the vanity. "The Marquess and Marchioness asked to see you before the ceremony. And . . . Cath? You haven't asked me to continue on as one of your maids here in the castle."

Cath blinked, waiting for the words to seep into her clouded thoughts.

You should have died instead, she wanted to say. *If you hadn't gone to the patch, this wouldn't have happened. I should have let you die. I should have left you there.*

"No," she finally said. "I haven't."

"Cath, please," Mary Ann whispered. "I know you're hurt — devastated, even. But you're my best friend. You came back for me. You saved me."

You should have died instead.

"The White Rabbit is looking for a housemaid," Cath said. "Perhaps you can seek new employment there."

The silence that followed was stifling.

Cath picked a ruby necklace off the vanity, one the King had sent her during their pitiful courtship. She latched it behind her neck. The jewels sat heavy on her collar.

"If that's what you want," Mary Ann murmured.

Cath didn't watch her go. Didn't turn even when the door shut behind her.

Somewhere in the castle, the people of Hearts were gathering. Music was playing. The King was wondering whether he was making a mistake, and whether it was too late to stop it.

She stared at the girl in the mirror, the one who looked as though she had never known a smile. Even as she had the thought, her reflection's lips curled upward, revealing a delirious grin beneath her sullen eyes.

She scowled. "This had better not be your way of telling me to be happy."

The reflection's eyes turned yellow and developed slitted pupils. "Were you aware that this is your wedding day?" said Cheshire. The rest of his face formed, furry cheeks and long whiskers. "To look so sad seems a travesty."

"I'm not in the mood. Go away."

"All due respect, Your Soon-to-Be-Majesticness, you do not seem much in the mood for anything. I have never seen such an empty expression." His face vanished, leaving the outline of fur and whiskers topped with pointed ears.

Catherine pushed away from the vanity.

Cheshire's face reappeared. "You needn't be so cold to Mary Ann. She's worried about you. We all are."

"What is there to worry about? I am going to be a queen. I'm the luckiest girl in Hearts."

His whiskers twitched. "And won't we be lucky to have you, miserable wretch you've become."

"Mind my words, Cheshire, I will have you banished from this kingdom if you tempt me."

"An empty threat from an empty girl."

She rounded on him, teeth flashing. "I am not empty. I am full to the brim with murder and revenge. I am overflowing and I do not think you wish for me to overflow onto you."

"There was a time" — Cheshire yawned — "when you overflowed with whimsy and powdered sugar. I liked that Catherine better."

"That Catherine was a fool." She whipped her hand toward the cat. He vanished before she could strike him. "You knew the bakery would never happen. You've known that I would end up either destitute or married to the stupid King, and any other hopes were meaningless."

"Yes. That's true."

She spun to see Cheshire floating in front of the door.

"But hoping," he said, "is how the impossible can be possible after all."

With a scream, Cath grabbed a vase of white roses and launched them at Cheshire's head.

The door opened. The cat vanished. The vase flew right between the White Rabbit's ears and shattered in the corridor.

The Rabbit froze, his pink eyes wide as saucers. "L-Lady Pinkerton? Is everything quite all right?"

Cath straightened her spine. "I despise white roses!"

The Rabbit shrank back. "I . . . I do apologize. I'll — er — have something else sent for, if you prefer —"

"Don't bother," she snapped, marching toward the window and thrusting her finger against a leaded pane. "And I want the gardeners to take down that tree."

The White Rabbit approached hesitantly. "Tree?"

"The white rose tree by the arches. I want it removed immediately."

The Rabbit's nose twitched. "But, my

lady, that tree was planted by the King's great-great-great-grandfather. It is an extremely rare varietal. No, I think we had better leave it as it is." He cleared his throat and pulled a watch from his pocket. The watch Jest had given him during the black-and-white ball. Seeing it brought blood rushing into Cath's face. "Now then, your parents will be here soon to escort you to the ceremony, but I wanted to be sure you had everything you needed before —"

"Mr. Rabbit."

He looked up and ducked at her glare.

"That tree is to be gone by nightfall. If it is not, then I will find an ax and cut it down myself, and your head will be soon to follow. Do you understand?"

His gloved hands began to shake around the watch. "Er — y-yes. Certainly. The tree. Quite an eyesore, I've oft said so myself . . ."

"In fact," she continued, scanning the gardens below, "I want all white roses to be removed before springtime. From now on, the gardeners are to plant only red roses, if they must grow roses at all."

"Of course, my quee— my lady. Red roses. Excellent choice. Your taste is immaculate, I daresay."

"Exuberantly glad you agree," she deadpanned, brushing past him. She paused at the vanity and Raven hopped off the mirror and came to settle again on her shoulder before she swept into the corridor.

She paused.

Her parents were there, standing over the shattered glass vase and drooping roses, waiting to escort their daughter to her wedding ceremony. Their faces held on to wobbly smiles.

"Oh, my sweet girl," said the Marchioness, taking a step forward. Hesitating. Glancing at Raven. Then she closed the distance between them and took Catherine into her arms. "You are a beautiful bride."

"Are you sure?" said Cath, still livid over the roses and the pocket watch and Cheshire's insolence. "Look again. You might find that I actually resemble a walrus."

Her mother pulled away, shocked. "What do you mean?"

She had to bite the inside of her cheek to keep from rolling her eyes. "Nothing at all."

"Catherine," said the Marquess, placing one hand on Cath's shoulder and one on his wife's. "We know you've been through some . . . difficult things recently."

Anger, hot and throbbing, blurred in her vision.

"But we want you to be sure . . . absolutely

sure this is what you want." His eyes turned wary beneath his bushy eyebrows. "We want you to be happy. That's all we've ever wanted. Is this what's going to make you happy?"

Cath held his gaze, feeling the puncture of Raven's talons on her shoulder, the weight of the rubies around her throat, the itch of her petticoat on her thighs.

"How different everything could have been," she said, "if you had thought to ask me that before."

She shrugged his arm away and pushed between them. She didn't look back.

Chapter 52

The traveling hat shop was empty when she squeezed her heart-studded dress through the doorway — empty but for the marvelous Hatter himself. A cackle reverberated off the wooden walls the moment she stepped over the threshold. Catherine drew herself to her full height and let her gown fall around her feet. She met Hatta's gleeful laugh with firm-pressed lips.

He was on his throne, feet up, hiding his face behind his purple hat. Mannequin heads were set on all of the chairs, adorned in elaborate hats. None were whispering now. They stared blankly ahead at the assortment of ribbons and felts and half-empty teacups.

"Good day, Hatta."

He lifted the hat and set it onto his white hair. Hair that was in desperate need of a combing. His cravat was undone, his coat wrinkled. There was a mysterious stain on the handkerchief that was crumpled inside his breast pocket.

"Is it six o'clock already?" he said, picking up a pocket watch from the table. "Why — barely noon. That can't be right. Perhaps I shall make it forever six o'clock, forever time for tea. Tea in the morning, tea in the middle of the night. Then I shall always be an accommodating host. Would that suit you and your early arrival, Lady Pinkerton? Or shall I say — *Your Majesty.*"

Cath shut the shop's door. "Am I early? I did not realize I was expected."

"I'm always expecting someone. Always coming and going, coming and going." He tossed the pocket watch onto the table with a clang. The face popped open and Cath could hear it ticking, too loud and too fast, like a manic countdown. If Hatta noticed it, though, it didn't show. "I hope you haven't come here seeking my marital blessing."

"I don't need anyone's blessing, least of all yours."

"Indeed, sweetness. You are the epitome of a royal bride. Tell me, does it make it easier, knowing the union had been foreordained? It was all laid out for you in stone and ink. You didn't even have to make the decision yourself, just go along with all fate expected of you."

She approached the table, narrowing her eyes. "That's cruel of you to say, after my one choice was taken from me."

"That is cruel of *you* to say, after being given a choice to begin with."

She frowned.

"What do you want, Lady Pinkerton?"

"I came to see how you're faring."

"Liar." His white teeth flashed in a sardonic smile. "You came to see if I've gone mad. You want to know you're not the only one to succumb to the Sisters' prophecy."

"I no longer care about the Sisters' prophecy."

"Convenient," he growled, "as you're the one who dragged us back here."

She clenched her fists. Then slowly unclenched them, smoothing her palms along the stiff fabric of her skirt. "Where's Haigha?"

"He went to get more tea." Hatta picked up his cane and stuck the end through a teapot handle. He lifted it clean off the table and the lid clattered onto a saucer. A few lonesome drops dribbled from the spout. "As you can see, we're out."

She let out a slow exhale. "I half expected you to have gone back to Chess."

The teapot slid back onto the table and crashed against a cracked porcelain cup.

"Without either of the Rooks, or the heart we came for?" One side of his mouth twisted into an ugly grimace. "You should be afraid, Lady Pinkerton. You are a queen now." He jutted a finger toward her chest. "That has value."

"I am not afraid of you. Tell me your riddle again, Hatta, and I will tell you that my heart cannot be stolen, only purchased, and mine has already been bought."

His cheek started to twitch. "You want to hear a riddle, you say? I know a very good one. It begins, why is a raven like a writing desk?"

She lifted her chin. "Have you gone mad, Hatta? I can't seem to tell."

"They are both so full of poetry, you see. Darkness and whimsy, nightmares and song."

"Hatta —"

His voice dropped to a conspiratorial whisper. "I figured it out, Lady Pinkerton."

She pressed her lips together and swallowed. "You figured what out?"

"Everything. Peter. The Jabberwock. The Mock Turtle. We are both to blame."

Catherine gripped the edge of the table, staring at him across the turmoil. The mannequins said nothing.

"You see, many years ago," said Hatta, as

if she'd asked, "I brought a pumpkin back from Chess. It was going to be a pumpkin hat. A toothless, smiling Jack-O'-Lantern that would light up on the inside. Oh, it would have been marvelous." He sung the word *marvelous,* letting his head tip back over the side of the chair. "But the pumpkin kept growing and growing. I couldn't make it stop. It got to be as big as a goat and no longer fit to be a hat, so I cut it up and carved out the seeds. I took them to the nearest pumpkin patch and asked if they wanted them. Ungrateful wretches they were, the man and his sickly wife. Told me something about wanting no charity, slammed the door on my face. So I tossed the seeds away into a corner of their patch." He smiled wryly. "I thought nothing more of it after that."

"And then they started to grow," said Cath.

"So they did. Lady Peter won a pumpkin-eating contest, did you know? She ate twenty-two of them, they say. Twenty-two bloody little pumpkins. And then she turned into a monster." His lips warbled into a mockery of a smile. Cath could see it now, the hysteria lurking beneath his amethyst eyes.

She thought of the destroyed corner of

the pumpkin patch. Peter had tried to kill them all, but one seed had survived and grown and thrived.

"And I made the pumpkin cake," she said, "and so the Mock Turtle was my doing, and yours, and maybe Peter's too."

"Peter, Peter, pumpkin eater," Hatta quoted in a singsong voice, "had a wife but couldn't keep her."

Cath shuddered. Her gaze traipsed across the mishmash of ornamentation on the table. "What else? Have you brought any other dangerous things back from Chess that I should know about?"

"Only Jest, love. He was dangerous enough for us both."

Hearing his name opened a crack in her heart that she hadn't felt in days. She bit her cheek and waited for the pain to recede and dull again.

She started making her way around the table. "You lied to me. Your hats are dangerous. We can't trust anything you've brought from Chess." She grabbed the chair to Hatta's right and made to pull it out from the table, but he whapped the cane over its arms. The cane crushed through a chiffon hat and shattered the skull of the clay mannequin underneath. Catherine jumped back.

"Don't be rude, Lady Pinkerton," Hatta

said through his teeth. "Look around. There is no room for you at this table."

Rejection sliced through her. She sucked in a breath.

"You did not deserve him," he said. There was a sadistic glint in his eyes. He was watching her, like he was waiting to see which accusations would make her writhe the most. "I'm glad he cannot see you now. I'm glad he'll never know how quickly you fell into the King's arms. You couldn't even wait until the worms had tasted him."

She clenched her fists. "I made a bargain to avenge him. I did it for *him,* whatever you might think. I loved him. I still do."

"If you think you had a monopoly on loving him, then you should be the King's new fool, not his wife."

She stared at him. Her thoughts somersaulted, warred with each other — first, a mess of confusion. Then understanding.

She straightened. "Did he know?"

"Does it matter?" With a brusque laugh, Hatta swung his legs off the table and stood. "He came here meaning to take your heart, but it was clear from the night he brought you to the tea party that he was going to lose his, instead." His voice had a growl to it as he sauntered to the wall and pulled a hat off one of the shelves.

No — not a hat. A crown.

He tossed it onto the table. The tines of the crown were made of Jabberwock teeth, jagged and sharp, and strung together with purple velvet and gemstones in hideous mockery of the real crown she'd left at the castle.

"That's for you," he said. "Consider it a wedding gift, from your most humble servant. One mad hatter to his monarch."

Her eyes stung. "You are not mad yet. You don't have to be."

He planted his cane on the ground and leaned into it. "It is in my blood, Lady Pinkerton. My father and his father and his father before him. Don't you understand? I am always coming and I am always going, but Time is searching for me and he's getting closer, always closer. You cursed me when you went back through that gate. You cursed us all."

"You didn't have to follow me."

He snarled. "I had to follow *him.*" He took off strolling down the length of the table. "Did you come here to make a purchase, Your Majesty? A most marvelous hat, and all it will cost you is *everything.*" He knocked the butt of the cane into the mannequins' hats as he passed, tipping them onto the table. Many of the heads fell too, their foreheads cracking against the table's edge. "A hat to give you wisdom, or maybe compassion as you embark on your queenly role? Perhaps a charm of forgetfulness, would you like that? Would you like to forget this entire tragedy ever happened? Or are you so vain, Lady Pinkerton, that you would like eternal youth? Endless beauty? I could make it happen, you know. Anything is possible when you know the way through the Looking Glass!" He started swinging the cane like a battledore, hitting the hats so hard they soared against the room and crashed into the walls.

"That is enough!"

The Hatter hesitated, the cane prepped for another swing.

"Anything is *not* possible," she seethed. "If it were, you would have already brought him back."

He recoiled. His eyes had gone crazed. The pocket watch on the table was growing louder, the tick-ticking a constant buzz.

Catherine snatched the cane away. He let it go without a struggle.

"Whatever you say, these creations of yours are unnatural. I won't allow them — not anymore."

"I beg your pardon."

"Beginning this moment, all travel to and

from the lands of Chess is strictly forbidden, by order of the Queen."

His eyes narrowed.

"You started this, playing with things you didn't understand. You created a monster and it's your fault Jest is dead. You brought him here and you brought the pumpkin and you gave Mary Ann that hat, and it's all your fault!"

He inhaled sharply. "Yes. So it is."

She jerked back, surprised at the levity of his admission.

"I know it is, and I shall pay for it with my sanity, just as the Sisters said. I've seen the drawings too, Lady Pinkerton. I've seen them all."

Her blood pulsed beneath her skin. "If you ever return to Chess, you had better intend to stay there, for I will not suffer a single grain of sand to cross through that maze again."

A sneer twisted his once-handsome face. "You cannot stop me from coming and going. This is my business. My livelihood. And as soon as Time should find me —"

"I am a queen, Hatta, and I can do as I like. I will imprison the Sisters. I will destroy the treacle well. I will burn the maze to the ground if I must. Do we have an understanding?"

She held his gaze, letting their wills battle silently between them.

His cheek started to twitch. Just slightly at first, but it continued to flutter until one side of his mouth lifted into a painful grin. "Why," he whispered, watching her with glossy eyes, "why is a raven like a writing desk?"

Shaking her head, Catherine tossed the cane onto the table, satisfied with the crash of porcelain and silver. "It's a shame, Hatta. Truly it is. Madness does not suit you."

"Of course it does," he cackled. "Murderer, martyr, monarch, *mad.* It runs in my family. It's a part of my blood. Don't you remember? I know you remember."

The watch was ticking so fast now she thought it would burst, crack wide open — gears shattering across the table.

"Good-bye, Hatta." She swung toward the door, but his desperate laughter followed her. A shrill giggle. A sobbing gasp.

"But why? *Why* is a raven like a writing desk?"

Her hand fell on the doorknob. "It's *not,*" she spat, ripping open the door. "It's just a stupid riddle. It is nothing but stuff and nonsense!"

Suddenly, inexplicably, the pocket watch fell silent.

Hatta's face slackened. His brow beaded with sweat.

"Stuff and nonsense," he whispered, the words cracking. "Nonsense and stuff and much of a muchness and nonsense all over again. We are all mad here, don't you know? And it runs in my family, it's a part of my blood and he's here, Time has finally found me and I —" His voice shredded. His eyes burned. "I haven't the slightest idea, Your Queenness. I find that I simply cannot recall why a raven is like a writing desk."

Chapter 53

She was growing impatient. Her hatred was burning a hole through her stomach, and it flared hotter every day that passed. Her fury burbled beneath the surface of her skin, often flaring in bouts of unexpected temper. Servants began to avoid her. The King dwindled into nothing more than a babbling idiot in her presence. All the members of the gentry that had doted on her after the wedding stopped making their calls.

Cath despised court days the most. She was the Queen and she had envisioned her iron word falling down on the people of Hearts. Laws would be executed, wrongdoers punished.

Instead she was trapped in a courtroom of absurdity and pandemonium. The jury, which had no purpose other than to squawk at one another and interrupt the proceedings, was made up of herons and badgers, kiwi birds and otters and hedgehogs, and not one of them with a bit of sense.

Not that it mattered, given the cases. A mouse who thought it was unfair that his brother had gotten a longer tail, a stork who thought it species profiling that she was forced to be the kingdom's sole baby carrier, and so on and so forth. Court days were agony.

Catherine spared a sympathetic look for Raven, who was perched on the rail that boxed in the thrones. His head was tucked between his neck feathers, his beak tight with disgust.

The Rabbit blew his trumpet. "Calling to the court the Most Noble Pygmalion Warthog, Duke of Tuskany, and Lady Margaret Mearle, daughter of the Count and Countess of Crossroads."

Cath lifted an eyebrow and watched as Margaret approached, her arm linked with the Duke's. They both appeared nervous. Margaret was wearing that stupid rosebud hat.

They bowed. Margaret's eyes darted to Catherine before lowering again.

"Good day," chirped the King, who looked extra absurd wearing an enormous powdered wig beneath his lopsided crown. "What is your request?"

"Your Majesty," said the Duke, "we wish

for you to marry us."

A rustle of surprise flittered through the crowd.

The King wobbled gleefully. "Oh, I love these ones!" He plastered on his almost-serious face and leaned forward, clearing his throat. "Is the lady under the jurisdiction of her father?"

"I am, Your Majesty," said Margaret.

"And what has he said to your request?"

"He has blessed the union."

"And for what reason do you wish to be married?" asked the King.

The Duke smiled around his tusks. "Because we love each other."

The King beamed. The crowd swooned.

Cath rolled her eyes.

"What does the lady say?"

Margaret gripped the Duke's elbow and lifted her chin. Her eyes were glowing, with nerves, yes, but also joy. In that moment she looked not just pretty, but nearly beautiful. "He speaks the truth. I have come to understand that Lord Warthog is the only man I could ever entrust the protection of my most championed integrity to, a man who upholds himself to the same rigorous standards which I deem to be of utmost value, and for this, I love him very much. We love each other very much."

Catherine scoffed, but everyone ignored her.

The King gestured for Margaret to come closer. When she was close enough, he whispered, "You are aware that he's a pig, yes?"

Her mouth fell open in outrage. "Your Majesty! What a crude thing to suggest!"

A long, awkward silence followed, until the King started to giggle, embarrassed. "Er — my mistake! Never mind!" He waved his hands and sent her back to her groom's side. "As I see no reason to deny this request, I now deem you —"

Catherine shoved herself to her feet. "Wait."

There was a nervous squeak from the onlookers and several of the smaller creatures dove off their chairs and cowered beneath them. Margaret paled.

"Margaret Mearle, I have known you my whole life, and in that time I have heard you refer to the Duke as arrogant, rude, and excruciatingly dull. Now you expect us to believe you wish to marry him. Not for his wealth or his title, but because you claim to love him."

Margaret gaped at her, cheeks blotchy with mortification.

Cath leaned forward. "Do you know what

the moral of that is, Lady Mearle?"

Lips thinning into a line, Margaret barely managed to shake her head.

"The moral of that" — she inhaled sharply — "is that 'you can't judge a book by its cover.' "

Margaret said nothing for a long time, as if waiting for Cath to say more. Finally, she drew her brows together into an uncertain frown. "All due respect, Your Majesty, but that sounds like nonsense."

"Oh, it is," said Catherine. "I suppose what I mean to say is that you are well suited to each other."

Margaret was still frowning, like she was waiting for Catherine to deny their marriage request. But when the audience cheered and Cath sat down again, a grin shifted over Margaret's face. She peered up at the Duke and the look that passed between them was almost magical.

Almost impossible.

Catherine looked away when their marriage was granted.

The couple rushed from the courtroom to vigorous applause, tripping over themselves in their glee. Catherine's shoulders slumped once they had gone.

The celebration quieted and the creatures returned to their seats, though many were still beaming and congratulating one another over nothing.

Cath noticed Raven watching her.

"What?" she snapped.

Raven started to shake his head, but stopped and puffed up his feathers. His voice was melancholy when he spoke — even more melancholy than usual. "Once I was a lonely Rook upon a distant shore, and I would murder for my queen so we might win a war. Now mine eyes see the heart that once we did search for, and I fear this heart shall be mended, nevermore."

Cath's nostrils flared. "Your fears are correct. Such a heart can't be mended. I hope I won't be tasked with keeping such a useless artifact for much longer."

The White Rabbit blew his horn, saving her from the bitter taste that was crawling up her throat. "Next to the court is Sir Milton Mulro —"

The doors at the end of the courtroom slammed open, letting in a gust of chilled air.

An owl swooped in through the double doors, its wings spread to their full span as it glided down the aisle. Three more silhouettes emerged in the doorway. A sleek red fox and a sly raccoon, each of them holding a chain that attached to a bedraggled figure between them.

Cath's heart thumped. She didn't remember standing, but she was on her feet as the arrivals marched down the aisle. Her stomach twisted. Her breaths came faster.

When they reached the front of the courtroom, the creatures deposited their prisoner on the floor. He seemed smaller than Cath remembered — bruised and covered in mud.

Fury throbbed inside her, filling the hollowness she'd grown accustomed to.

Finally. Peter Peter had been found.

As one, his captors reached for their faces and shed their masks and skins like Cath might shed a winter cloak. The Three Sisters stood before her, their small hands gripping Sir Peter's chains, their black eyes peering up at the Queen.

"We had a bargain," said Tillie.

"We made a deal," said Elsie.

Lacie's pale lips stretched thin. "We have come to take our toll."

"Wh-wh-what is this?" the King stammered, looking at the Sisters like they were a nightmare turned real.

"That is Sir Peter," Catherine answered. The name tasted like iron and filth.

Peter Peter snarled at her.

Mr. Caterpillar, one of the jurors, blew

out a ring of smoke that swirled around the Sisters' heads. "And *who,*" he asked, "are *you*?"

Elsie clasped her hands together, as if she were about to recite a poem. "There were once Three Sisters who lived in a well. They were very ill."

"They were dying," clarified Lacie.

Tillie nodded. "They were dying for a long time."

"But they knew," continued Elsie, "that one day there would be a queen who would have a heart she had no use for. Such a heart could sustain them."

"That queen is here," said Tillie. "That time is now."

In unison, the girls drawled, "We have brought your vengeance, and we shall have your heart in return."

Cath's attention didn't lift from Peter Peter. "Take it. As you said, I have no use for it."

The Sisters' wretched smiles glinted and Lacie stepped forward, her long white hair swaying against her ankles. She pulled out a jagged knife, from where Cath couldn't tell.

Choking, the King pushed back his throne, putting more space between himself and the child. But Cath didn't move. She held Lacie's gaze and listened to the rush of blood in her ears.

Lacie climbed up the Queen's box with the grace of a fox. She sat back on her heels, her bare, dirt-crusted toes curled around the wooden rail. Cath smelled the treacle on her skin.

She raised the dagger and plunged it into Cath's chest.

Catherine gasped, and though there were screams in the courtroom, she barely heard them over the cackle of the Three Sisters.

Cold seeped into her from the blade, colder than anything she had ever known. It leached into her veins, crackling like winter ice on a frozen lake. It was so cold it burned.

Lacie pulled out the blade. A beating heart was skewered on its tip. It was broken, cut almost clean in half by a blackened fissure that was filled with dust and ash.

"It has been bought and paid for," said the Sister. Then she yipped and launched herself back to the courtroom floor. She was joined by her sisters, cackling and crowding around the Queen's heart. A moment later, a Fox, a Raccoon, and an Owl were skittering out the door, leaving behind the echo of victorious laughter.

Chapter 54

Cath stared at the doors still thrust wide open, her body both frozen and burning, her chest a hollow cavity. Empty and numb.

She no longer hurt. That broken heart had been killing her, and it was gone.

Her sorrow. Her loss. Her pain, all gone.

All that was left was the rage and the fury and the desperate need for vengeance that would soon, soon be hers.

"W-what happened?" stuttered the King. "What did they do?"

"They freed me," Cath whispered. Her gaze traveled to the prisoner who was kneeling on the floor, his arms shackled by chains but with no captors to hold him. Peter Peter, alone, did not look appalled at what the Sisters had done. He looked bitter. To be caught. To be brought here. To be kneeling before the Queen of Hearts. Cath's lips twitched upward. "They fulfilled their promise."

"But . . . your heart . . . ," started the King.

"Was no longer useful to me, and I am most pleased with what they brought me in return." She narrowed her gaze. "Hello, Sir Peter." She spat the name, her anger roiling, bubbling, steaming inside her, filling up all the barren spaces. Her knuckles whitened on the rail. "This man is the murderer of the late court joker of Hearts. He cut off his head, then fled into the forest. He is a killer."

When she had imagined this moment, she'd worried that she might cry when faced with Jest's killer again. But her eyes were dry as sifted flour.

Already the numbness was fading. Now her body was enflamed.

The King hesitantly stood. "That is — yes. Yes, indeed. It's so good of you to join us, Sir Peter. I believe this calls for, uh . . ." The King scratched beneath his crown. "What happens next?"

"A trial, Your Majesty?" suggested the White Rabbit.

"Yes! A trial. Excellent fun. Good distraction. Yes, yes. Jury, assemble yourselves. Write down the Queen's accusation."

The jury rustled and pulled out slate tabs onto which they began to scribble notes with white chalk. Peter Peter stayed on his knees, but his head was lifted, his gaze piercing Catherine. She stared back, unafraid, for once. She was filled with the anticipation of seeing his blood spilled across the courtroom floor.

"The jury would like to call a witness, Your Majesty."

The King clapped his hands. "Oh yes, jolly good. Who shall we call?"

"We would like to call the court joker to the stand."

Cath growled. Whispers and glances passed through the crowd. Everyone seemed to be waiting for Jest to appear on a silver hoop from the ceiling.

"He is dead," she said through her gritted teeth. She had to fend off a fantasy of having every imbecile in this courtroom beheaded.

"Oh yes, that would be so, wouldn't it?" the Badger muttered, punctuating the realization with nervous laughter.

"I am your witness," Cath said. "I was there and I have already told you what happened. He is a murderer and he deserves to be punished."

Everyone tittered, uncomfortable that their new queen was intruding on the court's traditions.

"Perhaps," said the Rabbit, "if there are no other witnesses present, the jury might consider a verdict?"

A wave of glee sparkled over the jury box and Catherine heard mutterings of *guilty* and *innocent* and *in need of a bath,* when Peter Peter cleared his throat.

"I got something I'd like to say."

Though his voice was hoarse, it roared through Catherine like a tidal wave. White spots flecked in her vision. She wanted to silence him forever.

The King, ignorant of how Cath's blood was boiling, pounded his gavel. "The murder — er, the defendant wishes to speak!"

Two guards came forward and grabbed Peter Peter by the elbows, hauling him to his feet. The chains the Sisters had abandoned clinked across the floor.

Raven hopped along the rail, putting himself in Cath's field of vision. It was like having a confidant at her side — someone else who had been there that night, who *knew.* He alone had not flinched when the Sisters had taken Cath's heart. There had been a time when he had planned on doing the same thing to her. When Jest had planned to do the same thing to her.

But that no longer mattered to her. Such a heart was worthless, despite what everyone said. There was no value to it at all.

Sir Peter planted his feet so he could stand

without the guards' assistance. Though disheveled, he was as intimidating as ever. His eyes darted from the King to the jury to the royal courtiers to the guards — and, finally, to Catherine. "I did kill him," he snarled. "But I was defending my wife."

The jury scribbled on their tablets.

Peter took a step forward. "These people — the maid, the Joker, and *you.*" He snarled at Catherine. "They trespassed onto my property. I'd asked none of them to come there. Nosy wretches they were, coming to see the 'monster,' the 'beast.' " He spat. "But she was my wife! And you killed her. Right in front of me, you killed her. You're the monsters. Not me. Not her!"

"She was the Jabberwock!" Cath screamed.

A gasp rose from the crowd.

"That's what he isn't telling you. The wife he was protecting was the Jabberwock. Mary Ann was to be the creature's next meal."

"She should not have come to my patch. Trespassers! Murderers!"

"You are the murderer!"

"As are you, and a thief besides! You stole that pumpkin from me, I know you did. She was getting better. The curse was going away, but then she saw that cake and had to have it and when she turned again . . . she wouldn't . . . she couldn't turn back again and it's your fault!"

The King pounded his gavel — each thud like a hammer on Cath's temple.

"Now, now," said the King, who was sweating profusely. "I think perhaps the jury would appreciate one little clarification . . ." He cleared his throat and adjusted his powdered wig. "Sir Peter, you claim that the Jabberwock was your wife?"

The audience rustled and Cath heard more than one member of the jury mention that Peter Peter's wife had been at the black-and-white ball. Sickly thing. Not at all monstrous.

"She was poisoned," said Peter. "Poisoned by bad pumpkin. I saw her eat them — she couldn't stop. Then she started to get sick. I thought it was just from the overeatin' but . . . then she started to change." A deep wrinkle cut between his eyebrows. "It happened the first time after we left your ball, after those courtiers talked to us like we hadn't earned being there. After *you*" — he pointed at Cath — "looked at us like scum on your shoe. I watched her turn into the Jabberwock. Saw it with my own eyes." He balled his fists. "Even when she was herself again, the cravings were too much for her. She'd eat anything orange, anything she thought could satiate her. But nothing did."

Cath's jaw ached from clenching her teeth. They said the Jabberwock had gone after Cheshire and Margaret that first night — after Cheshire's fur had been tinted orange and he probably still smelled of pumpkin pasties.

And in the meadow, she had taken the Lion, with his golden-orange mane. But the monster had probably been there looking for Hatta, the messenger who had brought that first pumpkin from Chess.

And in the theater, the beast had come after *her.* Wanting more of her pumpkin cake.

"After she turned a second time," Peter growled, his eyes cast in shadows, "I made the pumpkins pay."

"If I recall," drawled Mr. Caterpillar, "the Jabberwock was a nuisance. I say, good riddance."

"I tried to stop her," said Peter Peter. "I swear it. Built a cage even, but I couldn't keep her." His expression turned fierce. "It wasn't her fault though. It was the pumpkins what did it!"

Cath squeezed the rail until her fingers ached. "This is not a defense. You killed Jest. You cut off his head, right in front of me."

"You killed my wife!"

"You were going to feed Mary Ann to her!"

"She shouldn'a been on my land in the first place!"

THUD.
THUD.
THUD.

The sound of the King's gavel interrupted their argument and Cath sank her head in between her tense shoulders.

"Th-thank you, Sir Peter, for your — er, statement." The King's voice was shaking. "We have now heard the defendant's testimony. Jury, what is your verdict?"

The jury huddled down with their slate tablets and whispers. Catherine heard none of their discussion. Her ears were humming, her brain clouded with visions of Jest in the mud, the ax swinging at his throat, her own heart splitting down the middle.

"We have reached a verdict, Your Majesty." It was a toad who spoke, standing up with a slate in his webbed fingers. On it he had drawn a picture of Peter Peter standing on top of an enormous pumpkin and grinning. "We the jury find Peter Peter *not guilty*!"

The cheer was deafening. All around her, the people of Hearts embraced one another, hollered ecstatically. Even the King giggled with relief.

The Kingdom of Hearts had never seen such a ghastly trial, and everyone was thrilled that it was over. The man was not guilty. They could all go on with their silly, pointless lives.

Except Catherine. From the corner of her eyes she saw Raven puff his feathers.

She snatched the gavel from her husband. "SILENCE!" she screamed, pounding on the railing so hard a crack formed in the polished wood.

The ballyhoo stopped.

A courtroom of faces turned to gape at their Queen. Her reddened face, her livid eyes. A turtle ducked into his shell. An opossum rolled into a ball. An ostrich tried, but failed, to bury its head in the polished quartz floor.

"I reject the jury's verdict," she seethed. "As the Queen of Hearts, I declare this man guilty. Guilty of murder. Guilty of thievery and kidnapping and all the rest, and for his sentence — I call for his head. To be carried out immediately!"

Her words echoed through the courtroom, casting a cloud over the stricken faces. No one dared to breathe.

Catherine had eyes only for Sir Peter,

whose face was furious beneath streaks of dirt, whose teeth were bared.

The numbness began to settle over her again.

"You deserve no mercy," she said.

Peter spat again. "I want nothin' from you."

"B-b-but, darling," said the King. Soft, patient, terrified. His fingers brushed against her arm, but she ripped it away. "We . . . we have never . . . In Hearts, we don't . . . Why, sweetness, we don't even have an executioner."

The corner of her mouth twitched. Her gaze shifted to Raven. "Yes, we do."

Raven lifted his head.

"You were the White Queen's executioner," she said, "and now you will be mine. Serve me dutifully and we shall both have our vengeance."

He remained silent for a long while, still as a statue. Then he spread his wings and stepped off the rail. Like an ink splatter on stone he transformed into the hooded figure. His face cast in shadow, his gloved hands gripping the handle of the glinting ax. Now, in the light of the courtroom, Cath could see that his hooded cloak was made from raven feathers.

The guards drew back, leaving Peter Peter

alone in the center of the room. Though he held fast to his defiance, Cath could see him beginning to shake.

Raven's shadow lengthened across the floor, dwarfing the murderer. He hefted the ax onto his shoulder.

"For the murder of Jest, the court joker of Hearts, I sentence this man to death." She spoke without feeling, unburdened by love or dreams or the pain of a broken heart. It was a new day in Hearts, and she was the Queen.

"Off with his head."

AUTHOR'S NOTE

OR, WHY IS A RAVEN LIKE A WRITING-DESK?

It's commonly believed that when the Hatter posed his unanswered riddle in *Alice's Adventures in Wonderland* — "Why is a raven like a writing-desk?" — Lewis Carroll did not have an answer in mind. However, after years of being pestered, Carroll finally gave in with a response, recorded in the preface he wrote to the 1896 edition of *Alice:* "Because it can produce a few notes, tho they are *very* flat; and it is nevar put with the wrong end in front." (Note that the misspelled *nevar* is *raven* backward. Unfortunately, the misspelling would soon be caught and "corrected" by some industrious editor and Carroll's clever wordplay would be lost in future editions.)

All of that is to say that Carroll's "official" answer to the riddle was the inspiration for Jest's debut performance at the black-and-white ball in Chapter Four.

Over the years, countless fans and readers

have added their own interpretations of the riddle. The answer that Hatta gives in Chapter Eighteen ("Because they both have quills dipped in ink"), was one that I was quite proud of myself for coming up with, but soon learned that I was not the only one to think it. This answer was credited to David B. Jodrey, Jr., in *The Annotated Alice*[1], along with dozens of other brilliant and amusing answers recorded over time. (My personal favorite comes from Tony Weston, one of the winners of a contest posed by *The Spectator* in 1991: "Because a writing-desk is a rest for pens and a raven is a pest for wrens." I imagine that Carroll, with his love of wordplay, would approve.)

Speaking of the Raven, I was unable to limit myself to abusing the work of only one great author in this book, I had to meddle around with two. Most of Raven's dialogue is inspired by (and sometimes blatant reworkings of) lines from the poem "The Raven" by Edgar Allan Poe. Though readers are free to interpret the character however they see fit, I rather like the idea of

1. Martin Gardner, ed., introduction and notes to *The Annotated Alice: The Definitive Edition,* by Lewis Carroll (New York: W.W. Norton & Company, Inc., 1999).

Raven being the same bird that tormented the heartbroken narrator in Poe's classic work. As "The Raven" was first published in 1845, twenty years before *Alice's Adventures in Wonderland,* the timeline was too perfect to pass up.

Lastly, I'm sure it will surprise no reader, fan, or scholar that I have taken an abundance of liberties, not only with Carroll's story and characters, but also with the societal rules and norms of Victorian England. I hope you'll forgive any inaccuracies, or even chalk them up to creative license if you're feeling generous, and I sincerely hope that the spirit of Lewis Carroll will find more amusement than offense in my attempts to expand on his crazy, kooky, quirky world.

It is Wonderland, after all.

ACKNOWLEDGMENTS

I'd like to start by expressing my appreciation for Gregory Maguire, whose fantastic novels *Wicked* and *Confessions of an Ugly Stepsister* served as the inspiration behind this book. Years ago, I was out to lunch with my agenting team, discussing fairy tales and villains, when I told them, "I wish that Gregory Maguire would write the origin story for the Queen of Hearts." To which my foreign rights agent, Cheryl Pientka, looked at me and said, "Marissa, why don't *you* write it?" So I also owe a great amount of thanks to Cheryl for helping me see the obvious, along with the amazing Jill Grinberg and the whole gang at Jill Grinberg Literary Management for their constant encouragement, wisdom, and enthusiasm.

I am enormously grateful to Jean Feiwel, Liz Szabla, and the many, many, *many* dedicated and talented people at Macmillan Children's Publishing Group, for having faith in me and for taking such pride in the books you publish. It's been an enormous joy for me to work with you all.

A huge thanks to Lewis Carroll, who, one hundred and fifty years ago, gave us some of the most memorable characters in all of literature. I don't know if I've done your world justice, but I have done my best.

Thank you to my husband, Jesse, our beautiful girls, Sloane and Delaney, and all my friends and family, who fill my world with love, wonder, and Cheshire-like smiles.

And finally, I have to thank my mom, who sparked my interest in *Alice* early on with her Queen of Hearts Halloween costume, *Alice in Wonderland* Christmas tree ornaments, and collection of *Alice* figurines, music boxes, and more. This book is for you.

ABOUT THE AUTHOR

Marissa Meyer is the author of the New York Times bestselling series the Lunar Chronicles. She lives in Tacoma, Washington, with her husband and their three cats.

The employees of Thorndike Press hope you have enjoyed this Large Print book. All our Thorndike, Wheeler, and Kennebec Large Print titles are designed for easy reading, and all our books are made to last. Other Thorndike Press Large Print books are available at your library, through selected bookstores, or directly from us.

For information about titles, please call:
(800) 223-1244

or visit our Web site at:
http://gale.cengage.com/thorndike

To share your comments, please write:

Publisher
Thorndike Press
10 Water St., Suite 310
Waterville, ME 04901